Original Publication: Lulu Publishing, 2010 Second Edition

ISBN: 978-0-557-98273-8

FOR CAL, DEBBIE, SARAH, JOSH, ISAAC, ABBY,
    CRESSIE, DANTE, CAROL, SARAH, BRADY,

    AND

    ALL THOSE WHO ENCOURAGED AND
    SMILED ALONG THE WAY.

A Journal Away From Life

A Novel By Caleb Kearns

Prologue

18/10/08 09:24
Monterosso Al Mare, Italy

Le temps était beau.

Henri Levure was beginning to get frustrated with the pace set by his wife, Fionna. An outdoorsman like Henri had motivations that extended beyond a scenic walk—he wanted to conquer the inclining trails with an effort that resembled a body builder in peak training. Fionna, not entirely out of shape, didn't feel the same way—her almost dainty efforts were beginning to annoy him.

"Come on, Fionna," Henri urged her on in their native tongue of France. "We only have a little bit to go before it is all downhill."

"Can't we stop for a break?" She asked as she leaned against a large natural stone to the left of the inclining path.

"No!" Henri exclaimed. And then he muttered under his breath. "I told you not to come."

Henri did not like yelling at his wife, but he strongly felt she should have realized what he was setting out to do and stayed behind. He would have been far happier hiking to the music in his iPod than listen to her consistent complaining.

Henri continued up a few more steps ahead of her.

"Henri," Fionna said quietly.

"What?" He screamed as he spun around. When

he saw her leaning against the large stone, dejected and tired, he took a deep breath. "What," he repeated in a much softer tone as he took off his backpack and went down to her.

"I'm sorry," she whispered. A lone tear crawled down her face as Henri put his hands on her shoulders.

Henri took a moment to survey his surroundings to avoid eye contact with his wife. He and Fionna had almost reached the summit of the intermediate trail connecting Vernazza and Monterosso Al Mare. The view out from the cliff was nothing short of spectacular. The weather reports predicted a seasonal storm a few days out but in the moment the clear blue sky reflecting against the ocean created an enticing horizon worth taking a memorable picture of. Henri wanted to enjoy the view with his wife—he knew he needed to put his competitive spirit away.

"Oh, I'm sorry, dear," he said as she looked up into his eyes. "I'm sorry. I shouldn't have yelled at you."

"I know I shouldn't have come, but I just wanted to spend time with you," Fionna said quietly. She and her husband had planned this romantic getaway to Cinque Terre, the five secluded cities on the Northwestern Italian cliffs hugging the Mediterranean Sea, and they spent most of the time apart while he went off hiking on the more advanced trails. Fionna had been lonely—a terrible thing to be at one of the most romantic places she had ever been.

Henri could see the sadness in his wife's eyes. "I know. I'm sorry Fionna," he said as he pulled her into his arms. "I've been a complete jerk, haven't I?"

"Not a complete jerk, just around seventy-five percent worth," Fionna said as she held her husband.

"I'll tell you what," Henri said as he pulled away from her enough to look into her eyes. "When we get down to Monterosso Al Mare, we'll take the train back to

Corniglia, wash up, and go to that restaurant in the castle that you've wanted to go to for wine and lunch."

"Oh Henri, we don't have to, I just—"

"I insist," Henri cut her off to display his certainty.

"That would be great," Fionna said as she smiled. Henri kissed her forehead.

"Now, we're almost to it. Can you get up these last few steps? Or am I going to have to carry you?"

"I think I can make it," Fionna played sarcastically as she stepped away from the rock.

"Then let's go," Henri said with a smile as he grabbed his pack off the step and led the way up the path.

After they reached the step summit, Henri and Fionna strode down a fairly level stretch that led around a corner.

"There it is," Henri said. "It's just around that corner."

"How long has it been here?"

"The locals say it's been exactly as it is for a couple hundred years." Walking side by side they began rounding the corner. "Sometimes you'll see candle vigils around the—"

"Oh my God!" screamed Fionna.

In the path directly in front of them lay a body of a young man.

"Oh shit," Henri said.

"Is he alive?" Fionna said in a panic. Henri rushed next to the body, and put his fingers around his neck, checking for a pulse. "Henri. Is he alive?"

"No, he's dead."

"*Oh mon Dieu.*"

PART ONE

THE BLACK LEATHER JOURNAL

1.

10/20/08 5:53 A.M.
Sacramento International Airport

A thin veil of tears glazed over Peter Sebastian's eyes as he sat staring out of the Boeing 747 window still parked in the terminal. A stewardess walked by and noticed the obvious grief on his face.

"Is there anything I can get you sir?" she asked softly. Peter looked up from his hand, straightened up his back, and cleared his throat.

"Water, please, water would be great," he muffled his reply. The stewardess complied with a nod and continued on towards the back of the plane.

Peter glanced down at the journal sitting in his lap. He ran his index finger over the black leather cover, feeling the roughness of the leather strap which felt as if it had been opened and closed a thousand times before. The mere sight of the journal made Peter shake his head; he diverted his eyes in an attempt to clear his thoughts to keep from tearing up once again.

I have to find some strength, he thought.

The journal was not his. It belonged to his son, Luke. Thirty-eight hours earlier, Peter had gotten a call at his Hardware Store that Luke's body had been found on a hiking trail in Monterosso Al Mare, Italy. There was no explanation given; no facts, no clues, and no details about how his son had died. Captain Roberto Caligno, the Cinque Terre Policeman in charge of the case, asked Peter to come immediately to identify the body. Luke had been traveling with a young man named Chris

7

Ludlow, but due to International Law only a family member could identify a corpse if found on foreign soil. Captain Caligno suggested Peter fly into *Fiumicino* Airport in Rome and take the earliest train to Genoa where Luke's body was being held at the *camera mortuaria*. Peter booked the first available flight he could find. Captain Caligno made arrangements upon Peter's flight check-in to have an envelope with some local Italian currency and his train tickets given to him in advance to prevent out-of-pocket expenses. Peter could afford the trip but thought it was an extremely kind gesture considering the circumstances.

As Peter looked at the journal in his hands, he began to think about the tragedy of his son's life. When Luke was fourteen years old his mother died in a horrific car accident after dropping Luke off at school. Luke had witnessed the accident from only a few yards away; Mary Sebastian ran a red light as a heavy garbage truck was racing through the intersection. In the last moment of her life, Mary was looking at her son who stood stunned, unable to breath, and motionless.

For years Peter tried to get Luke to talk about that day, but he was never successful. Luke distanced himself from the reality of the world in which he lived for most of his high school years. He became engulfed in music; Luke played both the piano and guitar from the age of seven. Peter always encouraged his music, but refused to believe his son did not want to play sports. *Luke*, at over six feet tall, lean but strong, *would have been a great quarterback*, Peter thought. But those days and options had expired. All of Luke's days and options had expired.

The stewardess came back with two bottles of water, a pillow, and a cup of ice. As she handed the items to Peter she said, "If there's anything else you need, just let me know."

8

"Thank you," Peter replied with a half smile. The stewardess smiled back, nodded, and continued towards the front of the plane. Peter thought she was pretty, but dismissed any possibility of flirtation by interpreting her kindness as professional courtesy.

Since Mary's death Peter had never tried to find love again. He always assumed Luke and his older brother Jake would have preferred him to spend the rest of his life alone than attempt to replace their mother. He could not have been more wrong. Only months earlier he and Luke had talked about the issue for the first time. He remembered how passionate Luke had been about his father moving on and looking for happiness. It had confused Peter. He never really put much thought into the idea. He had loved Mary while she was alive with everything he had. He still did. Every day since the accident seemed trivial and redundant to Peter—the redundancy, in large, due to his stagnant and perpetually mundane business—a medium-sized hardware store that kept him busy from early morning till late evening—just to pay the bills.

His two sons were distant. Luke graduated from high school and moved down to Los Angeles to attend UCLA. Jake went to law school at the University of Maryland and never moved back. He made partnership in a law firm in New Hampshire, married a pretty young woman from the east coast, and decided not to call his father anymore. Peter saw it as best—surprisingly, the awkwardness of not speaking to your son three thousand miles away   did not even compare to the awkwardness of not talking to your son while he sat across the dinner table. When their mother died, both sons became independent and cold to the everyday family ideals, which had all but disappeared in the Sebastian home over the years.

Mary is probably rolling in her grave right now, he

9

thought, *Luke has just died and I haven't talked to Jake in six months. What a great father I turned out to be.* He wondered how Mary would have reacted to Luke's recent activities. Peter could not figure them out and he, quite frankly, did not know how to react. Luke had been in the perfect situation—living a successful life with a beautiful young woman named Rochelle Dobbs he had met at UCLA.

Luke and Rochelle were both Business majors—Rochelle developed a crush on Luke in their Socio-Economics class. She had always said she couldn't get her eyes off the brown-haired blue-eyed "wonder boy" who could play the piano so beautifully. In fact, it was Rochelle who asked Luke out on the first date. Luke was playing at the university's "Bruin Night"—a weekly venue geared to showcase a student's ability to their peers. Luke was frequently asked to perform, and on that night a rather large crowd attended as he played tribute songs to Jason Mraz, John Mayor, and The Counting Crows. As was Luke's custom he ended his performance with an original song he had written, one he never shared with Peter.

After the grand finale and some rousing applause, Rochelle walked up to Luke as he was putting away his gear and asked him to dinner. Luke agreed and the two had been dating for just over two years when out of the blue, four months before Luke's death, Luke told Rochelle the best thing she could do was simply forget he ever existed.

Soon after their mysterious break-up, Luke drove home to Sacramento to visit Peter. Luke informed him of the occurrence. Peter was not only confused but awe-struck at the thought of his son letting go of such a catch. Luke tried to explain the situation, but Peter's visible disappointment grew outwardly and then out of control. As Peter expressed his feelings, Luke inherently banished his father from further influence—Luke then exploded with pent-up feelings and thoughts about his father's lifestyle. Peter retaliated by telling Luke he was making a huge mistake. The argument soon reached a climax and Luke walked out.

Horrifying and altogether atypical, Peter's argument with Luke was the last time he saw his son alive.

Desperately trying to recount every detail of Luke's life, Peter's memory seemed drawn and attracted to that closing moment with his son. And even when he tried to fight it, he could not seem to get passed the feeling that Luke had something else he wanted to tell him that evening. *It's these moments*, Peter thought, *that make me a bad father. Luke had something to tell me and I wouldn't listen. Mary would have listened. God, I miss her.* But now, both Mary and Luke were gone, and Peter didn't know what he was going to do.

"Good morning ladies and gentlemen," the pilot's voice interrupted Peter's thoughts. "We've got a little bit of a delay on the runway, but don't worry; we should be getting airborne here in about ten minutes. We're sorry about the delay folks; a few planes are ahead of us, and we're waiting for the tower to give us all the go-ahead. We thank you for your patience and for flying with us here at United. It should only be a couple minutes, so sit back and get comfortable, please make sure you lock in your tray tables into their upright positions, please turn off any portable electronic devices, and get ready to fly non-stop from Sacramento to Rome."

Peter ran his fingers through his hair and began rubbing his temples. He was tired—he had not slept well the previous nights. The delay did not pose much of a problem as long as the "ten minutes" didn't turn to an hour—his proposed travel itinerary to Genoa was demanding but not tarnished by a short runway jam. It also did not matter because Peter was not the type to complain—about anything.

He took a deep breath and looked down at the journal in his hands.

He had no idea what was in the journal as he had simply found it by chance. As soon as he found out about Luke's death, he drove down to his apartment near the UCLA campus. He looked for something that would help make sense of the situation; sleeping pills, drugs, anything that might have indicated an overdose. But just as he thought, his son, as well as his belongings, were clean. The only thing he found that might be useful was the black leather journal.

Peter had been hesitant to read the journal—he had only flipped the pages enough to see the entire journal was full of entries. Luke was always creative. He loved to read, write, and play music. The absence of a ball in his hand was pure choice, rather than a lack of potential. But now, Peter thought if he could find any information that would help answer the questions about his son's death, it was worth invading his late privacy. Peter simply had to know—he needed to know. Luke was too smart, too capable just to vanish from the earth on a whim—the story of his death had to be monumental; it had to be worth knowing, and most importantly, worth understanding.

Unhooking his tray table and laying the journal on top of it, he took off his jacket and hung it up on the hook next to the window. From his breast pocket, Peter pulled out his reading glasses. The sixty-one year-old father was about to enter his twenty-three year-old son's world. Peter took a drink out of one of the water bottles and set it to the side as he unwove the leather strap holding the pages tightly together. Opening the leather flip cover, he thumbed to the first page of text dated "5/16". He instantly recognized the handwriting

12

and felt a striking pain in his heart; *the pen that touched this paper*, he thought, *was held by my son*. But as he read the title, Peter felt like a father who was doing what he had to in order to help his son who could no longer help himself. So Peter began reading the entry.

5/16 Rudolph's with Rochelle

Tonight, for the first time ever, I fear for the future. Rochelle and I have been together for so long, I don't know if it's simply comfort that I'm still with her, or if I actually love her. Her beautiful imperfections, indulgences, and morals...even her soul...I connect with it partially, but I don't know if I connect with it completely. Maybe I don't know what I'm saying—I just feel as if no matter what I keep hitting the wrong chords, and shouldn't the soundtrack of your life be the most beautiful...

Peter glanced up from the journal. He was unaware his son spoke like this—or at least he had never heard him speak like this before. Peter felt a small amount of pride that his son was an imitation Keats. He then focused his attention to the last line:

I just feel as if no matter what I keep hitting the wrong chords, and shouldn't the soundtrack of your life be the most beautiful?

Peter smiled; he thought his son hit it dead-on. Was the soundtrack to Peter's life beautiful? He didn't dwell on the question, and instead kept reading the lengthy entry written by his son.

Around eight or so, I went to pick up Rochelle at her parent's house...

13

2.

05/16/08 7:42 P.M.
Home of Rick and Paula Dobbs
Anaheim, California

    Luke Sebastian tilted his rear view mirror down so he could look at his reflection. His straight brown hair was having a tough time staying waved across his face; he suddenly realized he should have gelled his hair for Rochelle. Ultimately he wished he could put on his North Face Buster beanie like he did almost every day, but Rochelle insisted they go out to a nice dinner which meant "no beanie". She had chosen the restaurant, Rudolph's, a place he figured would involve a thirty-dollar-a-plate meal that served three pieces of asparagus with a three-ounce wedge of lemon chicken. It would be absolutely wonderful for two minutes and then the bill would come.

    Luke opened the driver's side door of his black Pathfinder after adjusting the mirror. Most men do not care if they are late because most girls relish the extra thirty minutes to an hour to get ready—not Rochelle. She would chastise him with a look that said it all; he was twenty minutes late and his navy blue collared shirt was slightly wrinkled. He knew as he walked up the steps to her parent's front door that she would soon be asking him to take off his shirt so she could iron it. The certainty of that fact made him smile. His jeans were a little wrinkled too, but she would have to wait until they were alone to get them off.

    Luke rang the doorbell to the right of the two

large cedar doors. The Dobb's house was enormous; a three story, six-bedroom, five-bathroom, cedar paneled home with all the latest amenities; for three people. Luke always thought it was an incredible waste of space, but he loved being able to visit. The Dobb's had a heated pool, an incredible game room, and his favorite, a soundproof state of the art recording studio. They had the room installed when Rochelle decided she wanted to learn how to play the saxophone. The walls that had been engineered and constructed to lock in sounds that reached high pitches and certain decibels proved immensely valuable. Luke loved the room, but tonight was not that kind of night—tonight was a night for Rochelle—the romance-driven-family orientated-pretty-little-princess daddy's girl that Luke had grown to love.

Luke heard footsteps followed by the door being swung open by Rick Dobbs, Rochelle's father. He was in his middle fifties, tan, and in unbelievable shape. He was one of those men who almost looked better in his fifties than he did in his thirties. The gray slowly creeping in his hair testified to his age, but his personality and youthfulness disguised him otherwise. Rick reached out to give Luke a hug.

"Luke, how are you doing?" he asked as he pulled Luke close.

Luke *hated* hugging men.

"I'm good Rick, how are you?" Luke replied. Rick beckoned him to come in. Luke followed suit and stepped inside the large cedar home. The entryway was elaborate. Antique looking furniture mapped out the "sitting room" next to windowed cupboards full of glistening fine china and silverware. Above them hung a crystal chandelier that Paula Dobbs, Rochelle's mother, always told her guests belonged to one of Benjamin Franklin's Masonic churches in the 1800's. Luke always loved the story, whether true or not.

"Luke, Rochelle—"Rick began.

"Is right behind you," a soft, small voice interrupted. Rochelle was at the top of the spiral stairs that led to the two master bedrooms. She looked amazing—she always looked amazing. Her beautiful blonde hair accented her deep blue eyes. Her curvy figure showed a conservative vivaciousness that was unparalleled by anybody Luke had ever seen. She was wearing tight blue jeans tucked into a pair of brown European boots, a black low-cut see-through shirt layered a tight black tank-top outlining a "definite" push-up bra that caused a plethora of modernly acceptable cleavage. Luke always thought she didn't need to push anything up, but if Gustave Eiffel wanted ten more feet of steel to make his tower one floor higher, no one was going to argue with the creator of such a masterpiece. Luke didn't know who to thank for Rochelle's amazing breasts; Rick and Paula? God? Victoria's Secret?

As she started walking down the steps she noticed his shirt and stopped for a moment before continuing. "Baby, look at your shirt." Luke smiled. "Give it to me; I'll go iron it for you." Luke wished he could place bets with himself, but that seemed rather superfluous.

"Babe, it's fine, don't you think?" Luke replied. "I mean, Shakespeare used to rock a few ruffles and wrinkles back in 1594—it was considered the dress of a nobleman." He didn't want to take off his shirt.

"No, it's not fine, and you're not Shakespeare."

"No? Let me write you a sonnet right now—" Luke started to say.

"Oh, this will be good," Rick interjected with a seemingly sun-burnt smile. Rochelle and Luke just paused as they shared a look at him.

"Give me ten minutes." Rochelle said getting back on topic as she reached Luke at the base of the stairs, kissed him on the lips, and helped him unbutton his shirt.

"Ten minutes. Then we have to go, the reservation is at 8:30."

"Okay," she replied as she glanced down, "Babe, your pants…"

"Later. Patience is a high profile quality, you know," Luke said quietly so Rick couldn't hear—he offered a private wink that Rochelle returned with a smile. Taking his shirt, she turned to leave but stopped.

"Babe, is it cold outside?" she asked.

"No, it's actually warm."

"You mind if I go out in this?" she asked as she took a stance to model what she had on. Luke turned to Rick, who had been pretending to read the paper so he could stay in the room.

"What do you think Rick?" he asked. "Should we let her go out like that? If we post her on a corner she might make some extra money."

Rick smiled. "It would be the first job she ever had," he suggested.

"It could be good—she could definitely pay for dinner," Luke chimed, pushing the joke forward.

"Guys, I'm standing right here," Rochelle playfully sniffed at them. Rick turned to Luke.

"I gave up on getting her to dress how I wanted her to dress years ago. It's your problem now, son." He replied. Luke instantly was taken aback. Rick had never called him *son* before, but Luke quickly dismissed it as meaningless.

"Babe, you look great. It might cool down, so you should bring a jacket." Luke said with a wink. She smiled, winked back, and disappeared around the corner.

"Luke, come with me to the den. You have ten minutes; have a drink with me. There's something I want to talk to you about," Rick said as he put his arm around Luke.

"Sure thing, Rick," Luke responded shrugging his shoulders. He suddenly felt a chill walking with Rick's arm around his shoulder in just a plain white T-Shirt. Luke didn't like men touching him. The two turned the corner, passed through the kitchen, where Rick let Luke head down the stairs to the den first. As they went down the stairs, Rick began speaking with an almost *Brady Bunch*-like charisma.

"So where are you two headed tonight?" he asked. Luke took a seat at the bar as Rick positioned himself behind it pulling out two glasses and some ice.

"Rudolph's—over on Fifth Avenue. You've been there right?" Luke replied. Rick put the ice in the two glasses and turned to grab the spirit.

"Yeah, I took Paula there last week and recommended it to Shelly." Luke never called Rochelle "Shelly" because it was her dad's thing. "It's a little pricey, but good. Do you need any money to pay for dinner?" Luke shook his head no.

"No, I've got it covered. It's the two year—I saved some money for the occasion."

"Really, it's been two years?"

"Yes sir."

"Wow. Have I ever told you the story about when Paula and I had our six month and I was stranded in Baltimore?"

"Yeah, when you sent the eleven real roses with the one fake—"

"Yes—"

"But they got delivered to your neighbor on accident; single mother of three."

"Yes, but—"

"And she had a crush on you for two years." Rick clenched his lips together and nodded.

18

"Right—"

"What was her name again?"

"Claudia May, but—"

"How's she doing these days?"

"She's *dead*." Luke's eyes went wide as he deemed it appropriate to give Claudia May a moment of silence during his brief embarrassment.

"Oh," Luke said quietly after a moment, before springing back to life. "Wasn't there a note involved with this story?"

"Yes, the note said, "I'll love you till the last rose dies," Rick replied. Luke shifted in his seat.

"Uh huh, and what was the—"

"The point I'm getting after Luke, is that I put myself out there."

"I'm sure Claudia May appreciated that," Luke returned with a smile.

"That was an accident; Paula got it shortly after. Look, that probably wasn't a great example, but you have to show a woman your level of commitment."

"I guess my neighbor is kind of cute—" Luke started in with his patented sarcasm.

"Forget the neighbor bit, will you? You and Shelly have a good thing going, and I mean that. You're a great guy and I wouldn't want Shelly with anyone else."

"Thank you Rick, that means a lot." Luke gave Rick a "pound" with his fist. Rick liked to feel young as a middle-aged man. "What are we drinking?" Just as he asked, Rick turned around with the bottle of Crown Royal. Luke loved Crown Royal—he always ended up hating it the next day, but for the moment one would be great. "Ah, the good stuff." Rick poured the two stiff drinks and slid one to Luke.

"Luke there's something I wanted to talk to you about." Rick said, taking on a more serious tone. Luke took a big drink, preparing himself for what Rick was about to say. Rick had a way of pressuring Luke to do things, like the time they went to the lake, and Rick got Luke to water-ski; bad idea. He ended up taking more head dives then Paris Hilton. "You graduate in less than a month. Business school, music minor—what are your plans after that?"

Luke knew this question would arise eventually; hell; it was his father's favorite question to ask him. Luke shifted his weight in his seat before answering.

"Well, Rick, I guess I haven't really thought about it too much. I mean, I just wanted to get to graduation and use the summer to figure things out. After five years of school I'm a little burned out, you know?" Luke thought it was an honest answer, even if it was a lame one. Rick was nodding his head in agreement.

"Yeah, no, I get you. You've worked hard. You've done well, and I totally agree that you should take the summer off." Luke was wondering where this was going. "But I think I have something for you son." He paused to take a drink. Luke followed suit. "How about, say after Labor Day, you come and work for me?" Luke did not see that one coming.

"Work for you; at ODS?" Luke asked surprisingly. Rick grabbed his drink and moved around the bar to sit on the stool next to Luke.

"Yeah; you are exactly what ODS is looking for." *Probably not*, Luke thought. "Due to recent growth we have a new position opening up. It's a publicity position; you would be working alongside our commercial coordinators, our slogan designers, and the corporate message board. You'll have a BS in Business, and I know you're creative with all of the artistic things you do, music and writing and what not. I think it would be a perfect position for you. What do you think?"

If Luke was supposed to be hiding his shock he was doing a horrible job at it. Rick was the president of a billion dollar dental supply manufacturer called Organized Dental Supply. Rick Dobbs, to his employees, was a shark businessman who could control any room he walked into. His one weakness had always been and would always remain his lone daughter who had become the center of his attention and object of affection.

"Wow, Rick. I don't know what to say...I mean do you really think I'm qualified for that type of position within your company? I guess in the grand scheme of things I'm sure I could write a nice limerick with a few chords like, 'ODS, Dental's Best' as a corporate slogan... It just seems there are other people who already work for you that would love all that...you know the job of handling your public message." Luke wanted to seem humble but grateful for the opportunity, but all he seemed to be doing was speaking before thinking.

"Don't worry about that," Rick replied with a shake of his head. "I think you would be perfect for ODS, and who knows, you may take over the company for me one day."

There it was. He just said it; if Rick was trying to conceal even one card, it did not matter now; he just threw them all over the table. This was the way of bringing Luke into the family. He wanted Luke to marry his daughter.

This time Luke thought for a moment before speaking. This was a particularly interesting situation. He loved dating Rochelle, but two years had just "passed" in the same amount of time as a Prefontaine mile. To Luke it didn't seem like they were reaching a point in their relationship where marriage was even a possibility; but then again, maybe he was wrong. Either way it was a lot to take in at that moment. Luke turned his attention to the million-dollar man with the "literal" million dollar question looming in front of him.

"Rick, wow, I can't believe you're seriously

considering me for this. And it's an honor that you have even thought about me, but can I think about it? I mean, I just want to look at everything, and graduate first." Rick smiled. "I'm just not ready to say yes for sure, you know?" Rick patted Luke's thigh, which made Luke instinctively grimace in the form of a smile.

"No problem, son." *There is that "son" again*, Luke thought. "Take the first part of the summer to think about it. I'll give you till July 1st to give me an answer. Just remember, this would be a great opportunity for you. Plus, it will pay very well. If you and Rochelle were to, you know, get married; you would be in a good position." Luke nodded in agreement before finishing the bottom third of his glass in one swoon. "Just think about it."

Rick got up and grabbed Luke's glass and put it in the sink. Luke sat there playing with his bracelet on his left hand, always his left hand, and thought about the conversation he just had. He tried to escape an imminent feeling of claustrophobia. *The Dobb's clan just put it out there for me*, he thought, *it's all or nothing.*

3.

10/20/08 6:16 A.M.
United Flight 7742
Airborne

Peter took off his glasses and wiped his nose with the handkerchief from his pocket. He couldn't believe what he had just read. Luke had never mentioned anything about a job offer from Rick—especially an offer that would set him up for life. As Peter sat there reading Luke's journal, he thought how ungrateful Luke seemed to be passing up such an opportunity. *What did Luke want to do with his life? Nothing?*

Peter could feel he was getting shaken up without reading the rest of the story. It was extremely hard for him to read the journal in the past tense. The conversation with Rick Dobbs had been almost five months earlier—time was shifting in Peter's mind—almost as if he was reading a book.

He calmly put his reading glasses back on while putting his handkerchief aside. He opened the journal back up to the page where he left off. He was intrigued—for in this moment, in some odd way, he felt himself communicating with Luke for the first time in a long time. He read on:

Reeling from my conversation with Rick, I got my shirt back, ironed of course, and set out to dinner with Rochelle...

4.

05/16/08 8:17 PM
Anaheim, California

Luke pulled his car out of the Dobb's driveway and turned left down Reverend Street heading towards the I-305. His shirt was still extremely warm from the fresh ironing. He unbuttoned the top button.

"Don't, you look good babe," Rochelle said in reply to his action. *No, you look good, h*e thought. Rochelle always looked good though.

"I'm just overheating a little, babe," Luke replied. "I'll button it back up when we get to the restaurant." She seemed satisfied with his response and faced forward smiling. Luke could hear the distant sound of Pearl Jam from his speakers. While he instinctively reached out his hand to turn up the volume, his internal hunger to join Eddie Vedder in song was denied when Rochelle spoke out.

"So what did you and my father talk about?" she asked with a smile. *As if you don't know*, he thought. *Who knows, maybe she doesn't know*. Luke decided against the volume and pulled his hand back. *Damn, this is a good song.*

"Oh, we talked shop...you know, he was wondering about my post-graduation plans." Luke turned the car onto the interstate and sped up a little. They were twenty minutes away from the restaurant and he was hungry.

"Is that it? What did you tell him?"

"I told him it was time to fulfill my destiny and set

forth on pilgrimage to Mecca."

"What did you really tell him?"

"That the real five love languages are French, Italian, Buffalo Wings, a touch of Whip Cream, and the Mile High Club."

"Luke—"

"I told him I didn't know exactly what I wanted to do. I just want to graduate, babe." He could tell by her visual response she wanted to know his thoughts about the job opportunity. "And he...offered me a job."

Rochelle spun and faced him. She was clearly excited about the possibilities and implications the job had. He had never seen it from her before, but now it was as clearly written as a children's book; Rochelle wanted to marry him.

"Well? What did you tell him?" She asked excitedly. He looked in his mirrors to give him the extra second to think about his answer.

"I told him I wanted to think about it. It's clearly a charity job Rochelle; there's no way I'm qualified to handle a corporate message or commercial ideas."

"But you'll learn. You'll get the experience. A couple years under my father and you'll be in position to take over the company when he retires. Luke—"

"I don't know the first thing about Organized Dental Supply! "They manufacture surgical tools and miles of floss. That's all I know," he interrupted. "Rochelle, I'm a musician. I want to play, or find a way to stay in the music industry. If my daily conversations consist of #3 Molar Clamps and High Ridging Molding Gels I will be extremely disappointed with my life."

"High Ridge Molding Gels?"

"I just made that up. All I really want is to keep playing somehow."

"But babe, you can always teach private lessons or write your own songs. That will always be there. But this is secure, something we can build a future from."

"You and I...I mean, you're father was talking about marriage and things like that...Rochelle, we've never talked about getting married before," Luke pointed out as he passed a car on the left.

"Slow down."

"What?"

"Slow down, it rained earlier." Luke, annoyed by this comment, chose to ignore it. "Well, come on, Luke; what's the next step if it isn't getting engaged? We've been dating for two years. We're twenty three—you can't tell me you haven't thought about it."

"Honestly, I haven't. I've never imagined myself getting married."

"You've never thought about getting married?"

"No."

"Then what; a common-law marriage? Partnership?"

"I was definitely leaning towards a partnership, particularly because we're unbelievable on the racquetball court."

"Luke, Will you be serious for five seconds? Do you want to just date forever and continue visiting my parent's house on the weekends?"

"No, I just haven't thought about getting married yet. We're young."

"Luke, your parents got married at twenty-five. My parents got married at twenty. Age doesn't decide when you should get married."

"No, but being *ready* should decide when you get married. Are you ready?"

"I could be."

"But I'm not. Sixty-three percent of marriages—"

"Here we go with the numbers—"

"Sixty-three percent of marriages end in a divorce; forty-nine percent of marriages have one or both of the individuals committing adultery; of the sixty-three percent of the marriages that end in divorce, forty-two percent have children, and seven out of ten of those children are still in Elementary school or younger. The world today stands for something different—the United States alone has marital success rates down to below forty percent for the first time in history. Lately, when a person says their wedding vows it doesn't mean they're certain the other is the 'one', it means 'you're the one until you die or I find someone better'."

"Why do you have to be so cynical about everything?"

"Those are facts!"

"But you can be the difference maker—you can tilt the percentages in the opposite direction just by being legitimate with your life. When you say 'I do' and 'Till death do you part', you shouldn't assume you might be one of the five out of ten that cheats on your wife!"

"Sometimes it's not cheating—sometimes it's starting over."

As soon as he said this he knew the reasons why for saying it, though he imagined it sounded awful to her. *I've never wanted to be married*, *not since—*

"Look out!" Rochelle screamed as she grabbed his arm. Luke turned his attention to the red lights of the car in front of him and hit the brakes. His Pathfinder screeched to a stop with about a foot to spare. He could see the glasses of the driver in front of him looking in the rear view mirror probably wondering why he was so damn close to his car.

"Jesus! Will you slow down? Please?" Rochelle pleaded.

"Yeah, I'm sorry babe. Are you okay?" He leaned over and kissed her apologetically.

"Yeah, I'm fine, babe. You just..." She paused. "You mean to tell me you really haven't thought about marrying me?" Luke closed his eyes for a brief moment. He knew this was not the conversation either of them wanted to have on their two year-anniversary evening.

The car in front of them started moving again and Luke slowly moved the car with the rest of traffic.

"I have," he lied. "I just don't want us to have to put ourselves in a trapped position."

"What do you mean?" she asked. Her facial expression had changed from all smiles to a small scowl in a matter of minutes. Luke knew he had that affect on people when it came to a debate.

"Well, if I tell your dad I'll take the job, and everything starts out great, what happens if we break up later for some reason? Then your father is in a bad position, I'm in a bad position; we're all in a bad position." He thought that sounded logical.

"But you're making the assumption that we'll break up down the road. Why would you do that?"

"Because things happen, I don't know. I'm not saying we will, but I am saying that there are unseen possibilities."

"What if Alpha Centauri blows up to a Red Giant and we're all incinerated? That's an unseen possibility."

"Actually scientists are predicting that to happen sometime in the next ten thousand years. But due to it's relative distance we wouldn't be incinerated, we would slowly—"

"Luke, What the hell are you talking about?"

"Unseen possibilities. I'm talking about what I don't know at twenty-three. Hindsight is perfect because of the experiences we go through—the unknown is unclear. It's a haze we walk through until we wake up one day on the other side of the bed, educated by the nightmares we've just had."

"You just lost me."

"I'm talking about the things that could happen,

that we can't possibly see yet, but we may be more ready for with time."

"What, like you meeting someone else?"

"No, of course not." He was digging himself into a hole.

"Then what, exactly?"

"I don't know."

"You can't do that Luke, you can't plan everything out on what may or may not happen, you have to simply choose the best option for you and act on it." Her logic was beginning to trump his logic, but he wasn't finished.

"But doesn't that take the adventure out of not knowing something? Like, where you'll be in five years; secure situations create schedules and redundant lifestyles."

"And what's the problem with that if you're with the person you love?"

"It's not a problem. But look at my dad; when my mother died, he never moved on. He has been doing the same thing day in and day out for nine years."

"You're not your dad. He chooses his lifestyle."

"But it was all based on an unforeseen event. One random day his wife was gone—that can happen to anybody."

"Luke, you're scared of commitment."

"I am not."

"Yes, you are. You think if you decide to marry me, you're trapped. Then one day, the same thing could happen to you that happened to your dad."

"Maybe. Maybe my father would have been a better man if he hadn't met my mother."

"How can you sit there and say that?"

"My father grieves—everyday he grieves. He mourns the loss of my mother, but the problem is he's been mourning *silently* for nine years. His heart has been left in shattered pieces so small they're like grains of sand—big enough to be examined in the palm of your hand but so small they can never be put back together."

"But your father had to give his heart away for it to be broken; isn't there something beautiful about that? Yes, there are tragedies, but aren't there great things before a tragedy that define the action as a tragedy?"

"But at what cost? A few moments of bliss before a lifetime of heartache? That sounds terrible."

"Luke, I love you, but you are a walking, talking contradiction sometimes."

"How so?"

"You sing and write songs that define everybody's dream about love, happiness, and heartache, but you don't believe in them. You think what happened to your mother will happen to everyone; it won't. You have to take a leap of faith every once in awhile. Take a risk."

It's not what happened to my mother, he thought, *it's what happened to my father.*

"Look, I told your dad I'd think about the job. He said I have till July 1st to give him an answer. We need to graduate first. We're sitting here talking about marriage, when we're inches away from finishing school. Can't we just ease into one life-changing moment at a time?" He tried to smile after this last part, but when he looked over at her, the damage had already been done. She was disappointed in his response. *What a night already, a job offer, almost an accident, and an argument; if I get a big plate of shit at the restaurant the night will be complete.*

Just then he could feel his phone vibrating in his pocket. He pulled it out while making sure he was paying attention to the road. It was a text message from his friend, Jay. Jay was the coordinator of a program they had at UCLA called "Music Mentors". Luke gave free private piano and guitar lessons to high school students for college credit. Without it, he wasn't going to graduate. Jay thought Luke was great and gave him all the hours he could. The message said:

Dont forget manana afternoon at Douglas

Luke read the message and was slightly confused. *Don't forget tomorrow at Douglas*, he thought, *what does that mean? I don't remember him scheduling me for a lesson.* Rochelle could see his confusion as she leaned over to read the message. Luke held up the phone so she could read it with her own eyes.

"Do you know what that is?" he asked. She always knew his schedule better than he did.

"Yeah, tomorrow at two," she said with a sigh.

"What's tomorrow at two?"

"You have a guitar lesson at Douglas High School," she replied. He looked at her still confused. "Remember? It's that foreign exchange student who was hoping for a few lessons before she returns home. A German girl named...Saskia?"

He couldn't remember the name, or the meeting, but she was most likely right. He thought about that name though, *Saskia*. He liked it. He hoped she knew something about how to play—starting from scratch was always a headache. Luke looked over at Rochelle who was clearly replaying their conversation in her head. He decided it would be better to keep quiet as he took the exit off the interstate towards the restaurant. Another year had passed, and he wondered when it would start getting better before it would start getting worse. All he knew at that moment was that the Pearl Jam song had long since passed and the world's divorce rate wasn't changing. It seemed he and Rochelle had been standing in line for a happy ending to a great day for a long time without admission.

5.

10/20/08 7:24 A.M.
United Flight 7742
Airborne

Peter had hardly noticed the plane had been airborne for about an hour. He was reading Luke's words very carefully and at times had to retrace and re-read. Luke was a good writer, but his penmanship wasn't always perfectly legible.

Luke's feelings about Peter had been true. Peter knew his life had been in neutral for a long time. Mary's death had destroyed him, and in the process, destroyed his relationship with his sons. He could dwell on the thoughts all day, but he decided to push past them.

Peter had wondered why his son, even in his own journal had not clearly articulated his feelings for Rochelle. *Maybe*, he thought, *at this moment in time he just didn't know. I didn't know how I felt about Mary until I married her; and even then I didn't know I loved her as much as I did until the day she died. It's hard to know.* He glanced back at a couple of the pages and felt a great deal of sympathy for Rochelle. He always liked her. She was kind, sweet, beautiful, and responsible. Peter knew, long before reading his son's entry that Rochelle was very much in love with his son. If love was tested by the Tour De France, Rochelle was Lance Armstrong; unequivocally one of the best and resilient to the test of time.

Peter kept his mind on Rochelle as he thumbed back through the previous pages describing in great detail his son's skeptical nature—a trait he got from his old man. Peter always knew Rochelle to be supremely charitable and unbelievably selfless. Her raw nature and intuition was to take care of Luke, comfort him, and always see his point of view as clearly as she could. She was a modern day wife to the soldiers of the great wars—a dying breed amongst young and independent women today—so independent it's almost detrimental to their cause.

Rochelle will be a great wife for someone, Peter thought, *I just wish that someone had been my son. I wonder if Rochelle even knows about Luke's death.* Peter did not like the question—he had not called her, in fact, he hadn't even called Jake. He didn't know what to tell them. He didn't know what had happened. The thought of not calling his only other son, and Luke's lone brother, made Peter feel ashamed of himself. *Mary would not be proud of me right now.*

Pushing the thought aside, Peter reached for his water in the pouch in front of him, took a nice long drink, and returned it to its place. He settled back into his comfortable reading position, put his glasses back on, and turned the page to the next entry in the journal. He read:

5/17 Saskia
Today was an interesting day...it was the day I met Saskia Einreiner...

6.

05/17/08 1:37 P.M.
Douglas High School
Music Room

Luke took a sip of his caramel mocha as he set his guitar case down in the Douglas High School Music room. He looked at his watch; it read 1:37. He was tired. The night before he and Rochelle had stayed up late, talking about the future and finishing their conversation from the car. No solution was ever reached, so the two threw in the towel for some great anniversary sex. Luke was exhausted from such a late night and no chance to sleep in. He had driven from the Dobb's home in Anaheim to his apartment near the UCLA campus to pick up his guitar; then he had to head back south to Lakewood where Douglas High School is located; it consumed his entire morning. He liked to arrive early so he could set up before the student arrived.

Luke pulled out his Les Paul Gibson and began tuning it to perfection. Sometimes he would tune and retune his guitar because he enjoyed doing it so much. When he was satisfied with how it sounded, he played the first few cords of "Outside" by Staind, a group he had come to love and respect. Being a room engineered to absorb sound to relieve any echo, the sound coming from Luke's guitar was clear and precise. He reset himself, took another drink of mocha, and started over again, but this time hammering through the introduction. When the lyrics came, he didn't slow down. Luke was in his element—he closed his eyes as he often did and sang:

"And you
Can bring me to my knees
Yeah

All this time
That I could make you breathe
Yeah

All the times
That I felt insecure
Yeah

And I leave
A burning path of flames
Yeah"

Luke began tapping his foot, feeling the connection between the three elements of music; the instrument, the man, and the words. When he reached the end of the verse, he was about to sing the chorus, when he opened his eyes to see a young woman, a beautiful woman, standing at the door watching him intently.

Luke stopped playing, and set his guitar to the side.

"Oh please, don't stop," the young woman said with a hint of German accent. "I could come back if you would like." Luke smiled and moved towards her.

"No, believe me, I should stop," He replied with a smile. "You must be Saskia?"

"Yes. And you are Luke."

He couldn't stop staring into her eyes. She had

deep blue eyes that stood out in perfection. Rochelle had blue eyes as well, also beautiful, but they were far from Saskia's. Luke was having trouble placing the discrepancy—the shape? The shade of blue? The gold streak of Rochelle's compared to the dark triumph of Saskia's? Poseidon versus Zeus? Luke came back to earth when he realized he was taking it too far.

"I am," he said with a smile. In fact, he realized, it was more of a blush, which, he didn't understand why it was more of a blush. Shaking the thought out of his head he returned his attention to her.

"Am I late?" Saskia asked with genuine sincerity.

"No. I got here early. It was a long night, and I had to drive a ways to get here," Luke said, not realizing how it sounded.

"I see," Saskia said as she raised her eyebrows.

"No, not a long night like that," Luke defended as he thought about how his previous statement sounded. "It was just a late night...of nothing."

Saskia smiled. "Okay."

"Please, come and sit down." Luke held out his hand as if to direct her to her "patient's" chair. "What can I do for you today?"

"I think I came for a guitar lesson." Saskia said sarcastically but playfully.

"Of course," Luke replied with his own sarcasm. "I just meant, what are we going to be working from? Are you a beginner? Have you ever played before?"

"Yes. I have played a little before. I am not very good at getting my fingers to the correct frets. Did you have similar problems when you first started?"

"I think everyone does. I had really small hands when I first started because I was, like nine, I think."

"Nine? You have been playing that long?"

"Yeah."

"Wow. I think I was still playing with the mud in

my pigtails at nine," Saskia shot back. "Did you teach yourself or did you get lessons?"

"A mixture of both. But a few lessons are how I got started. It's an interesting story actually." Luke and Saskia sat down in the two chairs next to Luke's guitar case and cooling mocha. "I had this next-door neighbor who was great at playing. This guy had to have been straight out of Woodstock—long hair, big side-burns, glasses; always smoking a cigarette. He was playing on his back porch one day during the summer, and I thought it sounded so cool, so I snuck over to his house while my mom was inside making lunch."

"You daredevil," Saskia said with a smile. Luke instantly thought she had one of the most beautiful smiles he had ever seen.

"Yeah, I know. I was just this curious George of a nine-year old standing in front of this guy, and I started asking him all these questions about how he was playing, what he was playing, and if he could teach me how to play. So he starts to teach me how to play, or at least a couple chords, when we both hear my mom screaming my name from the other side of the fence. Alex, that was his name, told me I better go home but promised me he would give me a few more lessons. When I got home, my mom was so pissed, but when I told her the whole story about what I was doing, she agreed not to tell my dad that I snuck off and said she would get me some guitar lessons from Alex."

"Ahh, that was nice of her."

Luke smiled. "Yeah."

"So Alex taught you how to play the guitar?"

"I guess. I only took a few lessons from him. My parents bought me a guitar later that year, and I started teaching myself how to play. When you love something enough, the work becomes easy I guess."

"I think that is true with anything," Saskia replied

as she folded her hands in her lap. Luke picked up his mocha to take another sip.

"Oh yeah? What do you love to do?" Luke asked inquisitively.

"What do I love to do?" Saskia questioned in a way that she didn't expect the conversation to go back on herself.

"Yeah, what is your passion that made the work easy?"

"Oh, lots of things I guess. When I was younger I loved to dance. I saw Madona's "Like a Virgin" music video and wanted to be a dancer so bad. My parents didn't love the motivation, but they supported me. I danced for like five years before I got tired of it. I love movies, jogging, drawing—recently I have loved being on the debate team over here, but it is hard for me to debate in English, so that takes work...I guess I have never really found something that I love that takes work."

"You're young still. Actually, how old are you?" Luke asked, actually surprising himself as the question slipped out.

"I'm eighteen."

At least she's eighteen, Luke said to himself. *Jesus, Luke, no! Get that thought out of your head.*

"Yes, well you don't look it," Luke stated thinking out loud. Saskia raised her brows in pleasant surprise, and Luke, realizing what he had said and how it might be perceived, clapped, smiled, and looked at Saskia. "To our lesson?"

"Yes." Saskia said with a smile.

"Getting the finger positioning takes time and practice, but there are some tricks I can show you. First we'll find out what you know, and then we'll look at new things. Sound good?"

"Of course, Luke." Luke didn't know what was just

said that made his hair stand on end, but he wished the feeling would pass and not return.

"Well, how about you get out your guitar, we'll tune together, and get started," Luke said as he sat back down in his chair next to his cold mocha and case.

"Okay," replied Saskia as she put down her case and took off her jean jacket. She was wearing a green long-sleeved v-neck cardigan with a white tank top underneath. It went well with her tight blue jeans that sunk down into her calf-high brown snakeskin boots. She wore a little silver necklace with a flower at the end. Luke noticed his eyes traveling down her neck to her chest to identify the necklace when he quickly repositioned his eyes. Her long brown hair flowed to the midpoint on her back, near her very thin waist. Saskia was petite and gorgeous. Sensuality shined with every movement of her body. This was no regular high school girl.

Over the next two hours, Luke and Saskia continued to talk about themselves, while mixing in about a total of fifteen minutes worth of guitar lessons. The guitars basically sat in the laps of the young man and woman as they shared stories, jokes, smiles, and playful flirtatious banter. Luke had completely lost track of time. His world and Saskia's seemed to unite into one—it was a world separate from reality, from the way things are, but it was all real at the same time. He was twenty-three years old, graduating from college, a proud U.S. citizen, in a two year relationship with Rochelle, the son of a widowed father; and here he was, engulfed and completely trapped within this moment, this very real moment with an eighteen year-old exchange student. Luke didn't doubt his actions, but he knew there was a possibility for consequences if things went further than discussion.

"So my buddy—" Luke was finishing a story about

his best friend, when the door to the music room swung open. A stout man with a briefcase was walking in. Under his arm was a clarinet and a flute case—Luke was guessing it was the Douglas High School music instructor.

"Saskia, how are the lesson's coming?" asked the man. Saskia smiled.

"Great, Mr. Bennett. Luke is a great teacher," Saskia turned to Luke and dropped her smile for a face that Luke could never forget; it was a face of burning longing and adult passion.

"I think we were just wrapping up..." They both looked at each other as if to share the secret that they had indeed not worked on Saskia's lesson at all.

Mr. Bennett smiled in oblivious acknowledgment.

"Yes, please do, I need the room in ten minutes for a choir rehearsal for the performance next week."

"Of course," Luke said as he started to pack up his guitar. Saskia followed suit, and when the two were loaded up Luke looked up at her. *I'll walk her out, that's it*, he thought, *but then I need to go.* "Can I walk you out?"

"Yes, please," she said politely. Luke put out his hand as to say "you first" and the two walked out of the music room saying their goodbyes to Mr. Bennett. When they reached the open air, Luke noticed the parking lot was empty. He remembered it was a Saturday. He also noticed only two cars; his, and probably Mr. Bennett's. When they reached the center point of the parking lot near his Pathfinder, Luke turned to Saskia. He knew he shouldn't ask the question, but it didn't stop him from doing it.

"Do you have a ride home?" he asked. She balanced on her toes in heightened tranquility.

"Oh, I'll just take the bus. It's only a few stops from here," she replied. "It will be fine." Luke took a deep breath. He couldn't just let her take the bus.

"Can I give you a lift? I'm sure it's not out of my way," Luke said with little reluctance.

"Really?" then she paused, "Luke, really?" The way she said it made Luke's hair stand on end.

After a moment of warfare with his conscience, Luke went over to the passenger side of his Pathfinder, and opened the door for Saskia.

7.

05/18/08 5:05 P.M.
Lakewood Community Park

Taking in his surroundings, Luke thought Saskia had chosen a good meeting place. The park was quiet— a few people from the surrounding neighborhood coming and going, most of them walking their dogs. The tall oak trees provided a shade against the evening sun breaking through in patterns all over the manicured grass. The cedar-chip paths twisted and turned in random intervals—the tracks of joggers left on the surface— some fresh and some old. The playground was on the other end of the park—Luke could hear the laughter of children in the distance as they played without a single thought or care in the world. Luke wished he could be so lucky.

His legs were tap dancing on the seat of the park bench—his hands clutching the table top he was sitting on. She was a few minutes late, but he had been a half hour early. Luke had parked his car a few blocks down from the park entrance, about a block away from a remote music store he'd heard of but never shopped at, just in case. Guilt had led to paranoia, and paranoia had led to over-analyzing and over-thinking every possible scenario which included wintergreen gum and pre-cautionary condom in the hidden pocket of his book bag. He had brought a "Introduction to Music" textbook in case anyone asked why they were there together—he would tell them he was a music tutor, and the two wanted to get out of the building they were studying in because it lacked air conditioning. *Should I be reading through the textbook when she walks up?* He questioned to himself. *In case anyone she knows or I know, sees her walking up to me? Or in case she changes her mind about walking and wants to actually talk about music? What if she doesn't want to walk anymore? Then...I'm being paranoid.*

Luke tried to relax. He tried to convince himself the ride home had just been a "ride home". Saskia rode quietly in the passenger seat, but just before they reached her host family's home, they had caught eyes; he imagined they had been missing each other's glances the entire ride since then; but when they finally caught eyes, she had been the only thing on his mind ever since. Luke had trouble sleeping that night. He always had trouble sleeping. When she was getting out of the car, she proposed they meet in the park and go for a walk. *Walks are fine*, he had thought, *everyone goes on walks in the park*. They agreed on a time and meeting place, and then she left.

Rochelle had called him shortly after and asked him if he wanted her to come stay the night. He made up a list of things he needed to do and told her it would be best if she stayed at her place. The guilt of *possibilities* made him act as if he had cheated already. But Luke didn't want to cheat—he never wanted to hurt Rochelle—she was the best person he had ever known. But Saskia had blown him away—she made him feel sixteen again, when he had a crush on the first seat clarinet in his high school band, but didn't know what to say to her.

Luke reached into his book bag holding the textbook and pulled it out. He opened the book to chapter one then quickly closed it again and put it back in the bag. *What am I doing? I'm an idiot.* Instead of closing the bag, he pulled out a stick of gum. He had been chewing gum like a chain smoker. Closing his eyes, he could sense the oncoming anxiety, urging him to stand up and do jumping jacks to calm his nerves, but instead he opened his eyes to see Saskia entering the park.

Frozen in place, he watched her turn the corner down the path heading towards him. For lack of a description that would do heaven justice, she looked beautiful beyond all recognition. Wearing black leggings diving into short black boots, her legs moved sensually in unison and harmony with the twisting and turning spring breeze. A long black "Helen of Troy" top acted as a skirt—it was low cut, highlighting her full breasts. Her long dark hair waved around her shoulders—the breeze creating a photo shoot without a photographer in sight. A red handbag sat on her shoulder. As she got closer the sun fighting through the trees reflected the gloss from her lips—some of it fading away as she bit her lower lip when she saw him.

Her eyes—Luke couldn't get over her eyes. Since the beginning of time, it seemed the creator of all things absolutely knew what he was doing when he created a woman's eyes—Saskia was his ultimate model. As Luke watched her walk towards him, he simply forgot…everything. Breathing, swallowing, moving, talking, motioning; simply "being" didn't seem to function.

When she was ten feet away from him she stopped as his senses return.

"Hey," he said while rubbing the lust out of his eyes.

"Hi," she replied with a smile. "How are you doing?" Luke slid down from the park table top and stood, putting his hands in his pockets.

"I'm good. It's a beautiful day out." Luke realized he didn't know what to say. In the music room he could focus on the guitar lesson and that led to other things. He needed a starting point, and the weather sounded about right.

"Yeah, it's gorgeous." She looked up at the park around her.

"Yeah," Luke replied as he followed suit, even though he had memorized the tree-tops around him during his forty minute wait. The silence began to grow heavy.

"Do you want to go for a walk? / Do you want to see this textbook?" They said at the same time.

"No you first / No go ahead," They spoke again. Luke laughed a little. Saskia smiled then said before he could, "What?"

"Nothing, what did you ask?" Luke asked. He thought she said something about a walk, but between his nervousness and his conscience arguing in his stomach, his ears didn't seem to work.

"I asked if you wanted to go for a walk," Saskia

said smiling. Luke smiled back. Reaching for his bag from the table, his hand slid across the top of a rough board and dug a sliver into his index finger.

"Yeah...Ouch!" he exclaimed as he pulled his finger into view.

"What did you do?" Saskia asked with genuine curiosity.

"Nothing, it's just a sliver." Luke replied as he tried to start pinching it out. Saskia moved closer to him.

"A what?" she asked as she stood next to him looking at his finger.

"A sliver; you know a small piece of wood or something that digs in to your skin at the most inopportune times. I guess...when you're stupid like me." He explained, trailing off at some parts, feeling dumb at others. Saskia moved in really close.

"Oh, a "sliver"; I will remember that word. Let me see." Saskia moved in to touch his hand.

"No, you don't have to," he started to say when she grabbed his hand. The warmth of her fingers, the skin on his skin made his hair stand on end. She examined the sliver as he examined her hair—her close proximity, with the slight breeze, carried a scent of flowers and female perfume. Luke was taking it all in when she pinched the deep sliver from both side of his finger. He grimaced with a small amount of pain and let out a little yelp

"Don't be so immature," Saskia said with a smile. She looked up at him, and with a small motion, brought up her finger to reveal the small sliver on the tip it. He smiled down to her, the pain from the short moment, gone.

"I thought that would've been my line today," he teased. "Being the grown up and all."

"A grown up with a 'sliver' that makes him cry.

More like a baby in Germany." Her rebuttals never seemed to take her much thought. "And when a baby has a "sliver," we kiss the finger after it is out."

Saskia, still holding his finger with her left hand, raised it to her lips and kissed the end of it. Luke took a large inhale, his heart speeding up. *What am I doing?*

"Thank you," he said when she lowered his finger, and then finally, separated her hand from his. "So that walk...?" She nodded and smiled as he turned and reached for his bag this time; the three seconds she was out of his view, annoying him. "This park is pretty big, where do you want to go?"

"Everywhere," she replied. "Or at least everywhere we can go in three hours."

"Is that all the time you have?" Luke asked as they started down a cedar chip path.

"Yes. My host family wants me home for dinner," she answered. "They think I am at the library."

"Oh," Luke said. It had just dawned on him the event was a secret all around; from her host family, and from Rochelle. "Are they cool people?"

"Oh yes. I have come to like them very much. It is hard for me though."

"Why?"

"They have a lot of rules."

"Don't all parents?"

"Here? Yes."

"What is so different about here?"

"Well, culturally we have a lot of differences. I think my parent's looked at me as if I was an adult at fifteen. They trusted I was old enough to make decisions, but not just decisions, but actually the right decisions."

"Fair enough."

"In Germany, most kids are more independent than American kids. It is not uncommon for them to move out of the house at sixteen, or not have a curfew anymore at sixteen since it's the drinking age."

"I was born in the wrong country." A jogger passed by them. Luke looked at him suspiciously.

"It is just how it always has been. American kids are dependent. The system makes them this way. High School ends at the age a person is considered an adult. So most students need their parents until they go to University; and even then I imagine most still need their parents."

"True. But try not to generalize that statement. Not all American kids are like that; some have to work really hard."

"And some don't work hard at all."

"Do you like the States? I mean, from what it sounds like you despise it." Saskia stopped him dead in his tracks by putting her hand on his forearm.

"Oh no, I don't mean to sound like that. I do not like most of the high school kids but I love California. The sky is so big here. The weather is always so nice." Luke didn't know a lot about the climate of Germany, in fact, he didn't know anything about Germany. "And Christmas in America—how wonderful is Christmas in America? The decorations, the candy, the presents, the family time; it is all so beautiful."

As if by instinct, Luke dropped his eyes when she spoke about family time—it had been so long since his whole family shared a Christmas together. Saskia noticed and moved in with the questioning he'd hoped to avoid.

"Please, tell me about your family. What are they like?" The innocence in her voice softened the blow that Luke felt every time someone asked about his family.

"I agree that Christmas is probably great for most people—it used to be for me. My mother died when I was fourteen—in a car accident when she was taking me to school."

"Oh Luke, I am so sorry. Why didn't you mention this yesterday?"

"I didn't see the need to then. I didn't want to be like, 'Hi my name is Luke, by the way my mother died when I was fourteen.'"

"It wouldn't have been like that but I understand…wow, you were only fourteen. That must have been terrible for you and your family."

"Yeah. Well, my older brother, Jake, graduated from high school that year and moved to the East Coast. I haven't seen him for two years. We hardly ever talk. I hardly talk with my father and he just lives in Sacramento—he owns a hardware store up there. He always seemed to love the store more than his own family." Luke looked down to the ground, but when he glanced up he noticed Saskia's eyes were glued to him. There was a brief silence—Luke realized she was waiting for him, intently listening on anything he wanted to tell her. "I guess my family isn't what you've read in books; the white picket fence and the American Dream. It's more like a nightmare actually, but I've learned to deal with it."

"Do you miss your mother?" Luke stopped for a moment. He hadn't been asked this question in a long time.

"Yeah, I do," he began, "she was an awesome mom. She always wanted to help Jake and I; she always thought we could do whatever we wanted, like with the guitar lessons. She just wanted us to have dreams and to chase them." He paused—he didn't even know what he was saying. "But I was young. When she passed away my father never tried to remarry—I know he really, really loved her." Luke turned and began walking down the path—he was starting to shake on the warm, spring day. Saskia followed and he used the motion for a role-reversal.

"What about your family?" he asked. "Do you have any siblings?"

"Yes. I have two older brothers and two younger sisters," she said with a smile.

"Big family."

"I guess my parents loved their bed."

Luke laughed out loud and nodded his head in agreement.

"My parents are still married after thirty years. We have lived in the same apartment all my life. It has three bedrooms. My sisters and I shared a room, and my brother's had their own room."

"Wow; did you ever hate not having your own room?"

"Oh no; I love my sisters. I always thought it was a good way to be with them more often. I would get to comb their hair, and help them with homework. My family is very close."

"Very cool." Another jogger passed by and Luke hardly even noticed him. "What do your parent's do?"

"What do they do?" she repeated.

"Yeah, for a living? What are their jobs?"

"Oh, yes, well my father heads the Safety Committee at BMW. Do you know it?"

"Of course."

"He makes sure all of the new engineering patents are safe for the cars. Other than that, I have no idea what he does, exactly, but I do know he loves his job. He normally saves his work conversations for my brothers." Luke smiled.

"And your mom?"

"My mother was a...what's the word for the "Food Choices" class?"

"Oh, Home Economics?" She didn't quite understand but agreed with him anyway.

"Yes. She used to teach students how to cook but then she had too many kids at home. She wants to work again when my younger sister Mia gets to the seventh grade."

"Nice. How old is everyone?"

"My parents are both forty-eight—they met at University whatever year that was. My older brother Jonus is twenty-four, Timo is twenty-one, Hannah is fifteen, and Mia is ten...no eleven, I think. It is hard for me to remember since I have been gone a long time."

"Do you miss them?"

"I do. A few days ago I couldn't wait to get back to Munich." Luke stopped and turned to her—the two were now standing in the center of the park. Luke noticed nobody was around them, the distant voices of the children playing on the playground were closer, but still out of sight.

"What about today?" he asked.

"Now...I could wait longer." She replied. She finally broke and looked down to the ground, toeing some leaves to the side.

"And why would you want to wait longer?" He was playing the game—a game he had not played in over two years.

"Because now," she started and paused before continuing slowly. "There is you." She smiled as her eyes returned to his.

"And what is it about me that would make you want to stay?"

"I don't know exactly. Not yet anyway."

Luke laughed out loud. He knew what she was talking about but he also couldn't put it into words.

"And, are you trying to figure it out?"

"I am. I don't know," she paused. "You're just so easy to talk to. Didn't you think that the two hours we spent together yesterday just flew by?"

"They did."

"And?"

"And what?"

"Time doesn't just fly by. Smiles don't just sit on people's faces. The world isn't this happy."

"Maybe it is."

"Do you honestly believe that?"

Luke paused for a moment. He was bating her before, but now he was honestly thinking about her question. His world had never been simple, easy, carefree, or happy. But was he actually happy now, or was this just some flash-in-the pan infatuation?

"No, I guess I don't."

"Then what is this?"

"I don't know. A walk?"

"Yes it is. A walk with you."

Over the next three hours Luke and Saskia circled the public park as they continued to talk about their pasts, about their dreams, and about their problems and solutions for mankind. Luke could feel the strangest feeling in the pit of his stomach as he kept up stride for stride with his walking companion—a feeling of wonder that ignited a smile every step of the way, even when they were arguing about impossible declarations, for instance, what movie would go down as the greatest movie ever. He could see his life coming full-circle in a moment as if meeting Saskia was a re-birth, a new beginning to the order of his life—almost as if she was always meant to be next to him. Their views, their thoughts, and their distinct beliefs combined at times, repelled at others, but weaved together as a DNA strand of an extinct variety; without one, the other could not exist, fully.

As the sun began to set behind the tree tops revealing a coming time when they would have to part,

Luke found himself staring less at the ground as they walked, but more at Saskia's profile. Her beauty was truly a vision, but she had somehow grown more attractive in their time together. She grew less iconic; he began to see her for who she was completely. Luke let his thoughts become vocal as he stopped mid-stride.

"Saskia, I see you."

"What?" she asked with a smile as she stopped and turned to him.

"I don't know why I'm telling you this, and I shouldn't be telling you this, but I see you."

"What do you mean, you "see" me?"

"We've been walking and talking for three hours. Three hours which feel like three minutes. I would spend the next three years talking to you if you didn't have to go home. I don't know what's happening...but, if I thought you were beautiful when you walked up to me, it doesn't even compare to how I see you now...you are absolutely gorgeous."

"Thank you...I don't really know what to say." Saskia said blushing as she made herself keep her face up so she could look at him. "What are we doing here?"

"Walking," Luke said with a grin.

"Yeah...but Luke, you have to have a thousand girls who would "walk" with you. With how you think and how you sing—with how you look—how can I even compete?"

"I see your modesty and raise you some bullshit." Luke said as they both laughed. "You compete. You win. I just don't...I don't really know what's next."

"Me either."

"Does that worry you?"

"I don't know what to be worried about," Saskia said as she smiled—it wasn't the same smile as before. It was a smile that contained a hidden agenda—some plan that made sense to both of them even if it couldn't be scripted.

Luke threw his hands up over his head and quickly paced away from her as he chuckled to himself. In all of his life, he never thought he would feel, almost in an instant, how he did in that moment.

"I don't know either," he said out loud. "But..." Luke turned around to see Saskia had approached him, and in the same time as a flash of lightening, Luke couldn't wait a second longer. He grabbed the back of her head with his right hand and pulled her face to his. The second their lips touched the energy alleviated to a beautiful harmonious slow dance as they explored each others style, pace, and feelings. Luke brought his left hand up to her face and quickly felt the softness of her skin with his rough fingers. Luke could feel his body trembling as he reminded himself not to lock his knees, for in that moment he was as nervous as he had ever been before. This was *her*. And he knew it with total certainty.

As he pulled away from Saskia's face, he stared in her eyes to convey a message that only they could understand. At the same time, he could feel his cell phone vibrating in his pocket. He knew who it was. He would need to speak with her; one final time.

8.

Peter sat in stunned disbelief. He felt as if he had just witnessed an illegal act of some sort—the kind you see on the evening news. The young woman was eighteen but how could Luke even consider it? *Who in the world is Saskia Einreiner?* He thought, *and what was Luke doing with her?* Peter hoped it would remain a mystery, but he knew an answer would come in the following entry, especially when he read the date.

For so long he wondered what went through Luke's head—what the actual reason for breaking off his relationship with Rochelle was—he presumed he was about to find out. *But why now? Why this way?* Why couldn't Luke have told him himself? The answers Peter was searching for were just illuminated points for the reason why his relationships with his son's had failed. Peter was never in a position where he was listening; he was always explaining, condemning, wishing, hoping, reeling, forgetting, and patronizing; but he was never listening.

At that moment a sad realization hit Peter like an anvil; by reading Luke's journal, Peter was in a position that required him to listen. Luke was gone—his body was at the Genoa morgue—Peter would never talk to his son again, except through what was left behind in his written journals. Peter looked to the heavens as he stretched his neck; it is the same with Jesus Christ, the

54

Son of God. Christians for two thousand years have communicated with their Lord and Savior through his divine word, the Bible; a series of stories left behind after Jesus' crucifixion.

Luke is not the Son of God, he thought, *but he is my son, and I won't give up on him. I'm listening Luke, speak to me.* Peter prepared himself for the next entry. He was amazed at how much his son wrote in his journal.

Four hours into his flight to Rome, with most of the surrounding passengers fast asleep, Peter opened up the journal to his marked page, and began reading again:

5/20 "Goodbye My Lover"….

Two weeks ago I listened to James Blunt's "Goodbye my Lover"; at that moment I didn't think anything of it, but yesterday morning, I heard it again…"Goodbye my Lover, Goodbye my Friend." I am in utter termoil—because no matter how right the situation is for me, there isn't enough selfishness within me to forget about Rochelle, and the Dobbses. The world is what we make of it—through action…it is not always what we want it to be, and even then, opinions differ from person to person.

What I did last night was one of the hardest and easiest things I have ever had to do in my life…

9.

05/20/08 8:12 P.M.
Luke's Apartment
Los Angeles, California

I'm an adventurer. She's not. She doesn't want to be with me. She wants a family, a life, and security. I can't give that to her. Children? If parenting were genetic, I'd be a horrible father. I have to do this. I have to.

Luke sat impatiently waiting for Rochelle to arrive. He was on edge; he was nervous. He sat in his brown armchair his brother had given him when he moved to the East Coast. It was an older chair, but the brown leather was still a great commodity not many college students encountered. It was side thoughts like these that prevented him from pulling out all of his hair in the present moment. He heard the knock on the door.

When he opened the door the sight of Rochelle almost sent him reeling into an emotional collapse. As she walked by, he knew she had no idea what was about to happen.

"Hey babe," she said. "I went to Blockbuster and got "Half Baked" and "Scary Movie II" for you and "Armageddon" for me." She smiled as she put the movies down on the coffee table. Luke's mouth was dry as he attempted a half-hearted smile.

"Thanks..." he started to say, but the words left him after that. He looked down as if his feet might have a prompter he could read from.

"Are you okay baby?" Rochelle said as she moved towards him. "Let me feel your temperature. Do you feel

56

sick?" Rochelle had put her palm up to his forehead. As she felt the warmth of his cerebral sickness, Luke knew this would be one of the last times that she would touch him. He pulled her close and hugged her tight—a selfish gesture if anything.

"No, Rochelle, I'm fine. We need to talk," he said. The tone in his voice was sincere. Luke was going to go through with this.

"What's wrong Luke? Is everything okay?" she asked as she sniffed the air. "Have you been smoking?"

Luke worked to convince himself that almost every person in the world had been in this position before, and all of them seemed to get out alive. Ignoring her question, he pressed on.

"I think we need to sit down Rochelle," he replied. She nodded suspiciously as she pushed aside the DVD's to clear room to sit on the coffee table. Luke sat down in his armchair, face to face with Rochelle.

"Rochelle, this is hard for me...there's no amount of practice you can put into a speech like this...to make it perfect...I..." Luke trailed off, but when he looked into her eyes, he saw she was leaning forward in excitement. She was smiling. *Oh no! She thinks I'm going to propose.*

"It's okay Luke, just try," she said with a smile. Luke put his hands up and beckoned her to stop.

How in the world did she think I was going to propose? Especially after the anniversary dinner argument? The mediocre sex. Well, no, it was great sex. But I've been missing...Hadn't she noticed? I've been sneaking around with Saskia for three days...Saskia...tell her, Luke.

"I've met someone else."

The words stood alone. A moment of silence was granted from both parties. Luke had said it with a diabolical confidence so she wouldn't confuse it as a joke.

"What? Wha..." Rochelle trailed off as her forehead cringed. Her hands dropping into her lap.

"I've met someone. I never planned it..." Luke convinced himself earlier he would stay away from clichés. "I have fallen for this girl. I have fallen hard, Rochelle, and I'm sorry. I can't even begin to tell you how sorry I am."

"Luke," she began to tear up. "Is this for real? Are you serious right now?"

"Yes."

"But, when? How? I don't understand—"Rochelle was reaching, searching for any answer she could.

"The guitar lesson at Douglas High on Saturday." He didn't want to lie to her. He never wanted to lie to her—he decided to be as honest as he could be, all the way to the end.

"What?" Rochelle stood up and paced away from him covering her mouth with her hands to keep from bursting out loud. "Her?" Rochelle wheeled around. "How old is she Luke? Isn't she in high school?"

"Yes. She's eighteen." He didn't want to give anything more than what she asked. This wouldn't be an interrogation—it would be a lie detector test he would pass with flying colors.

"Eighteen? Are you serious? What the hell...I mean..." Rochelle was trying to find the words, but who can at this point? Luke sat patiently in the chair. She stood in the archway to his kitchen, crying, taking moments to figure out her next move. "Eighteen...Luke, why are you doing this?"

"I didn't mean for this to happen. I was happy with us, Rochelle. I was happy with everything—"he started.

"Don't! Don't say—"she interrupted.

"I have to say it. I was happy. But she, she

makes me feel invincible. She makes me feel alive in ways I didn't know could happen. I don't even know her, and I feel this way. I can't—"

"You don't even know her! That's right, Luke! You're going to throw away our two years together—our future, for some high school girl? One you've known less then a fucking week?" Rochelle was screaming now.

"Rochelle, she's young, so be it. I can't do anything about her age."

"But you can do something about your dick! Have you slept with her?"

"No," he paused. "I've kissed her. That's all."

"You've kissed her?" Rochelle questioned with rhetorical force. Moving from the counter she walked straight over to the adjacent wall and pulled down a framed picture of the two of them, and threw it on the ground, shattering the glass all over his carpet.

"Rochelle, don't..."

Rochelle slapped him in the face. Then again. Then again. After the third slap she formed a fist and started pounding on his chest, shouting the entire time, until it faded into a sob. Her hands slowly started to lose their energy, until she was soon holding his chest. She drove her head against his body, and wept.

Luke withstood the abuse; he deserved it. And as Rochelle wept against his chest, he wrapped his long arms around her small body and comforted her. When she could catch a breath, she looked up at him almost apologetically.

"Luke. What did I do? What..." she said, the words shaken.

"Nothing. Rochelle, you did nothing." He wanted to say something meaningful, but he couldn't find the words.

"Luke, don't you love me?" she asked, her voice soft, but abused.

"I do. I do love you, Rochelle, but not enough to stay with you." When he said the words, she cried even more. She held onto him tightly, as if she never wanted to let go. From the voice muffled by the clinging to his chest, Luke heard her say something that brought tears to his eyes.

"I want to marry you. So bad. I want spend the rest of my life with you. You're the only one I've ever wanted to be with. I love you Luke."

Luke lifted his eyes skyward. Rochelle was without a doubt, the best person he had ever known. Even in this moment, after being told a total stranger had replaced her, she fought for what she wanted, for what she loved. Tears rolled down Luke's face—he could never repay her for her kindness and support.

"I know. I know you do." It was all Luke could think to say.

Rochelle's tears heightened, then weakened, and softly ceased. The two held on to each other for what seemed like hours, but was only a matter of minutes. Luke didn't budge—he held still, his body warm against hers—his tears occasional, like wandering rain drops. When he felt her head lift, he looked down into her sad and dejected face.

"Is there anything I can do? Anything to change your mind?" she asked. His chin began to tremble—he almost wish she would have broken the picture and stormed off in a fit of rage—but this, her procrastination and unrelenting cling was more then he could bare.

"I'm sorry, Rochelle. I'm so sorry," he said as his emotions hit climax. It was Luke this time that pulled her close. He held her tight, for one last time.

When he regained his composure, the two separated. Rochelle whipped her eyes, but a cloud of mist remained.

"Luke, if I leave, I'm not coming back. I don't care

what you've done—I don't care who she is. So please, don't let me leave. Don't make me leave.

Luke listened intently to her heeded warning. A small part of him wanted to drop to his knees and beg her forgiveness, but Saskia had already done the damage. Rochelle stared into his eyes, motionless, brave, but without hope.

"Rochelle..." he stopped as he saw her eyes drop. He didn't need to say another word.

Every day, decisions are made. Most people do not think about them, they just act. Very few decisions are made that most people consider life changing. Luke had just made, and stood strong on a decision that would change the world forever. A woman like Rochelle only comes around every once in awhile, but a woman like Saskia is even rarer.

He made no excuses. He had not lied to her. He did not step on her, but neither did he coddle her. He was just a boy, standing in front of girl, illuminating the reality that had come to be. Pain swept across the room—darkness had fallen into night. The two stood for a moment—memories creeping in, but driven away by the present moment—Luke had just broken a woman's heart. A woman he respected and indeed loved.

Rochelle took a deep, hard breath, and to Luke's surprise knelt down in front of the broken glass. Luke began to die inside. With all that he had done that night, Rochelle still wanted to help him by cleaning up the glass from the picture she had broken.

"Don't...please, Rochelle. Don't." Luke said as the tears began to rush back. "Don't."

Rochelle looked up at him with her pained eyes, nodded her head, and stood up. Walking over to the table, she collected her purse, and slowly moved away towards the door. Just when she was about to reach it, she stopped and started to turn back to Luke, but dropping her head she decided against it. She opened the door, and left Luke standing there.

When he heard the door shut behind him, silence echoed in the room—Rochelle was gone, and he was alone. The emotions of a young man are a delicate thing, and sitting alone Luke let one thousand thoughts race through his head. Rochelle had been the best female influence on Luke since the passing of his mother. He had loved her, and now, by his own bidding, he had lost her forever.

Luke sat beside himself in his armchair. His initial instinct was to cry, but he resisted. He dug his hand into his pocket revealing his cell phone that he illuminated with the touch of a button. There were no new messages to scroll through, no voice-mails to hear; he just stared at a picture of him and Rochelle that had been on his home screen for the better part of a year. It was taken on the entryway of the Dobb's home before Luke took Rochelle to her sorority dance. It was a fun night. And as he scrolled though his options Luke realized it was one of many he would be able to clear from his "memory" but not one he would soon easily forget.

10.

10/20/08 11:44 A.M.
United Flight 7742
Airborne

Peter pulled out his handkerchief to wipe the tears from his eyes. He had never known any of this; the break-up, Saskia, his son's..."life". Peter again felt a deep sympathy for Rochelle, but it was not nearly the sympathy he felt for his son. In all of his years Peter never read something so heartfelt and sad as he did his son's last entry. He could tell by the words that his son cared deeply for Rochelle. And from his best guess, the evening had pained his son terribly. Peter felt responsible for it all.

Peter re-read the line that hurt him deeply:

Rochelle, if parenting is genetic, then I will be a horrible father...

Oh Luke, have I been that bad of a father? Wasn't I there for you when you needed me? Peter examined these questions as he lifted his head in exasperation. He felt heavier—Luke had never intended for his secret journal to pain his father, but in his death it had happened. Peter tried hard not to let Luke's personal thoughts become a real-life villain. He had to let the words on the page exist—the good with the bad. Everyone is allowed his or her personal thoughts, and Luke was no different.

Peter raised the window cover to look out the window. High above the cloud cover, the plane was flying over the North Pole. Below the low, sparse cloud line was a thick layer of ice covering the vast area Peter could see out the window. It was bright from the sun's reflection. Peter found the view to be incredible.

Peter had always believed in God—he considered the view below him to be one of many clever creations. He also thought about the Grand Canyon, the Swiss Alps, the Mississippi River, and the Cayman Islands. He had never been to any of them, but he had seen pictures. He recalled Luke saying in his last entry that he was an "adventurer." He smiled as he thought that correct; Luke took after his mother.

Mary was always trying to get Peter to travel, but early in their marriage Peter was still trying to get his hardware store off the ground. Peter worked around the clock—always assuming he did not need to hire one more person if he stocked shelves at night, and did his own inventory aside from the many duties that come from being a small business owner. Once, Mary planned a road trip for the family to Texas to see the Cowboys play the Oakland Raiders, but at the last minute Peter backed out because an employee was in a car accident. Mary took the boys and ended up staying an additional night. Peter could remember when Mary called him from a Best Western in Parcel, Nevada; he remembered Mary passing the phone to Luke, who was seven years old at the time:

"Hey buddy. How was the car ride today?" Peter recalled asking.

"Hey dad! It was cool. We sang songs; played games...Mom let us stop at Dairy Queen." Luke spoke excitedly into the phone.

"That sounds like a good day." Peter replied. "Were you and Jake good boys for your mother?"

"Yeah...hey dad, what does it mean to be "adopted"?" Luke asked curiously.

"What? Why do you ask bud?" Peter replied.

"Well, Jake told me I was adopted. Mom said he was wrong. She said that I was definitely not adopted." Luke said. Peter smiled. He knew why Mary would say "definitely." He let out a small chuckle.

"Luke. Adopted means you would have a different mommy and daddy. And that isn't true. I want you to know son, that I love you very much." Peter said in a soft voice.

"I love you too dad. I wish you were here with us."

"Me too big guy; I *promise* I'll be there the next time." Peter said.

"Do you promise, promise?" Luke exclaimed to his father over the phone.

"I promise, promise. In fact, how about you and I go to the Raiders game next week when they play the Packers? We can watch Brett Favre."

"Wow! Really?" Luke said excitedly.

"You bet. Tell your mom and brother too. We'll all go together." Peter said smiling into the phone. Before he finished his last sentence Luke was already talking loudly to his mom and brother without lowering the phone. Peter had to hold the phone away from his ear because his son was screaming into it.

"Alright, dad. I told them. We're going to bed now. I love you." Luke said.

"I love you too son. Be good to your mother." Peter replied.

"Bye dad." Luke said.

Bye Luke, Peter thought. Peter never did take the boys to the game the following week. A wrong shipment came in that his assistant manager had stocked on the shelves; Peter spent the weekend re-boxing the wrong merchandise and sending it back. Mary scolded him for a week for promising to take Luke to a game and then breaking it. Peter told Luke he would make it up to him somehow, but he never did.

And now, staring out the window on his way to find out what happened to his son, Peter wondered if he had been dead to Luke a longer than Luke had been dead to him.

11.

21/10/08 3:55
Fiumicino International Airport
Rome, Italy

Bump. Bump. Peter opened his eyes he realized he was holding the journal tight against his leg. He couldn't believe he had fallen asleep. He had not been sleeping well lately. All at once it came flooding back in; the entries, Rochelle, Saskia, Luke...Luke was dead.

Peter suddenly lifted his head from the window he had been sleeping against and looked around. All the passengers around him were awake and seated upright. When he took a second to listen he could hear the thudding of the plane tires on the pavement, and the de-acceleration of the 747's engine. *We've landed*, he thought. Peter found it hard to believe that he slept for four straight hours. He turned and opened the window cover surprised to only see the wing lights blinking before the interior lights from Rome International Airport came into view. *What time is it?* Just then the Pilot's voice was heard overhead.

"Good morning ladies and gentleman. Welcome to Fiumicino International in Rome. The time is 4:03. The temperature outside is 17 degrees and climbing..." The Pilot spoke as if he had said that same speech a thousand and one times.

It took a minute for Peter to realize the Pilot had been referring to the temperature in Celsius rather than Fahrenheit. He chuckled to himself, *if it was 17 degrees Fahrenheit in Rome during October, then Al Gore should make another movie.*

When the plane reached the terminal, the Pilot turned off the "seatbelts" sign, as Peter and the rest of the passengers unbuckled and began rooting around for their luggage and personal affects. Peter always hated the process after landing; the impatient wait to get off the plane, the airport terminals and lengthy walks, and Peter's least favorite, the checked luggage retrieval. Checked luggage caused Peter such great grief in his lifetime that he simply stopped checking luggage if he could. This particular trip was one of those treasures— Peter had carried-on his smallest suitcase. Once he got off the plane, he trekked through the lengthy airport, found the main entrance, and waved down a taxi.

The taxi took Peter to the Rome Central Station where Captain Roberto told him to board the 6:03 Train heading for Genoa. During the cab ride Peter nervously glanced at his wristwatch; he didn't want to miss the train. After a long forty-nine minute ride, the taxi pulled in front of the main entrance to the station at 5:49. Peter quickly paid him some of the money Captain

Roberto had sent him. The fare was sixty euros—Peter had given the driver eighty, unaware that tipping wasn't as common in Europe as it was in the States. The driver thanked him gratefully in Italian and Peter started for the steps up through the large station doors.

Peter had never ridden on a train before. The railway system in the States was well behind Europe's. Walking into one of the larger train stations in all of Western Europe was a little overwhelming. He was thankful Captain Roberto had sent him his ticket already—the lines were ten or fifteen people deep, and Peter didn't know if the ticket vendors spoke English. Peter was very surprised to see a cornucopia of American stores and fast-food places within the station; Subway, McDonalds, Burger King, and a bookstore featuring books in english. It wasn't at all what he imagined it would be. He figured there would be steam whistle trains, large luggage carriers, and men in top hats and canes. *I watch too many movies*, Peter thought.

Peter was happy to see on the large board listing trains coming and going, the word "Departure" next to its Italian translation, "Partenza". *Thank God the Italians respect the American traveler*, Peter thought to himself. It never dawned on him that the citizens of Great Britain, the original English-speaking country, frequented the Italian countryside far more than the likes of American citizens.

Peter found his train leaving from *Plattaforma 9*; he didn't need a translation. Glancing down at his watch he read 5:58. He quickened his steps as he past the platforms numerically from three. As he walked through the hoards of people walking and standing, he kept hearing *scusami*, while he was saying, "excuse me." *Scusami, excuse me...wow, they sound a lot alike*, he thought, *just like plattaforma and platform...Italian might be easy to pick up.* He had no idea how wrong he was.

Peter reached the platform with two minutes to spare. He boarded the third car, only to figure out his seat was in the ninth car. Rather than exit and walk down the platform, Peter elected to walk through the five cars in between to ensure he would not miss the train. When he finally reached his seat, he was tired, overheated, and hungry. He realized in his haste, he should have stopped to grab an orange or croissant for the four-hour train ride. Of course, this being his first train ride, Peter was unaware the tenth car was a café.

Shortly after Peter hung his jacket on one of the hooks above his seat, he felt a short jolt and the train was rolling slowly out of the station. Peter pulled the black leather journal and his reading glasses out of his jacket packet and settled comfortably in his seat. It was still dark outside but the interior lights in the train were more than adequate for reading. The seat next to Peter was unoccupied, but directly across from him sat a snuggling couple already attempting to fall asleep.

Peter was not tired. The few hours of uninterrupted sleep on the plane had been enough for the entire day. He was wide-awake, and anxious to get back to Luke's entries. After thumbing through a few pages, Peter found the last entry he read on the plane before falling asleep. Turning over one more page he read the title:

5/22 "The Infamous Thursday"….

Peter thought the title was interesting, but nothing could have prepared him for what he was about to read.

12.

05/22/08 3:06 P.M.
Douglas High School

Luke couldn't believe what he was doing. Every three seconds he was checking one of his mirrors; looking for her...or anything else. He thought if he parked under the large tree he would be less visible by anyone because of the shade reflecting against his tinted windows on his Pathfinder. Luke looked in his rear-view mirror and saw a man in a blue jacket walking down the sidewalk towards his car. Luke straightened up and turned on his engine. *Oh shit*, he thought*, it's a cop. If it's a cop I'm driving around the block.* He didn't want to look in his mirror again, because people who constantly looked in their mirror were guilty of something; like a person going fifteen over the speed limit at night when all the sudden they see two lights turn on behind them; just try not looking in your rear view then; guilty.

Luke could tell the man was getting closer as he pushed in the clutch and put his car in first gear. He was ready to slowly pull out when from his right peripheral vision he saw a stick tapping the ground followed by two slow moving legs. The man in a blue coat wore sunglasses to hide his blind eyes. Luke felt foolish and let out an exhale as he put the car in neutral and turned the ignition.

I can't believe I agreed to pick her up from school, he thought. Luke continued to glance in his mirrors as he sat forty yards from the football complex, just down the street from Douglas High School's central campus. He looked down at the clock. 3:13. *Come on.*

Saskia had said she would ask her History Teacher if she could get out a few minutes early, but it didn't appear she had any luck. Luke couldn't get the idea out of his head, that he placed the entire success of his afternoon on Saskia's fucking History Teacher. *I'm going to jail. She's eighteen, but I'm going to jail somehow.* The paranoia had reached an all-time high when all the sudden a knock on the passenger window made Luke jump.

He turned to see Saskia smiling at how she startled him. He reached over and manually unlocked the door. She threw her bag on the seat behind her, and jumped in the seat. Luke was about to start the engine as she shut the door but her hands grasping at his head interrupted him. He turned his head to meet her gaze and moved in quickly for a long and surprisingly relieving kiss. Her smooth hands took off his beanie as her gentle fingers ran through his straight brown hair. She finally separated about an inch or two from his face to stare at him with her Greek goddess eyes.

"Hi," she said in the softest voice possible.

"Hi," he replied with a smile. Luke finally took notice of the whole picture. Saskia had curled her hair; Luke remembered telling her he wanted to see what it looked like curly; and she had done it. It looked gorgeous. She was wearing a loose v-neck that announced her curves with authority; around her neck hung a plethora of silver and blue necklaces. Her tight blue jeans displayed every curve in her lower figure which made Luke feel very blessed and cursed at the same time; he doubted he could ever take her anywhere without every guy staring at her. Luke loved her fashion sense. Around her wrist was the crucifix bracelet he had given her the night before. "We should get going, don't you think?"

"Of course," she said as she raised one eyebrow

quickly; Luke always loved sexual body language, but he liked the fact it was universal now more than ever.

Luke started the ignition, turned on his left blinker and pulled out of his space away from the school. In his rear view he could see the rest of the student body starting to exit the school. *Perfect timing*, he thought. Saskia was eighteen, and far from a child, but it doesn't look good in any circumstance for a soon-to-be college-graduate to date a high school student; especially a foreign exchange student.

Luke turned to Saskia, buckling her seatbelt.

"So, where to? How long do we have?" he asked.

"I told my host family I was going to the library, and then to a movie...So I think we have about till nine, ten o'clock." She replied with a smile.

"Where do you want to go? Back to the park? Or that place last night?"

"What about your apartment?" She asked with a hint of a grin.

"Really? You want to see my apartment?" Saskia kissed the side of his cheek as he kept his attention on the road.

"Are you kidding, can I live there?" she exclaimed. She wasn't serious but she wasn't holding anything back either. Luke knew what she wanted. It didn't take him long to agree.

"Let me show it to you first. I've got some food there if you're hungry." Luke said as she hung on to his arm. He realized he was in fifth gear heading down the highway so he put his hand on her lap. "How was school today?" She laughed.

"It is so easy, Luke. German schools are much harder. Some days my toughest class is Food Choices." He nodded and smiled. "Also, three out of my six classes had "work days" for projects I finished last week. I mean, how many days do students need 'in class' to finish a speech about a fifty word law amendment?"

Luke smiled. *Yep*, he thought, *that sounds about right. High school was a breeze. College, not so much.*

"And Luke," she started, "the teachers here don't even teach. They hand out worksheets, and projects, and expect the students to figure out the information on their own. Why are they there? I caught my calculus teacher on facebook the other day."

"Really?"

"Yes!"

"That's bad. Public schools in the states are getting worse."

"It's worse than 'worse'...the diploma I'm going to get in two weeks is absolutely meaningless. I'll still have another year when I get back to Munich, and that diploma actually means something."

"I bet. But don't forget, you're going to a public school. There are a lot of great private schools in the area."

"Yeah, that only the rich kids can go to. Why is the government here against funding private vouchers or actually putting money into the public school systems so that the European kids don't come over here and take all of your great jobs? Because you know that is what is happening."

"Probably true."

"Probably?"

"Most of us just don't worry about it..." Luke trailed off as he realized, "That's the problem isn't it?" Saskia laughed.

"Yes. A person's education needs to be valued. I see the problem with most American kids, which I'm not saying that we Germans are perfect, but most kids just want to get to college to party and drink. And the other kids can't go to college because they can't afford it."

"To each his own."

"I guess. I know I voice my opinion too much, but I just see so many differences; there are problems that can be fixed if the people in charge would just realize that a fifteen year old today will be tomorrow's parent and taxpayer."

"Well, listen to you," Luke said with gusto. "I'm putting your name on the ballet for governor of California. I'm sorry to say you won't win since you weren't the "Last Action Hero"."

Luke took the next freeway entrance and sped up to the traffic speed. For ten minutes they headed down the I-9 towards Palmetto. At Bookings, Luke exited the freeway. When he reached his parking space, he put his Pathfinder in neutral, set the parking break, and turned the engine off.

"Well, this is it," he said as he turned to Saskia. She smiled and pulled on the door handle. As she exited the car, Luke took a deep breath. *What the hell am I doing*, he thought. Luke reached over and locked her passenger door, climbed out, and locked his door with his key. Saskia stood on the sidewalk in front of his complex looking at it as a tourist looks at the Eiffel Tower. When Luke reached her he wrapped his arms around her from behind, smothering his face into her long brown hair, inhaling the wondrous scent he would never be able to forget. Saskia ran her hands to his elbows convincing him to hold her tighter. Then she ran her hand up his shoulder to his face, turning as she did so. When they were face to face, Luke once again found himself staring into her deep hazel eyes. He moved in for a long, slow kiss—the taste of her lips transferring to his. Luke knew, in that moment, there was absolutely nothing wrong with the world.

"Do you really want to go up?" he asked pulling away from her.

"Yes." She replied.

"We shouldn't be doing this. You know that right? I shouldn't be doing this. You are so young—I mean, I know you'll graduate soon, but you're still in high school."

"Age is just a number, Luke. If you don't want to, I would understand—"

"No, no." He interrupted. "I do. I want you to come up."

"Then lead the way, Mr. Sebastian," she said with a smile. He let out a small laugh, reached for her hand, and led her to the front entry.

Luke's apartment was on the second floor. He led Saskia up the flight of stairs, got his keys out of his pocket, and opened the door. Luke, knowing the extreme nature of summers in Los Angeles, had bought a window air-conditioning unit when he first moved in to his flat. By May, he never really turned it off. When he opened the door, a blast of cool air flooded into the hallway—Saskia smiled in immediate approval.

"You live in a refrigerator," she joked. Luke led her into the kitchen where he placed his keys and Saskia's purse on the counter.

"I like to keep it cold. I hate being hot."

"And you live in California?"

"Tuche," Luke replied with a flip of his index finger.

"Do you live alone?" Saskia asked.

"Yep. I sure do. I never really liked having a roommate."

"Why?"

"I guess I just like my personal space. Plus, I don't like annoying anyone and I love to play my guitar at night rather then watch T.V."

"You don't like living with anyone?" Saskia said as she batted her eyes playfully.

"There are exceptions to every rule if it came

down to it." Luke said as he winked. He loved their ability to flirt openly about even the most serious of topics that would be miles down the road.

"How can you afford it, if you don't mind me asking."

"I don't. I work during the summers, but I saved all of my mother's life insurance money after she passed. I got academic scholarships for school, so I never had a real reason to spend any of it. I'm a simple guy."

"YOU are not simple!" Saskia shot back. Luke just laughed.

"Okay, maybe...I'm not that simple."

"But I like it," Saskia said as she reached for his hands and pulled him in for a kiss.

"Well, do you want a tour of the flat?" he asked. Luke had been saying "flat" instead of "apartment" since living in the dorms his freshman year; his roommate was an Englishman named Lyle who was studying abroad.

"I thought you wanted to dance?" she said looking at their arms positioning.

"I would love to dance." He said as he started swaying with her. He began to whistle Neil Diamond's "Sweet Caroline" when she stopped and laughed.

"I would prefer the tour," she said. He smiled and kissed her on the tip of her nose.

"Okay. One tour coming up," he said as he switched voices. "If you please miss, keep all hands inside the tour guide's pockets at all times," she reached behind him and put her hands in his butt pockets. "And if at any time you have a tour question, or if you want to remove clothing, please feel free to do so." She smiled, but then pretended to be serious as if it were a real tour. "Our first stop is the kitchen. Built in...well whenever the hell this flat was built, the kitchen has been the birthplace and home to many horribly cooked meals, late night Chinese takeout, beer drinking games, and stubbed toes on the counter stools early in the morning." Saskia laughed at his humor and quick improvisational wit.

"Sir," she said, "There was a rumor that current food was being homed here; would you care to comment on that?"

"Ah food, yes," he started as he walked her to the refrigerator. Opening the main door he scanned the almost empty shelves. "Food, yes, food….no. There is no food. That rumor is a myth and the creator of such a fallacy should be spanked." She laughed again, and shut the door for him.

"Oh, he will be punished." Saskia kissed the side of his neck and then straightened in front of him. "But please continue with the tour, Sir." She replied.

"Right. Our next stop is the T.V. room," he said as he led her through the archway into his living room. "There is a T.V., coffee table, and armchair and…well, that's it, actually."

"Excuse me, but if there are two people, where does the other sit?" she asked. "I mean, one arm chair is hardly enough to…accommodate a party." Luke's eyes went wide as he turned around.

"Oh to the contrary Miss; if a party is what you want, that armchair is plenty big enough for two. Parties of three or more are always encouraged, but only one male is allowed; house rules." She hit him on the chest as he smiled. "Now, a person with personal space issues, well, they should sit on the floor." He winked. She rolled her eyes. "And now for the last stop, the bachelor's humble sleeping grounds."

Luke led Saskia into his master bedroom. Through the door directly in front of them was Luke's work-desk surrounded by a chair, a framed autographed poster of

Dave Matthews, and two guitars sitting on racks. To the right was a queen-sized bed with black coverings; above it was a shelf with framed pictures, collector's items, and an old Seven-Eleven Big Gulp cup. Running along the adjacent wall were two doors; one to his walk-in closet, and the other to his bathroom. Saskia moved into the room freely, looking at the posters and pictures hanging on the wall thoroughly while Luke plopped down on his bed.

As Saskia roamed around the room, Luke could sense building emotions. He felt that with each passing moment he climbed higher and higher into the limitless sky—a sensation synonymous with the fear of falling. Luke was in love with Saskia—he felt more for her in two minutes than he did in two years with Rochelle. In a matter of days, Luke believed in love again—he witnessed its power first hand—the jubilance and joy; the invisible feeling. Luke wanted to commit his music to explaining the wonders of it all—to make others believe in the search for the whole self—a journey to find a soul mate.

Luke could not believe he was lying on his bed, twenty-three years old, watching the woman he knew to be the future of his existence. She consumed his thoughts; he spent his days scribbling lyrics in an attempt to write the perfect song; the song that would explain it all. She held his heart by a thread; and knowing this scared the living shit out of him.

When Saskia finished her scan of his desk, she crossed over to his bathroom door, peered in and nodded in approval. He lay motionless atop his covers as she moved towards him.

"I love your room," she said as she positioned herself on top of him.

"Really? I've always thought it could use a feminine touch...maybe someone to clean it and pick up after me—" he joked.

"You wish," she replied as she ran her fingers through his hair. She leaned down and kissed him. When she separated, Luke could see the look of longing in her eyes. She bit her lower lip in sexual anticipation. She wanted him and she wanted him bad. No amount of air conditioning could cool her down—Luke ran his fingers up her shirt, feeling the smoothness of her back—the warmth making his palms balmy. As they continued long, slow, and sensual kisses Luke slid her shirt high over her head—her black bra the only thing keeping her perfect breast from visibility. She followed suit and removed his shirt; his olive tan skin reflecting the light coming in from the window; the daylight exposing his lean physique.

Throughout the ages there has been a difference between lust, sex, and making love. Lust can be triggered by merely one of our human senses—the way a man looks at a woman without knowing a single thing about her, and wanting her. Sex can almost be described as a mutual lust agreement between two people—with this commencement, one or both of the parties should realize the inevitable hurt that awaits them down the road. Making love is for the distinguished—it is beautiful, timeless, and controlled. For Luke and Saskia, and the love that they instantly shared that day in the music room, there could be no better description of the ensuing hours woven in passion as their first time making love.

In one motion Luke rolled Saskia to his right, repositioning himself over the top of her. Luke took her hand in his. He looked into her eyes as his hand ran down her arm and behind her back. With the appropriate amount of pressure from his right thumb and index finger, Luke unlatched the clasp on her bra, and slowly went down to kiss...

13.

21/10/08 7:39
Train 24504

Peter closed the journal before he read another word. He wanted to find out information about his son, but couldn't bring himself to read about his sexual endeavors. Peter knew a picture was worth a thousand words, and at that moment Peter wished his son had taken a Polaroid picture that he could easily place in the back of the journal like a bookmark, never to be seen again.

Peter removed his reading glasses and ran his face through his hands. He glanced over at the couple sitting next to him. The young man was still asleep against the window, but the young woman was awake and now reading a book. She glanced over at him and smiled, holding up the book as if to say, "good book" in universal hand gestures. Peter raised the journal and gave a closed mouth smile in a similar reply. *If only she knew what I was reading*, he thought. He turned to glance out the window. He hadn't even noticed the sun had risen. Out the window the rolling Italian hills moved slowly by. Peter guessed the train was traveling at a speed of seventy miles per hour. Captain Caligno had told him it wasn't a high-speed train, but Peter didn't mind. He enjoyed the comfortable sway as he glanced out the single-pane window—the view surreal, new, and surprisingly breathtaking despite the circumstances.

At that moment it dawned on him that Luke had traveled down these exact tracks. The young man, Chris Ludlow, whom Peter had never met, had told Captain

Caligno their route during official questioning. Chris had flown into Amsterdam, Netherlands; after two days of God knows what, he met up with Luke in Munich. Peter had wondered why Luke wanted to meet Chris in Munich, but now it all seemed clear; Luke had gone to see Saskia before his travels. From Munich the boys headed east to Prague in the Czech Republic. According to Chris, the boys spent a few days in each city before moving on. From Prague, they traveled southwest to Bratislava, Slovakia. Next, Peter thought they would go to Vienna, Austria, but for some reason the two boys skipped it—they headed to Budapest, Hungary instead.

In the official report Chris said they had taken the overnight train from Budapest to Venice, Italy. Peter knew Luke had an interest in Italy; he had always said he wanted to visit Vatican City, as well as Sicily. Luke was a big fan of "The Godfather"—when he was younger he would put cotton swabs in his mouth and mimic the character Vito Corlioni put to life by the late Marlon Brando. Mary had always encouraged Luke to become an actor. In middle school Luke performed in all the school plays and musicals. His talent was noted and praised by all of his teachers and friends, but shortly after Mary's death Luke lost interest in drama and never set foot on the stage again. Peter always thought it was a shame.

After Venice, the boys headed to Southern Italy; they stopped in Bari, but never made it as far south as Sicily, which puzzled Peter. He hoped to ask Chris about it when he arrived in Monterosso Al Mare. After Bari, Chris explained they went to Rome for the obvious attractions and almost a week later, going through Genoa, the two headed to Cinque Terre.

In the whole of his phone conversation with Captain Caligno, Peter had been told of his son's death, Chris's description of their rout, and where they were taking Luke's body. This left a lot of information that Peter needed to discover. But with all of the information he wanted to know pertaining to what happened to Luke on his Europe trip, it didn't even calculate to the amount of information Peter let slip through his fingers when his son was alive and well, living in California. The entries had been proof of it. And even now as Peter traveled in his son's wake, he felt a sense of duty to uncover it all. He wanted the truth. He wanted his son back.

Looking out the window, Peter exhaled. He pulled the journal up to his chest as if it were a newborn child, smothering it with the warmth of his arms. The journal was all he had left—the last connection to Luke.

Clearing his mind of previous speculation, he focused his eyes on the journal. He knew, or at least could imagine, what happened next with Luke and Saskia in the comfort of his private abode. Peter didn't want to invade his son's privacy, so he decided to skim read the following pages to hopefully skip the intercourse and get back to what might actually be useful to his investigation.

Glancing down at his wristwatch, which he had already changed for the 9-hour time difference, it read 8:13. *A little over an hour*, he thought to himself. He was supposed to arrive at Genoa Central Station around 9:30. Peter once again positioned his reading glasses and opened the journal to the marked page. His eyes scanned the page:

Thrust...She moaned...Music in the background..."I love you"

Peter's eyes stopped at the words. They were clear and concise. The ink was darker, as if his son had applied more pressure to the pen in his exuberance to publish the three words. *Oh boy Luke*, Peter thought, *Oh boy.* Peter repositioned his hands, and began reading from there:

14.

05/22/08 6:01 P.M.
Luke's Apartment

"I love you," Luke whispered in Saskia's ear. Time had stopped. The two lay naked, interlocked, under a maze of ruffled sheets, attempting to fend off the cool sensation of the air conditioning on their sweating skin after the physical flurry. Saskia's eyes opened as she slowly turned to meet his illuminated gaze. She started to speak but hesitated. "I do. I feel crazy for saying it, but I can't help it. I love you. I fell in love with you the moment I opened my eyes and saw you standing in the doorway at Douglas. I love everything about you...I mean there is so much I don't know, but I want to learn." He let out a small smile, and then a deep exhale. "Shit. Am I making sen—"

Saskia immediately moved in and kissed Luke with a passionate force that transformed into a soft sensation. His head went spinning—he thought the sheer power of the kiss would bring peace to the world, ending hunger and war forever. He couldn't tell if his heart was beating fast or if it had just stopped beating altogether. He didn't want to open his eyes—the kiss felt like a dance—a harmonious dance he never wanted to end. When he felt her pull her head away, he realized he was gripping her shoulder with undue tension and eased his grip. When he opened his eyes he saw her lips move, and with delayed effort, heard her response.

"I love you too."

Luke couldn't believe the world he was in. He was scared it was a dream—but it wasn't a dream. He was scared it was a movie where the director was about to scream, "that's a wrap"—but there were no cameras or trailers. The reality was indeed upon him—the world was actually a marvelous place. Luke had fallen head over heels for this woman. She defied practicality; she was unlike anyone he had ever met; and Luke hoped history would hold them high in regard, as one of the greatest love stories ever documented. Luke would do anything for this woman.

At that moment, Luke decided his place was no longer in California. Staring into the eyes of the woman he couldn't stand to spend ten minutes away from, Luke wanted nothing more than to follow her to Germany, and leave his past behind him. He wanted to tell her of this epiphany, but figured the conversation would come later. He smiled at the thought, grinning ear to ear; and pulling her closer to him as she again closed her eyes, he glanced at his wristwatch and noted the time; they had four hours until he had to take her home...

"Or she may get grounded".

15.

21/10/08 8:26
Train 24504

Luke had not written that Saskia would get grounded if she was late, but Peter figured that would be the case. In his mind he was mocking Luke's confession of love for the young woman. *How can you love her*, he thought, *when you don't even know her?*

Peter considered himself old-fashioned; born and raised in a conservative home, Peter did not believe in love at first sight, and whimsical relationships. Peter believed in the process; you date one woman at a time, you respect her, and if it worked out, you married her. You always ask for a father's blessing, and divorce is never an option. It was very clear to Peter his son did not follow the same code of conduct as he did—his son sounded like a Liberal Existentialist—he believed in new thoughts and new ideas while living by a universal truth of sex and happiness. Peter no longer wondered who his son had voted for in his absentee ballot—clearly Barrack Obama had won his vote.

Peter paused and backed off the thought for a moment; it wasn't fair for him to be judging his son. He also realized he was a thought or two away from picking a cognitive fight with Luke's journal. He was fighting the truth—the written words of his son's life. Luke didn't love Rochelle; he didn't want to settle down; he fell quickly in love with Saskia; he traveled to Europe and weeks later he died there.

Peter closed his eyes in anguish. *That can't be it. There is no way the ending to Luke's life is so easily explained!* There were still so many loose ends, so many gaps that didn't equate. He removed his reading glasses once again and rubbed his eyes. Between the lengthy entries, his son's penmanship, and the ungodly weight of the situation, his eyes were fatigued. Peter looked down at the journal's pages and realized there were only a few pages left to read. Peter thought there could only be a single entry remaining the way Luke wrote in great detail. A sudden panic hit him; *is there another journal in his room that I missed*? He tried to recall if he saw anything else in his apartment that could have been a journal, but nothing came to mind.

Peter glanced down at his watch and read the time: 8:35. He had enough time to finish reading the journal before he would meet Captain Caligno in Genoa. With the train steadily moving along the western Italian coastline, Peter opened the journal once again and positioned his reading glasses to their familiar place. When he read the title of the last entry, Peter froze in a nervous shock. He did not know the exact date before he read it, but he knew all too well what happened that day. He could recall the evening as if it were yesterday, and did not need the journal to tell him what happened. The entry was about him.

Peter wanted to read the entry, because although he knew what happened, he wanted Luke's perspective—the only perspective that actually mattered at the moment. Knowing the entry would probably pain him Peter started from the top and began to read:

6/12 Cold Food from my Return Home...

Today I drove five hours to my father's home to have dinner—I had told him I was coming for dinner but apparently he forgot. When I arrived he had already eaten and put away the leftovers. Against my will, he pulled out the plastic containers full of chicken and rice and made me a dish...but I didn't go to eat; I went to tell him about Saskia...

16.

06/12/08 8:23 P.M.
Peter Sebastian's Home
Sacramento, California

Luke sat at the familiar table while his father pulled out the chicken and rice containers from the refrigerator. He straightened up his back to stretch; he stopped only once to refuel and stretch his legs on the drive from LA to Sacramento.

"I'm sorry son," said Peter as he pulled a plate from the cupboard above the sink. "I thought you were coming tomorrow for the weekend." Luke rose from his chair to remove his hooded sweatshirt, tossing it on the chair next to him.

"Don't worry about it dad. I'm only staying tonight; I have to get back tomorrow afternoon." He replied as he sat back down. Peter glanced behind him as he scraped the chicken and rice from the containers onto the plate.

"Really?" he asked. "That's a long drive just to stay one night." Peter put a napkin over the top of the full plate and placed it in the microwave. *Beep beep*. The microwave started and Peter turned to his son.

"Yeah, it is, but I have to get back to take care of some stuff." Luke said as he fidgeted with his bracelet.

"Like what?" his father asked sitting across from him.

"Oh you know, music stuff. I also have to talk to Randy about getting my summer job back."

"I thought you weren't going to work there this summer?"

"Yeah, I'm going to try to work one more summer there. They have a new line of six-strings that I want to look at. I might get one and having that employee discount is great."

"But what about that internship you were talking about? Didn't you say you wanted to do that because of the doors it may open?" Peter shifted his weight forward and folded his hands on the table.

"I was going to, Pops, but after I looked into it..." Luke trailed off. "I have other options though." Luke took a deep breath. "Look Dad—" he started.

"What time does graduation start next Saturday?" His father interrupted him, "I want to be there early. I got this new camera—"

"Dad, I'm not walking." Luke said.

"What?"

"I'm not walking. I already had my diploma sent to me."

"You did what? Why?" Peter sat back in obvious disappointment.

"I didn't want to go through that whole deal, you know? It didn't seem worth it." *Ting*. The microwave announced it was finished; neither of them seemed to notice.

"Luke, walking is a big deal. You're announcing your accomplishment to the entire university. You worked hard for that moment. I am proud of you, and I wanted to be there."

"Like you were proud of Jake?" Luke said as he looked up at his father with an exhale. Luke knew it was a low blow, but he had to prove his point.

"Listen Luke, I couldn't be there. I had an emergency at work. I've apologized to your brother a hundred times."

"But that's how it always is, Pops...what if you had an emergency at the store next Saturday? It's just easier this way." Luke tilted his chair back.

"Now hold on. If you walk, I'll be there. I promise." Luke chuckled—his father's promises weren't worth much.

"No, Dad, don't. It's already done—I'm not walking. I didn't come here to talk about this—" Luke leaned into his comments.

"What does Rochelle think about this? I mean, she's walking, right? And Paula and Rick no doubt want you to," Peter interrupted in confusion.

Luke took a moment to gather himself; for once in his life he really wanted his father to listen and understand, so Luke thought of the words he wanted to use. He knew his father would have a tough time understanding what he was about to say.

"Rochelle and I broke up three weeks ago." Luke put it out there. The present situation would be harder to explain.

"No. What happened?" Peter asked.

"Nothing really happened, I just knew...I mean, I..." Luke trailed off and paused before continuing. "I couldn't be with her anymore. I didn't love her, Dad."

"Wait. You broke it off with her?" Peter's voice was full of surprise.

"Yeah, I did." At his reply, Peter shook his head and pushed his chair back. He rose and walked over to the cordless phone that sat on a small dresser table in the next room. He took the phone off the receiver and walked over to Luke.

"Dad, what are you doing?" Luke asked as he watched his father move around.

"Call her, Luke. Call her and tell her you made a big mistake." Peter replied. Luke could have predicted this reaction from his father. He was a surface-looker—he didn't unfold the layers—Luke wondered if his Dad ate a banana without peeling it first. "She'll take you back; that girl loves you."

"No, Dad. Put the phone down." Peter held it out further to Luke.

"Son, I'm serious. Call her—you won't find anyone better than Rochelle. I promise you that."

Luke stared at his father—he couldn't believe the amount of ignorance in the old man. Luke tried not to let himself escalate; he didn't come to fight with his father.

"Sit down Dad, please." He coolly replied. Peter dropped the phone on the table and paced over to the counter where he leaned against it.

"Jesus, Luke. What are you doing? Rochelle is a great girl. You two have been together for what, two years? A successful girl—I mean, what are you looking for?"

Luke was about to answer his question with his story about Saskia when Peter continued his lecture.

"Son, I love you, but your mother would be so disappointed—" he started when Luke interrupted with a kick to the chair next to him, sending it toppling over.

"Don't you even start to tell me what my mother would think! I know who she was—and I know she would've told you to shut the fuck up about ten minutes ago." The restraints were off—the two were going to have this conversation—it was overdue.

"Now you watch your tongue, Lucas!" his father growled. "Your mother raised you boys better than to talk to your father like that."

"Yeah, she did raise us. When were you going to raise us, Pops? You have been so blind and consumed..." Luke paused. He decided not to reveal it today. Not this moment, not now. "What about you? Look at yourself, Dad; mom has been dead for nine years. When are you going to start taking care of yourself?"

"This isn't about me. This is about you, and your future. I've already been married. I've already had my family. Your mother is the only one I have ever loved, and I don't think she would appreciate me with another woman."

"Mom is dead, Dad! She's gone. She's been gone a long time. Yes, my mother raised me better than to talk back to my father, but she also raised me to believe in doing what's right; to believe in happiness and compassion." Peter loosened his stance a little as Luke pushed forward towards his father. "Don't you think mom would've wanted you to be happy? She's been gone a long time, Pops, and you've been stuck in the same routine for nine years. Don't you think she would've wanted you to move on?"

"No I don't, Luke. I think she would've wanted me to continue raising my boys and that's it."

"Then your job's done! Your moral obligation to mom is done. I'm twenty-three years old Dad. Jake is twenty-eight, and he's gone. You're right, you've had your family, but now your family is all but dissolved. When's the last time you talked to Jake? When did you ever come to visit me at school? You obviously don't want anything to do with us, so why not find someone you can love?" Peter just stared in anger. "Move on with your life."

"This is my life!" Peter exploded. Luke stood back. "I worked my ass off to provide for my family! For what? My wife was taken from me; my oldest son won't speak to me; and my youngest son is throwing his life away, for what? Music? I built that company for this family. I worked every day to provide for you. What did I sacrifice so much for, Luke? You tell me. What is happiness?"

Luke knew this would be the finale of the conversation. He turned and grabbed his hooded sweatshirt from the chair and faced his father.

"Happiness is living each day knowing the good outweighs the bad. Happiness is not being so self-absorbed that you can't afford to smile at a complete stranger. Happiness is being able to wake up each morning excited at the different possibilities." Luke began in a cool, rational voice. "You say that you sacrificed everything for Jake and I, but all you did was hide from us. You worked twelve-hour days because the sight of us reminded you of mom. We didn't kill mom—I didn't kill mom, despite what you may think. I just got out of the car Dad, that's all. And now, nine years later, you are just a scared old man. You think if you open up to someone else, you also open up the possibility of getting hurt again. And that includes Jake and I. Well you know what, Dad? You're right. You might get hurt again, but that risk has to be better than this—this obsolete life you lead. You work, for nothing. Every day you don't face reality you lose a day...Rochelle was not the girl I was meant to be with. She is a great girl, and you're right, I may not ever find another girl like her, but that doesn't mean it's a mistake. It doesn't mean that I'm not going to be happy."

"Luke—" Peter tried to say.

"No, you listen to me. You say that I am wasting

my life. You think my music is a waste of time. You're wrong. You think marrying Rochelle was the only thing that would have made me successful. What kind of message does that send me, Dad? That I can't do it myself?"

"No, Luke—" Peter tried again.

"Who has the ultimate power to measure success? Nobody. Success is an individual measurement of happiness. Dad, I am so happy right now that I can't even begin to describe it to you. I am successful—I don't have a lot of money, but I have a treasure beyond wealth...you, you are the least successful person I know. Mom would've wanted you to move on—to try—"

"Alright, Luke, that's enough! I don't want to hear it anymore! I don't want to hear another word about your mother! You didn't just get out of the car, Luke. You killed her! You got angry with her! You got out of the car and it got her killed. She couldn't bare to see you angry for one minute; she sped up to catch you and that was it!"

"That's what you believe? That's what you think?"

"Yeah, I do. You killed this family; so don't lecture me on my life! I won't have it! You hear me? I won't have it." Peter punctuated these last words by slamming his hand down on the counter.

Luke stood in front of his father in disbelief. His father had no idea what happened that day, nine years ago. Luke wanted to scream it at him at the top of his lungs, but he didn't. His father was right—the family was torn apart—and Luke in an instant gave up on ever trying to mend the tears. Holding his hooded sweatshirt in his hand, Luke moved past his motionless father and headed towards the door. When he reached the arch, Luke turned around and said his last words. He felt he owed his father the privilege of the information.

"I'm leaving for Europe in three months. I don't

know when I'll be back." He paused for a moment, and then shaking his head finished with, "I didn't kill her Dad; Mom was already dead." Luke took one more look at his father, before turning and leaving.

Peter stood in his kitchen alone—an all-too familiar feeling. He heard a door shut, an engine warm, and the sound of crackling rubble under tires driving into the distant night. Peter walked over to the microwave and opened the door; pulling out the plate, he noticed the food had gone cold once again.

17.

21/10/08 9:17
Train 24504

Peter stared out the window, watching the passing land. He remembered those words with such clarity and precision.

I didn't kill her Dad, Mom was already dead.

Those were words he remembered vividly, but

had tried to forget ever since that night. *What happened that day in the car?* Peter thought. He figured he would never know—it was a secret that died with Luke. He knew now why Luke had come to see him that night. It didn't have anything to do with Rochelle, graduation, or his mother; Luke was going to tell him about Saskia.

It overwhelmed Peter to think about the possibilities. What if he would have sat there and listened? Luke would have told him about a young woman he had fallen in love with. Peter could have smiled and listened—asking questions when they came up. He imagined Luke would have quoted Shakespeare and Keats to describe Saskia's beauty. The two would have sat at the kitchen table till the late hours of the night. They would have been father and son. And when he had to leave the next morning, Peter would have hugged him—telling him he supported his decision and could not wait to meet the young woman. Luke might have told his father he loved him.

Peter shook his head at the hopeless daydream. There were so many days in his life he wished he could take back. Maybe Luke was right, maybe Mary had been dead long before the accident. He was unable to tell—every night he would crawl into bed and Mary, asleep or not, would roll over and kiss him, telling him she loved him as she curled up on his arm. Peter knew he would give anything for that feeling back—for the warmth of her skin against his.

The sun outside the window was shining bright—the salt air was clean and clear as the train began to slow. Peter glanced down at his watch. 9:22. He knew they would be arriving soon but he saw no sign of the town. Outside, the train went dark as night as it passed through a tunnel. It remained dark for a little over a minute—Peter guessed the tunnel was a little more than a mile long. When daylight peered back through the window, a small city came into view.

Like clockwork, his fellow passengers roused and began packing up their belongings and bringing their luggage down from the racks. Peter noticed no one put on their coats; he figured the locals knew the temperature so he followed suit. Standing up, Peter pulled down his small carry-on sized suitcase and put his jacket inside. While he had the suitcase open he placed the small black leather journal inside it. He surrounded it with his undershirts and dress socks to protect it from the outer shell of the suitcase. The contents of the book were more valuable to him than his wallet—it was his son's story.

The train passed an array of colorful buildings, apartment complexes, and walkways busy with people going about their everyday lives. The train continued to slow until Peter saw the beginnings of the central train station. Six platforms, extending past the covered portion, slowly rolled into view. A small number of people sat waiting for the incoming train, no doubt returning to Rome. Peter put his reading glasses away and stuffed the case into his breast pocket. *God, I'm old*, he thought as he stretched his back out. Lifting his suitcase Peter exited the train knowing in a short time he would see his son for the last time.

18.

21/10/08 9:34
Genoa Train Station

Qui andiamo, Captain Roberto Caligno thought as he saw the train arrive at platform five. His drive from his station just outside of Riomaggiore was a lonely one. The last seventy-two hours had been draining; his youngest son, Elmo, had broken his wrist in a *calcio* match and with his wife, Ella, gone to a funeral in Milan, Elmo was being watched by his older brother, Petri. Roberto wanted to be there for Elmo, but Luke Sebastian's death had taken precedence.

He didn't know how to explain to Mr. Sebastian that he had no idea how his son died. The investigation contained a large, unanswered gap of time. Most of the information he'd received from Luke's traveling *compagno*, Chris Ludlow. Chris had explained to Roberto that the two had gone to dinner, drank some *vino*, and retired to their hotel, *Hotel di Armi*, around 22:30. Everyone in the surrounding area, the restaurant, as well as the hotel receptionist confirmed Chris's story.

But yet somehow Luke's body was found by two French hikers the following morning; the emergency call came in at exactly 9:27. From 22:30 to 9:27 the following day, there wasn't a single person who saw Luke Sebastian leave Monerosso Al Mare. *Merda*, Roberto thought. The brown file under his arm contained photos, a list of Luke's personal belongings, a copy of the official report, a copy of the Missing Person's Report filed by Chris Ludlow, a copy of the Possible Correlation Statement, and copies of the written statements of Chris

Ludlow, Marisa Fericceli (the hotel receptionist), Henri and Fionna Levure (the French hikers), and Priscilla Venetti (the waitress at *La Linea di Riva*); he planned to share them with Mr. Sebastian over lunch. But that was it—that was all he had to offer the man who flew 9,000 miles to hear the autopsy report and identify his son.

As the passengers began to flood off the train, Roberto looked for the man who would be wearing Kaki pants with a blue long sleeved dress shirt. When he saw the man getting off the fourth car, he knew it had to be Peter Sebastian. The man took three steps and started looking around. From about fifty meters Roberto could see the heavy bags under his eyes. He was about the right age—described as sixty years old, slightly overweight, thinning gray hair, with a gold wristwatch.

"*Questo è l'uomo,*" Roberto said as he started towards him. When he was close to him, the man had turned around and motioned with his eyes as if to confirm Roberto's identity. "Mr. Sebastian?"

"Peter, please. Captain Caligno?" Peter butchered the pronunciation. The two shook hands.

"Roberto, please. *Vieni con me.* This way." Roberto led out his hand and Peter followed. "We are due at the *camera mortuaria* in two hours. Have you eaten?" he asked.

"I guess I haven't since the plane. I'm very hungry." Peter replied. He followed Roberto through a large archway heading towards the exit.

"*Bontà.* We shall go to a *ristorante* where you can eat and we can talk. I know a place. Good food." Roberto led him out the exit, where a plain brown, unmarked car was parked.

"That sounds great," Peter replied at Roberto's hospitality. Roberto moved to the trunk of the car and opened it with his key. Peter handed him his suitcase. Roberto could feel the weight of the case. "You have packed lightly." He said in surprise.

"Yes. I guess I don't need much," Peter replied.

"Not like most of the tourists in *Cinque Terre*. I think sometimes they pack their satellites and televisions." Roberto joked. Peter barely smiled.

"I didn't come to watch television," Peter responded with a hint of sadness. Roberto felt as if he had said enough. Roberto locked the suitcase in the trunk and climbed in the driver seat; Peter climbed in the passenger side and the two shut their doors. Roberto glanced at himself in the rear view mirror—he also hadn't slept much the last two nights and wondered if visible bags were also under his eyes. Not noticing anything, he turned on the ignition and pulled out onto the main street.

Standing just less than two hundred centimeters, Roberto had a commanding stance to him. He always slicked his hair back despite the Italian stereotype. He was never seen in uniform—always a black polo shirt tucked into black cargo-style pants. The region almost always required the aviator sunglasses he donned as soon as he and Peter pulled out of the train station. He would have preferred silence, but feeling sorry for Peter's loss, he struck up conversation.

"Was it a good flight?" he asked.

"Yes. It was quick. I slept for a bit." Peter replied. Roberto noticed the tension in Peter's posture. He was *un pesce fuori dall'acqua*. Roberto could relate.

"That is good. We are almost there." Roberto replied. He had been driving down the main street for about a half a mile, but suddenly turned his left blinker. He was taking him to a local *pizzeria* that he liked; he also knew at that time of day it would be near empty, allowing Peter some quiet and space as the two men spoke of sorrowful details.

"You speak great English," Peter said. "Even on

the phone I understood everything. Where did you study?"

Roberto turned left down a side street.

"I studied in school when I was a boy. I loved "The Beatles" and hoped to live in America one day. At the time there were jobs in Miami for Italian immigrants. But when I was sixteen, my father died, and I was left to help provide for my mother and younger sisters. So I stayed here...continued with my English...and joined the *Polizia* when I was twenty. I still study the language, and I still listen to "The Beatles." Roberto smiled. He could see a slight chuckle from Peter as well. He was happy to give him a small, even if meaningless, amount of happiness.

Roberto pulled into the *Pizzeria* parking lot and found a space close to the entrance. As he and Peter exited the car, Roberto remembered to grab the brown file from atop his dashboard. He doubted the lunch would have any effect for Peter other then fulfilling his appetite. Roberto didn't know the investigation had just begun.

19.

21/10/08 9:54
Luigi's Pizzaria

Peter had never eaten so quickly; the two square slices of mozzarella cheese pizza Roberto ordered for him had disappeared from the plate in a matter of minutes. The combination of the pizza and Pepsi was more than sufficient to fend off Peter's western appetite. Peter was still hungry, but he was also anxious to begin discussing the contents of the brown file. After ordering for Peter Roberto had excused himself to use the restroom—he left the file sitting on the table, and Peter was moments away from plunging in when Roberto shut the restroom door behind him, as he returned to his seat.

"Peter, you have eaten quickly. *Era buona?* Good, eh?" he asked as he made himself comfortable by removing his side arm and placing it on the table. Peter glanced at the automatic handgun; he never really liked guns.

"It was. Thank you, very much." Peter replied as he finished the last of his Pepsi Light. Sliding the plate and bottle to the side of the table, Peter wiped his hands with a napkin. "Is that what you have so far?" Peter asked, gesturing to the brown file with his eyes, hoping to indicate he wanted a look.

"Yes. Of course," Roberto answered as he opened the brown folder. Instantly Peter could see the outer edges of photos he knew he didn't want to see hidden behind a short stack of papers. *Lord, give me strength*, Peter thought. Roberto began to organize the stack of papers in front of Peter so he could view more than one at a time. He began to describe their details in the simplest language he could think of.

"This is a copy of the official report I filed through my office in *Riomaggiore*; it contains the outline of procedure details, the incident details, and the licensed *camera mortuaria* we have sent the corpse to." Peter didn't like hearing his son's body being called a corpse but he remained silent. "These are copies of the statements made by Luke's friend, Chris Ludlow, the hotel receptionists, Marisa Fericceli, the waitress Priscilla Benitti, and the two French hikers who found the corpse, Henri and Fionna Levure; all statements are pertaining to the night of 17, October, and the morning of 18, October." Peter had pulled out his reading glasses to take a closer look at each report, which thankfully, had been translated into English.

"This is a copy of Mr. Ludlow's Missing Person's report that he filed 18, October around 16:00. At the bottom, we stapled the Possible Correlation Report; this report allowed us to make the immediate connection between the missing person, and the recovered corpse." Peter looked closely at the correlating times and statements between all the parties involved as he let Captain Roberto continue.

"Also, we were able to get a full list of your son's personal belongings left behind in his hotel room; as well as the list of personal effects sent with him to the *camera mortuaria*." Peter began looking at the two-page list of Luke's personal belongings; it was detailed down to the Swiss Army toothpicks he used. Peter had not yet reached the end of the list when Roberto returned his attention to the last contents of the file. "And these are photos of your son...*dopo la morte*. You do not need to look at them of course."

Roberto closed the folder and slid it to Peter; he

was being courteous by giving him the option to look or not. Peter hesitated for a brief moment; he had already read his son's personal journal entries in order to understand the full truth; he knew he had to look at the photos as well. Peter slowly opened the brown folder as Roberto looked out the window, as if to give Peter a moment alone.

As Peter slid the first photo out of the file, his heart sank into his stomach as he covered his mouth with his hand and closed his eyes. The photo was taken about ten feet from the top of Luke's head about three feet off the ground. Peter could see Luke's right arm laying perpendicular from his body flat on the ground. His right index finger was pointing while the rest of his fingers curled in. His left hand lay palm down over his chest, almost as if he was covering his heart. His right leg lay straight, while his left leg was slightly bent inward. Lying on his back, his head lay to the right. His son was wearing blue jeans, tennis shoes, a black t-shirt, and a blue hooded sweatshirt Peter recognized very well. His son was lying on a dirt path under a group of Olive trees; the ocean horizon was distant in the background; the mountain trail snug against the Italian cliff.

Peter could hardly breathe as he looked at the photo. *That's my boy, that's my baby boy, Luke. That's my son.*

Tears welled in his eyes as he searched for air. He knew, no matter how hard he tried to prepare for this moment, there was no way he could do so. He was a father, riddled with regret, looking at a photo of his son's lifeless body. His mind was reeling—in a world that seems to move faster and faster all the time, this moment seemed to be the beginning of some sort of haunting that would last forever. No father should ever have to outlive his child.

Peter felt Roberto touch his upper forearm. He looked up and nodded.

"No, I'm okay. I just..." he began. Roberto squeezed his arm as Peter took the napkin in his left hand and wiped his eyes. "I just haven't seen him in so long, I didn't...think...I'm fine."

"I am a father too, Peter. Do not think for one moment I wouldn't swear to the Heavens if something happened to either of my son's." Roberto said. Peter hardly listened to his words of encouragement. He picked up the other photo behind it. The initial sight of it again made him close his eyes momentarily before summoning the courage to analyze it.

The position was still the same, but the view had changed; Peter was looking straight down at his son as if he were standing over the top of him. From this view he had a clear view of his son's face; his straight brown hair, longer then usual, was flowing over right side of his face. His blue eyes were slightly open—his stare was intense as if he was searching for something. Luke's mouth was open about a half of an inch as if in his dying moment he was trying to communicate something. The view altogether was terrifying to Peter, but not horrific. There was no blood. His son was not covered in mud; he was in fact clean, preserved, shaved; just lifeless.

Peter's eyes suddenly fixated on a shining silver item that was barely sticking out of his son's t-shirt. It was necklace of some sort, but Peter had never seen it before. *Luke never wore a necklace*, he thought, *or did he?*

"Captain," Peter summoned his voice. "What is this necklace my son is wearing? Do you have the list from the coroner's office? Maybe another photo—something clearer?"

Roberto looked surprised at Peter's interest; his change in demeanor, as if the necklace contained an answer to a long, lost question.

"Yes, a moment," he answered as he rustled through some of the papers he laid out. When he happened across one, Peter noticed the small pictures stapled to the back of the report. "Here it is. It is identified as a "half-heart" engraved with an "S"." Roberto thumbed through the small pictures stapled to the back; when he found the one he was looking for he tore it out and handed it to Peter. "Yes, this. This is it, I believe."

Peter took the small photo and looked closely through his glasses. It was exactly as the coroner had reported; a heart split down the middle, with what appeared as a half "S" engraved in the middle. Looking at the picture in his hand, he had no doubt what the "S" stood for. The necklace around Luke's neck was his other half of his heart—the "S" stood for "Saskia." Somewhere, miles from where they were sitting, Peter imagined a young woman was going about her day wearing an identical necklace; her necklace engraved with the other side of the "S"; for "Sebastian".

"Captain, has there been word from a young woman named Saskia?" Peter asked with angst. "She's a young German woman my son may have been dating. She's young—eighteen or so." Roberto looked surprised by the name.

"No, I don't believe so. Why do you ask?"

"My son kept a journal before he left. On my flight over, I read it—I wanted to see if there was something to make sense of his death. He had—it's a long story, but he had fallen in love with this girl. Saskia. She may know something. I don't know what it would tell us, but if we could contact her, somehow, maybe she received emails, or text messages from Luke."

"Peter, what are we looking for? We haven't ruled out homicide, because the autopsy is not complete, but—"

"You haven't ruled it out," Peter interrupted. "And until we do, it's worth investigating. Please Captain; help me find out what happened to Luke. If we try, we may find something." Peter paused. He could sense his emotions getting the best of him. "My wife was killed in a car accident nine years ago. Just before she died, Luke had gotten out of the car. She ran a red-light—the investigation closed. *Snap*, like that. There were so many unanswered questions. I can't go through that again. Please, Captain, help me find out what happened to my boy."

Roberto shook his head in agreement. Peter hoped Roberto was a man who admired courage, but also was a man that possessed a great deal of it, because Peter needed help. Then he got his answer.

"I can have a lieutenant check the phone records and postal codes for the young woman." Roberto said in a re-assuring voice.

"Have him do that, please. Have him look for a Saskia Einreiner. E-I-N-R-E-I-N-E-R. I think she lives in Munich."

"I'll have him look, *scusami*." Roberto replied. He got up from the table, exited the restaurant, and went to his car to radio the station. Peter, meanwhile, scanned the documents laid out before him. He began reading each document more intuitively—looking for information he could connect, if there was, in fact, anything to connect.

According to Chris Ludlow's statement, he and Luke had gone to dinner after a nap around 20:00. The two went *La Linea di Riva*, a seafood restaurant on the main street in Monterosso. According to Chris, and later confirmed by Priscilla Venetti, the waitress, the two "ordered two bottles of Red La Châteaux Wine, and shared a platter of miscellaneous seafood". Peter knew

Luke wasn't allergic to anything, which ruled out an allergic reaction to the shellfish and oysters. "Sometime around 22:00, the boys paid for their meal and returned to the hotel room". In Chris's statement, he "left his wallet at the restaurant, but was too intoxicated to retrieve it". Marisa Fericceli said she saw "the two young gentlemen return to the hotel around 22:00, but then saw the younger man leave again around 22:13, only to return immediately around 22:19"; this was confirmed by Ms. Venetti as she commented, "the younger, good looking man came to retrieve the wallet left behind, thanked us for our kindness in Spanish, and left again around 22:15."

Everything connected, but didn't return any valuable information. Peter didn't see a gap of time in all of their stories. It was actually very easy to understand; Chris and Luke went to dinner; the two drank wine and ate seafood; they returned to the hotel; Chris left his wallet but felt too drunk to get it, so Luke returned to the restaurant to retrieve it; and then Luke returned to the Hotel room. Peter took a deep breath—he was thinking too bluntly—he put down the paper and thought about home. *What did I do when I couldn't solve something in the hardware store? What would I do if an order I received didn't make sense? If everything appeared normal, but I knew it wasn't?* He suddenly thought he was looking for something when he should not. When an order was wrong, say, the number of shovels he got from Garden's; Peter counted the merchandise for the purpose of finding what was missing, instead of what was there.

This all seemed basic, but Peter knew he had to find what was missing. He picked up the statement by Chris Ludlow and began reading through it again when Roberto came through the door and returned to his seat.

"I have my Lieutenant looking for a trace on the

young woman you requested. He said to give him till the morning." Roberto said. Peter nodded his head in thanks. "What do you think?"

Peter was surprised by the question—almost as if the Captain was asking his advice. He appreciated being in the loop, but Peter was not a detective. But scanning his surroundings, he noted the environment; Cinque Terre was probably not accustomed to random deaths or inquiries of discovered bodies.

"I'm just reading over—" Peter started when he stopped. He re-reads the information from Chris's statement and then looked up at Roberto. "Did the coroner find my son's camera?"

Roberto looked at him surprisingly as he slowly started for the coroner's report again. "I think so. Why?" he asked. Peter shifted his weight to share the information with the Captain.

"Well, according to Chris's statement, the last thing Chris remembers is asking Luke to switch out their cameras." Peter replied. He began to read the statement word for word:

I was about to pass out when I asked Luke to switch out our cameras. I wanted to take pictures of the beach the next day...

"Yes. What does this mean, "to switch out"?" the Captain asked curiously.

"I'm guessing Chris wanted his camera charged. If Luke took his camera off the charger and put Chris's on—" Peter began.

"Then Luke would have his camera during the time of death. *Merda!*" Roberto finished Peter's sentence. He turned the page of the coroner's report quickly and scanned the list again. "Yes, it is here. A Samsung camera. I thought maybe it was a disposable camera."

"No, it's a digital camera with a memory card. Luke's girlfri—ex girlfriend, that is, gave it to him as Christmas gift." Peter noted.

"A nice gift," Roberto suggested.

"Okay," Peter started new. "Luke loved taking pictures. It's possible he took some pictures during the missing time. If he did, the camera will show the recorded times and dates. Then we can start to fill in the gap between 22:30 and 9:27 the following morning."

"Very good, Peter," Roberto said instinctively as he looked at the coroner's report. "I'm sorry I did not see this."

"It's okay. We need to work together on this when we can."

"I understand. After we finish at the *camera mortuaria* I will take you to Monterosso Al Mare—maybe there we can find answers together, if indeed, there are answers to find."

"Why do you say it like that?" Peter was not defensive, just curious—he hoped his tone portrayed his demeanor.

"We do not have the results of your son's autopsy. There are many things that may have happened that could be explained after we receive the results."

"Permit me to ask Captain," Peter replacing "Roberto" with "Captain" to insinuate professional courtesy. "What do you imply when you say that?"

"Peter," Roberto began in a softer voice. "I do not imply or pretend to know your son. I have met and spoken with his traveling friend who met him after a short time in Amsterdam, might I add, and drugs or foreign toxins may come up in the toxicity report." Peter shifted in his seat. "I am just saying, there are possibilities that may be answered after we receive the report."

"And," Peter quickly followed. "There may be things we can find out or get answered without the toxicity report. This is an open investigation, right?"

"It is."

"Then let's treat it like one, please."

"Peter, I just don't want you to look for a phantom killer just to find out your son overdosed on some hack European drugs."

"No, Luke wasn't into drugs. He had too much purpose for any of that. This Saskia girl...she changed him. She changed him for the better. I have to believe, by what I read in his journal, that after meeting her, he became the best version of himself."

"You say he was a detailed writer?" Roberto asked with genuine curiosity.

"Very detailed. On the flight here, I read his journal almost like a book. Why?"

"I shall get you his other journal as soon as we get to Monterosso Al Mare. Maybe that will shed some light on the situation."

Peter's eyes went wide. *Luke has another journal.*

20.

Roberto sped along *Via Vittorio Veneto*; the two were heading to the *camera mortuaria*. He noticed Peter glancing at an extra pair of aviator sunglasses sitting in the center console.

"Put them on, it is a very bright day," Roberto said.

"Thank you," Peter replied as he put the sunglasses on with pleasure. For the first time since watching Peter slump off the train Peter looked semi-relaxed. With the window down, and the cool ocean breeze blowing through the car, Roberto could sense Peter taking in the beautiful country side. The Mediterranean Sea was unusually blue and the site of it was comparable to the pictures of tropical islands in traveler's magazines.

"We will be there in five minutes," Roberto pointed out as he took a left turn at *Via del Cappelleto* which ran into *Via Fontevivo*. "The coroner does not speak English. I will translate as best I can. Okay?"

"Thank you," Peter replied.

"After we finish at the *camera mortuaria*, we will go to *Monterosso Al Mare* and visit with Mr. Ludlow. He flies out in the morning to return home."

"He's returning home?" Peter asked surprised.

"Yes. With what happened to your son, his travels seem meaningless." Roberto replied.

"But you're allowing him to leave?" Peter shifted

in his seat.

"Yes, of course. Should I not?"

"I don't know. I've never met him. He traveled with Luke for a month; then Luke dies. I don't know if—" Peter started.

"You have never met him?" Roberto questioned; his voice more serious.

"No, I haven't. He and Luke met through a friend." Peter glanced over at Roberto; he was now looking at Peter with a small amount of shock in his eyes. Without replying Roberto reached down to his radio.

"*Uno a base di,*" Roberto said into the radio. A voice came in response.

"*Andare avanti uno.*"

"*Si prega di annullare Señor Ludlow's di volo e di trasporto di Monterosso Al Mare. Egli sarà più necessaria per mettere in discussione.*" Roberto said with authority and precision.

"*Copia che.*" Roberto put the radio back in the slot and continued driving.

"What did you say?" asked Peter.

"I made sure one of my men detained Mr. Ludlow. I thought he was a family friend." He replied as he pulled the car into a parking lot of a small medical complex.

21.

21/10/08 10:44
Hotel Di Armi
Moterossa Al Mare, Italy

Chris Ludlow lay on his bed at the *Hotel di Armi* waiting for the return of Captain Caligno. The room felt like a jail cell. He hoped in a few hours the Captain would return with Luke's father, Peter Sebastian. He had no idea what he would tell the man, but meeting him and telling him what he knew about Luke's death was his ticket out of there. He was unsure what happened to Luke that night after blacking out, but he could surely tell him about the adventure of getting to know his son. Luke was a one of a kind—a Jedi master of his crafts; music, romance, and bullshit.

Chris had been living in British Columbia when Luke called him—working as a bartender at an Irish Pub, he had saved enough money for what he considered, "the trip of a lifetime." Luke had been good friends with Chris' best friend Jay at UCLA. Chris had planned on backpacking Western Europe alone until Luke called him in June. Luke had asked him if he could join him from Munich. Chris thought the company could be great, and immediately called Jay to ask about the legitimacy of Luke.

"He's legit," he remembered Jay said. "And make sure you find a guitar for him to play along the way."

That was all Chris needed; confirmation from his best friend the kid was "alright"; the fact he played the guitar was a bonus. Chris never imagined that all this would happen.

As he lay in bed, he ran his hands through his face and hair. Sitting up he turned off the television. None of the channels were in English. He lowered his head, trying to remember every detail from that night—any small, new recollection might put the pieces together.

Cinque Terre had been everything the two hoped it would be, with the exception of one item; there wasn't a single female tourist there that week. A day after the two had arrived Chris wanted to leave, but Luke refused—Luke had his reasons but he wanted it to be a surprise. All throughout Europe Chris had been on a roll—German girls, Russian girls, Slovakian Girls, Italian girls—you name it, he'd done well. But Cinque Terre was full of senior citizens, locals, and tourists' vendors; none of which appealed to Chris. Sure, the sights were beautiful, but the whole of Cinque Terre can be explored and admired in one day.

But Luke's death, his body being found on the trail between Monterosso Al Mare and Vernazza should never have come to pass. The two should have been in Nice, France. *Why did Luke want to stay here so badly?* he kept thinking. The night of 17, October was Chris and Luke's fifth night in Monterosso Al Mare. Every day, Luke would vanish somewhere for hours. Chris had no idea where he went, but whenever he would ask Luke, Luke would smile and tell him to be patient. Chris, bored out of his mind, finally decided to go on a bender. The two went out for a seafood dinner, and Chris ordered two bottles of red wine despite being fairly drunk already. They ate, he drank, and they went back to the hotel. *How did Luke end up on the trail?* The question nagged at him.

Chris stood and pulled out his pack of cigarettes and opened the window. He reached into his bag next to the bed and pulled out the lighter. Once it came into clear view he winced at the sight. It was Luke's lighter—he had bought it in Venice at a cheap souvenir shop. The Italian flag waved over the body of it. Chris afforded a small smile when he noticed the ignition wheels on the head. They were bent outward making it hard to spin them for the spark; the lighter barely worked; Luke had broken it right after they bought it. *The first light*, Chris thought. Luke always joked about the "Fucking First Light" and had even written a small song about it.

Chris missed him. Luke had become his friend, and above all things, his hero. Not because Luke was extraordinary, but more or less because he was real. He never quivered, never complained; he always reminded Chris to "kill 'em with your kindness."

Chris lit his cigarette and pushed his head up against the cracked window. His tall frame looking down at the outlet below—a European converter was plugged in; it was also Luke's. Chris had asked the Captain if he could use it until his return home—the Captain had complied. As his eyes headed back towards the window, Chris remembered something. It had just dawned on him; Luke came back to the room. He remembered telling the Captain he asked Luke to switch out their cameras on the charger, but now he was certain even after that Luke came back to the room.

Chris sat down on the bed to try to clearly remember the event. *Yes, he came back,* he thought, *it wasn't light yet but he came back a second time, after he brought my wallet back.* He was certain of it. *For what though?* Chris tried to piece the event together but couldn't. He had been wasted—three pounders and two bottles of red wine—none of which Luke helped him drink. He had lowered his head again and closed his eyes when he heard the knock on the door.

Chris put his cigarette out on the ashtray sitting on the windowsill as he walked over to the door.

Unlocking the dead bolt, he opened it to find an officer at the door.

"Hi," he said to the officer. He wondered why he was there—Captain Caligno had been the only one in communication with him.

"*Señor* Ludlow," the officer began, "*il volo è stato cancellato. Vi rimarrà qui.*"

"I don't know...I don't speak Italian. English." Chris said with a confused voice. He had almost been used to it by now; sounding like a dumb Canadian. The officer took a moment and tried again.

"Flight cancelled," he stated. "You stay here." The officer turned to leave as Chris walked behind him a step.

"No, wait. There is a mistake. I fly out tomorrow morning." He spoke rapidly in pursuit.

"No. Flight canceled. You stay here." The officer repeated himself with more authority. He turned to leave again when Chris stopped him.

"Wait. Who told you so? Who says?" Chris asked in hopes the officer would get the message.

"*Captain Caligno.* Now stay here. Please." The guard turned and exited down the stairs. Chris stood in the hallway in disbelief. He had no idea why the Captain wanted him there—He had been through enough.

Chris had no idea what happened to Luke Sebastian that night, but he feared he had just become a suspect.

22.

21/10/08 11:37
Camera Mortuaria,
Genoa, Italy

Peter sat near the front desk of the *Mortuaria* while Captain Caligno went in to make sure the pathologist was ready for them. Peter sat with his hands folded in his lap. He found the mortuary to be a very solemn and bland place. The reception desk sat alone in the hallway—a few clipboards clinging to the empty wall behind it. A woman sat at a computer typing away at the keyboard while staring at a file containing notes.

Peter had a moment of doubt. Every person has these moments; where they believe a present situation too big and difficult to be handled. Even when Peter read Luke's second journal, what would it tell him? What would Peter do then? Chris was most likely innocent, and now they were delaying his travels home. Peter wondered if he had family on the other side worrying for him; Peter did not want to be responsible for the delay of a reunion—something he wished he could have done with Luke. At that moment, there was absolutely nothing right with the world.

Staring at the black and white checkered linoleum floor, Peter heard doors open and feet approach. When he looked up, Roberto was heading towards him with a small, gray man in a white lab coat. Peter stood and met them halfway.

"Peter, this is Dr. Beniamino Patra," Roberto said as the two men shook hands.

"Pleasure to meet you," Peter said with a small

smile. Dr. Patra looked at Roberto.

"*Piacere di incotrarvi,*" Roberto relayed. The doctor nodded his head in acknowledgment, and motioned the two to follow him.

"Dr. Patra said as soon as you identify the body, we can retrieve the camera from Luke's personal belongings after they fill out a form and copy your passport. It is standard." Roberto said in a quiet voice as if they were in a Church.

"Okay, sounds good." Peter replied. He was happy to be carrying his passport with him, rather than having left it in his suitcase.

"Dr. Patra says the official autopsy report should return in one or two days maximum. It has to travel to Rome and back. I am sorry, it cannot be faster."

"I understand." Peter said. The three men left the front room and walked down a corridor containing windowless rooms. Each room was numbered. When they reached room "13", Dr. Patra opened the door and ushered the two men in.

As soon as Peter stepped inside his mind and body trembled. The room was cold, and dimly lit; gray metal shelving covered the far wall. There were two chairs, a desk and computer. In the center of the room was a gurney; on top of it was a body-shaped bulk covered by a gray sheet. Peter fought back the tears with everything he had. Roberto took one step into the room and leaned against the front wall. Dr. Patra motioned for Peter to come towards the corpse.

Before the unveiling moment, Roberto stepped forward and spoke.

"Peter, for the report, you have to speak directly to Dr. Patra. He will ask you, *'ti individuare tale organismo come tuo figlio?'*; 'do you identify this body as your son's?' You may answer 'yes' or 'no' in English if you like." Roberto spoke steadily. "Do you understand?"

"Yes," Peter answered as he took a deep breath. Roberto motioned to the Doctor with a head nod; the doctor nodded back and pulled back the grey sheet.

Peter gasped at the sight. His hand immediately covered his mouth to restrain his outward speech. He could no longer fight back the tears as they slowly clouded his vision and moved down his cheek. His lip trembled furiously; he bit down, fighting for composure.

"Peter," Dr. Patra began, "*ti Individuare tale organismo come tuo figlio*?" The question was soft, compassionate, but professional.

"Yes," Peter spoke quietly fighting for the words. "That's my boy."

Dr. Patra nodded to Roberto and moved towards the door. Roberto stepped forward, and shook the Doctor's hand in thanks. Roberto moved to Peter placing his hand on his shoulder.

"We will give you some time alone," Roberto said quietly as he removed his hand and exited the room, closing the door behind him.

When Peter was alone, his emotions exploded. His eyelids crushed together in anguish as he reached for Luke's hand. The light made his son look a slight shade of blue; his half naked body stretched out on the gurney. Peter stood over the top of him clutching Luke's hand. He bent down and kissed the top of it—rigor mortise had prevented him from bringing it to his face. Peter let out a loud howl—his lungs fought the air for a moment of silence. Bending down and placing his head on Luke's chest, Peter began to fight for words.

"Luke," he whimpered. "My son, I am so sorry." With unsteady hands Peter moved his son's hair across his face; it was how Luke liked his hair. "I am so sorry, Lucas. Dad's here." Peter put his hands in his face, whipping the tears from his eyes. "I'm here now, son. I'm listening. Damn it, Luke, I'm sorry!" He looked at his son's face—his chiseled chin and cheekbones—his soft flush lips now cold with death. He reminded Peter of Mary; Luke had always reminded Peter of Mary. "Please, son, tell your mother I love her. I miss you both so much."

Peter could feel his heart racing. He prayed for a heart attack to end his misery. But staring at his son he knew he had to make up for his years of being a bad father. He had to make up for so much lost time; the times where Luke was a phone call away; his wit and charm on the other end of the line. Peter would've given up his own life just to be able to tell his son he loved him, and have him hear it. He had so much to say, but he couldn't find the words. His memory of the last time he saw his son flooded his mind—the night Luke came to tell him about Saskia.

"Luke...when you came to tell me about Saskia...I should have listened, son. I should have been there for you. I...I just wanted what was best for you. You know that, right? I'm your father; of course I just wanted what was best for you." Peter paused as he wiped his nose. "When I told you that you killed your mother...I didn't mean it, son. I didn't mean it. You were right. I'm so sorry son. Lucas, I'm so sorry." Peter paused again to summon his weakened voice. "I'm going to find out what happened—who did this to you. I won't sleep until I know son. I promise you..." Peter trailed off in a burst of tears. He knew Luke didn't hold much stock in his promises, but he hoped his son was looking down on him to see that he meant it with all of his heart. "I promise you son."

Peter ran his hands over his son's face for the final time; bending down he kissed Luke's forehead. "I love you son. I love you. I'm dyi...I love you, Lucas. God rest your soul, son." After his final farewell, Peter placed the gray sheet back into position over his son's body.

Unable to leave, he sat down on one of the steel chairs against the wall. Not knowing what to do exactly, Peter sat in silence. The light above the gurney highlighted the corpse as Peter sat staring at the outline of Luke's body. Without even thinking, Peter folded his hands and dropped to his knees. In moments of tragedy, in a world filled with lust and greed, everyone hopes for a higher power in the final hour.

"Lord, I know I haven't spoken to you in a long time; since Mary died," Peter prayed. His voice was desperate, rough, and strained. "But I have one more favor to ask you again. Could you please watch over my boy, my Lucas." Peter paused. The tears wouldn't cease. "He was so young, Lord; so young. I know it's not my place to ask "why", but why God? Why him?" Peter bowed his head in resentment, looked skyward, then bowed again in restraint. "Lord, I am not much; this you know. But Lucas...he was a creation you could be proud of. Lord, if he's standing at the gate of St. Peter, ask him about all the kids he's taught; all the volunteer hours he put in at the homeless shelter—even when I asked him to stop; and ask him about his good grades— he worked hard." Peter paused in his plea. "Please, Lord, let him through. I wouldn't deserve to pass, but Luke does. I swear it. Please Lord, let him pass...let him pass. Please, Lord, please watch over my boy...Amen."

Peter coughed as he choked on his words. Kneeling next to the gurney, Peter remained motionless for fifteen minutes, alone in silence. Peter could feel the energy expelled from his body. Pushing one leg up, he worked his way to his feet. He could see the spots on his khaki pants left from the dust on the floor. His shirt felt ragged and dirty. He felt his years for the first time in a while—the age sagging from his waist like an anvil weighing him down. Clearing his eyes, Peter took one last look at the gurney, Luke's brown hair just barely visible from under the gray sheet; Peter nodded his head, and turned to leave; completely motivated on fulfilling his last promise to his son.

        When Peter reached the reception area, Roberto and Dr. Patra were standing together talking over a piece of paper. When they noticed Peter, Roberto put two hands on his shoulders and brought Peter in for a hug.

"*Dio sia con voi*, Are you okay?" Roberto asked. Peter couldn't thank this man enough for his friendship and warmth in his time of need. Roberto Caligno was a good man, and a new friend. Peter pulled away and patted Roberto's side adding a warm smile before they fully separated.

"Yes. As good as I can be." Peter replied. Dr. Patra turned Roberto around to speak with him.

"*Non appena i segni della relazione, siamo in grado di darvi Luke's apartenenze. Egli non desidera che il corpo extradited in America?*" Dr. Patra said. Peter could make out "extradited" and "America." He did want the body returned home to be buried in Sacramento next to Mary. Roberto turned to translate.

"He says, as soon as you sign the report we can get your son's belongings. Also, do you want the body to be sent back with you to America?" Roberto translated.

"Yes. I do. Can it stay here till I leave? I would like to travel with him if I can, and I'm not ready to leave." Peter asked. Dr. Patra stood patiently waiting for the translation. When Roberto asked him, Dr. Patra responded, nodding his head as he did so. Roberto turned back around.

"Yes, the corpse can stay here, but for no longer than forty-eight hours. Then it must be sent back to America. Normally, once identified, it must be extradited

122

immediately, but the Doctor will not turn in his official report until the autopsy comes in."

"Thank you, very much. *Grazie*." Peter said to Dr. Patra while shaking his hand. Dr. Patra pointed to the report sitting on the receptionist counter, and Peter nodded moving in to sign the report. Peter then handed the receptionist his passport—the young woman copied down the passport number and returned it to Peter. Then reaching down and unlocking a cabinet below the desk, she pulled up a large plastic sack with Luke's clothes and affects. "*Grazie*," Peter said again taking the plastic sack into his possession.

Peter shook Dr. Patra's hand again as the men said their farewells. Roberto waived back to the receptionist as the two men headed for the exit. Peter was already searching through the sack to locate the camera. Roberto walked through the double doors as Peter stopped before leaving. His hand hit the bottom of the bag when he felt a small plastic ziplock bag. When it came into sight, Peter found himself looking at the silver necklace he saw in the photos at the Pizzeria. Examining it, he thought it was very beautiful, and probably very expensive; sterling silver or maybe even white gold. Pushing through the double doors, he put the necklace in his pocket telling himself he would look at it later. Pushing his hand back into the plastic sack, he felt the small solid square at the bottom of the bag; it was Luke's camera. Walking to Roberto's brown police car, he opened the door and sat inside, not closing the door.

"Does it still have... how is it said...battery left?" Roberto asked.

"Let's see," Peter replied as he touched the small power button on top of the camera. To his surprise, the camera turned on. He noticed the low battery level in the top right corner of the digital screen; it was enough to scroll through the memory card. Peter put on his reading glasses to look at the camera's array of buttons. He noticed the small "play" sign to the right of the screen. Pressing it, the camera thought for a moment and then showed them Luke's last picture.

In the small screen Peter could see a small building in the moonlight. He had never asked before, but it appeared the weather that night was as clear as could be. The small building had the inside lights on. Olive trees surrounded the eastern side, and a small path led up to the stairs of the main entry. A green neon light was barely seen around the left side of the house.

Roberto leaned in closer to get a better look at the photo; doubling back and leaning even closer, his head popped up and looked at Peter.

"I know this place," he exclaimed.

"Where is it?" Peter asked.

"It is close to where your son's body was found. Just up the hill. It is a small pub for hikers to stop. It is owned by a Spaniard." Roberto said with a confused look on his face. "How did Luke know how to get up there? It is a nasty trail."

"I don't know." Peter replied. He scrolled to the next photo. It was an illuminated boy, smiling at the photographer; the night was dark all around from the flash.

"This boy," Roberto began. "I believe he is the Spaniard's son. They are olive tree harvesters. They do not speak English."

"Maybe not, but Luke is fluent in Spanish," Peter replied.

"Let's go. We are heading to Monterosso Al Mare now. We will visit them." Roberto said as he started the ignition.

"Wait," Peter said. Roberto looked at Peter. "The time, the date."

"*Permettetemi*, What is it?" Roberto asked. Peter

pointed to the time and date in the lower left side of the screen.

"The picture was taken the night before Luke died. It was taken on the 16th. It doesn't fill in the time gap. Luke didn't take a picture the night he died."

23.

21/10/08 16:20
Hotel Di Armi
Monterasso Al Mare, Italy

Chris was waiting impatiently in his room. He wanted to go down to the lobby and e-mail his mother about the delay, but he was terrified to do so. The lieutenant had asked him to stay in his room; if he was an actual suspect in Luke's death, Chris wanted to follow every instruction. His watch read, 16:21. He began to calculate how long it had been since he last ate. Outside, the rain had been howling for three hours. Chris thought Cinque Terre was every meteorologist's worst nightmare—an unpredictable coastline with amazing and horrific weather.

Chris began to feel nauseous so he stood up and

paced the small cubicle of a room. The question of why Luke had come back to the room had plagued him all day. Luke was a surprising person. Chris learned very early on in the trip to stop asking so many questions of Luke. Chris could never figure out Luke's heightened sensitivity to the world around him. Thing things that drove Luke crazy seemed to be a contradiction to his personality. Luke was a convicted liberal—a man torn between a thread of uneasy faith and experiencing the plethora of earthly ideas and experiences. When Luke spoke, he spoke with centered intelligence and poise, but when Luke played, he played with reckless abandonment.

During one of their long conversations on one of the countless walks they had taken in the cities they visited, Luke examined a character in a book he had read called, *The Razor's Edge* by Somerset Maugham. The character's named was Larry Darrell—a person Luke felt a great likeness to. Larry, a nomad in pursuit of truth and meaning, found himself spending months at a Monastery with a certain Father Ensheim. Luke had explicitly remembered a line Father Ensheim had told Larry at the end of their acquaintance; he said, "Larry, you are a deeply religious man who doesn't believe in God. The distance that separates you from faith is no greater than the thickness of a cigarette paper." Luke explained to Chris the value of this synopsis—he felt it was dead on with the confliction he felt.

Chris still couldn't believe Luke's body had been found on that trail. *What the fuck happened?* He kept thinking. Chris had been inspired by Luke's outlook on life—as if each gasp of air actually meant something. Luke had always portrayed the excitement of life. During long conversations over pints of ale, Luke would describe the world they lived in. He would rationally point out the wonders as well as the discrepancies. Chris

126

always nodded in agreement, as if Luke had just introduced him to water from a faucet—so clear and easy to understand.

Chris had always run away from understanding. Born and raised in Billings, Montana, Chris had never seen a rational world. His parents divorced when he was a sophomore in high school. His father was an alcoholic, and never a recovering alcoholic. After a series of DUI's and spurts in the county jail, Chris's mother had had enough. She took Chris and his two younger sisters to their Grandparents' house, and that's where they remained as he finished high school. Chris had tried to keep a relationship with his father, but it never stuck. His father had given up on life, and eventually, a small piece of Chris did as well.

Prone to weekend benders and lackluster relationships with women, Chris graduated from High School and left with his best friend, Jay, to work on a charter fishing boat in Alaska for the summer. Chris and Jay had been glued to the hip most of their lives, and that summer was a memorable one for Chris—the open air, the salt of the sea, the four inch beard he grew—a freedom he had never felt in all of his life. All summer long Jay had tried to convince Chris to come to UCLA with him in the fall, but Chris declined. He had been touched by the travel bug, and wanted to experience the world. Continuing his education had no appeal to him— his father had his M.A. in Psychology—a lot of education for a man who spends most Wednesday afternoons cuddling up to a brown paper bag on a park bench pissing himself. No, Chris didn't want education—he wanted freedom—the ability to move from one place to another with little or no dependence or responsibility.

After Jay moved to Los Angeles, Chris stayed in Alaska until the charter season ended. After six months of work, he had compiled enough funds to sustain his new life style. Moving through Canada, staying in places in three or six month increments, Chris had a decision to make; either fly down to Central America, or make the trip across the pond to Europe. Central America would have been cheaper, but Europe was an opportunity he wanted to capitalize on immediately; his impatience plowed over logistics; the Euro was killing the dollar, flights were an arm and a leg, and the global economy was heading into a depression and the president had been deemed by the media a 'lame duck'; and although there was a lot of hype surrounding the ensuing election, the economy remained depleted.

And here he was, six weeks after flying out to Amsterdam to meet Luke Sebastian, a guy he had never previously met, his world turned upside down. Chris believed traveling with the same person over an extended period of time creates an almost "marital" relationship—not in the intimate sense—but something like it. Three weeks into their travels, out of blatant curiosity, Chris found himself wondering what Luke was thinking about sometimes; not because he needed to know, but more or less because he wanted to know. Some of Luke's perspectives helped Chris see his own problems in a new light. Luke also had a troubling relationship with his father—the two had a big argument the last time they spoke—similar to Chris's conversation with his dad, which of course Chris couldn't understand with all of the belligerent bellowing.

Luke always reminded him that the resemblance between a father and son can't stop at a physical description; that human instinct is to mold into the shape of our examples, but, if our examples prove themselves to be washed-up, disappointing drunks, then a new example is required. Luke's insight did not affect Chris when thinking about his father, but they did affect him when he thought about his sisters. Jane and Lisa

128

Ludlow were nineteen and fifteen. They had the same father, same situation, and same miserable father-figure; it pained Chris to think he had made the situation worse by running away from the problem; a problem he never knew existed until Luke had given him some perspective. When Chris explained his epiphany to Luke about Lisa and Jane, Luke smiled, as if that was what he was trying to sweep under the rug the entire time.

What happened to him? What was he thinking? Those two questions   haunted him. Chris had not killed Luke. He did not have the first clue as to what did. Chris could, however, conclude that Luke had been hiding something from him the entire trip—some deep secret that now would never surface. Chris could tell by the way Luke stared out the window when they traveled on the trains. It was the same stare Chris' mother had before the divorce; she would spend hours looking out the kitchen window, a cold cup of coffee in her hands. But when Chris would ask his mother what was wrong, she would turn, smile, and dismiss the idea that a problem existed. But inside, she was dying—the man she had fallen in love with no longer shared her bed, her home, her life—he had died, somehow, drowned in a bottle.

That night at dinner, before the bottles of wine cut Chris's night short, he had told Luke of his future plans. Chris was flying home. He was going to help his mother buy a house, and support Jane and Lisa as they headed to college. He wanted to be an example—he wanted to be a man, and a father figure to his younger sisters. He spoke about making sure they found good men to be with—he spoke about getting his mother back on her feet. And in all the time he spoke, Luke sat and listened—a silent supporter of the proclamation. When Chris had finished, Luke made a toast; "To Killing them with our kindness." Chris then toasted, "to Saskia".

Saskia...Does she know? Chris thought as he sat on his bed. He had not thought of it in midst of all the chaos of the last couple days. He knew first-hand how much Luke loved her; the way he spoke about her; the way he described her; it was poetry to Chris. And Chris never thought of himself as a "deep" or "enlightened" person, but traveling with Luke made him want to reach a certain amount of life understanding. Chris thought people were born with that gift, but in Luke's case, he figured Saskia brought out that which most people considered surreal.

And now, Chris wanted to help Luke out—he wanted to remember what Luke came back for—anything would help, any bits and pieces he could pull together that might help Peter and Captain Caligno. But more importantly, he needed to let Saskia know what happened. She needed to know how much Luke loved her. He needed to find Luke's journal and get it to Saskia—the contents, although he never read them, would no doubt paint a picture for the ages.

24.

21/10/08 18:17
Ristorante Sulla Scogliera

Alonso Eloy admired the fury of the storm from

his porch. The sunset in the distance declared the coming night. The wind swirled as the Alonso heard the bang of two shutters against his front window. He started to move towards the door when he heard the voice he had been waiting for.

"*Papa, acabo de hacer con los tres últimos árboles.*" Said the young voice heard running up the path.

"*Muy bien, Jacobo,*" Alonso said to his son. Jacobo continued his long strides with the basket in his hands all the way to the porch. Wet, cold, and shaking, he handed the basket to his father, and walked into the cabin.

Alonso opened the basket to find a full harvest of olives—his son was a hard worker. Walking inside and shutting the door, Alonso could see Jacobo already huddled by the fire in the next room. Walking over to the window, Alonso opened it and closed the shutters— shutting the window behind them, the sound of the storm outside ceased to a distant hiss. Alonso also figured he should turn off the neon green "Pilsner" sign hanging in the window. He didn't think any hikers would be stopping in tonight.

He was curious about the young American—the one who spoke Spanish. Alonso had enjoyed the company; he imagined the young man would be back— he had to come back.

I hope to see Luke Sebastian again.

25.

21/10/08 19:03
Via Delle Cinque Terre SP 370

Holding the black leather journal in his hand, he couldn't wait to get the second one from Luke's belongings being held at Roberto's station in Riomaggiore and begin reading it. He knew it had to offer answers to questions that could bring justice and closure to Luke's cause of death. After digging it out of his suitcase in Genoa and skimming the entire contents for the second time, Peter placed the journal on the dash of the car.

Peter was exhausted. He wished he could fall asleep, but the storm outside had kept him awake. The twisting road made him nauseous—glancing at Roberto, he could tell he didn't like it as well. Roberto had told him another fifteen minutes, fifteen minutes ago; it was obvious he didn't leave Riomaggiore very often. The wind hammered against the car as the rain washed down in buckets. Roberto had been driving slow, cautious, and attentive—Peter appreciated it, but he wanted to get there—so much to do, so little time.

"Is this normal for this time of year?" Peter asked breaking the silence between the two men.

"Storms like this come and go quickly. Not often, but usual around now," Roberto replied.

"In Sacramento, we don't get storms often, but when they come, they come."

"You have storms in California?"

"Yeah, sometimes, in Sacramento the weather is fairly mild."

"I thought all of California was a tropical paradise." Peter smiled. The American stereotypes were even climatically incorrect.

"No. Southern California is normally very nice all year around, but he further north you go, you start to hit the Northwest jet stream and weather."

"What does that look like?"

"You're driving through it. Seattle never gets a break from the weather." Roberto looked out the window with his hands remaining ten to two; his facial expression showed that of disgust.

"I don't like this weather. I would not like Seattle. You should go down to Sicily. Beautiful weather, all the time; the coastline is very beautiful. Inland, not so much, but the women are very beautiful, Peter."

"Sounds great...Luke wanted to go to Sicily. I wonder why he didn't go."

"He probably heard there were thieves, crooks, and crime in Sicily. Most tourists are scared into not going."

"Well, are there?"

"Well, yes, but I enjoy—"

A loud *thud* accompanied by broken glass and a dented hood interrupted Roberto as he lost control of the car. They rushed towards the edge of the cliff along the Riomaggiore coastline. Peter could hear Roberto scream when the glass broke, and the few tree limbs broke through. Peter was in shock by the feeling—his left arm sliced on the bicep by an intruding limb. He was lucky not to have his entire arm run through like a spear.

The moment seemed to hit them with blinding force—the conversation, the thud, the skidding of the tires, the open gashes, and the screeching halt. When the car finally stopped, it was Peter who first noticed the tilt. The car was balanced on the edge of the cliff, the seemingly insignificant guardrail fighting to hold the car. Peter looked out his window to find the side of the hill looked as if it had erupted—mud slid down flowing underneath the car and down the rocky cliff. From out of Roberto's window, Peter could see the height of a fall they could not survive.

Peter screamed Roberto's name. He was unconscious, leaning up against his window, a large gash on his forehead, a smaller one on his cheek. "Roberto, wake up!" Peter started to move his arm, the sting of the open wound rising above the shock. "Ugh! Roberto, wake up!" Peter shifted his weight towards the driver side. A sudden *creak* of steel made him stop moving. He knew if enough weight was transferred over to Roberto's side, the car was going over. *Think! Think!* He thought to himself as he looked again at the mud and water sliding under the car. Time was running out— if the mudslide continued, it would send them tumbling down the cliff.

Peter started looking around the car—looking for something that could help him out. He titled his seat back to keep the balance of the car while looking in the back seats. A black rope was tucked under Roberto's seat, and with slow, painful movements, Peter reached for the rope with his left hand. The weight of his arm moving towards the driver's side again made the car *creak*. Slowly lifting his arm, the gash made the rope feel like it weighed fifty pounds. It was good rope— strong and braided tightly multiple times. At the each end of the twenty foot rope, were "eye" loops, and a mountain hooks. Peter didn't think he could have gotten any luckier, but staring at the cliff outside Roberto's window, he knew it could be useful to a Captain of the local Police force.

Peter hooked the rope around his waist, looping it once around his belt, hoping to keep it tightly around the core of his body. He took a deep breath—the next part would be hard—he had to unbuckle Roberto, and get the rope around his waist without shifting his weight towards Roberto's side. Peter knew he could get out of the car and safely touch land without Roberto, but the Captain would be sent over the cliff with the car. The same tree that was holding them to the cliff would also push it over with the weight change. Peter's heart raced.

We either both live, or we both die, he decided.

Rain and sweat mixed together as Peter slowly lifted his dead arm—shifting his weight to the right, he used the length of his arm to determine how far he needed to move to the left.

"Roberto! I'm going to take your seat belt off if you can hear me. Don't move!" Roberto groaned a little. Peter let out a sigh of relief to hear his companion was at least still alive. "Roberto, don't move!" Peter reached down and pressed the silver button on the seat belt, releasing the belt as it coiled up to Roberto's neck. Retreating his hand, Peter latched the hook to the body of the rope so it would lasso tight to Roberto's body. Taking a deep breath, Peter reached for the belt first; sliding it down around Roberto's right arm, he managed to set it free, releasing Roberto's attachment to the car. Trying to put Roberto's right arm through the lasso of the rope, Peter's armed stung in intense pain. He needed to use both hands.

Wiping the sweat and rain mixture from his eyes, Peter positioned himself to lean with his body towards Roberto. Using both hands, he slid the rope up under Roberto's right arm. When it was about halfway up his arm the entire car shifted towards the cliff—Peter froze, readying his mind for the fall, when the car stopped again, tilting at an even greater angle then before. Breathing heavily, Peter noticed the shift actually helped his cause—the tree limb that had been creating a barrier between the two, had now moved closer to window, allowing enough space for Peter's plan to actually work. Looking out the window, Peter also noticed through the buckets of rain the tree was still rooted to the side of the cliff. The tree now became his landing point. Moving slowly again, Peter reached the lasso to Roberto's under arm, and wrapped the loop around his head. One last *creak* of the steel under distress told Peter it was time. Just as he was about to open the door, Peter noticed the journal on the dashboard. When the tree had struck the car, the journal that Peter had placed on his side of the dash slid to the driver's side—in a moment of panic Peter reached for the journal. The car started to shift again, and Peter retreated, his head hitting the head-rest with a *thud*. An agonizing moment passed in Peter's mind; he would have to leave it behind. He looked at the black leather journal with the strap longingly. *I'm sorry Luke, I'm sorry son*, he thought to himself.

"Roberto!" Peter exclaimed as he tightened the rope around his waist. "Roberto, I'm going to open my door, and jump to the ground. I'm going to grab the trunk of the tree! Just hold on!" Peter looked at Roberto's legs; in the instant the car would go over the cliff, it was highly probably that Roberto's legs would get stuck, and they both would fall to their deaths; a risk Peter had no choice but to take if he was going to save the Captain. The adrenaline rush surpassed Peter's fear as he opened the passenger door. Swinging it wide, Peter reached out his right foot and kicked the door, breaking the swing joint to open the door even wider. Taking one last look at the journal on the dash, Peter didn't notice Roberto had opened his eyes. Turning back to the door, Peter shouted, "Here we go!"

Lunging out the door, Peter hurled himself towards the tree trunk. His left arm reached out and grabbed a limb. His right arm hit the ground and instinctively bounced up to reach around the trunk. Feeling around with is right arm, he found another limb and held it for dear life. Just as he thought would happen, the car tilted from the weight shift, and slid down the cliff out of sight. Peter prepared for the worst—hoping the weight he felt when the rope tightened wasn't that of a mid-sized car. In a terrifying instant, Peter felt the mountain hook tighten—he thought it might rip his body in half, when all of the sudden the squeeze loosened to a comfortable fit. In the distance, Peter could hear the sound of the car hitting the surf below. Trying to shift his weight, Peter raised his head to see his feet sitting in the mud a few inches away from a thick limb about three feet in length; the rest of the limb had been snapped off in the fall. Bracing his legs on the limb, Peter was able to let go of the limb with his right hand; his left hand still clutching to the near limb. Sitting up slowly with his feet braced, Peter brought his right hand to the rope, pulling hard to loosen some of the weight from his waist.

"Roberto! Roberto! Can you hear me?" Peter yelled into the stormy night. He couldn't hear a response. He waited for a few seconds before calling again. "Roberto! Robe—" Peter felt something. The vibration of the rope felt like a signal as if something was moving on the end of it. Then out of nowhere, the rope slackened. Peter's eyes went wide. The weight of the rope was gone. "Roberto!"

Peter couldn't control his heart rate—a fear for the worst engulfed him. Thoughts of the rope being cut, or breaking filled his mind. Moving quickly Peter unhooked the mountain clip, and removed the rope from his waist. His hands moved with trembling speed as he re-hooked the rope to the trunk of the tree. Making sure it was tight and secure before he moved; he yanked on the rope twice. Crawling to the edge of the cliff, Peter didn't want to stand with all of the slick mud around him.

"Roberto!" he cried as he inched closer. "Can you hear me!"

When Peter got to the edge, his eyes squinted in the rain; following the black rope to the best of his ability, he scanned the Cliffside.

"Peter!" cried a weak voice from the cliff. Peter inched as far as he could until he could see him. Clinging to the rock face of the cliff, Roberto looked up as Peter came into view.

"Roberto! Are you okay?"

"I'm okay! I have a flat footing!" cried Roberto from below. Peter couldn't help but smile, and nervously laugh in surprise. "Peter, can you pull me up? I can climb as you pull!"

"Yeah! Let's try it! I have a footing!" Peter braced himself and began to pull the rope with all of his strength. The rope moved swiftly between his aching palms as Roberto's dead-weight was reduced by his moving feet up the cliff face. Peter was beginning to feel exhausted in a way he had never felt before, but his adrenalin pushed him to keep pulling with all the strength he could muster. With one large heave, Peter could see a hand grab hold of the cliff's edge—with one last effort Peter and Roberto found themselves laying on their backs as the rain continued to pour down. Roberto finally rolled over and picked up his panting and heaving friend.

"Peter, thank you. *Eterna benedizione del Signore*," Roberto said with exhaustion. As Peter nodded his acknowledgment, Roberto pulled something out of his belt loop on his back—it was Luke's journal. When Peter's hand touched the black leather of the journal, he pulled it close to his chest. Just then, Peter could see lights out of his peripheral vision. When he turned his head, two lights closed in on him in the distance.

Headlights.

Thank you God, he thought as he stored the journal under his shirt and turned to a smiling Captain Coligno.

26.

21/10/08 21:34
Hotel Di Armi

Chris was starving. He had been sitting, laying, standing, and smoking in his room for eight hours. At that moment he should have been sitting in an airport terminal waiting for his flight. But now, he felt like a prisoner. But he wasn't a prisoner—he was a bystander in Luke's nightmare.

All day long he thought about why Luke came back to the room, if anyone had contacted Saskia, and how he could call his mother. Chris opened the front zipper to a small pouch on his backpack. He figured chain smoking would help control his hunger. Reaching in for the dwindling pack of cigarettes, his hand felt a bulge from the pocket underneath. Wondering what was in the small pocket he smoothed the fold over and unzipped the small but not hidden pouch. His eyes went wide when he saw the small item he had forgotten about—it was his cell phone.

Chris had never used it on the trip. It was very expensive to call internationally, and Chris had never considered the need for it. When he flew out of Billings he had meant to leave it at home, but at the last minute turned it off and stored it in the small pouch. Now, he didn't think twice about using the phone to call his mother. Excited, he opened the flip-phone and turned the power on. The AT&T signature tone played as the phone powered up...

That tone? Chris thought as his eyes widened. *Luke's Blackberry!*

With a simple sound that triggered his memory, Chris remembered why Luke had come back. He came back for his phone.

Just as the thought hit him, there was a knock on his door. Putting the phone in his pocket, Chris stood and moved to the door.

Peter sat in the armchair in the lobby of the *Hotel di Armi* still reeling from the experience on the cliff. The headlights of James Russo's truck had been a beacon light sent from the heavens. James was a hired currier to deliver a package to Monterosso Al Mare from Genoa. The package was marked as urgent, and against his will he traveled through the stormy night to make easy money.

James was a large man—half Italian, and half American. On any other day Peter would've guessed that James would have delivered the package tied to the back of a Harley.

With the road blocked, James parked his truck up the hill, and the three men hiked the remaining two kilometers to Riomaggiore. While Roberto and Peter slightly limped, James kept pace while carrying the long and large package over his shoulder. Once getting to Riomaggiore, James shook hands with the two men and continued to Monterosso Al Mare alone to deliver the package, collect his pay, and get back to Genoa. He didn't want accolades; he didn't want dinner; he just wanted to collect and leave.

Once in Riomaggiore, Roberto took Peter to the police station for warm clothes and bandages, as well as the box that contained all of Luke's affects confiscated from Chris's hotel room. If there was any question in Roberto's mind about whether or not Peter wanted to continue to Monterosso Al Mare that night, Roberto disregarded it as an insult—Peter was on a mission, and he would not be denied. Peter had saved his life, and he would repay him with whatever he could. And Peter needed help. His suitcase was now sitting at the bottom of the Mediterranean coastline, inside of Roberto's police car. All he had left was drying on the table, pulled from his pockets; his passport, wallet, phone, Luke's camera, the half-heart shaped necklace, and because of Roberto's heroics, Luke's journal.

Peter would never be able to repay him for that.

After leaving the station tired, wounded, and hungry, Peter and Roberto boarded the train for the ten-minute ride through the five cities ending up at Monterosso Al Mare.

Roberto had arranged for three small meals to be brought over to the *Hotel di Armi* for himself, Peter, and Chris Ludlow. Peter had requested the three sit down and talk and Roberto didn't hesitate to make it happen. With the landslide and weather, Peter knew it would be impossible for them to make a visit to the Spaniard, and decided it would be best if they waited till morning.

The hotel lobby was very nice for the small, quaint hotel. For Luke and Chris to stay there, the hotel had to offer small and extremely affordable private rooms. The lobby contained a mass of comfortable chairs and tables, a fireplace, and a mini-bar that was now closed. At the front desk sat a plump man with a ponytail playing racing games at his computer. Roberto had gone to get Chris from his room, but when he came within eyesight outside the large windows escorting a young man, the receptionist quickly shut off the monitor and stood to his feet.

When Roberto and Chris entered the lobby, the receptionist nodded his head and disappeared through a door behind the desk to give the three men privacy while they ate. Peter stood to greet the two men.

"Peter, this is Chris Ludlow," Roberto introduced the two men as they shook hands.

"Chris," Peter said with a small smile.

"Mr. Sebastian," Chris replied out of respect.

"Please, call me Peter." Chris nodded as he took his seat. Peter and Roberto did the same, but a little more slowly and gingerly.

"The food should be here any minute," Roberto said to them.

"Great. I haven't eaten all day," Chris responded. Peter thought he seemed nervous. A part of him wanted to believe he had something to do with Luke's death, but most of him knew he was a friend who was terrified of the situation.

"Chris," Peter started, "I need you to tell me about Luke; what happened that night, the trip, everything." Peter sat up straight and could feel his spine snap and pop in about thirty places.

"Mr. Sebastian—"

"Peter, please."

"Peter," Chris started as he leaned forward and folded his hands on the table. "I don't know what happened to Luke that night." He paused. "I was drinking, and Luke took me back to the room to pass out. I mean, it was normal for me to pass out early. It happened in Prague, Budapest, Rome...everywhere we went."

"Why?" Peter asked.

"Because I was always drinking; Luke drank too, but never to get drunk. He was always casual about it. He was quiet. I would talk to girls and he would just chime in whenever he saw fit."

"You two met up in Munich; did you know Saskia?" Chris looked surprised—Luke had always told him his family didn't know about Saskia. He didn't want to question Peter's finding out—instead he answered as honest as he could.

"I never met her. But Luke talked about her every day—not annoyingly or anything like that, but he told me stories. I felt like I knew her."

"Do you know how we could contact her?" Roberto chimed in.

"No. I don't. I didn't even know where she lives. When I met up with Luke, he had already said goodbye, we hopped on a train for Prague."

"You left Munich immediately?"

"Our train left at six in the morning. I got there the night before. We went to dinner and then decided to sleep in the train station." Peter glanced away. *Nobody can sleep in a train station*, he thought. "I would get up every now and again, I mean, I hardly slept, but one time I got up and saw Luke sitting next to some guy playing a sitar. I went out there and listened to them awhile, before going back to sleep. The next morning I asked him if he slept and he said 'no'."

"And in the other places?" Roberto asked trying to get them on a time track.

"When we were in Prague, we got word of a pharmacy that sold Ambien over the counter. Luke and I

143

both went in at separate times to get two separate bottles."

"What is Ambien?" Roberto asked. Peter figured the word had a translation or something.

"It's a sleeping pill," Chris replied. "Luke was an insomniac. He just couldn't sleep."

"He wasn't an insomniac—he is just a very light sleeper. When he was younger, he had to have a fan on, the window cracked, every light out, and absolutely no noise in the house. When he hears things his mind has to focus on them—he has to listen."

"Yeah, he talked about that. We tried ear-plugs, music, everything, but sleeping pills were the only way he'd get to sleep."

"Did he ever need more than one?" Peter asked.

"No. Not that I saw. He would take one, and be good most nights. But I was always asleep. I wouldn't know for sure."

"Peter," Roberto said quietly. "His belongings report did not have a bottle of pills in it." Peter remembered that as well.

"Belongings report?" asked Chris. He looked as if he wanted to take the question back as soon as he said it.

"We have a report on all of his belongings taken from your hotel room. Do you have the pills?" Chris shook his head "no."

"No, you can search my things if you want. I didn't take them. I didn't need them."

"But you can get high off of sleeping pills, can you not? Maybe you wanted them to get high." Roberto pushed.

"No. We were going to Amsterdam for that." Chris replied, again not thinking before speaking. Peter wasn't amused, but he didn't argue the fact. Peter looked away for a moment—he figured Chris was a smart-ass kid who

144

probably couldn't help them a whole lot, but the questions had just begun.

Chris could feel his heart beat out of his chest. Captain Caligno, whom he thought was nice now scared the shit out of him. They were sitting at a place setting with knives and forks, both of which could be used as weapons if the Captain wanted. Peter was intimidating also. The two had bandages covering war wounds—they were wearing identical light brown law enforcement shirts—Chris thought Peter was a hardware store owner, but now he thought he was a general of some sort.

He knew he needed to get the attention away from him—the pills? Where did they go? He had never touched them; alcohol had the same affect for him and Europe never ran low on that.

The belongings report, he thought, *if it didn't have Luke's cell phone he was right about him coming back for it.* Chris was about to say something when he stopped. He would be changing his story from the initial report—that could mean jail time for false information to a police officer. His paranoia led him to believe he could be hanged for it. He remained quiet—waiting for them to ask him questions.

"Did you ever read his journal?" Peter asked as he leaned forward.

"No. He read me a couple of entries, but nothing in-depth. He wrote in it all the time—twice a day at least."

Chris watched as Peter leaned to his left beside his chair and pulled something out of a large plastic bin. When Chris could see the familiar brown leather journal come into sight, he knew the bin contained all of Luke's belongings. Peter set the journal on the table.

"You're sure, you never read any of these

entries?" Peter asked.

"No. Have either of you?" Chris replied curiously.

"Not yet, but I will. And I have to tell you that my son is a very detailed writer and anything you don't share with us could not be in your favor if it is discovered in this book."

"Like what?"

"Like anything," Peter pressed.

"I'm sorry Peter..Captain, I don't follow. I am not a suspect, because I didn't kill or have anything to do with Luke's death. I swear on the lives of my baby sisters, I didn't have anything to do with it." Chris took a deep breath—he was so nervous—he also didn't have any idea what was in that journal, but he still had a lot of faith in Luke, and believed nothing would be in there to convict him of murder.

"Chris, listen. You were the last person to spend a great amount of time with Luke. Forget about being a *suspect*—just concentrate on the details. Just focus on what Luke would do on a daily basis." Chris relaxed a little.

"He was very private about a lot of things he was doing. Every day he would wander off for a few hours—I never knew what he was doing. I would ask him, and he would say it was a surprise."

"What? Wander where? Around here?" Peter asked with interest.

"Yes. I wanted to leave Cinque Terre after the first day. There were no girls here...I mean, I wasn't interested in staying here for four days. Luke...Luke had some surprise—some *thing* he was working on. He asked me not to question it, and that we would leave as soon as he got it done."

"Why didn't you say something about this before?" Captain Caligno asked.

"Because you didn't ask about the days prior—you

asked about that night. And you asked when I was hung over. I have spent all day trying to put the pieces of that night together."

"And?" Now Chris had to tell them.

"I think he came back to the room after midnight."

"You think? Or you know?" Chris wasn't a hundred percent sure, but he knew deep down that Luke had to have come back to the room.

"I'm sure."

"Why did he come back? Did he take anything?"

"I think he took his phone. His Blackberry."

Whatever doubt Chris had about revealing this information disappeared when he saw Peter's face.

Peter figured he was probably wearing his emotions on his sleeve. *Luke's Blackberry*, he thought. *Why am I forgetting the simplest things?*

Roberto was one step ahead of him in handing the copy of the belongings report they had gotten in Riomaggiore to Chris.

"Look at the report. Look at it carefully. What is missing?" Roberto asked as he reached for the second report—the belongings found on Luke from the trail.

Chris surveyed the items with great intent. Peter now wanted Chris to help them. He didn't suspect him anymore—Chris was Luke's friend and now he could help them—Peter didn't feel he had any other choice.

"You traveled with him for over three weeks—all you two had were backpacks. You know what was in his. Concentrate."

Chris looked up at Peter, and then returned to the report.

"I don't see his camera. He must have taken it with him when I asked him to charge mine." Roberto handed Chris the second report.

"Yes. It was on him. This is the list of belongings we recovered from the corpse." That word still sent shivers up Peter's spine. Chris looked over both lists very carefully while Peter and Roberto waited quietly.

"I see what you guys see; the pills and his Blackberry."

"Can we get a record of his call logs?" Peter asked Roberto.

"We can try first thing in the morning. The storm has made communication very tough. My Lieutenant said he would try the German embassy again tomorrow to locate Miss Einreiner."

"You're trying to contact Saskia?" Chris asked out of curiosity.

"Yes."

"So, she doesn't know?" Chris replied. Peter's eyes went wide. He hadn't even considered the thought.

"I don't believe so, no." Peter responded. "I have never even seen the girl."

"But you have Luke's camera, right?" Chris leaned in.

"Yes. Does he have a picture of her?"

"Yeah, a ton of them; here," Chris motioned for Peter to hand him the camera with his hand. "We have the same camera."

Peter retrieved the camera from his pocket—he hadn't attempted turning it on since the event—he didn't even know if it still worked. Handing it to Chris he hoped for the best. Chris took the camera and turned it on. Pressing the "Play" button, he began to scroll through the pictures. Once he found the one he was looking for, he returned the camera to Peter. Roberto leaned in to see the contents as Peter held it from his face at a distant because he didn't have his reading glasses; they also went over the cliff.

The picture was taken in downtown Munich, in

front of an old church. Luke was standing with his arm wrapped around a beautiful young woman; long dark straight hair, blue eyes, a petit curvy figure, a blue scarf around her neck.

"*Lei è molto bella*," Roberto said as he inched closer. No translation was needed.

"We need to get a hold of her, Roberto. She needs to know what happened to Luke." Peter said as he turned the camera off.

"Yes, first thing tomorrow," Roberto replied. Peter noticed Chris looking at something in his hands, out of view from the table ledge.

"What do you have there, son?" Peter asked Chris. Chris looked up and held up his cell phone.

"Oh, I just have my cell phone. I was going to call my mom, but there's no service."

"There isn't service?" Peter asked Roberto somewhat surprised.

"Correct. There is no...signal that can get down into the towns. Our station satellite can transmit from on top of the hill."

Peter thought a flash of understanding passed him by, as if what Roberto said was a piece to the puzzle. He tried to focus in on the flash, but the thought had eluded him. He was tired and he was hungry. The day had been the longest of his life.

"Chris—" He started when a door behind him opened. It was the receptionist—he was carrying three circular plastic containers and a plastic bag filled with water bottles—it was the food. The receptionist handed the plastic containers to a standing Roberto, nodded, and walked back through the door.

"It looks like chicken, rice, and vegetables," Roberto announced as he opened one of the containers. Peter silently praised the Lord as he took one of the containers and removed the lid. Chris did the same,

149

thanking Roberto as he took it. The three men took bottled waters from the sack and began their meals. Peter thought the chicken tasted amazing, although it had cooled down considerably during its travel from the restaurant to the hotel.

"Chris," Peter began again, "did Luke ever talk about how he met Saskia?"

"Yeah," he replied, "He told me the story about how they met; how they kept everything a secret—the late night car rides, the park walks, the engagement—"

"Excuse me?" Peter interrupted, "engagement?" Chris looked up from his fork.

"Yeah...you didn't know?" he asked. Peter dropped his fork into the container and rubbed his eyes with his hand.

"No. He never told me." Peter felt as if the blows kept coming—he wondered if they would ever stop. His son had told him nothing about his life—absolutely nothing.

"I'm sorry—" Chris tried to say.

"No, no, please, tell me about it. Tell me the story." Peter sat back in his chair as his appetite diminished. Roberto ate quietly, but his attention was locked on the young man across the table. Peter knew he would have to fill Roberto in on the whole story about Saskia, but it would have to wait till later.

"Wow, let me think. He asked in June I guess, right before she flew back to Munich. They had been dating about a month...he told me he never thought twice about asking her...it was just meant to be..."

27.

06/21/08 8:21 P.M.
Los Angeles, California

All of his life Luke associated music with moments in his life. A single song could help relocate past feelings and emotions. For example, whenever he heard Andrea Bocelli and Sarah Brightman sing "Time to Say Goodbye," the memory of his mother's fatal accident flooded his mind with the fury of a hurricane. Bocelli's voice accompanied the sounds of steel crushing steel, shattered glass spraying into the street, and distant ambulance sirens edging closer and closer. Every finite detail would come tumbling back as Bocelli hit his high notes; arguing with his mother over the secret he had long kept from his father; getting out of the car four blocks early; turning in time to see her accelerating to catch him; her blue eyes locked on his while screaming his name in tears the moment before the truck came crashing into her side; and the immediate silence followed by his wailing agony harmonized with an onlooker's cry for help.

Luke had often wondered if Andrea Bocelli ever thought his voice could co-exist with such a tragedy; his mother's life taken in the finale. The song had been playing the moment before Luke slammed the door shut, leaving his mother alone, causing her to accelerate after him; a moment that has haunted him every day since. Mary Sebastian had been a great woman when she was alive—a perfect mother, always loving, always caring. Luke didn't know if he would ever meet another woman like her; until he met Saskia.

Luke had other memory associations to songs; "Freshman" by the Verve Pipe reminded him of his older brother Jake because of an old cassette he played in his Jeep as they zipped down the highway together; "Man of the Hour" by Pearl Jam reminded him of his father and his failing promises; "You're Beautiful" by James Blunt recalled the many afternoons lying in Rochelle's arms while she ran her fingers through his hair. Music had a way of creating a timeline for Luke's life. Tonight, he wanted to create his own memory from his own song—a memory worth repeating time and time again. He was going to ask Saskia to spend the rest of her life with him, an unequivocal happiness that would make up for all the losses he had endured; his mother, his distant brother, and recently, his decaying father.

She would be flying out in two days—with her visa expiring she had little choice but to return home to Munich. Luke had graduated without walking—his ties to the area were cut, and now he had the freedom to make the choice of where he wanted to be and who he wanted to be with. Fluent in Spanish and trained for business, he wanted to see the world. After arranging a backpacking trip over the phone with a guy he'd never met, he was set to leave for Europe after a summer of working and mentoring with the intention of never returning home.

Driving down Interstate 5 towards downtown Los Angeles, the warmth of Saskia's hand pinning his to the shifter gave him confidence in the decision he had made. Tonight he would tell her of his new dreams and ideas; tonight he would ask her the question that would show his highest level of commitment. As he sped up, the warm summer night seeped through the open windows, tossing her straight brown hair back like a bulk of ribbons. He would glance at her every chance he had, wondering what she was thinking, and how she would answer him when the time came.

Luke knew the circumstances; she was young; they had only been together a short time; in no time at all she would be flying home to Germany to finish prep school; and he was a jobless twenty-three year old musician banking on love and luck. There were obvious obstacles, but he believed the obstacles were problems caused by the expectations of western society. How many people are truly happy in this world? How many men have a love story they can't wait to share with every new person they meet? How many people can consider their lives exciting and unique? Saskia was young, but in a few years the gap between their ages would vanish into obscurity like a trial without verdict or consequence.

Luke thought Shakespeare had gotten it right. The greatest love story ever told was rash, exciting, and whimsical. Why is love at first sight cliché? Because time and time again, throughout the ages, it has existed—the power of infatuation caused by a person's inherent attraction to beauty, personality, and intelligence is, indeed, love. Love doesn't have to be the respect a person has for their spouse after living together twenty years; love doesn't have to be what remains after the physical torch is left a slow burning candle; it doesn't even have to endure, it just has to exist to create beautiful possibilities.

Luke looked over at Saskia who was singing "Outside" by Staind; a song they couldn't get enough of since he had sang to a lone audience with his eyes closed in the music room at Douglas High. As he listened to her accented words combined with the wind in his ear, a philosophical thought came to his mind. She existed, therefore he existed; the same way the rose lifts towards the sun by a ray of light on a fresh spring day; a unity constructed by the hand of creation.

Rochelle had told him he was scared of commitment—a statement that was true in light of their relationship; but Luke never intended to settle for a lifetime of wealth and security—he intended to settle for happiness. He had found that happiness with Saskia; he had committed the moment he opened his eyes that day in the music room; he somehow felt throughout his life he had been waiting for her to come sweep him off his feet.

Taking Exit 303 towards Interstate 10, Saskia turned the volume on the stereo down to a whisper as she grew suspicious. He hadn't told her where they were going.

"Where are you taking me?" She asked with an eyebrow drawn down in curiosity.

"I would tell you, but that wouldn't be as fun," he replied with a grin. She reached over to him with her left hand and began rubbing the back of his head.

"Come on, tell me," she replied as she picked a battle she hoped to lose, but persisted in for nothing more than playful conversation.

"Nope."

"Are we going to dinner?" she started to probe.

"I'm not telling."

"Are we going to a movie?"

"Yeah, I want to spend one of our last night's together watching a movie."

"We could have sex in the theater," she replied with a smile as she leaned over and kissed him on the cheek. Luke's eyes widened as his hair stood on the back of his neck.

"You would have sex in the theater?" he questioned back, his romantic stream of conscience fading to the back of his mind.

"Yeah, with you, anywhere," she said convincingly.

154

"But in a theater? How would we get away with that?" The question seemed logical.

"Sit in the very back and try not to make noise," she said as she ran her finger slowly down his thigh.

"You are not right, you know that?" She inched her way over to him until he could feel her breath in his ear.

"I know, but you make me that way." Her whispered accent drove him insane—she always knew what to do to make him want her, anywhere, anytime, even while driving.

"Have you ever had sex in a movie theater before?"

"No, but it sounds fun. Wouldn't it be exciting?" She asked as she pulled away.

"Of course, but I think we would be arrested for public indecency if anyone were to see us."

"Where are we going, Luke?" Her voice softened; she was being tactical.

"You'll see when we get there." He wanted to change the subject again in case she persisted. "Do you have that playlist you said you'd make?" She reached down for her purse.

"I do," she said excitedly, "do you want to hear it?"

"That's why I asked if you had it." She pulled out her iPhone from her purse and plugged it into the stereo converter. Scrolling through a list of playlists she selected one. The day before he had asked her to come up with a list of her favorite songs to see if their musical compatibility was consistent with their physical one. He had joked that it would be a "deal breaker."

"I do not think you know these songs, so tell me if you do."

One by one they went through her playlist of songs—Luke loved it because he got to listen to music he potentially had never heard before and it killed time while they drove into the night. The playlist consisted of the following:

1. "Lover's in Japan"—Coldplay
2. "My Moon, My Man—Feist
3. "1,2,3,4"—Feist
4. "Realize"—Colbie Calliat
5. "Forever"—Chris Brown
6. "Take a Bow"—Rihanna
7. "We Belong Together"—Gavin DeGraw
8. "New Soul"—Yael Naim

Luke had recognized a couple of the songs, but it wasn't until Saskia played the ninth song that his full attention was grasped. The song was from an Italian movie called, *"Tre Metri Sopra il Cielo"*. The title of the song was "Gabriel" by a group called Lamb. When the woman's voice started to sing, Luke was captivated—he was drawn to the words (which were in English). The voice of an angel sang for her lover to take her out of the darkness—to be her angel. When the song was over, Luke asked Saskia to play it again as he turned up the volume, so he could hear the words more clearly:

I can fly, but I want his wings;
I can sigh even in the darkness, but I crave the light that he brings;
The song he reveals, my angel Gabriel.

The soundtracks to life—the words we live by.
Luke knew this song was his interpreted cry to Saskia. He didn't want to live alone, in fear of turning into his father. He wanted to fly with her, as far as her wings would take them; he wanted her to be his angel. Luke didn't know if he believed in God or not, but in that

moment he figured God gave him a sign—it was all he needed to gather the courage to ask her the ultimate question in the coming hours.

As they continued to listen to the song, Luke took the South La Brea Exit off of the interstate. Driving about a half mile, he turned on San Vicente Boulevard, and then took a right on Wilshire Street. He could see Saskia scoping out the area for clues as to where they were going. When Luke saw his destination, he pulled to the right, parking the Pathfinder in front of a large building. Turning off the ignition, Saskia finally noticed what he had hoped she would—the large illuminated German flag flying atop a large flag pool in front of the dark building.

"Is this the German embassy?" she asked as they stepped out of the car.

"Well, no; it's actually the German Consulate. The German embassy is in Washington D.C." He replied as he opened the back door of the Pathfinder. He pulled out his guitar and strapped it to his back. He also pulled out a backpack and lunch basket as he shut the door and walked around to the front of the car. Taking his right arm, it was Saskia that led him closer to the flag.

"What is all that?" she asked glancing at the items he now clutched in his hands.

"You'll see."

"That's my flag!" she exclaimed as she looked into the air towards the flag. "The Bavarian flag is so much prettier."

"I hoped you'd say that."

"Why?" Luke put his finger up to his lips as they entered the Consulate courtyard. Luke couldn't have asked for a better night to do what he had planned. In the square courtyard stood four tall palm trees, in the center was a patch of lawn surrounded by a Dublin Cobble paver-stone walkway that led to the street. On a bench that was bolted to the ground, Luke put down his guitar, backpack, and basket. With the flag flying high above on the poll just beyond the bench, Luke opened the bag to reveal a blue and white-checkered blanket.

"They didn't fly the Bavarian flag, so I brought our own." He said with a grin.

"Oh my God, thank you," she said as she kissed him. He spread the blanket down on top of the cool summer lawn, and urged her to sit down.

Luke then pulled out a couple of small round candles and placed them in the center of the blanket. Saskia sat in amazement at the romantic gesture from her boyfriend.

"Will you do the honors?" Luke asked as he handed her a long stove lighter.

"Of course," she replied as she took the lighter and lit the candles. Luke then opened the picnic basket and pulled out a bottle of Champagne and two plastic cups. Setting them on the blanket, he kissed Saskia on the forehead and retreated back to the bench. In the basket were two plastic covered containers full of food. Taking off the lids and grabbing two forks, Luke sat next to Saskia on the blanket.

"What is for dinner?" she asked as he set the containers down.

"Tonight, we are having Bavarian *Schweinebraten* with *Knödel*, soft pretzels, and *Weisswurst*. I know I butchered all the translations except 'pretzel' so we can move past that," Luke smiled as he spoke. Saskia laughed as she took Luke's face into her hands, and kissed him once again. "Eat, or it'll get cold...if it's not already."

"It's perfect," she replied "You're perfect."

Luke peeled away the protective covering on the Champagne bottle, and opened the bottle cap. He poured the contents into the plastic cups and handed

158

one to Saskia.

"Also, if we see any cops, throw the Champagne away and suck on a penny," he said, trying to sound serious. "Otherwise I'm going to jail tonight for this." Saskia smiled as she raised her glass.

"To us, to the adventure," she said as she inched towards him. The plastic cups touched together in a gentle *tap*.

"To us, to this moment," Luke replied as they both took a small swig of the bubbling white Champagne. "Eat, please, I promise it was all store-bought." Saskia laughed again—she loved his humor. Luke stood up and walked over to the bench.

"What are you getting now?" She asked as if he had already done enough.

"What is a romantic picnic without music?"

"You're going to play for me?" she asked as she sat up a little, a torn piece of pretzel in her hand.

"Of course; for you, anything babe," Luke said as he took his guitar out of its vinyl soft case. Saskia sat and ate while he began to tune the guitar to perfection. He hadn't considered the noise he was about to make by playing and singing—he hoped security wouldn't come around any time soon—they would surely kick them off the premises, although the courtyard was a place designated for public sanction. *Here we go*, he thought to himself. "Where do you want me to sit?"

"Can you play sitting on the ground?"

"I can. I can also play on one knee, both knees, criss-cross-apple-sauce, laying down, or in a playboy pose—centerfold only."

She laughed out loud. "Sit next to me."

She was there—in the moment. Luke had done almost the same dinner with Rochelle on the fifty yard line of his high school football stadium during a visit home; the evening was fun, but Rochelle wanted to talk about other things; problems, gossip, trivial Hollywood stories—she hadn't been there, in the moment. Luke bet that if Saskia was asked that age old question of 'if you could be anywhere in the world and with whom' she would answer 'right here, with him.' Some may confuse Luke's confidence with vanity, but it wasn't—it was beyond it somehow, in a good way.

Luke put his pick in his mouth and carried the guitar to the blanket. Sitting next to her with his right leg straight out, and his left leg curled in, he positioned the guitar until he was comfortable.

"I wrote a song for you," he said as his hair rose with his nervousness causing a knot in his stomach he doubted would go away.

"Really?" she said with wide anticipating eyes.

"Yeah. I want to play it for you, but I want you to close your eyes."

"Can I lie against your leg?" she asked innocently.

"Of course, get comfortable." She moved the plastic containers aside, and lay on her back; her head against his outstretched leg as the candlelight warmed her face with an efflorescent glow. Reaching back, she gently rubbed his calf, if anything, to show him she was there. "Now please, close your eyes, and listen to the words." She did as he asked, and looking up to the stars for support, Luke positioned his fingers and began to play.

The introduction was short, only two bars; a few climbing chords that tumbled down to the base; followed by some hard, sharp notes before he began singing the important lyrics:

Give me time to explain,
But before I begin, please take my hand girl.
I might laugh, I might cry,
I might have to say goodbye,

160

but know you're my world.

You're my angel; I'm your man,
You're the sun on my sand,
so I know I have to try hard.
To be your day, to be your night,
To keep us close in the fight when we are apart.

To keep us close when we're apart.

As Luke played the chorus, he could feel her hold on his calf tightening. If she were touching his chest she would feel him shaking uncontrollably. The next verse, and the final chorus would be the point of no return; his voice was pure, concise, and beautiful.

Because time tends to go, it just goes to show,
You're the queen of my cards.
Face the falling sun, and I'll turn to the moon
And we'll both know it's all ours...

To keep us close when we're apart.

And I can't, tell you, enough,
How much I feel in love,
And what we are, it feels, so right,
Take me, and be, my goodnight.
Be my light, be my bride.
Please, be my wife.

Luke had closed his eyes—he feared to open them. Saskia was no longer touching his calf; he didn't feel her head against his leg. He could no longer play the guitar as his hands nervously slipped from the positioned frets. The last two lines would be sung a capella. His heart had stopped—his body went cold. He said the words one more time for clarity—slowly, like a blind reach searching for her heart in his palm.

Be my light, be my bride.
Please, be my wife.

When he opened his eyes, she was sitting up—tears rolled down her cheeks, passing her wide smile. When their eyes connected, she nodded her head in a simple 'yes'.

Without speaking a word, he reached into his pocket and pulled out the small blue box, the contents a secret for two weeks. When the box came into sight, Saskia's eyes went wide. Asking in a song had been the first step; the next words out of his mouth had to be the truest thing he would ever say in his entire life.

"Saskia, I love you more than I can ever possibly express. When we're not together, I feel like a piece of me is gone—I find myself wishing you were with me; like the stars on a clear night, I can see you, but I can't feel you," he paused. "You're the best thing I have ever known, and I would be the happiest person in the world if you would marry me..."

"Yes," she said before he could finish. "I will marry you, of course, yes." She wrapped her arms around him, kissing his lips, his cheek, his neck, before resting her head between his neck and shoulder in a warm embrace.

Luke pulled away so he could open the small blue box. When he did, she smiled at the sparkling silver necklace inside. The silver chain held a lone silver plate that was cut in the shape of a broken heart. An engraved "S" was cut in half—she had the right side of it. She pulled the necklace out of the box to take a closer look.

"I didn't want to get you a ring yet. I want to ask your father's permission, but I haven't had the chance yet," he said as she looked at the necklace.

"Luke, it is beautiful," she exclaimed.

"And I want to ask your father...in September." He had just revealed the final part of his master plan. Saskia looked at him in surprise.

"In September?" she asked.

"I'm coming to Germany. That is, if you'll have me." She looked as if she was going to cry—she sat staring at him with wide eyes that closed in an exhale. With both hands she pulled the necklace to her heart.

"Really, Luke? Really?" she asked. He had heard that sincere question before. He nodded his head in a 'yes' as he smiled. "Oh my God, of course I'll have you," she exclaimed as she hugged him again. Then she whispered in his ear, "Stay forever. Please, stay forever."

"I'll love you forever," he whispered in her ear, "always and forever."

"I will love you too," she whispered back, "you and no one else."

Luke took the necklace from her hands, unhooked the small silver clasp, and put it around her neck. She looked down at in exuberance.

"Where's the other half?" she asked. Luke pulled down the collar of his shirt to reveal a matching necklace with a slightly thicker chain; the left side of the broken heart dangling at the bottom; put together, the "S" was complete.

Saskia laughed as she got to her knees and put his face in her hands. She kissed him with passion, with eagerness, and with unabated love. The kiss continued as he laid her on the blanket—the small candles burning through the night, the flames seemingly brighter then ever before.

28.

21/10/08 22:38
Hotel di Armi

Peter and Roberto sat in complete silence as Chris finished his story. When Peter glanced over at Roberto, he noticed his friend's chin dug into his hand, his attention glued to every word coming out of the young man's mouth—Peter sympathized as he had done the same. Chris had promised he would tell the story exactly as it was told to him, and a splendid job he had done. With the food containers empty of their contents, the three men sat at the table in a brief silence—one man registering the reaction to the other two.

Peter didn't know the first thing about Chris Ludlow—an hour earlier Chris had been a suspect in Luke's death—but not now. Whatever power Luke had given Peter with the words left behind in his journal, the feeling of love and passion had also been passed to Chris.

"Luke always felt guilty he hadn't asked her father first, so it was one of the first things he did when he got to Munich," Chris continued. "Saskia had apparently told her entire family about Luke when she was in the States. So when Luke got there, it wasn't a complete shock to her father when he asked permission."

Peter ran his fingers through his thinning hair—he imagined by the time he returned home his hair would finally disappear, frightened off his head by the stress of the situation.

"So he asked her father then? For permission to wed his daughter?" Peter asked exhaustedly.

164

"Yes, he did," Chris said as he opened his bottle of water to take a drink. "Luke said her parent's were very supportive of the idea."

"I'm sure they were," Peter responded hopelessly; he had been on the other side of things; unsupportive and uninformed.

"When we left for Prague, Luke told me after ten days in Munich, he had considered not going on the trip with me; but Saskia urged him to go, saying that it would be an unforgettable experience," Chris paused as he shook his head. "But no one wanted this—it's so fucked up. We have to get word to her."

"We will," Roberto started, "first thing tomorrow, I will have my lieutenant try to contact the German officials."

Peter pulled his hands from the table and ran them down his thighs, suddenly feeling an unfamiliar shape in his pocket. Reaching in, he pulled out the small plastic baggy with the half heart-shaped necklace in it. Reaching in to the bag, he slid out the silver necklace and held the silver plate between his thumb and index finger. Running his thumb over the top of it he could feel the slight indent of the "S" engraving carved into the smooth finish.

"His necklace," Chris said as he put his head in his hands. "He never took it off..." he paused as he tried to clear his throat, but the obvious emotion of seeing the necklace anywhere but around Luke's neck had taken his voice. "He said he would die before taking it off." In one swift motion Chris stood up sending his chair skidding on its side behind him as he walked over to the far wall.

"Chris," Roberto spoke as he stood. Chris backed against the wall and slid down to the floor as a few tears of rage crept down his face. Peter didn't know if it was the first time Chris had mourned the loss of his son, but he certainly felt a great deal of empathy for the gesture.

Roberto walked over and crouched next to Chris, putting his hand on his shoulder in comfort.

"We will find out what happened. You have done enough tonight. What do you say; you go up to your room and get some sleep. We will wake you in the morning when we need you."

Peter only slightly observed the conversation between the two as Chris asked Roberto for a minute to regain his senses—he had been focused on the necklace dangling from his fingers.

You certainly loved her, didn't you son? He thought to himself, *What a girl she must be. I'll tell her myself, I'll make sure of it. I don't know what I'll say, but I'll tell her myself, son.*

With Roberto still crouched, consoling Chris about the evening's events, there was a knock at the main door. Standing, and moving towards the door, Roberto could see it was his lieutenant, drenched, with a man behind him—the man was James Russo, still holding the large package.

Roberto opened the door as James and the lieutenant stumbled in to get out of the storm. Peter stood and walked over to James, tucking the necklace back into his pocket.

"James, what are you doing here?" Peter asked as Roberto began to speak to the lieutenant in Italian.

"Peter, I think this package is for you," James replied as he wiped the water from his bald head.

"For me?" Peter was puzzled as he turned to Roberto who finished speaking with the lieutenant. "Roberto, what's he talking about?"

"It is for Luke," he responded with heavy eyes. "The package is post marked for your son. From Germany."

29.

21/10/08 22:43
Risturante Sulla Scogliera

Jacobo Eloy sat in his bed as the wind pounded against his window—the porch light his father promised to keep on throughout the stormy night cast shadows of the moving trees across the heavy comforter he curled up inside. Jacobo, having just turned eleven, hated the stormy weather. It reminded him of a distant memory involving bright lights, a covered face with glasses, and cries in anguish—a blur of a memory, but one he could never forget.

Jacobo turned on the small green flashlight in his right hand to look at the photo of the woman again. He had memorized her long, curly brown hair, her beautiful wide smile, and her perfect blue eyes. The woman in the photo had been described by the American as an angel— one that would guide and protect him wherever he went—he knew the American had told him the truth. Running his finger over the frayed edges of the photo, Jacobo didn't fear the storm anymore—he convinced himself to welcome it as one of God's creations.

The sound of footsteps through the open door made Jacobo hurry to turn off the flashlight and roll to his side as he pretended to be asleep.

"Jacobo," his father said in the native tongue of Spain. "It is late, you need to sleep."

Jacobo peaked an eye open, but seeing he had already been made, sat up to address his father.

"I'm trying to sleep, Papa, but the wind is keeping me up." He replied in a soft young voice. His father sat down on his bed and ran his hand through Jacobo's hair.

"It is just wind, son," he said with a smile, "tomorrow the storm will pass and the sun will come out again."

"I am not scared papa, I have an angel with me" Jacobo said as he pulled out the photo from under the covers. Handing it to his father he continued, "the American said she will protect me from the darkness."

Looking at the photo of the woman, his father smiled at the gesture by the young American man.

"The American gave this to you?" he asked.

"Yes, he said the woman was very dear to him, and to take good care of it," replied Jacobo.

"He was a wise young man; you must take good care of it until he returns," his father said as he handed the photo back to his son.

"Do you think he'll come back?" Jacobo asked curiously.

"I hope so, but surely not tonight. We shall look for him tomorrow. In the meantime," his father began as he stood and pulled the bed-sheet up to his son, tucking him in, "try to get some sleep."

Alonso kissed his son on the forehead and started for the door, stopping when he heard Jacobo speak.

"Papa, do you think Mama is an angel?" he asked with a crease in his brow. Alonso turned from the door and smiled at his son.

"What do you think?" he returned with a question.

"I don't know; I hope so," he replied.

"Look in your heart, and one day the answer will be given to you; now get some sleep and no more flashlight."

Jacobo smiled, turning to his side as Alonso turned to leave once again.

Alonso closed Jacobo's door a little more than

usual as he made his way to the bar to finish his nightly cleaning. It was late, and he was tired. Picking up a broom he smiled as he replayed his son's question in his mind—he wished with all of his heart that Jacobo had known his mother.

Sweeping up the bar, Alonso turned a chair upside down on a table. When he did this, he dropped the broom stick to the ground; reaching down to pick it up, his eyes saw a flash of orange beneath the old steam heater against the nearby wall. Leaning down for a closer look, he saw a small container of some sort. He reached under the heater to discover a small orange pill container with small white tablets inside. Curious as to the identity of its owner, Alonso analyzed the container, but found nothing written on it.

Assuming someone may return to look for them, Alonso put the small cylinder container into his pocket and resumed cleaning; hoping to finish quickly so he could join his son in a restful night's sleep as the storm raged on.

30.

21/10/08 22:47
Hotel di Armi

"It's for Luke?" Peter asked as he looked over the large box. "Who is it from?"

"It's tagged by United Airlines," James said as he removed his jacket. "The package is about three days late; that's why they hired a private carrier from Genoa to here, they couldn't find a chartered carrier all the way from Rome."

Peter could see Chris from the corner of his eye, composed, standing tall, and earnestly interested in the package.

"Did Luke say anything about a package?" Peter asked Chris.

"No...but I think I know what it is," Chris replied as he moved towards it. "That night I was telling you about, when we slept in the train station; I remember Luke telling that guy he was playing the guitar with that he had brought his, but the baggage claim lost it, accidentally sending it to Turkey...It's Luke's guitar."

"Is that what he was waiting for? Is that the reason you guys stayed here so long?" Roberto asked as he stepped forward. Chris stared at the floor as if he was deep in thought, trying to recall everything from the previous weeks in an instant.

"It had to be. I don't know how he would have contacted them from here, but he must have known they had it, so he requested they send it to Monterosso."

"How would he have gotten a hold of United?" Peter asked Roberto. It just dawned on him they were still speculating what was inside the package. Peter sat down and began opening the cardboard flaps.

"I do not know, Peter; we have the only communication tower in the area. There are land lines running through the five cities, but a cell phone would have to clear the hills."

"But even on *Rupe di Roccia Caduta* you can't get a signal," James added. "It definitely sits higher than the hills." Peter had no idea where "whatever he said was;

he wanted the guys to think logically—Luke had to hike wherever he used his phone, and he had to do it under the radar because of Chris; wherever it was, it couldn't be that far.

As Peter opened the last flap, the black hard case came into sight—it was a case he recognized. Chris had been right; sitting in the packaged box was Luke's Les Paul Gibson. Peter knew his son would never move without his "musical baby", and he would never fly with it unless it was a serious move. Peter slightly smiled at the thought of Luke's panic when he landed at the airport to see all of his luggage except the Les Paul Gibson—*Luke probably wanted to kill someone*.

"His Les Paul Gibson," Peter shared with the small audience. "It was his favorite guitar." Peter pulled on the guitar case as James helped him clear the cardboard box. When the two did this, a small note that was attached to the bottom of the case fluttered to the ground; Peter didn't notice it, but James did. He picked it up and without knowing its significance, read it to himself.

"Luke loved this guitar," Peter continued. "He bought it three years ago for an incredible price that I always fought with him about. But Luke never touched his mother's life insurance checks granted to him, so he always had the money—I'm sure that's how he paid for this trip."

"I am amazed he had it shipped here," Roberto replied. "James, you are a great man, but anyone could have taken it when they hired a private carrier."

"I bet Luke didn't think about it that way. I'm sure he wanted the guitar for when he returned to Saskia— and Luke's patience isn't exactly—"

"Did you say Saskia?" James interrupted as he looked up from the note.

"Yes. Saskia was Luke's fiancée in Munich," Peter

replied, surprised by James' interruption.

"There's a note from her," James said as he held up the note. Peter set down the case and stood up, his left arm aching at the swift movements.

"Where did you get that?" Peter asked, as Roberto moved to join him.

"It was underneath the case; in the box." James replied as he handed the note to Peter.

Peter took the note and held it at a distance; without his glasses he was having trouble reading the note. Trying to clear his eyes, he attempted to read it in private one more time, but soon gave up on the notion. Handing the note to James, he asked him to read it to him. James cleared his throat; looking up he realized everyone's attention was directed at him.

"Luke, when you have received this note, you will no doubt wonder why I sent you your guitar after all that has happened. Those in charge assured me it would get to you this time. I couldn't wait to hear my song again any longer, and when I arrive on the 18th, I want you to play it for me. I miss you more than ever, my bed misses you, and my family and I can't wait for the future—they think you are part of the family already. I love you more today than ever before. Always and forever, your future wife, Saskia"

When he finished, James handed the note to Roberto who read the contents once again. Peter was more confused then ever. *Saskia was coming here?* The question grinded into his already aching mind full of details, facts, and questions. Turning to Chris, Peter began to feel angry.

"Did you know anything about this?" he questioned with authority. Chris's eyes went wide.

"No, Luke never said anything to me." In a quick movement, Peter ran towards Chris and threw him up against the wall.

172

"You knew! You know everything! What happened to my son!" Peter screamed as Roberto and the lieutenant rushed over to separate him from the young man.

"I didn't know! I don't know what happened to him!" Chris yelped as Roberto separated Peter.

"Peter!" Roberto screamed as the fire in Peter's eyes glared at Chris but then quickly retreated as he began walking the other way; kicking over a chair Peter let out some of his anger.

"Damn it!" he yelled out as brought his hands to his hips—his mind searching for control.

"Peter," Roberto said softly as he moved towards his friend, "we will find out what happened. I promise you that. The pieces do not finish the puzzle, I know, but we will find out what happened."

Peter dropped his head in exasperation; it was all too much for the moment. Picking up the chair, he slumped into it and put his head in his hands. No one in the room, not even Chris, blamed him for the outburst; they just stood quietly, giving him a moment to collect his thoughts.

Pushing his head up, and looking at Chris, Peter felt foolish for his rage.

"I'm sorry...I just..." He trailed off as everyone in the room exhaled in momentary relief.

"It's okay, don't worry about it," Chris said as he slumped down against the wall. "We're all in the same boat."

Peter glanced around the room till his eyes met James Russo's. The man was completely in the dark about what was going on. Peter wanted nothing more than to fill him in, but he was too tired to do so. The heavy silence filled the air—Peter wanted to be left alone but out of respect to all those in the room, he didn't immediately seek it.

"Roberto," Peter began, "can we get Mr. Russo a room so he can stay out of the storm tonight? It's the least we can do for him." Roberto nodded his head as he headed towards the door behind the receptionist counter. Peter was calling the shots now—he had risen to the occasion, and Roberto didn't argue with the man's integrity.

"Chris, you should go on upstairs and try to get some rest," Peter said to the young man. "We'll wake you in the morning...I'm going to need you tomorrow, son." Chris rose from his crouched position.

"Of course, anything I can do to help." Chris replied as he followed the lieutenant out the door. Roberto returned with a set of keys.

"James, please, I will show you to your room. You will have clean linens, a warm shower, and a dry place for tonight, on us," Roberto said as he motioned his hand towards the door.

"Thank you. I appreciate it," James said to Roberto. Turning his attention to the aging man slumped in the chair he said, "Peter, I don't know what exactly is going on, but if you need me for anything tomorrow, I would be happy to stay and help."

Peter nodded his head, too exhausted to reply, but still grateful at the hearty offer. Roberto led James to the door and then stopping, turned back to Peter.

"I will be back down in a minute," he said. Peter acknowledged the comment as the two men left out the door and into the stormy night.

Sitting alone in the hotel lobby, a scatter of chairs, cardboard, and plastic food containers sat highlighting the black guitar case sitting on the floor in the center of the room. Peter's arm ached; he looked down at the bandage wrapped tightly around the wound; when they were at the station Peter guessed he needed stitches, but dismissed it in their haste. Finding the energy to stand up, Peter walked over to the chair next to the guitar case and plopped down once again. Running his fingers over the smooth, hard case, Peter took a deep breath as he began to open the three latches. Swinging the case open, Peter's morbid state continued when he saw his son's treasured Les Paul Gibson. Like the case, the guitar was black. The glossy reflection easily showed Luke's handiwork. Peter could tell he cleaned it meticulously before travelling.

Peter pulled the guitar out of the case and positioned it in his arms. The hopeless feeling returned as his body felt numb; his fingers began to shake as the tears rolled slowly down his face. With a strum of the strings Peter lowered his head to the guitar and began weeping uncontrollably. He felt the same way as he did at the *camera mortuaria*—the item of grief being his son's guitar rather then his son's lifeless body laying on a gurney. Peter began to wonder if every small bit of memorabilia would trigger the empty feeling he felt inside—if it did he wouldn't be able to survive.

Wiping his eyes and nose with his right hand, Peter sat back in the chair, clutching the guitar tightly against his chest. It all seemed surreal—Peter looked around the room—*where am I? How did this happen?* A week ago life had been normal, if you can even call it that; Luke was traveling around Europe, Jake was home in New Hampshire, and Mary had been gone a long time. A week ago, Peter was bothered by a misplaced stapler from his desk. Now...things were different. Peter was changing in the wake of a complete tragedy—he was hardening and opening up simultaneously. He thought the world was cruel; but clutching the guitar and replaying the words written by Saskia in the note to his son, he knew it wasn't for at least two people. Last week, Luke was exploring the endless joys and possibilities life had to offer with a young woman who loved him with all she had. Last week, Luke had been alive, and life was beautiful.

Peter could sense the rage returning. His tears had ceased and now his face began turning red. It was a nightmare—the whole thing was a nightmare. He couldn't stop thinking about Luke's final moments; how scared he must have been; how he needed his father. Peter thought about Mary; the husband she needed him to be wasn't the husband he had been. He thought about Jake—the son living as far away as he could possibly run in order to escape his father. Peter shook his head as he grinded his teeth together—he was repulsed by his own life, by his actions of abandonment for the sake of what was seemingly nothing of real value.

In a sudden explosion of insulated frustration, Peter placed the guitar down on its case and sprinted for the door into the stormy night. Taking the stairs down onto the side street, Peter failed to hear Roberto calling him from the second story stairs of the hotel. Running as fast as his old, aching legs would take him, Peter ran until he hit the main street in Monterosso Al Mare that led straight to the ocean. Very late on a stormy night, not a soul could be seen. Peter felt the rain splashing into his face—the wind forcing him to shield his eyes as he sprinted. In the distance he could hear a voice, but he couldn't make out who it was or what they were saying; he didn't care. He passed by a series of restaurants with their outdoor chairs stacked on top of each other, a canvas fighting the wind to protect them from the rain.

Seeing the train tracks in front of him, he sprinted through the underpass; a white gate was open, leading to the lone deserted beach split between the cliffs of Vernazza and the uninhabited. Peter, completely soaked and filled with rage, his left arm aching as the rain soaked through the bandage, picked up a piece of drift wood and hurled it as far as he could into the crashing waves—the noise of the wind covering the ensuing *splash*.

"What did you want with him?" Peter screamed into the sea salt air, "He was just a boy! He had his whole life in front of him!"

Peter picked up another piece of driftwood and hurled it into the seas. He stumbled as the wind almost knocked him over—the fury of the storm reaching a climax. Regaining his balance, he arched his head back and let out a long, continuous cry towards the heavens. A bolt of lighting streaked across the sky in reply, followed almost immediately by a *boom* of deafening thunder. Peter caught his breath as he sank his hands and knees deep into the sand in submission to the mighty storm.

"Why didn't you take me instead?" his words carried into the wind. "Why did you take my boy? It should've been me."

The waves continued to crash into the shore as the sixty-year-old man knelt motionless. He couldn't move—his rage had been extinguished with his recent cry to the ocean. Behind him, Cinque Terre, one of the wonders of the world, stared at Peter like a Chagall painting; dark, and mourning for the decrepit man taking on the sea. Peter closed his eyes as his heart raced beyond a controllable state. With the adrenaline running low he began to feel the affects of being completely soaked in the middle of stormy night. Beginning to shiver, Peter suddenly felt a hand on his back. Turning in surprise, he saw Roberto with his right hand raised to shield the oncoming elements of wind and rain.

"Peter," Roberto said, lifting his voice over the noise of the storm, "Come back inside."

Peter lowered his head again, he had given up. With the hand on his shoulder he heard Roberto speak again.

"Please, Peter, come back inside."

The words were hollow, empty; thrown to the wind just as Peter's had been. He considered the world to be a decaying place as his inner voice told him to hurl himself into the sea to end his misery. Then Roberto spoke again.

"Peter, you will freeze out here, please come inside."

Peter listened to the swirling wind around him as the crashing waves boomed in front of him. The rain was relentless as the thick sheets disciplined Peter for his decisions. The lightening streaked across the sky again, an even louder boom of thunder following it. And then Peter heard a different voice, a woman's voice.

"*Peter, bury your anger in the sand. Fight for your son.*"

Unable to recognize the voice Peter turned quickly to Roberto.

"What did you say?" Peter snarled at the man who ran into the night after him.

"Please, come inside." The difference in the two voices was unmistakable. Peter rose from his knees, looking around to find the source of the second voice. But realizing the two were completely alone on the deserted beach, Peter looked down in confusion. "Please, come," Roberto said as he signaled for Peter to follow him.

Peter, bury your anger in the sand. Fight for your son. The voice had been crisp and clear—the sound of the wind and rain silencing for a moment. Looking up, Peter saw something he would never forget. In a crease of the dark and looming clouds, Peter saw a small opening. A single star shown through the raging storm.

178

Peter stood motionless, awestruck at the phenomenon. *A lone star amidst the chaos*, he said to himself, *that's my son.*

The crease in the clouds quickly closed as the fury of the storm returned to Peter's attention. Roberto was still beckoning for him to follow, the strength of his voice lessening as the storm raged on. Peter lifted his right arm against the wind before stumbling a few steps in Roberto's direction. Stopping, he turned back, taking one last glance at where the star had appeared. Peter smiled before turning to leave the beach.

Once the two men reached the inside of the lobby of the hotel, Roberto quickly went behind the desk and opened the closet door—grabbing two towels he tossed one to Peter and used the other one to dry himself. Peter, now totally wet and aching to the core, nodded his head at Roberto in thanks.

"Peter, you have got to get control over yourself," Roberto started as he moved around the desk. "Running into the stormy night, screaming at the ocean, screaming at God even...it will not bring your son back."

Peter nodded his head in agreement. "I know. I'm sorry."

Roberto inched closely to Peter so he could lower his voice. "I have two sons. I would die inside if anything happened to them. Anything. But I would do my best on the outside to make things right."

"Yeah," Peter replied as he lowered his head.

"To make things right," Roberto said again with emphasis as he put his hand on Peter's shoulder. When Peter nodded his head in agreement, Roberto slapped his shoulder and nodded. "I will see you in the morning. Get some rest. It is a nasty trail we are going to be hiking tomorrow."

"I will. Goodnight." Roberto gave a slight nod of his head and turned to leave when Peter spoke up. "And thank you. For everything." Roberto stopped and turned at the door.

"You're welcome. By the way, welcome to Italy," he said with a smile, as he turned and exited.

Peter was left alone, the water dripping from his clothes beginning to saturate the carpet below. In an attempt to be momentarily productive, Peter quickly wiped off his head as he walked over to the table housing the empty food containers. Picking up Luke's guitar case and the plastic bin with Luke's belongings Peter headed off to his room. Walking out the main entrance under a covered portion of his hotel, he quickly turned down a corridor. His room was the third door on the right; Peter set the guitar down to pull out his room key, his dripping towel still wrapped around his shoulders.

Once inside, Peter turned on the light, which illuminated the small, but efficient room. Placing the guitar on the bed, Peter set down the plastic bin and opened it. Pulling out the brown leather journal still sitting on top, Peter walked over to the desk and pulled out the chair. Realizing how difficult it was going to be to read the journal without his glasses, Peter turned on the desk lamp to completely illuminate the tabletop.

The brown leather journal.

Peter just stared it for a moment. He hadn't gotten a chance to even open it yet since arriving at Monterosso Al Mare. *Luke, what secrets do you have to share with me now?* Putting both hands on the back of his neck and looking skyward, Peter took a deep breath. If he were a drinker, he would have poured a drink; if he were a smoker, he would have lit a cigarette; but Peter was a vice-less doubter, so he only sighed for comfort.

Opening the journal to page one, Peter continued his deep breaths when he saw Luke's patented penmanship—all caps and high rising "A's" and "H's"—a

180

unique style that would always be identifiable to he, and he alone.

Peter fluttered his eyes to focus as he read the title of the first entry:

9/9 "The Arrival"

PART TWO

THE BROWN LEATHER JOURNAL

31.

09/09/08 4:17 P.M.
Munich International Airport
Munich, Germany

Standing at the baggage claim in the Munich International Airport, Luke couldn't control the moisture in his palms—the air-conditioning flowing through the building proved inadequate as he sweated profusely. The thought of seeing Saskia again in a matter of minutes made him as nervous as he had ever been before. Unable to read the exact words of the German signs overhead, he had a pretty good feeling the green "exit" signs pointing towards the corridor down the hall would lead to the woman he had traveled halfway around the world to see. The moment he had waited for and dreamed of was close—it seemed almost ridiculous that it was being stalled by the always-annoying retrieval of checked luggage.

During their last phone conversation before he flew out, Saskia had promised she would be at the closest possible point security would allow—waiting in uncontrollable anticipation. Shortly after this statement, they had said their lovers' goodbyes, and Luke told himself it would be the last time he had to dial the thirty digits on the phone card, which over the last two and half months had become second nature.

Calling cards and long phone conversations had

become their main source of communication. Almost every day through the long summer months, Luke would take his hour-long lunch from the In House Music Store and sit on a bench outside talking to Saskia who was nine hours ahead and winding down her evening. He had memorized every detail of the bench and the surrounding area during their conversations; the twenty-year old oak tree standing tall next to him; the regulars eating lunch at I-Hop each day at one-thirty; the parking space in front of him occupied daily by the black convertible Mustang, owned by the manager of the Dollar Tree in the building next to them; and the strange series of lines Luke had carved in the bench with the metal clip off his name tag.

Luke thought the creator of the old adage "distance makes the heart grow stronger" was terribly misinformed on a level that was almost tragic. He missed Saskia with a reckless abandonment he felt could never be understood by anyone of his generation. The summer of '08 would go down as the longest summer in history, bar none. But now it was over, and she was one corridor away.

The conveyer belt started to move as the bevy of fellow passengers started to huddle around to claim their luggage. Luke had to check his two larger pieces, a large black suitcase and his backpack, because his laptop satchel and carry-on black suitcase were all they allowed him to take on the plane. A fiasco with his connecting flight in Philadelphia had already left him one very important piece of luggage short. His large black suitcase came out with the first group of spilling luggage, enticing him to believe it would be a short wait, but due to popular airport luck, his backpack came out fifteen minutes later.

Looking like a tourist with his luggage spilling over as he tried to mobilize, Luke finally headed towards

184

the exit corridor. When he turned the corner, the sizable group of people who obtained all of their luggage before him obstructed his view from venturing into the large crowd of relatives, friends, loved ones, and security officers standing ready to greet the travelers. As a man started to move, Luke thought he saw the long brown hair he could never forget, but it quickly vanished behind a large woman hugging an even larger man. Moving at pace that allowed him to advance while keeping from spilling his luggage all over the floor, Luke headed in the direction of the large couple. When the conventional greeting hug between the large couple ended, they slowly started to walk away, revealing the wandering and excited blue eyes of the young woman wearing the silver half-heart shaped necklace around her neck. Before she spotted him, Luke stopped. Time stopped. Luke didn't know if life after death was more important than life itself, but he knew love had them both at its mercy. Taking a deep breath of air, he took his first steps aimed at a new life with the last person he figured he'd ever love so deeply.

When their eyes finally met for the first time in what seemed like an eternity, Saskia completely abolished the idea of the yellow security line that restricted her up to that point as she sprinted towards him. Setting down his laptop satchel gingerly, and dropping his Columbian backpack, Luke opened his arms as she raced into them. A security guard took two steps towards them, but quickly stopped when Luke threw up his right hand, pleading for him to allow the intrusion.

Saskia clung to his body as if she would never let him go. Luke ran his fingers through her long brown hair as he held his face tight to her head. The smell of her hair he'd all but forgotten flooded his senses while the shape of the small of her back through the light brown leather jacket formed in his hand; the memories of their long hours in his bed returning to his thoughts. And they had yet to speak a word to one another.

Pulling her away only enough to touch his forehead to hers, Luke smiled as he could see light tears roll down her soft cheeks.

"Hi baby," he whispered to her as he raised her chin to look into her watering eyes. "I made it."

Every literary genius has attempted to describe the ensuing kiss—the defining moment of every lover's reunion—all in imperfectly beautiful words, but imperfect by nature. If a picture is worth a thousand words, then a thousand pictures couldn't even begin to describe the moment Luke softly touched his lips against Saskia's—a moment that expressed and exemplified their very existence. It was simply, eternal.

Every person has those moments in life where they are completely content with every situation and outcome they have faced because it brought them to a single moment of happiness. Luke; with his mother dying tragically in a car accident, his father seemingly lifeless and stagnant, and his brother excusing himself from the family; was in a new territory of emotions. Every moment spent with Saskia was an introduction to a new level of happiness never obtained before. His world had become ultimately unpredictable, adventurous, and worth living in.

The kiss had been long, soft, sensual, and passionate. Saskia reached up and took the chiseled bone structure of Luke's face in her right hand. Ending the kiss, she ran her index finger over his once dry lower lip, examining the shape through the sensation of her hand. "Hi," she said softly as she smiled.

"*Entschuldigen Sie bitte, wenden Sie sich bitte Ausgang zum Haupt-Terminal,*" the security guard said behind Saskia as he motioned for them with his hand. Luke imagined he was telling them to keep moving.

186

"Sorry, *ja natürlich*," Saskia replied as she turned to speak to the guard. Luke began to re-mount his luggage. Saskia picked up his laptop satchel, and the two started for the main terminal.

"Luke, where is your guitar?" she asked curiously. Luke noticed her accent was a little thicker than when she was back in the States—slowly over the summer it seemed to creep into her dialect as she was back in her homeland.

"That's a story. When I checked in for my connecting flight from Philadelphia to here, there was a message at the counter saying my guitar was left in Los Angeles."

"It was left there?"

"Yeah, the lady said they 'failed to load it.'"

"How does that happen?"

"I don't know; it didn't makes sense to me," Luke said as they continued to walk towards the airport exit. All around him he heard conversations passing and going in German—a language he wasn't even remotely familiar with. Luke was in another world, but for the first time in months, he felt like he was home. "They told me they would try to get it on the next flight to Munich."

"Which guitar did you decide to bring?" Saskia asked in reference to one of their previous phone conversations—the short of it being Luke's ultimate indecision on which guitar he would bring on his trip.

"My black Les Paul Gibson." His reply made Saskia's face cringe. She knew it was his favorite.

"I am sorry, honey. I am sure it will be here soon."

"Yeah. Hopefully before Chris and I leave." Saskia quickly noticed the brown paper bag in her hand—in the fury of the immediate moment, she had forgotten all about it.

"I brought you some food," she said holding the

bag up.

"Oh, thanks baby. What did you bring me?"

"A bottle of water, some fruit, and a pretzel...that I have eaten half of already," she said with a smile. Luke laughed.

"Of course you did."

"I am sorry?" she said in more of a question tone. Luke stopped and leaned down to kiss her again.

"It is fine, babe. Thank you for bringing me food." Luke started to move again when she asked him if he had talked to his father before he left. Luke paused for a moment, biting his upper lip as he often did when he was pained by a thought.

"I tried. He wouldn't listen." Saskia touched his open arm in support. She was obviously sad for him—he didn't want her to be—he wanted her to be his new family. Re-arranging his luggage so his left hand was free, Luke reached for her hand as they walked slowly out of the airport into the light of the Bavarian sky.

The journey to her family's apartment in Schwabing wasn't short. Taking the S-8 from Flughafen München to Marienplatz took close to an hour. Half of the subway ride was above ground—the view outside the window would have been anything but spectacular if Saskia wasn't in his arms the entire time. She was so excited to point out things and places she wanted to take him—her tone of voice was that of tour guide who absolutely loved her job. Fellow passengers sat quietly as the two spoke in an abundance of English over a wide range of topics from what they were going to do that night, the meeting of the family, the backpacking trip with Chris, and a hint of Luke possibly living in Bavaria permanently.

When they arrived at Marienplatz, Saskia led him

up a series of escalators to the U-6 line. Four stops later they arrived at Giselastraße—the closest U-Bahnhopf stop to Saskia's home. Entering out to the street, Luke's head began to swim in his new environment. The crisp, warm late summer day had a fury of citizens swarming the busy corner of Giselastraße and Leopoldstraße. Luke felt like he was on a different planet—he had never left the United States before, and now more then ever, he prepared to leave the "Sebastian way" of disappointment behind him.

"So, they will put your guitar on the next flight and mail it to my home address?" Saskia asked in reference to their ongoing conversation about his rogue guitar.

"Yeah. I gave them your address, so even if it comes after Chris and I leave you can either find a way to get it to me or keep it here," Luke replied as they continued to walk down Giselastraße; grey, looming, six-story apartment buildings on either side of them.

"Oh, I see," Saskia began. "Would you want me to bring it to you?"

"I wish," Luke shot back at the suggestion. Saskia reached out and took hold of his free arm.

"I could do it," she suggested.

"What? Come and meet me on the road?" Luke wheeled around to face her.

"Yes."

"Really?" Luke asked in surprise.

"Yes. I would love to come see you—I have fall break in October—second or third week. I could come travel with you and Chris for some days and then come back."

"I would love that. I don't know how he'll feel about it, but then again, I don't care." Luke said with a smile. "Second or third week in October? We should be in Italy, I think."

"Perfect."

"Really? You want to do this, really?"

"Of course. I would go anywhere in the world with you." Luke pulled Saskia in and kissed her.

"We'll find the exact date of your break and figure it out," he replied.

"Deal," Saskia said as she kissed him again. Luke pulled away to re-adjust the heavy backpack on his shoulders. He was growing tired of packing the luggage around.

"How much further?" He asked. "I have to put this stuff down."

"About twenty meters," she replied. Luke's face lit up with excitement but quickly cringed. "What's the matter?"

"I'm nervous." Saskia laughed as she took steps forward, beckoning with her open hand to follow.

"Don't be. Luke, come meet my family."

32.

22/10/08 00:18
Hotel Di Armi

Peter wiped away the fatigue in his eyes. He wished he had his reading glasses, but they would soon be part of a fish carnival, along with the rest of his things lost in the accident earlier that night.

Peter's instinct was to skip ahead to the last couple entries in the journal, but he decided against it. He didn't want to miss possible important information that Luke was clearly outlining in each entry. Peter knew Luke had a way of capturing images, events, and emotions, but the more Peter read, he thought it very strange to read another person's personal and private thoughts—even if it was his son's. He found himself paralleling Luke's life with his own in abstract forms.

Peter sat hovering over Luke's journal with his hands clasped together. From what Peter could tell as he read Luke had obviously, and very clearly found the love of his life in Saskia. Peter recalled when he met Mary for the first time. It was a day, thirty-seven years earlier, which coincided with so many things; the last time Peter had a drink of alcohol; the last time he saw his father; and the first and last time he would ever fall in love.

On November 3rd, 1971 Mark Peter Sebastian, Peter's father, died in Arcata, California due to internal hemorrhaging when his liver burst. Mark, a World War II veteran turned alcoholic, had a disdain for life that saved him a special place in the afterlife. Peter remembered countless times finding his father sitting at the dining room table with a full bottle of permissible whiskey along side a lone shot glass. His father would pour a shot then stare at the deaths of hundreds of fellow soldiers, friends, and countrymen before attempting to release their memory in one swoon. Shots were devoured until the bottle was empty or his tolerance denied the use of his hands. Nowadays, kids go out and drink for new memories—in past times, a lot of them drank to forget old ones.

To his credit, Mark never once belligerently cried in pain and anguish at Peter or his mother—he simply died long before his natural death. But when his blood finally distilled, Peter was left a twenty-four year old farm hand without a single bit of fatherly advice to pass on as an heirloom in the future.

The night of his father's death, Peter went to The Wrangler's Lagoon—a small tavern his father frequented with other well-known bottle bastards in the area. Taking a seat at the bar, Peter sat patiently waiting for someone to serve him.

"What can I get you?" a voice said. Peter turned to his left to see a beautiful young woman circling around the bar. His eyes, which only seconds before burned with disgust, softened when he met her gaze. She was absolutely gorgeous; her long curly brown hair had been pulled back into a ponytail as her perfect blue eyes patiently waited for his answer. Even standing behind a bar, her upper half physic showed promise to an even better half below.

"Jack Daniels," he managed to say, in awe at the sight of her. She turned around and reached for the bottle of whiskey. Wheeling back around she grabbed a shot glass and was about to pour a shot when Peter interrupted her. "The whole bottle, please."

"You want the whole bottle?" the young woman said curiously.

"Yes." The young woman sighed the way a

blackjack dealer sighs when a gambler pulls out the last of their money after the being run by the table for the third time in a row.

"Looking for a rough night?" she asked almost in pity.

"No," Peter replied. "I've already found it."

"Do tell."

"Do you know Mark Sebastian?"

"Sure. He's a regular here." The young woman said as she shifted her weight behind the bar.

"Not anymore. He died tonight."

"Oh my God," she replied.

"He's my father."

The young woman just stood in silence for a moment before placing her hand on top of Peter's in support, the warmth of her hand a rare occurrence to him.

"I'm so sorry," she said.

"Don't be," Peter said stoically. "He played the hand he was dealt, and now the game is over." The young woman forced an empathetic smile and patted his hand before retreating it back to the corner of the bar.

"He was always so quiet when he came in here. You could never get more than two words out of him."

"Yeah, "One more" no doubt."

"Is there anything I can do for you?" Peter looked up into her sad blue eyes that read wholeheartedly.

"Yeah, will you take a shot with me? Not in his honor—we'd salute his honor —but rather take a shot with me in his damned eternity." The young woman paused to weigh heavily on his request, and then slowly pulled out a second shot glass. Peter grabbed the bottle and poured himself a shot, then filled hers as well. After both of them shared a heavy breath, they took the shot and lightly placed their glasses on the counter. Peter glanced down at the unusual scene; a bottle of whiskey and two empty shot glasses. Sensing some higher meaning to the symbolism, Peter looked up at the young woman still looking at him.

"What's your name?" he asked.

"Mary."

"I'm Peter. Peter Sebastian."

Peter always wondered how Mary could find him the least bit interesting or attractive that night at the tavern. He imagined he looked like an angry, lost sailor in the middle of the desert when the two shook hands across the bar. But for whatever reason he and Mary continued to talk for the rest of the evening. They spoke so long, Peter eventually watched Mary shut down the bar and politely walked her out to her in the early hours of the morning. In the haze of their conversation, she completely lost track of time. Mary hadn't even cleaned up the bar before they left. Peter remembered standing at the door as she turned off the lights—a near full bottle of whiskey and two empty shot glasses still sitting on top of the counter.

It pained Peter greatly to think he hadn't learned anything from his relationship with his father. He had the chance to be everything his father wasn't, but ended up squandering the opportunity by focusing on a medium sized hardware store that rarely showed signs of growth. He never realized he had the best of the world at his fingertips; a beautiful wife, two great sons, and a life that was worth living if he had just realized the stars people are shooting for has everything to do with family, friends, and love.

But Luke knew. He knew how to break the mold—and his sledge had been Saskia.

Peter ached for Mary now more than ever. He was alone, sitting in a room reading his late son's journal, aching for his wife. Such loneliness couldn't be found on the proverbial deserted island.

Unclasping his hands, Peter tried to focus—the journal beckoning him to keep going, to keep fighting. Pushing aside his ascending depression, Peter picked up the journal and started reading from where he left off.

33.

09/09/08 5:23 P.M.
Home of Otto and Tuvia Einreiner
Munich, Germany

Luke felt loved—not of the intimate variety, although Saskia offered plenty of that, but loved in the way a family makes you feel when coming home for Thanksgiving after a long absence. Sitting at the dining room table with the Einreiners, Luke couldn't help but smile with genuine happiness. The three-bedroom condo was an inviting place to walk into when he and Saskia arrived. Saskia's mother, Tuvia, had painted a banner with her youngest daughter Mia, that read "Welcome Luke Seßastian"—Saskia had laughed when she read the sign to her mother, saying the German Eszett in place of the "B" would make his name sound like "Se-ZA-tian". Luke found the banner perfect, and an extremely nice gesture to welcome him.

The condo didn't look all that different than an American condominium that you would find in the eastern cities. The only discernible difference he could see was the absence of a washer and dryer. A flat-screen television was hung on the wall of the modern living room connected to the kitchen and dining room. One mistake Luke made was pointing out the "Foozeball" table in the corner—Saskia's father, Otto, was quick to point out that it was indeed a *Futbol* table, and "soccer and foozeball were 'hack' American concepts that took away from the real concept of *Futbol*, the only real global sport".

Thirty minutes after the arrival introductions Luke sat silently observing the organized chaos around him as the Einreiners prepared the last remaining details to the home cooked German feast in his honor. Mia and her older sister, Hannah, helped their mother put vanilla frosting on the cake that would eventually make it's way to the table later in the evening with multiple signs of premature fingers having dipped into the icing. Saskia with her older brother Timo, who had came over from University for the occasion, and Otto were debating in German as they routinely peered into the oven to check on the pork basked in laurel and chives, indicating to Luke they were playfully arguing about when it was cooked to perfection.

Luke felt a hint of sadness when he thought about his family compared to the Einreiners. There was so much happiness in the room filled with smiles, random hugs and defining roars of spontaneous laughter. The Sheen family couldn't pull off such a performance if it was indeed fabricated for Luke's arrival.

Luke could vaguely remember the last time his

family sat down to a celebrated meal just before the untimely death of his mother. It had been Jake's graduation celebration, almost ten years prior to Luke's trip to Germany. Luke had indulged in plenty of the Dobb's posh dinners with family friends and acquaintances that Luke deemed the "Seven Figures Club", but those events were not the same as what he was witnessing before him. Saskia had told Luke the family attended a Roman Catholic Church a few streets down for her entire life—Luke didn't know if having a purely eccentric religious ideal was the difference maker, but looking at Saskia's family, he was seriously starting to wonder if God was the absence in his life, the void that needed to be filled on his personal pathway to contentment and happiness.

"*Es ist geschafft, weil ich sagen, es ist getan,*" Luke heard Otto say to his children. Luke didn't understand a word but he was enjoying the beauty of the language. For Otto, Tuvia, Timo, and Saskia, German was the easier language for them to freely converse, but each had remarkable English that Luke understood easily and for which he was extremely grateful.

"He says the pork is done, but I don't agree," Saskia said in Luke's direction to clear up any lingual gaps he had.

"Yes, Luke, the pork is done, and it is time for feast," Otto said with a large smile. "It is done, I am the head of this house, and I say it so." Luke laughed at Otto's soft nature and choppy sentence structure.

"Luke, would you like beer? We have, um, water, milk, wine..." Tuvia started to ask when Timo interrupted.

"Luke, have an Altbier. It is very good," he said over his mother.

"Sounds good to me. I mean, I have to get ready

for Octoberfest, right?" Luke said with a smile. The family laughed out loud when Otto spoke up while bringing in the seasoned pork on a platter from the kitchen area.

"Luke, you can drink day and night for the next two weeks, and you will not be ready for Oktoberfest," he said with a smile. "Old men will drink the table on you." Luke found that an interesting way of saying he couldn't keep up with the German beer drinkers.

"They drink that much?" Luke asked.

"We drink that much," Timo said with a wink. Luke cracked a big smile as the group started to take their places around the table. Tuvia brought a tall glass containing a dark amber beer for Luke with a smile. Luke thanked her as Timo continued. "If Saskia will let you go for but a minute, I would like to take you around University and show you some cool bars."

"Yeah, that would be great," Luke started to say when he looked at Saskia, "that is, if it's okay with your sister. I know how she gets a little greedy."

"You can go over to University with him," Saskia chimed in as she took her seat at the table next to Luke.

"*Dies ist mein Gabel oder sein?*" Mia asked in a seemingly directionless way to the group.

"*Das ist Ihre Gabel, ist sein das andere,*" Hannah said in a response that made her smile. Luke had no idea what the conversation was pertaining to, but he had this intricate feeling that everything spoken in German was about him. Hannah could see the confusion on his face, and with her limited but still outstanding English, she tried to explain.

"Mia asks which fork is hers," she said to Luke. Luke nodded his head in understanding.

"This fork, my dear, is yours," Luke said as he picked up the fork and bowed his head as he held the fork in the air as if addressing the child as royalty. Mia started to laugh and giggled out a German phrase. The family then laughed together. Luke laughed along as if he knew what the joke was.

"She says that you are a fool, or silly. But it's more of a historic phrase, like a "jester" or something." Luke smiled at Mia.

"Surely, you jest?" Luke said, laughing to himself. Mia had no idea what he was saying, but she erupted in laughter nonetheless.

Luke took a moment, as the laughter died down into conversation amongst the family for a brief minute. The German language was being flung around the table in panoramic fashion. As was his entire relationship with the woman sitting next to him, the whole ordeal seemed like a fantasy—a dream that he would eventually have to wake up. The day before he was signing a rent check for three months advancement on his flat, staring at his luggage that had been packed for what seemed like an entire week in anticipation; and now, he was in Munich, sitting next to the most incredible and inviting family.

Otto said something and the family reached out and took each others hands.

"A prayer to bless the food. Forgive me, Luke, it will be in German," he said as Saskia took his hand, and Mia nearly took his arm off with a smile and warm squeeze of his palm.

"No worries," Luke said as he bowed his head after winking at Saskia. As Otto began his prayer in his native tongue, Luke said his own silent prayer to whomever was listening.

Thank you for this day. Thank you for this wonderful family that I hope to call my own one-day. He thought for a second as he felt his hand shaking in Saskia's—the feeling of her hand sending shivers down his spine. *And thank you for Saskia, I love her so much, she's such a gift from Heaven. Thank you for sparing one Angel to look after me. At this moment, there is absolutely nothing wrong with my life. Amen.*

      After dinner it was decided by Saskia that she and Luke were going to take a walk. The sun was starting to set, but being early in September, it was such a warm and inviting evening, a walk was the most logical choice to get to spend some alone time together, while touring the new city for Luke. Leaving the condo the same way they came in, Luke and Saskia got on the subway once again, going three stops from Giselastraße to Marienplatz. Being a Tuesday night, Luke figured the streets would be fairly empty, but the Marienplatz foot traffic was amazing. People flooded the lamp-lit streets, as most of the stores were still open. Bikers, walkers, joggers replaced the usual cars and buses as it became more and more apparent of why Europeans were in better shape then Americans.

      Saskia led him to the Marienplatz, also known as St. Mary's Square. The huge courtyard was an attraction that resembled a theme park replication in the States. Luke's eyes went touristy and Saskia smiled.

      "This is Marienplatz. Normally, or at least especially around any sort of holiday or festival, there are a ton of vendors and food stands everywhere," Saskia told Luke as she took his arm and put it around her shoulders.

      "This place is amazing," Luke said as he erratically moved his eyes from one thing to another. When his eyes met the largest structure to his left from the side street they had walked down, he could feel his eyebrows rise. The structure had to be at least two hundred feet tall, gothic architecture gracing one terrace to the next. The dark building had steeples rising out of it to give it a churchlike presence.

"What building is that?" Luke asked in amazement.

"That is the *Neues Rathaus*, or Town Hall. Do you see the figures in the center column about halfway up?" Saskia returned. Luke moved his eyes to the center of the building, which was well illuminated with exterior lighting. He could see motionless figures that resembled older versions of the Disneyland attraction figures on the ride, "Small World."

"Yeah, I can see them."

"At eleven, noon, and five o'clock, they come out and perform the famous *"Glockenspiel"*—a traditional dance that is a reminder of the end of the plague."

"The plague? How old is that building?" Luke asked naively.

"Oh, five hundred years or so," Saskia replied, but Luke's attention was already diverted to his right, as he looked at a fountain that stood in the center of the Square. "That is the *Mariensäule*, or the "Column of St. Mary"."

"It's gorgeous."

"It was erected after some Swedish invasion to celebrate the end of all the wars and problems they had—we had to learn all of this stuff in school, but I would make an awful tour guide with how much I have forgotten." Luke smiled as they made their way towards the beautiful fountain. Luke could see at the top of the column in the center of the fountain was a gilded statue of the Virgin Mary.

There were only a few people around the fountain, giving them a chance to get close and stand in front of the ledge of the cement bowl containing the rare art form of the enclosed statues. Four Putti's were symmetrically surrounding the column looking skyward towards the Virgin Mary.

"You just don't see things like this in

Sacramento," Luke said as Saskia stood in front of him and wrapped his arms around her, his height allowing him to comfortably rest his chin on the top of her head.

"Well, Sacramento probably hasn't been invaded by an army from Phoenix, or lost hundreds of thousands of lives due to a plague," Saskia remarked.

"No shit. The biggest battle those two cities have is between the Suns and the Kings," Luke replied sarcastically.

"Watch your mouth in front of the Virgin Mary," Saskia shot back—causing Luke to wonder if she was being serious or not.

"Oh, yes, sorry."

"I'm serious. Many people come to this fountain with a bag full of Euros they got from the bank to pray and ask the Virgin Mary to answer their thoughts and prayers. They pray for protection from all of the awful things that happen in this world, that we, ultimately brought upon ourselves."

"Yes, but you just said we bring them upon ourselves. We should also be able to undo them ourselves, don't you think?" Saskia, for the first time since they held each other in the park, separated from Luke on her own free will to turn and face him.

"No, Luke. Not everyone has the power to change what powerful people have done. We here in Germany, above all know that. When I was in America, I don't know how many students asked me about Hitler, or if I was also against Jews. One man in power left the rest of us paying the price, which causes some of us to pray at this very fountain for forgiveness for our grandfathers and great grandfathers who bought into it."

"The students at your school were young and naive. Anyone with any reasonably working brain wouldn't think that."

"And you can say that for sure?"

"I can't. But those who stand and only reflect in the past have no real future."

"But the past effects who we are. Forgiveness is the only way to a fresh start."

Luke knew he was in a very foreign argument, but against his better judgment he pushed forward—a trait he got from his father. Press. Pursue. Don't back down, so in the end you come out with more answers then when you started.

"But that forgiveness is unnecessary, isn't it? Hitler doesn't exist anymore; Nazi's have been outlawed for six decades, haven't they? German's rebuilt Germany and brought the Berlin wall down—the people have caused a resurgence that allows us to stand in this unbelievable square. An all powerful God would render this statue as a water feature and nothing more."

Saskia was confused. "What do you mean by that?"

"An all-powerful God would have never allowed the plague to come. An all-powerful God would have stopped the Swedish invasion before it ever started. An all-powerful God would have never let Hitler exist, or for a group of Muslim extremists to run planes into towers."

"You look at it from one side Luke."

"How so? Do you not believe in a trinity of Gods that protect our mind, body, and soul? Do you not believe that he sent a man, of all things, with an ideal, to change the way we perceive the afterlife?"

"I do."

"How can you explain it?"

"Luke, I love you. You are the only man I ever want to be with. I have a belief that I hope you realize, or at least respect, and maybe believe in too, but it is not so easily explained."

"How complex does a belief need to be?" Luke was now wondering how they ever got into such a deep, perplexing conversation about God anyway, but he was grossly interested in her responses. "I believe in music, the power of melodies and their ability to move people. I believe in cardiovascular exercises because scientists have proof of it helping the immune system, prevention of cardiovascular diseases, and obesity. I believe—"

"Luke—" Saskia tried to stop him but Luke pressed on.

"I believe in the written word before a picture, because a thousand words can illustrate in time what a single moment can't explain. I believe in walking on the beach, Peanut Butter M & M's, sleeping in till noon, the unexpected staring contest, cinematic moments, deep breathing, and above all things, I do believe in love. I do believe it exists for I, for you, for us. It is not imaginary." Luke had a small smile when he said the last part—thinking the cleverness of his random thoughts would make Saskia smile and drop the conversation. But it did not. She remained quiet, patient, and waiting for rebuttal. "Saskia, come on. I can believe in those things because I know they're right there, in front of me, like you are right now. They are so easily definable."

"You think love is easily definable?"

Luke smirked. "Now I do. I didn't before, but now I do."

"You think you are so very clever, don't you?"

Luke placed his hands behind his back. "Yes."

"Do you love me?" This was not a question he was expecting.

"Of course. With all of my heart."

"If a person or friend you knew well walked up to you and asked you to describe your love for me, which you say is with all of your heart, would you be able to do it? Would you be able to convince them of your love for me, so that they saw it as you do?" Luke started to speak, as if to say, "that's different", but he stopped.

204

"No. I wouldn't be able to—they couldn't possibly understand."

"Well, that's how I feel about Jesus. Not to even mention, how Jesus feels about me. Or you. And in the Bible, he explains it so beautifully—like one of your songs that seems to be the oxygen people breathe when they listen to it—and when the Bible is read, or spoken by a priest, we still don't understand it to its full value."

"But how can you put all of your trust in a man that claimed to be the Son of God? I mean, the very Son of God! Especially a God that allows so many tragic and awful things to happen in the world—one that can stop so much heartache, but doesn't."

"If I were to turn around and fall, would you catch me?" Luke took a deep breath, and nodded at her simplistic way of viewing religion.

"Yes, of course."

"Well that's how I put my trust in him. I have faith that he will protect me, the same way that I have faith you will catch me, because you love me, and don't want to see me harmed."

"But if I catch you, you feel my arms catching you. You can look me in the eyes and thank me. You can see what you believe in. Can you see God? Can you feel Him?"

"As clearly as the wind," Saskia shot back with an unbelievable confidence that seemed to radiate from her body to warm him. He was nervous. But Luke wanted to keep pressing, to keep discussing this issue, if not "the" issue of all the ages. Saskia turned and sat down on the ledge of the fountain, Luke following in his analytical pursuit.

"As clearly as the wind?" Luke threw back her answer as he sat down beside her. The night was clear, cool, perfect—there were no gusts of wind to be felt.

"Yes, the wind. The way it comes and goes. How

it shows itself in both small and large increments."

"But the wind is just the wind. We feel the wind, and know it's simply wind. The existence of a God is not so easily proven." Saskia shifted her weight as she threw up her legs up on the ledge, allowing her to face Luke as she held his hand.

"And why not? Why can't a person want to see God as they do the wind? Why can't we say God is the feeling we get when we see a new baby, or the accomplishment of a career, or a good family dinner—or love? Why can't we see God in love?"

"Because humans...are flawed. Our judgment has devastating implications. We almost can't be trusted to make such a huge decision like the existence of a God. We can only strive to be the best we can be. That's it." Luke was bold to speak so openly, so cynically about human behavior—it was almost as if he knew, not thought, the hope of an all-powerful being would never reach its potential—that man would always be left in the balance.

"We are flawed Luke. The only way we can become whole is with help," Saskia said matter-of-factly. But after a brief pause her tone changed. "Have you ever had that moment, where you think everything is good in your life, that everything has lined up the way it should, but you still felt hopeless? As if no matter what you have, or what you've accomplished can ever really be meaningful?"

Luke knew exactly what she was trying to articulate. He thought everyone, throughout eternity, has probably felt what she was describing at least once. Luke had written a song called, "On Top of the World" that basically defined the life of a man as worthless—that even when a person is on top, after all the victory fades, there is a moment of extreme worthlessness.

"I have," he replied looking up at her.

"Good. That is God telling you there is something more," Saskia said as she came in to kiss Luke on the cheek. Luke smiled. "And as long as God continues to tell you things, you will have the chance to listen. But I have to warn you, he will never stop. He will be hidden at times, disguised as your conscience, but eventually, I hope, he will be a loud voice that yells 'Luke!'" Saskia screamed his name loud enough to make a countless number of passerby's turn their heads. Luke immediately brought his hand up to her mouth and playfully covered it.

"Stop!" Luke said while laughing. Saskia started to laugh as well as she came in closer to him, staring into his eyes, seeming to search for his inner soul.

"Luke, if you spend the rest of your life speaking against God, I will still love you. But I promise you, I will cry his existence so loudly it will drown your voice out to a whisper, because God led me to you. And for all of time I will thank him for that." Saskia pulled out a Euro coin from her sweatshirt pocket, and showed it to Luke. "And with this coin, I thank God for all that he has blessed me with, and I pray for your forgiveness—I pray for you to be saved one day, because that is the real eternity with me."

When Saskia was done, she flipped the coin into the fountain—the splash was small, but the impact of the coin was large enough to change the face of the water—the ripples joining forces with all the other wishes and prayers throughout the centuries.

The ten days Luke was in Munich fruitfully flew by. After a summer of some of the longest days of his life, the ten days spent with Saskia and her family were some of the shortest—like the days described by one of those grey hairs who can't believe what happened to their forties, fifties, and sixties—it all just sort of flew by.

The city of Munich had been very kind and welcoming to Luke. When Saskia had to attend school, he would take the subway between Karlsplatz and Rosenheimer Platz in the city center. Everything eight blocks either way from Marienplatz is something of an outdoor shopping center. Luke didn't have much of an interest in buying anything, but he loved the public venues, the interactions, and the language being spoken, not to mention the architecture. Every night, Saskia would try to teach him a little German, but he quickly found out it would take many classes and total immersion to pick up the language. Luke thought it a strange, but uniquely satisfying experience being the foreigner in a new place—it was starting over from scratch in almost every way.

Often, when Saskia was at school, Luke would visit Starbucks, a familiar coffee shop with familiar coffee. He would always bring a book, as there were certainly no shortages of American books or American bookstores in Germany. After his intense religious conversation with Saskia at the fountain, Luke felt led to dive deeper into his own understanding of what he believed. To Luke, organized religion had always seemed transparent at best—the idea of the masses with a leader who can cast happiness, doubt, and condemnation with a whisper had never been all that appealing. It should be noted the "leader" is, and has always been, a human. Luke always believed in the individual power each person possesses—some people are weaker in mind, body, and spirit than others—but was the difference made by an individual relationship with a higher being? Luke thought it was possible—he always considered himself an agnostic—his answer was always, "I don't know." But lately, a power greater than him had been at work. Through Saskia, Luke could see light for the first time in a long time. Her spirit radiated, and it all stemmed from a belief in God and Jesus Christ, and the love they have for their creations. Luke feared it couldn't be that simple but it was at least worth looking into.

Luke also believed in intelligence and what intelligent people have to say by way of passing along wisdom. This is why the first book he bought in Munich was by a local, but famous author, Albert Einstein. The book, *Ideas and Opinions* was a compilation of Einstein's articles, interviews, and journals that Luke found intriguing, satisfying, but somewhat computable.

In one of Einstein's most popular articles, he describes the world as he sees it—an honest rendering of the deepest human conflictions. Einstein describes the individual need to find a higher purpose in life, but pragmatically dismisses a decisive destination for all journeys to end.

As Luke read Einstein's personal views he thought about the human purpose—the vagueness of it—the unknown and how answers drive most people to fear. Luke remembered his conversation with Rochelle about the unseen possibilities in life—can it be that *religion is a conjured state meant to exhaust the human fear of what we can't possibly understand or know?*

Einstein likened religion with science—the mystery of the unknown captivating right action and the pursuit of answers. He felt mystery and fear caused most people to believe in the most beautiful and incomprehensible things, and in this sense, all people could share a common ground in spirituality. But Einstein couldn't bring himself to believe in a God that punished and rewarded his creations through a will that humans also experience.

How can a person stand on either side of the spiritual argument in total determination? How can one person scream at the top of their lungs in certainty, as the other across the way does the same thing in opposition? These questions were among the many for which Luke felt compelled to find answers.

Luke spent hours reading Einstein's theories, thoughts, and ideas, but came to the conclusion they were irrelevant to his own personal case. Luke couldn't believe in God merely because Saskia believed in God, and he couldn't disbelieve in God, because scientists didn't have enough facts or evidence that a God existed, because somewhere deep down inside Luke thought an all-powerful God wouldn't feel the need to privilege his creations with all the information. In either case, his journey had just begun, and like Somerset's Larry Darrell, it could be a long and unbelievable fight to truth and understanding.

The day before Luke had to meet Chris at the train station, Luke asked Otto if they could go to lunch. Being a Thursday, Otto had to take an extended break from work to meet Luke at the corner of Leopoldstraße and Franze-Joseph Straße for a short five minute walk to Bachmaier Hofbrou—a German restaurant of Otto's choosing. Otto had explicitly forbidden Luke to eat anything but the finest German cuisine while he was in town.

When Otto and Luke sat down, Otto ordered two pints of Pilsner beer which Luke thought was rather interesting considering Otto was going back to work after lunch.

"I just wanted to say thank you for meeting me for lunch Otto," Luke started, and then added for gravitas, "*Danke*."

"*Gern geschehen*," Otto replied with a smile before asking, "What did you want to talk with me about?"

Luke shifted a little in his seat as he smiled. He

210

was very confident about what he was going to say, but any man in his right mind is still nervous when asking a father for his daughter's hand in marriage.

"I wanted to talk to you about Saskia," Luke began as Otto pushed his lips together to form a small acknowledging smile.

"Yes, you and Saskia—the only thing being spoken about around the home."

"I know it all may seem lightning fast; how we met, our few weeks together, and me flying here; but, I just want you to know I love your daughter with everything I have to offer and above all I respect her family's wishes."

Otto leaned back in his chair as the waiter appeared, setting down the two large pints on the table. As Otto thanked him, Luke devised a quick schedule of sips he would take so he didn't get intoxicated at lunch with his potential future father-in-law.

"Then we shall cheers to that," Otto said as he raised his glass and tapped Luke's.

"Cheers," Luke said with a smile as he took a scheduled sip. When Otto had finished drinking he set his mug down and put his elbows on the table.

"Yes," Otto began. "You and Saskia have come a long ways in a short time, you especially." Luke got the pun. "But I do not see it as a bad thing. Saskia has always been very smart, and very grown up in her decisions. I have had a great joy in being her father and trusting her to do the right things in life."

Luke sat and listened—Otto slowed at points when he spoke with his thick accent searching to find the right translational words and pronunciation for the message he was trying to deliver. Luke was patient and appreciative of Otto's efforts with him.

"Do you see yourself as a good man, Luke?" Otto asked him.

"I try to be. I try to be the best man I can be."

"Trying to be a good man, and knowing you are a good man are two things separate from one another. Only you, as a man, can decide such things."

"I am a good man. I have never had much in the way of an example, but I guess I just ran from the inherited disease in my family."

"Your father?" Otto asked as he took a large drink from his beer.

"And his father. There has never been a strong father-son tie in our family." Luke also took a scheduled drink.

"And I am a man of faith, and I do not believe that for you," Otto said with a large smile. Otto was a very animated man. He was about six feet tall, lean, and his face appeared almost worn, like a chain smoker of many years even though Otto didn't smoke. His spiked salt and pepper hair pronounced a happy medium of adult adolescence. "But that is not why you wanted to speak with me. What is it Luke?"

"I want to ask you for Saskia's hand in marriage," Luke stated, feeling more and more comfortable at the private meeting with Otto.

"Ahh, you do then?" Otto asked with a smile as he folded his arms across his chest.

"I do. I wanted to ask back in California, but I wanted to wait for your permission first."

"A gentleman. I thank you." Otto started, "but what does my blessing mean to you?"

"What does it mean to me?"

"Yes."

"It means a lot, I guess. I would hate to marry Saskia without your approval."

"Ahh, but you would still marry her. Wouldn't you?"

"I suppose I would," Luke smiled, as he felt

somewhat trapped with that last question.

"Then it looks like this old man has nothing to answer for, but I can say I would be happy if you were to join my family, because my Saskia wants it so badly, and I can see how much love there is between the two of you."

Luke couldn't describe what he was feeling, but he knew it was beyond overjoyed. Otto was a good man, who had an interesting and almost charismatic way of delivering his thoughts and wisdom.

"Thank you, sir," Luke said with a great deal of respect.

"I must now tell you some fatherly advice that was once spoken to me. You'll have to excuse my delivery—the advice was given to me by my father, and in German, of course."

"You're excused," Luke said patiently heeding Otto's words.

"There are three rules when it comes to treating a lady of interest in order to show her respect that is always deserved. The first rule is as follows: Always remember to do those things that many young men have forgotten. Be a...chivalrous man. Listen, be courteous, remember to be self-sacrificing at times, and always remember fair play. Be a knight, as true knights were the noblest of all men, and it had nothing to do with money." Luke shook his head in agreement. "The second rule as a knight is to always treat your woman as a princess, because ever since she was a little girl she wanted to be one. Women want to be beautiful, and to be treated as such. But do not disguise disgust with too much flattery—a woman does not want to be mocked—if the beauty you believe in is deep inside, then you must acknowledge that. The third rule is the most important rule, and you may never get the chance to understand, but always remember that your girl is somebody else's daughter. My daughter. Long before Saskia was the love of your life, she was my princess. She was my little girl, and that title cannot be changed or replaced. To Tuvia and I, Saskia is the love of our lives—and my little girl will be treated fair, and shown a great deal of love. As her father I expect nothing less; do you understand?"

Luke nodded his head in agreement. "I understand. And I promise you; I will do everything in my power to make every day a great day in her life. I will wake up each morning, asking myself, 'how can I make her day better?' She is the object of my affection, and that title cannot be changed or replaced."

Otto unclasped his hands sitting at the table, and reach out his right hand. Luke followed suit and the two shook hands firmly—an agreement of trust forming in their grasp.

"Good then. Let's eat. I am hungry."

"Me too," Luke said glancing down at the menu for the first time.

34.

22/10/08 01:16
Hotel Di Armi

Peter closed the journal as he pushed it away—his eyes were in need of not only his glasses, but a three-week hibernation. The entirety of his body ached from his head throbbing head down to the tips of his toes. Saskia's God, Einstein, and Luke's formidable conversation with Otto had put Peter in a position of mild discomfort. He himself had grappled with the idea of organized religion and a relationship with Jesus Christ all of his life, but now more than ever it seemed no one or no higher power was looking over him.

Needing a glass of water, Peter stood up, stretched his back, and walked over to the bathroom. Pulling a plastic cup out of its plastic casing, Peter filled it up with Cinque Terre's finest city water; he hoped it was at least potable. Leaning against the sink, Peter began circling his neck to relieve tension. Looking up into the mirror, Peter stared at his own reflection—his aging, darkening eyes roaming from his receding hair line to his sagging jaw.

Time passes us all by, he thought to himself. *And there's not a damn thing we can do about.* He remembered a line from one of his favorite movies, "The Shawshank Redemption." In it, the character played by Tim Robbins says to the character played by Morgan Freeman, "We either get busy living, or we get busy dying." Peter always liked that line—but was he living, or was he slowly fading to an afterlife he never dared to predict the destination of out of fear of the unknown? *At least Luke and I could finally agree on something. He didn't know, and I don't know.*

Knowing it was getting later and later, Peter wanted to read just a little bit more before retiring for the evening. Sitting back down in his chair, he placed the glass of water in the top right corner of the desk and pulled the journal close. Opening up the soft pages, he returned to Luke's words—a new entry, titled:

9/19 "The Long Kiss Goodbye, Chris, and a Sitar Player"

35.

19/09/08 18:23
Einreiner's Home

"Passport," Saskia said as she sprawled out on her bed. Luke was sitting at the edge of her bed looking through his backpack.

"Check," he replied.

"*Eurorail* Pass."

"Check."

"Map of Europe."

"Comes with the Pass. So, yeah, check."

"Guide book."

"Check."

Saskia sat up and smiled. "Tour guide." Luke's head came up and turned around to look at Saskia with a sideways bent.

"A tour guide?" He playfully questioned.

"Yeah. If you're going to run around Europe, you'll need a good guide." She sat up on her knees and inched towards him with her seductive charm.

"I think you're right. Actually in "Let's Go" they have several references to great tour guides along the way. They even have photos and I was particularly drawn to a young blonde German girl named Eva."

"Oh, is that so?" Saskia shot back at Luke with a smile. "And this Eva, does she do it for you?"

"She does have blonde hair, and I like to mix it up every once in a while—I've been with this brunette for a while."

"And you want a blonde?" Saskia asked as she inched really close to his face—she could feel his breath against her chin.

"Come on, you can only have so many Snickers bars before you need a little vanilla chewy nougat!" At this comment Luke grabbed Saskia is his arms and lifted her off the bed. The two twirled in the air before Luke tried to lower her legs into his backpack—both of them laughing hysterically the whole time.

"And what do you think you're doing?"

"If you can fit into my backpack I'm taking you with me."

"Such a great offer, but I think I'll pass." Luke took her feet out of the open backpack and placed her to the right so she could stand.

"And why do you say that?"

"Two boys in small hostel rooms after large consumptions of alcohol, no thanks." She said with a smile.

"Two boys? If you were coming with me, I would ditch Chris right now."

"And I would hate you for it."

"I know." The mood in the room shifted as Luke glanced over at the clock on the wall. He would need to leave soon to meet up with someone he had never met.

"You two will have a great time. And I'll come meet you over fall break, wherever you are."

"I know. But I feel like I just got here and now I'm leaving again. I hate it."

"Yeah, but when you get back from all the traveling, think of all the stories you will have, and I will want to hear them all. Except for the ones about other girls."

"What other girls?"

"Oh, the ones you will have to play Chris's friend for, I am sure."

"You're probably right. But you have nothing to worry about."

"Of course. You have me." Saskia and Luke embraced. Luke had recently found the extreme joy in just holding her—he figured, at times, it was the best way to show his affection for her—to just hug her and hold her for as long as she wanted.

When she started to release her grasp, Luke took the sides of her face in his hands as he stared into her eyes. Starting to sway back and forth, Luke began to sing "Danke Schoën" by Wayne Newton. When he looked down at Saskia she had the largest smile spread across her face he had ever seen.

"Danke Schoën, darling Danke Shoën, thank you for all the joy and pain. Pictures show, second balcony, was the place we'd meet, second seat, go Dutch treat, you were sweet. Danke Schoën, darling Danke Shoën." Luke sang. Saskia buried her head in his chest as he sang. Luke did things in abstract ways, and this was one of his gestures aimed to reassure her that he intended to spend a lifetime with her, and her alone. Luke dropped the lyrics and slowly hummed the music, eventually fading down to nothing.

Saskia raised her head and looked into her fiancé's eyes. *"Danke,"* she said in her thickest German accent.

"You're welcome. I need to go, baby."

"Are you sure you don't want me to go with you to the train station?"

"I'm sure. I've been there a few times this week when you were at school. Plus, if Chris ends up being a total douche bag, I don't want him to have the pleasure of meeting you."

"Okay. You better get going." Luke clasped his backpack and pulled down on the lateral straps to secure his sleeping bag in one of the string allowances. Putting his arms through the large straps, he mounted the bulky pack on his back. Saskia led him out of her room, past the living room, and next to the front door. Her family had said their goodbyes earlier, before Otto and Tuvia took the girls to get pizza, allowing Saskia some moments of privacy with her fiancé. Stopping at the door, Luke took Saskia in his arms once again. He felt like a soldier going off to war—he didn't want to leave her for ten seconds, let alone three weeks. He had fallen desperately in love with her—this was the woman he was going to spend the rest of his life with—the last call of every night till the end of his days and hopefully after.

"Saskia. I love you so much," he said softly as he placed his hands in hers. Saskia's eyes started to glaze over a little.

"And I love you more, Luke." She replied.

"And you're sure?" he asked.

"About what, baby?"

"That I get you? That I'm the lucky one who gets you for all eternity?" He lowered his head and placed his forehead on hers.

"If you want me, I'm yours. Forever."

"Don't forget to email."

"I won't."

And with that, they kissed. It was long and passionate, and booming with a love from a world without end. And when it was over, Luke turned and walked out the door—the sun shining bright, reflecting the polished half-heart silver from both of their necks.

When Luke arrived at the Munich Central Train Station, he headed straight for the arrival reader board. Chris's train from Amsterdam was due to get in at platform A-23 at 19:02. His wristwatch read 18:47. Luke walked to the customer service desk to ask for a departure schedule. When he and Chris had spoken over the phone and through emails, Chris always reminded him that he would have the train schedule and know all the exact times they needed to be at the train station to leave on time. Luke liked the reassurance—he was never one to be a big planner.

When Luke thanked the customer service rep for pointing him to the pamphlet-sized train schedules on the wall, he walked over and grabbed one. Knowing that he was looking for "Munchen to Praha," he began to search until he found it. *Good first impression, Chris*, Luke thought as he learned the last train to leave for Prague had left at 18:05. Not wanting to venture a guess as to why Chris had him meet him at the train station at this time when they clearly couldn't leave for Prague till the next day, Luke walked over to platform A-23, took off his pack, and sat down on one of the benches.

Luke didn't have to wait for long—the train, Train 3407, was a minute early, arriving at exactly 19:01. Once completely stopped, the doors opened and passengers immediately began flooding off the train from the different car compartments. Luke was sitting at the central end of the platform, as he was able to see all the busy travelers as they got off the train. Then he saw Chris. Chris towered over Luke at almost six and a half feet. He wore jeans, a black polo and sported a University of Oregon hat. For Luke, there was no mistaking him once he saw him, and from their previous conversations he expected him to be a wild card.

"Chris," Luke called out as he waved his hand when Chris was about twenty yards away. Chris nodded his head and picked up his pace a little bit.

"Luke, my man." He replied. When he got close the two shook each other's hands. "How are you doing, brother?"

"I'm good. How was the ride down here?"

"Dude, it was great. Just before I got on the train, this guy I was hanging with in Amsterdam, Mossimo, rolled us a nice one. Had a killer buzz the whole way here." Luke laughed. He was never in to drugs, but quite frankly, smoking weed in Amsterdam was legal.

"So thanks for telling me we wouldn't be leaving for Prague tonight."

"Wait, I thought you knew?"

"No, I left my fiancée at home thinking we were boarding a train leaving tonight." Luke could see Chris beginning to feel the unnecessary weight of his pack as he unbuckled his straps and lowered it to the ground.

"Your fiancée?" He asked in surprise.

"Yeah."

"Nice. Nice. Terrible for a great time in Europe, but nice." Luke liked Chris already—there was a laxity about him that he found amusing. "So let's go."

"Go where?"

"To your fiancée's. I'm sure she has a couple of friends. I know we can get a couple of drinks, start off with a couple of memories. What do you say?"

"No," Luke said quickly and pointedly.

"What do you mean 'no'?" Chris put his hands on his hips.

"No. Saskia lives with her parents and little sisters. And I'm not taking Tommy Chong to meet them." Chris laughed at the reference.

"Come on. I'm not that stoned. I've had a five hour train ride to idle the effects."

"No, it's out of the question. Plus, if I go back and see Saskia right now, I may never leave her again. Then you'd be traveling on your own. Come on," Luke said as he shouldered his own pack. "I'm sure you have the munchies."

"I could eat. Where to?" Chris asked as he shouldered his own pack.

"I know about this Greek restaurant. I heard it was good."

"I like it. We won't make it to Greece so we'll just have to eat their food." The two began to walk down the remaining twenty meters of platform A-23 while they spoke. "So what have you been doing here?"

"A little bit of everything. Spending time with Saskia, exploring the city, reading books—staying pretty low key, you know?"

"Gay, gay, and more gay—excuse me..." Chris said to a young woman who was passing by smoking a cigarette. "Can I bum a fag?" Chris gestured with his hands to make it clear what he was asking for. The young woman complied with a smile, pulled out her pack of cigarettes and handed him one. "Grazie," Chris said as he bowed his head. The two turned to walk again as Chris tucked the cigarette in the breast pocket of his polo.

"It's 'Danke,'" Luke corrected him.

"What?"

"'Thank you' is 'Danke' in German," Luke said with a smile.

"Donkey," Chris repeated.

"No, Danke."

"Donkey, got it—excuse me..." Chris started again to another passerby smoking a cigarette. "Can I get a fag from you?" The man smiled and pulled out a cigarette and handed it to Chris. "Donkey," he said with little hesitation. Luke just laughed.

"Are you opening up a cigarette shop?" He joked as Chris tucked the second cigarette away in his breast pocket.

"Hey, it's free," he said with a wide smile.

"And what's with the word 'fag'? Do people even say that anymore?" Luke asked before realizing Chris's attention was focused ahead.

"I don't know, but watch this." Chris quickened his steps and veered right towards two fairly attractive girls leaning against a cement column next to the Burger King in the station. Luke stopped short of Chris, allowing him to either fail or triumph on his own. He could barely make out what Chris was saying to the two foreign girls but he could clearly see Chris's hands flailing in explanation. Hearing the words, "my friend", "join", and "dinner" Luke got the hint.

And when Chris turned around, grinning from ear to ear with the two young ladies following him whispering to each other, Luke just shook his head. The trip had begun even though they hadn't gone anywhere—and Luke, with Saskia at the forefront of his mind at all times, would have to be very careful or Chris would get him into an unbelievable amount of trouble.

The dinner had been a disaster. Chris desperately tried to talk to the girls who spoke very little English. After much agonizing, and a few awkward silent moments, the girls stood up and walked away. Chris and Luke figured they were going to the bathroom, but soon would realize after the passage of time they wouldn't be returning.

And to make things worse, when they had arrived, the waiter taking care of them also spoke little English—so it seemed, but he might have been a very brazen con man. Luke and Chris tried to read the German menu, but with no success, they just pointed at what they thought seemed best. The mistake they made was pointing to the menu and circling their fingers as if to say, "We'll all have the same thing." The waiter nodded his head, and eventually brought out a meal for 8. The dish Chris and Luke had pointed at was a double meal for a party of two or more. The waiter, Luke figured to be a scheming asshole, put in a double order for each of them. With more food than they could possibly eat in front of them, especially when the girls got up and left, Chris demanded for four plates to be boxed up. Contrary to casual belief, "boxing" up food is entirely a Westernized concept. The waiter had to get pizza boxes from the Pizza Hut next door in order to satisfy Chris's demand. Needless to say, Luke felt they both had learned a valuable lesson with their first meal together, and even more so when they got the bill.

Luke and Chris walked around Marienplatz for a while before they determined it was time to go back to the train station—which would act as their first hostel for the night. Over dinner and as they walked around, the two caught up on a great many details—who they were, where they were from, their acquaintance Jay, and the ensuing trip details. They actually had a lot in common, and despite the many stories Luke could share with Chris, he ended up listening more than speaking. It was as if Chris had longed for someone to speak to for a while, and once he found that person in Luke, there was an explosion of information. Luke heard all about Chris's adventures in Alaska and Canada, the trying times with his mother and sisters, and his failing and tumultuous relationship with his father. Luke could relate, and knowing the need to express all of the feelings that come along with a turbulent relationship with someone, he openly listened and supported Chris's thoughts and emotions. Luke instantly felt a bond with his new friend.

Laying on his Columbia roll-up sleeping bag in the central waiting room at the train station, Luke looked as his watch: 3:02. Their train was scheduled to depart at 06:55 and after a night filled with open conversation, he and Chris decided at 1:00 to try to get a few hours of sleep before they left for Prague. But sitting up, Luke soon realized he would not sleep any time soon. As one of the world's lightest sleepers, Luke knew it would be impossible to sleep amongst the masses; in the warm room was a full house of fellow travelers, both young and old, and a few seeming to compete for the loudest and most obnoxious snore. Chris had no trouble sleeping at all—when the two decided to get a few hours sleep, it was almost as if Chris fell asleep in between his last spoken word and the ensuing breath like a person suffering from narcolepsy.

Luke stood up, and unable to bear the intolerable breathing that surely was in need of medical help, he exited the room into the open-air veranda that looked out over the full tracks of paralyzed trains. Putting on his sweatshirt to combat the cool early morning air, he heard to his right an unfamiliar plucking of strings. Looking to his right, Luke could see about a hundred feet away, a man playing an odd-looking stringed instrument that Luke knew to be a sitar. Walking slowly over to him Luke listened to the high pitches combined with the slurring affect of bridging the strings. As he got closer he could see the man playing in better detail— Luke smiled at him, while the man continued playing. He was sitting against his worn and well-traveled pack with patches reading, "Florence, Italy", "Lyon, France", "San Sebastian, Spain", "Dublin, Ireland", and more. The man, Luke guessed, was in his early thirties, wore a braided beanie from which long brown hair descended. The man had a two-week stubble that engulfed his lean, chiseled face. It was then that Luke noticed the crutches laying behind him; at first glance it appeared the man sat with is left leg tucked under his body, but when Luke looked closer, the leg, in fact, wasn't there at all.

"Do you play?" The man asked as Luke leaned against the veranda railing across from him. His accent was English, as to what part, Luke had no idea.

"I do. The guitar." Luke replied.

"A Yankee," the man sad. "What a surprise. Where you from, Mack?"

"California."

"Well I'll be pissed. Don't say from Los Angeles or we'll both be in the movies now, won't we?" Luke chuckled to himself.

"I've lived there. Actually went to school there, but I was born in Sacramento. My name's Luke." Luke walked over and held out his hand.

"Paul. Pleasure."

"How long have you been playing?" Luke asked.

"About two years," Paul started. "It's been a long row to hoe but I'm starting to get the hang of it. Picked this beauty up at a trade show in Islamabad, Pakistan. The maker of this beast said it was the finest line of Teak wood they had in a grip."

"Pakistan, wow." Luke slumped down on the railing and leaned against a center pole as the two men sat across from each other.

"You ever been?" Paul asked as he set his Sitar to the side.

"No. This is actually the first time I've ever been outside of the states."

"Where you been so far?"

"Just here. I flew in ten days ago, staying with my fiancée. Tomorrow, a friend and I leave for Prague."

"Well done, Mack. You have a fiancée, do ya? She's not up the spout is she?" Luke had no idea what he was talking about.

"Up the spout?"

"Pregnant. With child. Like 'Oops we're having a baby'?" Paul asked. Laughing, Luke threw up his hand.

"Oh, no. She was actually an exchange student where I'm from. We met in May, and here I am."

"In May? Jesus, Mary, and Joseph—you're a true

blue Nascar-racer aren't you." Luke figured that was his idiom for "fast-moving" and he was right.

"Yeah, so I hear." He paused. "She's worth it though."

"I'm not one to argue. To each his own, I say. Let's just hope you're not all mouth and no trousers," Paul said as he pulled out a cigarette. He held out the cigarettes as if to offer Luke one, but when Luke waved his hand, he put them away.

"You travel a lot?" Luke asked.

"Yeah, Mack. I've been all over the world—except the states though."

"Why?" Luke asked as Paul lit his cigarette.

"Too many people who speak our language. I've learned the best way to learned Gilda from Lilly is to be all ears. There's a lot of talk these days. Talk, talk, talk, but does anyone really listen anymore?"

"Some," Luke responded coolly. "It's tough. The wise spend more time listening then they do talking—so it's hard to distinguish them."

"No it's not, Yankee. Look for the one in silence and sit next to him till he speaks...or burps, or whatever. It has to be better then listening to a suit talk about Wall Street."

"True."

"Did I tell you I'm from Wales?" Luke shook his head "no." Not that it mattered; Luke didn't really know where "Wales" was or what that distinguished.

"The Welsh always say it's better to know the devil you know, rather then the one you don't. I sit on my haunches with my one good leg sticking out, listening to people as they pass by. Some drop shillings at my feet because they think I'm poor. I'm in bad shape because I choose it Mack. I've probably got more money then the lot of them combined."

"Really," Luke started. "And if you don't mind me

asking, how's that?"

"Because I'm royalty."

"Royalty?"

"Yeah."

"Royalty to what?"

"To England you daft cunt!" Paul exclaimed playfully as he held up his arms.

"Okay. So what are you doing here, sleeping overnight in the Munich Central station with the peasants like me?" Paul's smile slowly crept to a painful look filled with skepticism.

"Because fuck 'em. Fuck 'em all, Mack." Luke knew what he was talking about. His relationship with his family had enticed him to feel that exact thought Paul just outwardly spoke of. Luke snickered at their similarity, and shook his head in agreement. After a useful pause to allow Paul to smoke some of his fading cigarette, Luke spoke up.

"Do you have a girl?" Luke asked.

"I did."

"What happened?"

"Life happened, Lucas. There's nothing to be done about it, either."

"So tell me."

"What?"

"What happened?" Paul smiled as he took a drag.

"What do you care?"

"I don't really."

"Then why?"

"Because I find it useful."

"Find what useful?"

"To learn."

"Oh you're learning something then? From me?"

"Of course from you," Luke said as Paul took another drag. "And maybe you want to talk about it."

"You think I want to talk about it?"

"Maybe."

"What kind of mind games are these, Mack?"

"They're not mind games."

"You're a real wanker, you know that? A real dirty wanker." Luke smiled from across the Veranda. Their tennis-talk dialogue had been a fun bout of wits—Luke could sense Paul's respect for him. Then Paul began.

"Fuck it then, eh? My story—she was a special bird, that girl. That was back when I had two good legs, Mack. Her name was Bethany, and I thought she was Lady of the Lakes, a real chestnut to be held close, you know?" Luke nodded his acknowledgment. "Bethany and I both came from the same roots—both our lineage is from the old money. I'm not exactly royalty but I do come from a wealthy blood. Bethany was sort of my childhood chum back in the day. She had this smile that was infectious. I simply basked in it. In our teens, I wanted to take her to this particular dance—the kind where all the boys look like penguins and the girls look like characters from Jane Austin. It had gotten fairly late, and she told me I had to go, but I told her I needed to ask her father something. She said he was in bed, and it had to wait till morning, but I just smiled, kissed her on the cheek, and raced up her stairs to her parent's quarters. I could hear the T.V. still on so I lightly knocked. When I went in, I was, well, like a piece of petrified driftwood—scared out of my stocks." Paul chuckled to himself in remembrance. "I asked her father if I could take her to the dance. I remember his shock. The old codger had been thrown and he didn't know how to handle it. His reply was outstanding. He said, 'Well I think you should ask her then. I'm not very good for a dance.'" Paul hesitated, his demeanor softening.

"I took her to that dance. We had an absolute blast of an evening. For four years she was my girl, and for two more after that we were engaged. She was a real pipe dream for me. Your fiancée, Mack?"

"Saskia," Luke revealed with a smile.

"Is she the first thing you think about in the morning, and the last thing you think about before the lantern's blow?"

"Absolutely."

"That's great. You Yank's normally just chase tail for a good pussyfoot. A bunch of cloth ears as well."

"I'm not like most 'yanks'," Luke said, using Paul's preferred phrasing.

"Yeah," Paul started, "and I didn't think Bethany was like most girls—but she, in the end, proved me wrong. My first year after university, I started to feel soreness in my right thigh. The doctor poking around at it said it was probably tendonitis from my water polo days. He told me to rest it, gave me some white candy, and sent me off. About a month later, the pain had nearly tripled. I could barely get out of bed some days, so Bethany and I went to the hospital where a new doctor said I should get an MRI. The MRI showed I had osteosarcoma. There was a tumor in my femur. During surgery to get it removed, my doctor's found it was too large, and it had dug deep into my leg, so with very few options available, they had to amputate it."

"I'm so sorry—" Luke started to say when Paul interrupted him with a slightly stronger voice.

"Bethany...couldn't stand the sight of me when she came into my room after the surgery. Bethany couldn't stand the sight of me in a wheelchair. And Bethany couldn't stand the sight of me on crutches, or when I had to hop to the loo..." He took a deep breath. "Bethany just couldn't stand the sight of me." There was a pause that just seemed to hover in the air for a bit. Luke didn't want to press. He patiently waited for Paul to speak.

"I never worried about how all of the masses

230

looked at me, but I did die inside with how she looked at me. To me, I just lost my leg—to her, she lost a whole husband." Paul started to laugh out loud—a forced, painful laugh. "I mean, could you imagine making love to a woman with one leg? It could make some give up their supper...yeah, Mack, that's why I say 'fuck 'em'. The world is too big, and the people are too different to throw yourself in with the bad lot. Have I loved? I loved like the stories say. Have I worshiped a goddess? Oh yes. But my story is a bit of a tragedy, don't you think?"

Luke let his question linger in the air before responding. "It doesn't have to end there does it? I mean, you can get back up in the saddle and ride, can't you?"

"I can have sex—"

"That's not what I me—"

"I know what you're saying," Paul joked, trying to break the mood before he slowly began again, "But once you've been with Aphrodite, it's hard to stay with May. And you, if you were ever to be snake-bitten by your sweet Saskia, you would know exactly what I am talking about. I'm not trying to be all blood and thunder about this, Mack. You asked about my story, and I told you."

"Thank you."

"Just remember, it can all be rock and dodger one minute, then shit the next. Life is all about half chance. Don't be afraid to wake up in the morning, and say, 'today my chances are as good as anybody else's. But never say, 'today my chances are better or worst then anybody else's—because they never will be. The real gritty stuff—the real shit stuff can happen whenever, to whomever, and they'll never see it coming. You know what I'm saying Mack?"

"Yeah, I do."

Luke thought about Paul's story—how terrible it must have been to be walking one day, and without warning, lose a limb. But he thought about Paul on a deeper level too. *What is he doing sitting here? Looking like that?* Luke thought. Thinking about Paul's timeline, he figured Paul had been traveling for close to ten years after losing both his right leg, and his treasured Bethany. Luke thought it was such a shame she didn't love him for who he was, and not for what he was without. His leg, sure, he could find an old tree branch to make a peg leg out of, but his heart, there was no prosthetic for that.

"Did you learn anything?" Paul asked, snapping Luke out of his own thoughts.

"I did," Luke said with a smile, grateful for having heard Paul's words. Paul picked up his sitar and pulled out his metal pick and began strumming and plucking strings. Out of the corner of his eye, Luke could see the door to the waiting area open as a yawning Chris stepped out on the veranda. When Chris saw him he nodded his head to acknowledge his whereabouts as to why he wasn't laying on his sleeping bag.

"So where's your guitar Yankee?" Paul asked.

"You have to hear this story," Luke began as Chris drew near. "When I got off my flight in Philadelphia…"

36.

22/10/08 02:24
Hotel Di Armi

Peter closed the journal and instantly stood up. Opening his door he walked out of his room and down the exterior corridor till he got to the room Chris was staying in. Knocking lightly, he could see a light turn on through the window. When Chris opened the door, Peter could easily tell by his appearance he had woken him from a deep sleep.

"Chris," Peter stated.

"Peter, what's wrong?" Chris responded somewhat delirious.

"Nothing. Nothing, I was hoping I could speak to you."

"Of course, come in." Peter walked into Chris's room, which was the mirror image to the design of his room. Chris plopped down on the edge of the bed and began wiping the sleep out of his eyes. Peter pulled out the chair from the desk and sat down.

"Chris, I've been reading Luke's journal, and I wanted to know...I mean, in it..." Peter trailed off. He didn't exactly know what he wanted to initially ask Chris, but he tried to force the words out. "You traveled with him. What did he say about me?"

"Peter..." Chris said with a deep exhale.

"I just want to know what he said about me, that's all. You were one of the last people to get to spend time with Luke—he trusted you, confided in you."

"Yeah, we talked about a lot of stuff. Most of the time, I think we staid away from the shitty stuff at home. But you have his thoughts. What he wrote in his journal, that was always private."

"I know," Peter started to say as he leaned forward in his chair. "He wrote about you, and your relationship with your father. That you and your father had a similar relationship to what he experienced with me."

"Well, not all that similar, actually. My father is a drunk. He knowingly abandoned his family."

"Mine too."

"Yeah?"

"Yeah."

"Did yours used to hit you? Did yours ever...strangle you for fun?"

"No. No, he would never have done that."

"Mine did," Chris stared at the floor for comfort. "He just didn't know how to handle anything...I provoked him more than anything, but I figured I should get him to take it out on me, rather then my sisters." Peter didn't know what to say. It all seemed bigger then he was. "It's funny, I've really never told anyone about this...except—."

"Luke."

"Yeah."

"Yeah," Peter said as he patted Chris on the leg and began to stand up.

"I learned a lot from him," Chris began as Peter froze as he stood, eventually slowly sitting back down. "But I think he learned something from me too."

Peter listened as he let his tired eyes rest on Chris.

"The night I met Luke in Munich, we had to sleep in the train station overnight because Luke thought we had a train heading to Prague that night, and when he found out we didn't, he didn't want me, still high from Amsterdam, crashing at Saskia's place with her family

234

there." Peter knew all this but he let Chris continue. "We ended up going to this shit Greek restaurant, and then just wandering around the city for a few hours. I don't know why, in those opening moments with your son that I felt the urge to tell him my life story, but it just sort of happened. I told him about my dad, and some of the things he used to do to me, and about how I just had to leave the area for a while, even though I was sort of abandoning my family just like he did.

"My dad was an asshole, Peter. He was on the darker side of a lot of things. He was just so smart, and when nothing went his way, he just drank, and drank, and drank. When he was still living with us, when my sisters were younger, my mom would tuck us into bed, and when she was tucking me in she would whisper into my ear, 'when I leave, lock the door.'" Chris paused for a second as he considered his words. Peter just stared at the young man, his full attention on every detail leaving his mouth. "A child shouldn't have to worry about feeling safe under their own roof. Ever. A teenager shouldn't grow up so angry with their father that they get into fight after fight just to feel the release. And a man shouldn't run to every corner of the earth to forget where he comes from."

Peter started to feel his eyes well up. He felt empathy for Chris—and sat stunned in silence.

"Now Luke, now there was a guy whom had it figured out. Which I don't know how," Chris chuckled lightly, "he never slept." Peter forced a small smile. "But he knew what it was all about—he knew how to make a difference in people's lives. And I firmly believe, after he met me, after hearing my story, that he knew he had a good father at home."

Peter's couldn't stop his face from cringing tightly as his eyes completely filled with water. His lower lip quivered in a way that produced anger, regret, frustration, loneliness, sadness, depression, but most of all gratitude for what Chris had just said.

Chris just sat in silence while Peter pulled his emotions together—he never erupted, but he needed a few seconds to stop his hands from shaking uncontrollably.

"Thank you, Chris." Peter choked out. Chris put his hand on Peter's shoulder in comfort.

"And you're here, you know? You're right here, fighting to find out the truth. From what I learned about Luke, he wouldn't ask anything more of you." Peter stood up, pulled Chris up, and gave him a hug out of gratitude. The young man's words had meant more then he could possibly thank him for. When the two separated, Peter dabbed his eyes.

"Go back to sleep. We need to hike the trail tomorrow," Peter said as he headed for the door.

"Okay."

When Peter got to the door, he turned around. "Did Luke ever say anything about his mother?"

"No."

"Nothing?"

"Only that she passed away when he was younger. I never brought it up again after that." Peter nodded his head before opening the door.

"Goodnight."

When Peter was back in his room, he sat on the edge of his bed in complete silence. The storm outside had subsided with only a light wind remaining, gently purring like an old space heater. He looked at the clock: 2:36. He needed to get some sleep. Standing up he turned out the light; forgetting to lock the door, he lay in his bed. For a few moments he concentrated on clearing his mind, he felt the tension in his temples fading, as a dark blanket swept over his eyes, casting

236

him into a deep sleep.

The night was thick in darkness. Luke trembled as he lay flat on his back in the middle of the dirt path, his eyes tightly shut. The end was near, but one thought endured, keeping him alive momentarily. A light swirling wind brushed across his face, sweeping his hair lightly to the side—the coolness of the earth vastly becoming the bottom of his coffin. The end was near.

Reaching for his chest, and pointing beyond the horizon, Luke opened his eyes in a panic—the fear igniting in his retinas—as he screamed:

"FATHER!"

Peter shot up in his bed. "Luke!" he exclaimed. Panic resonating from the nightmare caused Peter to break out into a cold sweat. Surveying his surroundings, Peter realized he was in his room at the *Hotel di Armi*. A fresh set of dark apparel had been folded and placed on the desk next to the journal. Peter guessed Roberto had slipped into the room quietly while Peter slept and left the items to be found later. Peter was having trouble adjusting his eyes as the morning light filled the room through the window with the curtains drawn back.

The dream had been so real—the darkness, the loneliness, and the eerie cry for help. Peter plopped back down in the bed as he rubbed his eyes for comfort. The devastating thought of how Luke spent his final minutes had surfaced as a high definition nightmare that begged to be actual reality.

Wondering what time it was Peter turned to the nightstand and glanced at his wristwatch: 7:10. The brightness of the morning light through the window told Peter the storm had pushed past completely as he threw back the covers and walked towards the desk containing the dark apparel. A note sat on the desk—picking it up

237

Peter read Roberto's chicken scratch.

*I am at the station trying to get our commu-
nications up. Here are some dry clothes. I will meet you
in the lobby at 09:30, Roberto.*

Peter smiled, thankful for the warm, clean clothes
to put on. Roberto was a good man—a friend that Peter
could not live without for the moment. Putting the note
down, Peter examined the black shirt, and black cargo
pants left for him. At the base of the desk were a pair of
dark socks and hiking boots—all standard police apparel
Peter figured. He wondered how Roberto got the sizes so
close to his own, but dismissed it as superfluous.

Taking a quick hot shower, Peter got dressed,
packed a small black pack with his wallet, the journal,
and the long sleeved shirt he'd gotten at the station the
night before, and headed down to the lobby. Passing by
a full length mirror in the hall Peter thought he looked
like an old FBI special operative—no one at home would
recognize the hardware store owner if they saw him
today—no one.

Once he reached the lobby, he noticed the mess
from the night before had been cleaned up. In place of
the empty food containers, a continental breakfast, of
sorts, had been laid out for the guests. Peter was
famished—eating had taken a back seat to all the
commotion over the last forty-eight hours. Even though
he had only slept for about five hours, he felt an odd
sense of refreshment. His talk with Chris had given him
some much needed relief that took away some of the
ache he felt deep inside his soul.

Taking a small plate and loading it with a couple
croissants, some fresh strawberries, and a bran muffin,
Peter placed the plate on a side table next to one of the
antique reading couches in the rear of the lobby.

238

Retreating for both a cup of hot coffee, and a cup of orange juice, Peter sat down on the couch and opened up his black pack. Pulling out Luke's second journal, he felt ready to continue his path of late knowledge as he vicariously traveled through Europe, hanging on every word written by his son. Concentrating his eyes which sorely missed his reading glasses, Peter opened the journal and turned to where he left off. The date:

9/25 "Prague, the Buddhist, and Professor Gerhard"

37.

24/09/08 13:12
Train 0013
Kolín, Czech Republic

Luke sat staring out the window, watching the hills go by as the train rolled smoothly down the track. Luke enjoyed the long train rides—he found it peaceful, and far more comfortable and less nerve-wracking than flying. The weather had been beautiful, and day trips on the train allowed Luke and Chris the chance to see the central European countryside by daylight. Many places reminded him of driving through parts of Northern California where green trees, hay fields, and small towns were in abundance.

Luke glanced over at Chris across the aisle. Chris, like Luke, had been listening to his iPod for the first hour of their train ride. They differed in the fact that Chris was nursing yet another self-inflicted hangover. Luke's final evening in Prague had lacked such dramatics.

Over the last four days, Luke and Chris explored one of the most beautiful places they had ever seen. Prague was quickly becoming one of the largest tourist attractions in Europe because of its accessibility, architecture, gorgeous skyline, modern clubs, and of course, the favorable exchange rate. Chris had come up with the motto soon after their arrival that everything was "free" in Prague. A pint of Stella Artois cost twenty Czech Crowns, roughly one dollar and twelve cents American.

Aside from the beer being essentially free, Luke thought Prague was the quintessential destination for any young traveler, a melting pot of tourists from all over the world. Luke and Chris stayed in The Manhattan, a hotel that sounded far more prestigious than it was, but for two young men on a budget it was absolutely perfect. The room had two queen sized beds, a tidy bathroom, and a dining room table where the two could sit, drink, and smoke while discussing lifetime stories, philosophy, and future dreams. Luke never got heavily intoxicated, but he did start smoking fairly regularly as it was a common ritual amongst young travelers; asking for a light was always a great conversation starter, and Luke and Chris used it often to meet girls, other backpackers, and locals with decent English skills.

The Manhattan was located in Staré Město, also known as Old Town. Old Town at night proved to be a labyrinth of narrow streets and quick dead ends, but Luke and Chris always navigated to destinations by pointing and heading in directions, rather than navigating by streets or signs.

Before the sun would set each night, Luke and Chris always found themselves standing at the center of Charles Bridge, which served as the link between Old Town and New Town. From the Bridge, they had the perfect view of the downtown lights, the glistening river, and the Pražský Hrad, also known as the Prague Castle. The Prague Castle is one of the world's largest castles and Luke found it to be breathtaking when lit from the gardens up to the highest steeple. In the evening, Chris would end up in nightclubs with beautiful women, while Luke would find himself sneaking off to some patio or veranda to admire at the beauty of the city. It was a wonderful blend of modern ingenuity combined with historical preservation—it was as if the city of Prague knew how to co-exist harmoniously with its forefathers without tarnishing their legacy. Luke couldn't get enough of it, and he couldn't stop emailing Saskia, telling her how much he wished she were there.

Luke often daydreamed about future trips he would take with her to the places he had been. Prague had an abundance of theatre—both small stage and large stage that Luke knew Saskia would love. One morning while Chris was deep in alcohol-induced slumber, Luke saw a great marionette show alongside an audience of no more then twenty people. Although the show was in Czech, Luke found it to be funny and full of anecdotal charisma—the type of humor he knew Saskia would enjoy.

When Luke and Chris checked out of The Manhattan, he took a business card of Wally's, the owner. He wanted to make sure he had Wally's number on speed dial because Prague was only a few hours train ride away from Munich, allowing it to be the perfect weekend getaway once Luke officially moved to Europe.

Out of the corner of his eye, Luke saw Chris put down his headphones and begin stretching his arms high above his head. Luke had been finishing an email to Saskia on his Blackberry, which he quickly sent off after writing at the bottom, "I love you and miss you, Luke."

Taking off his own headphones, the natural noises around him quickly flooded in.

"How are you feeling, brother?" Luke asked as Chris pulled out his Eurorail map of Western Europe.

"Good man, ready to get going again." Luke titled his head back and let out a little chuckle. He didn't know how Chris could drink so much, feel so awful, and then combat the feeling with more drinking. "Hey, where's your guide book?"

Luke dug into his pack sitting in the seat next to him; pulling out his "Let's Go to Europe: 2008 Edition," which he handed to Chris.

"I want to look at places to stay in Bratislava," Chris commented as he began scrolling through the pages.

"I don't know if we can find a place to beat The Manhattan."

"I don't think so either. Wally was the dude, wasn't he?"

"Yeah. He should get a website. That place would be booked solid."

"No kidding."

"You never told me what happened last night, with…" Luke tried to recall the young woman's name but couldn't.

"Ulga."

"Ulgaaaaaa," Luke sang, grinning from ear to ear. "Yes, Ugla."

"Not much happened." Luke sat forward in his seat to argue.

"Nothing happened? You almost missed the train this morning. I know you didn't sleep in your bed—"

"Alright, alright," Chris interrupted him as he

turned his Oregon Ducks hat around. "After we left the club, Ulga hailed a taxi. I was hammered. She told me she had a room at the Hilton next to the airport, so I got in the cab with her. The worst part wasn't till the next morning, when I woke up, and of course, No Ulga. She was a flight attendant. Had to catch an early flight, and there I was, butt naked, no idea where I'm at, and the cleaning ladies are knocking on the door." Luke couldn't help but laugh at the story. "So I get dressed, go downstairs to find a cab, and when I finally get a cab, the guy looks at me, and I tell him to take me to The Manhattan. After he gives me this blank stare, I say it again, 'Take me to The Manhattan.' Nope, nothing. I had to point to The Manhattan on a damn map before he would pull out of the hotel."

"Nice," Luke replied with a shake of his head, "so how was Olga?"

"Good. She kept yelling shit in Russian—I had absolutely no idea what was going on."

"Could've been worse," and then the two said in unison, "It can always get worse." The two shared a laugh, and Luke repositioned himself so his back was leaning against the window. Chris was scrolling through the pages of the guidebook when Luke asked, "So talk to me, tell me about Alaska." Chris closed the book and placed it on the seat next to him, mirroring Luke's position against the window.

"What do you want to know?"

"What was it like up there? How was the fishing?"

"The fishing is amazing. I was on an inland salmon charter that took out tourist fisherman. Jay and I were in charge of helping them bait their hooks, reel in their strikes, gut the fish, and clean the boat after we got back. We worked for this real Ahab-looking dude, Captain Burn—his boat was "The Gaffer". I worked my ass off, and I think I got his respect, but Jay was always a step behind. Burn nicknamed him "Lenny" after that character from *Of Mice and Men*." Luke chuckled—Jay was a good kid, but he imagined out there he was a little out of his element.

"The best days up there were when Burn would take Jay and I out alone," Chris continued. "The open sky, the brisk air—I never felt more free in my life. It was absolutely liberating. I would stand at the bow as Burn pounded the Gaffer against the tide—you could just see miles of open ocean. There was nothing like it, man. I could've stayed up there for—"

"Excuse me," a raspy voice behind Luke interrupted. When Luke turned an old woman stood up two rows behind them and walked forward. Standing above their row of seats with her rickety hands placed on the headboards, the old woman locked her gaze on Chris. She had short grey hair, a large nose, and protruding long whiskers stemming from all sorts of strange places on her face. In fact, Luke was merely guessing that it was, indeed, a woman.

"Yes," Chris asked in a surprising tone.

"I couldn't help but overhear you speaking," the woman stated slowly with a thick Czech accent.

"Okay," Chris said bewildered.

"You are a fisherman?"

"I am."

"Do you believe in morality?" the woman asked pointedly.

"I don't understand what you're asking me." Chris said. Luke had to agree—he had no idea what the woman wanted.

"You kill fish. And I was wondering, if you believe that is a moral thing to do."

"Well, a great percentage of the world believes in killing fish for food, and I am one of them."

"So you believe it is moral to kill a fish?" The

woman asked as she sat in the diagonal seat from Chris. Luke was merely a spectator to their dialogue.

"I don't think it is immoral to kill a fish. I kill the fish. I eat the fish. The circle of life continues," Chris stated with a harshness developing in his tone.

"But what did the fish ever do to you?"

"Nothing."

"Then why kill the fish? Why destroy an innocent life?"

"You think the fish is an innocent life form?"

"I do, and the morality is a fish desires life the same way you and I desire life."

"Hmmm...I'll have to think about that one. No! A fish is a fish. Humans have been hunters and gatherers since their beginning. If I don't eat the fish, another fish will eat the fish, and I'll be stuck eating celery. Ma'am—"

"Sir," the woman corrected him, but Chris steamrolled over it.

"I don't like celery. I hated it as a child, but I loved fish."

"Do you mock me?" the woman asked.

"I don't mock you, I just don't understand what you are trying to establish in terms of your argument. In every corner of the world, people eat fish. Are you trying to deter every meat eater in the world one by one, starting with me on a train ride?"

"What kind of person would I be if I didn't try?"

"Okay, excuse me ma'am—" Chris again started to say when he was corrected for a second time.

"Sir."

"What?" He asked surprisingly as Luke put his jaw in his palm.

"I am a sir. A him." The man stated with authority. Both Luke and Chris looked as if they had just seen the ending to "The Sixth Sense" for the first time— the information they had just been given baffled them to an extent beyond comprehension.

"Oh, I'm sorry about that." Chris had no rebuttal—he probably figured it was best to just move on. Luke stepped in to save him.

"From what origins come your convictions, sir?" Luke asked, trying not to concentrate on the previous gender discretion, which allowed the lengthy stubble to be acceptable in Luke's book.

"From the Dharma."

"You're Buddhist."

"Correct."

"And you speak from the Sīla—stating a person should act in a non-harmful way and have a non-harmful livelihood."

"Very good. Are you learned in the ways of Siddhartha Gautama?"

"I've studied him—I read Herman Hesse's *Siddhartha* in college."

"Then you know of what I speak."

"Sure. But the meaning of morality cannot be summed up in the decision of whether or not a person kills fish."

"That's what I was trying to say," Chris chimed in from his seat.

"Yes," the man started in again, "the act of fishing is premeditated and an act of harm. A fisherman goes out on a boat, and baits their hooks looking for blood."

"Because we need to eat," Chris exclaimed. Luke smiled and held his hand up to his less-than-stoic friend. The man glared at Chris before turning his attention back to Luke, assuming he was a more formidable opposition.

"Sir, you define blood all to easily, don't you think?" Luke questioned.

"How so?"

"Blood is a translational word meaning 'a life

246

source of some kind'—is water from the root of an apple tree not the life source, or blood, for that tree?"

"It is not the same—"

"But it is. Without a life source, an orange would be a dry, withering cesspool for insects to destroy. Siddhartha himself had to eat, and he himself ate living things. All life sources live off of each other."

"But humans and animals are so alike in spirit—a plant cannot think or move—"

"If that were true," an American voice said behind them. They all turned to him. "The earth would be a deserted dust bowl, as there would be no trees, because the still roots wouldn't grow. If the psychosis of a plant didn't recognize photosynthesis as its way of survival, all vegetation would be destroyed. Hi." The man, an obvious man, stood opposing the less then obvious man. He had a plaid shirt tucked into his white kakis—a pair of sunglasses sat on his shaved head. Luke guessed he was in his mid to late forties. "I overheard you guys— where are you boys from?"

"I'm from Montana, and Luke's from California," Chris answered, glad to be free from the Buddhists moral trivia.

"What part?" The man asked turning his attention to Luke.

"Sacramento, but I went to UCLA."

"Go Bruins. I'm a professor at the University of Virginia."

"In what subject?" the Czech man asked.

"British and American Literature," he shot back before he turned his attention back to Luke. "I heard your voices and was glad to hear Americans. Just wanted to say hello."

"So you've read Tolstoy?" The Czech man continued with his never-ending questions.

"No, no, I'm not getting into a lit debate with you.

Make an appointment to see me in my office at UV and we'll talk. I'm just heading to the café car for a drink." Luke saw his out and jumped all over it.

"Let me join you," he said standing up. The man shook his head and headed towards the end of their compartment "Chris, you want a beer?"

"Yes." Chris yelled out to Luke as he jolted ahead. Chris could see he was about to be left alone with the Czech, so he put his headphones back on.

Luke followed the professor down three cars till they got to the café car. A long bar with space for a single man to stand behind stretched along one side of the car, as a much smaller bar with stools bolted to the ground ran along the opposite one. A menu was posted on the wall behind the bartender—a few sandwiches and bags of chips were available to buy but Luke did not see any other food; but like most European retail there were plenty of beer options.

"Luke, wasn't it?" The professor asked, as he extended his hand for a formal introduction when the two got to the bar.

"Yes, Luke. Luke Sebastian." The two shook hands.

"Matthew. Matthew Gerhard," he said with a smile.

"Dr. Gerhard, I presume?"

"Only in a professional setting. Out here, Matt's fine."

"What are you doing out here?" Luke asked as he leaned on the bar getting a better look at their beer list.

"Probably the same thing you are—taking in the sights, drinking cheap beer, and forgetting for a couple of weeks the world that consumes me. Am I right?"

"Yeah. Chris and I met up for a six week backpacking trip—it's really just started but we're having fun so far."

"Did you enjoy Prague?"

"I did. Gorgeous place."

"Don't kid me. I've been married for seven years, but when I saw all the women in Prague, I thought that nowhere was it like that back home. How were the women?"

"I honestly wouldn't know." Luke said with a smile. "You'd have to ask Chris back there."

"I see. You married?"

"Not yet. Engaged." The bartender came over to help them.

"What do you want, Luke?" Matt asked.

"No, I'll get my own."

"Please, it's on me."

"Thanks. I'll take a Stella."

"Two Stellas please," Matt enunciated to the man. He nodded and went to the small refrigerator to get their beer. "Engaged, huh? Congratulations," Matt said, getting back to their conversation. "How long?"

"About three months—but it's all based on a technicality." The two got their Stellas, opened them, and took a drink.

"How so?"

"Well, I still haven't gotten her a ring; I actually just asked her father about a week ago, but the initial proposal happened in June; I've sort of done everything ass backwards." Matt smiled—he seemed intrigued.

"Tell me about it. How did you meet this girl?"

Over the next twenty minutes Luke outlined his story about Saskia—it was his favorite story to tell although he didn't have many people who wanted to listen. He always felt telling the story was a way of elevating himself from a common reality—over his life he had always been so pessimistic and impractical—Saskia was the first thing that came along that made him want to take huge risks. Matt was quiet and patient with Luke's story, smiling at some parts, laughing at others—he even seemed to sympathize with Luke when he spoke about his digressions with Rochelle.

"Do you have a picture of her?" Matt asked when Luke finally concluded.

"Yeah," Luke said as he fished his Blackberry out of his pocket. Pressing the roller ball the phone lit up. On the home screen a picture of Saskia appeared. She was standing next to one of the large Bayern Lions at the entrance of the Feldhernhalle in the Odeonplatz Square. The picture had been taken a few days after Luke arrived in Munich when he and his stunning female treasure were walking around eating gelato from a cone.

"She's a beauty, isn't she? Wow. What is she doing with a scruff like you?" Matt joked as he handed the Blackberry back to Luke.

"I have no idea, to be honest with you."

"And she's eighteen?" Matt asked as he leaned his back against the bar.

"Yeah. I've come to look at is an awesome thing. Because when most guys turn thirty, their wives do too. Me, I'll be turning thirty and my wife will be turning twenty-five." Matt laughed.

Matt finished his beer in one last swoon and turned to order two more, when Luke stopped him.

"I'm good, thank you."

"I'll get it for your buddy. He's probably wondering where you're at." Luke thought about Chris and laughed when he imagined he and the Czech still arguing about the morality issues of filleting a salmon. It was an argument a fisherman like Chris would never back down from.

"Hey Matt," Luke said switching gears.

"Yeah?" his brow lifted as he put the Euro change he'd gotten from the bartender into his wallet.

"You said before, every good story seems to end

in tragedy. Why is that? Being a literature expert and all."

"Well, I was generalizing of course, but every great story does end in tragedy. It's a simple equation—the greater the love, the greater the tragedy. Except in Hollywood, of course—have you ever seen one of those predictable romantic comedy plots— A guy and a girl who can't stand each other end up meeting, but eventually find some common ground that has to do with money, family, or sea turtles?" Luke nodded his head, actually unsure of what he was talking about but baiting him to continue.

"Yeah."

"Over the next hour of the movie the two fall in love, right? And then some miscommunication occurs which escalates into a lasting separation. The final minutes of the movie are dedicated to the reunion, the accumulating climax of love between the two characters—it often takes place at a distant cabin, a busy street corner, or an empty beach. The ensuing kiss after the make-up, supported by some great song that will sell thousands of soundtracks at Walmart plays, *da da daddaaaa dad* kiss, *dad a daa dad a*." Matt sang a melody then continued "And then, fade out. Credits." After saying this he froze, as if to allow Luke a chance to reply.

"What's your point?"

"My point, is what happens after the kiss? They still have to walk off that beach, probably get in the car and drive to one of their homes, right? They're in love, so one of them has to move in with the other. While he's carrying heavy boxes down the stairs he starts to get frustrated that she keeps talking to her best friend in Oakland. Two weeks later, she starts crying when there's no Peanut Butter in the cupboards—the laundry hasn't been done in two days, and he doesn't have work socks. He calls her a 'lazy ass,' they get into a fight that leads to her locking herself in the bathroom while he gets in his car, peels out, and joins a buddy down at the local tavern so they can talk about it and shoot pool. Doubt starts to cloud his mind as to whether the moment on the beach should even have happened. Maybe he was just feeling vulnerable in the situation, and seeing that he's in the prime of his thirties, maybe he shouldn't have to deal with all—

"Okay, I get it. So what, he's just supposed to let her go?"

"No. No, Luke that's not what I'm saying at all."

"Then what?"

"You asked me why the best stories end up tragedies. The best stories end up tragedies because they have the greatest risk, the greatest love, and most importantly the greatest obstacles. Human nature is to be inspired by the impossible, and to also want what we can't have. Romeo Montague. He was the ultimate example of a man who wanted the impossible, what he couldn't have. He loved two women—Rosaline and Juliet, both of the house of Capulet—his father's greatest arch rival."

"Okay. I see that as one example of a tragedy. It doesn't fit the mold for everyone—it's not even a true story. Not all people fall in love with impossible situations. Your generalization is a bit farfetched." Matt reacted to Luke's reaction with a flourish—almost as if that is what he wanted Luke to say.

"So let's break down tragedies into four different groups shall we?" Matt started as he held up his index finger. "Group number one: the tragedy through death—losing someone you love can be an absolute devastating experience. Group number two: the tragedy through infidelity—some of these people prefer death, believe me. Group number three: the tragedy through unseen

252

possibilities," Luke was just about to say 'unseen possibilities' but he remained quiet. "Things happen to people that can't be predicted or prevented, but can be devastating to their life." Luke quickly thought about Paul. His cancer in his leg had altered his life completely, and it was an unseen possibility to both he and Bethany. "Group number four: the tragedy of a wrong perception."

"I don't follow that one."

"How so? It is the vastest of the four groups. For instance, a mentally challenged person—can they experience true love?" Luke thought about it for a moment.

"I don't know."

"I don't either, but I know the greater percentage of people look at a human strapped into a wheelchair, unable to mechanically control the drool running down their chin, and they say, 'wow, what a tragedy. That poor soul.' I don't know if I buy into that. That soul may know or experience feelings in their mind that I will never know. That person may be the most cognitive-explosive person alive—but we would never know because certain brain function has shut down in the areas that allow them to function like you and I. They can't express themselves in the same way we do. It's possible their minds are simple, but it's also possible their minds are infinitely complex."

"Another example."

"Another example," Matt took a deep breath. "When I was in my twenties I dated a girl named Joanna Baker. She was a beautiful girl, but she and I didn't line up kinetically—she wasn't as aware of her surroundings as I needed her to be. It was like her world was constantly foggy—she couldn't read the signs until she was right up next to them. I liked Joanna—although two steps behind, she had a real kindred spirit that I liked for some reason my mother could never put her finger on while we dated. I always thought this was unfair, because I don't think I ever heard or saw Joanna say anything or do anything bad to anyone, ever. I didn't date her for very long, only about three months or so, but years after we broke up we kept finding one another—meeting for lunches, dinners, and late night movies that sometimes ended up being a touch bit more then that. One time, almost five years after we broke up, we decided to meet for lunch—I hadn't seen her in almost a year, and the last time we met she had been on a break with a new interest she had—a guy named Phil. At lunch I could see Joanna hadn't changed much. She was still gentle, kind, and as quiet as she had ever been—which, it was a shame she wasn't livelier, because she was absolutely gorgeous Luke. I remember the small talk we had that day. I asked her how her family was, how she was doing, and if there was anything new I should know about. She answered my questions and then the subject turned to her dating life." Matt paused as he took a drink of his second beer. Luke was listening intently as he finished drinking his first beer.

"She said that she had actually moved in with Phil and the two had been dating again. I thought this was interesting, as the last time I had seen her, while they were broken up, we had slept together, and after, she spent hours talking about Phil with little or no confidence that he was even a decent guy. I felt sorry for her. At lunch, again with little or no confidence, she talked about how good things had been, and how wonderful he was. The worst part was, I don't even think she believed what she was saying. It was almost as if I was a mirror that she was looking into, and the speech she was telling me she'd rehearsed over a dozen times. I called her out on it. I told her I didn't believe what she was saying. She smiled, but didn't react to what I had just said. Instead, she decided to switch gears and ask me about my love life. I told her it was non-existent. I was in my second year of my PhD and a relationship would be a terrible idea, at best. She said that was a shame, because I was so perfect—any girl's dream. I thought this was interesting, Luke, because the conversation tensed up around this point."

"Go on," Luke said as he buried his chin into his right palm as he often did when he was in full concentration mode.

"You see, when I asked her to lunch I had no idea she was living with Phil—had I known, I probably would have never met Joanna for lunch. She apparently didn't have a qualm with concealing the information from me, and when I got to the restaurant we decided to meet at, Joanna looked as good as I had ever seen her before—lean, fit, and well decorated with a plethora of make-up. So I asked her a simple question. I had been living in Tennessee mind you, and she was in Virginia, 'Joanna, if I were to move back to Virginia and come knocking on your door, would you leave Phil?' It didn't take her long to answer me at all. She said, 'Yes, I probably would.'" Matt paused for a moment before continuing.

"You see Luke, I see Joanna's life as tragic. She was settling for spending a lifetime with someone she didn't truly love. She woke up each day knowing there was something out there better for her, but she was afraid to go looking for it."

"Afraid of what?" Luke asked.

"Afraid of being alone I imagine. Because anyone who is not deeply in love with someone or some thing, is alone." Luke wondered why he said "some thing" but decided not to ask.

"And remember, your great story with Saskia is already a tragedy for someone else."

Luke looked puzzled as he sat straight up. "Oh

255

yeah, who?"

"Don't forget, in your haste to love Saskia, you still betrayed Rochelle."

38.

22/10/08 08:01
Hotel Di Armi

Was Luke starting to regret what he did to Rochelle? Peter asked himself as he placed the journal in his lap. He couldn't understand why Luke had written what Matt said as his final thought of the entry—in fact, he didn't understand much about the entry at all. Luke had barely described the city of Prague or all the wonderful things he saw in any detail. Instead, he chose to focus on some old Buddhist and a bald professor from the University of Virginia.

No Peter, think about it, he thought to himself as he stared off into the corner of the lobby. *Luke always wrote for a purpose.* Peter thought about the first journal. From May to June, Luke wrote his entries about Rochelle, Saskia, and the argument he had with his disgruntled father. All those things were important and key moments in his life. *Luke is still very young. All those things were a big deal. Now he's writing about Saskia, Einstein, and...philosophy I guess.*

And then it hit Peter. Luke had been changing. His

entries grew less about his romance and love for Saskia, because he knew how much she loved him—he already knew he would spend the rest of his life with her. Now it seemed that Luke was battling with the rest of the things he didn't know—religion, ethics, and cultural differences. Luke wrote a great deal of what other people had said to him in guidance, advice, or wisdom— whatever you want to call it.

Peter suddenly remembered the reference Luke used to a character in a book he had read about a boy on a journey. He couldn't remember his name so he scrolled back a couple of pages. *Larry Darrell.* Peter had never read the book his son mentioned, but he imagined it meant a great deal to him. Luke was on his own journey to self-discovery.

Peter put his hands on his head as he took a deep exhale. Everything he had been doing, everything he was reading was a lot to soak in. He felt privileged to be able to read Luke's thoughts and ideas at the end of his life, but it created a heavy pain that had to be endured in the worst of ways. Luke had been dead for a matter of days—the ink barely dry from his pen.

Glancing at his wristwatch Peter realized he only had time to read a few more entries before he, Chris, and Roberto would set off for the Spaniard's bar on the trail. He opened the journal and braced himself to read more in hopes of finding some useful information about Luke's death while simultaneously learning about how his son truly lived.

39.

01/10/08 19:51
Venice, Italy

Luke couldn't believe where he was. Chris had found the most unbelievable place to stay in all of Venice. After a few memorable days in Bratislava, Slovakia where the two partied the night away in the Sub Club—an old bomb shelter underneath a huge castle, which had been converted into a bar—they headed to Budapest, Hungary. Budapest proved to be a lackluster city where the majority of its citizens spent most weeknights getting plastered well into the morning. It wasn't Luke's scene, but Chris had the time of his life.

After a few days on the Pest section of the city, which Luke never knew was separate from the Buda side, he and Chris took a night train to Venice. Paying a few extra Euros, Luke and Chris upgraded to sleeping compartments, which proved worthless when border inspectors woke them up every two hours to stamp their visas—a courtesy Luke found entirely rude and unnecessary. But when they finally arrived in Venice, Luke's frustrations dissolved entirely. The city that floated on water was a timeless creation that Luke found exceeding his expectations at every turn, which was a surprise because most people found it dirty and overcrowded.

Since their train arrived so early in the new morning, Luke and Chris were forced to just wander the city with their packs in tow. Chris was frustrated at first, his impatience due to their lack of sleep and his growing fatigue from the two-week bender he'd been on, but eventually Luke convinced him it would be a good thing. Venice is a maze—if he thought Prague was a labyrinth, then Venice was a labyrinth without an entrance or an exit. The "Let's Go" guidebook Chris had worshiped proved to be worthless and navigating, even by direction, was almost impossible. Travelers simply had to wonder around until they found what they were looking for or until something else distracted them. Luke thought it was great, because it was an adventure within their adventure.

It eventually became late enough to necessitate securing lodging—whichever came first at the best price. After turning down a few offers of thirty or forty Euros a night, Chris saw a sign over a distant canal that offered room and board in what seemed like a decent building. Seeing the sign, and getting to the sign proved to be two different things entirely as it took them fifteen minutes and two double backs to reach it.

Once they reached the entrance, Luke opened one of the two heavy deadwood doors—inside was an elaborate courtyard that seemed to be alive from the array of flowers, green shrubs, and chiseled statues of Italian nobility. The building was actually an old Monastery within the city limits that rented out the old Monk sleeping quarters. The rate was a mere fifteen euros a night, and with that price, the two quickly agreed and put down a deposit for three nights. The woman at the counter took their deposits, copied their passport numbers down into a logbook, and handed them their keys. She quickly got the attention of a young novice who showed them up the stairs to the great room they would be staying in.

The room, or sanctuary as Chris called it, was unlike anything Luke had ever seen before. Ten cots were equally spaced along the two outer walls. To the left of the entrance stood five tall oak cabinets that housed two separate lockers in each cabinet. The novice, with her limited English, explained that five other renters had already claimed five of the beds, but Chris and Luke could have their pick of the remaining open cots. Luke thanked her, and after she left the two were left to explore the great room on their own.

Luke first noticed and couldn't get his eyes off of the twenty-foot ceiling that had been painted like a section of the famous Sistine Chapel. Two nude women with grain baskets sat at the foot of Jesus Christ while child-like Angels fluttered around in the background filled with a large, looming sun. The earth stretched towards a focal point that disappeared into a sea of large white clouds—the ceiling was a painting of Heaven.

Chris, meanwhile, had looked ahead to the two French doors at the end of the room. Opening one of the doors, it led out to a veranda enclosed by a white marble safety railing that extended over a wide canal of water. To the left, down the canal, a series of bridges could be seen until the water vanished out of sight around a corner of one of the neighboring buildings. To the right, Chris could see a gondola making its way down the canal as the traditional gondolier pushed his long stick through the water while singing an Italian melody to two lovebird tourists sitting on the large plush pillows inside the Venetian vessel.

When Luke joined Chris on the veranda, the warm sun spilled over his face. A cool breeze waved his lengthening hair across his face as the picturesque canal filled his thoughts. Chris had become a formidable traveling companion, but in that moment, standing on that veranda, he wished he could share the view with Saskia. A feeling of love filled his heart in a way he couldn't quite explain—the wonders of the world revealing themselves in mysterious ways. He and Chris had been searching for a warm room and bed to house them during their visit, but instead, found one of the closest things to a Heaven on earth.

"Can I bum a fag off of you?" Chris asked John. John, Molly, and Crum were the Aussies sharing the sanctuary with them. John and Molly had been dating almost their entire lives it seemed. Luke figured they were in their mid-thirties. Crum was their runt friend in his late twenties. The three were on a cross-country driving expedition across Italy in a VW Bus that belonged to Crum's uncle. Luke had come to like them very much over the past two nights in Venice. Along with their stray accents and loose terminology, the three were smart, and full of a dry humor Luke found hilarious.

"'Can I bum a fag,'" Molly mocked Chris in terrible impersonation of an American accent. "Who really says fag anymore Christopher?"

"It's my line. What can I say," he replied as John handed him one from his pack.

"And who wants to say 'cigarette' anyway?" Crum said from his seat on the veranda. The sunset had caused a flurry of colors in the sky, bursts of bright oranges and soft violets. Luke and Chris sat on opposite railings leaning against the building while Crum and Molly sat in the only available chairs—John centered himself, standing against the railing.

"Oh come off it Crum, fag sounds like 'fag' and 'fag' is used to describe homosexuals nowadays, and if Chris wants to bum a homo, he should go to Rio or someplace like that." Molly said as John handed her a cigarette, before offering one to Luke, who accepted it graciously.

"Wow, Molly, you have me pegged. I was trying

to slide it under the table that I wanted to curl up next to Crum tonight, but now you made me confess my intentions in front of everyone," Chris said with sarcasm.

"Is that how you American's are? Curling up next to one another when no one is looking?" John asked more in the direction of Luke.

"Not me," Luke replied as he lit his cigarette and tossed the lighter across to Chris who concentrated like crazy to catch it; otherwise it would end up falling down into the canal.

"Ah, yes, the mate with a 'fiancée'," John said mimicking Luke's accent from the previous times he labeled Saskia.

"I want to meet this dame, a girl willing to settle down with the likes of you," Crum chimed in. "She must be fidgety dealing with the likes of your mind. We've only known you about a day, and I'm willing to baptize you in a liberal pool of classical rebellion."

"What does that even mean?" Chris shouted as he threw his arms up in bewilderment. Molly and John laughed out loud.

"What's with you?" Crum asked Chris before continuing. "Luke is a modern day Joan of Arc, a crusader of wit, on some sort of exploration of understanding, don't you see?"

"And why do you say that?" Luke asked coolly.

"Isn't it obvious? You get squirrelly when you see two doves having a go at it. You look like you want to kiss Jesus Christ on the mouth, and you probably would if you could reach the ceiling." The whole group shared a laugh.

"You think so?" Luke asked coming down from his own laughter. The entire group, now smoking together nodded their heads in unison. "Well, seeing as I'm the wet blanket of the group, I have a surprise for you."

Luke disappeared into the sanctuary as he heard

John ask Chris what a "wet blanket" was. When Luke reappeared he was holding two large plastic shopping bags full of bulging containers the group couldn't identify yet. Luke set the bags on the ground, and pulled out sixteen-ounce Stellas and handed them around.

"Luke, how did you get these past the old ranger downstairs?" Molly asked in surprise. One of the conditions of the church was that alcohol wasn't allowed inside the premises. Making sure the group would drink the beers on the veranda, Luke felt no qualm about what they were doing at all.

"She wasn't there when I got back," Luke said after everyone received a beer. "Merry Christmas."

"And a happy New Year," John bounced back. "Thanks mate."

Luke held his beer up for a toast.

"To new friends, to a beautiful view in one of the most beautiful places, to new memories, and to great adventures. To Venice."

"To Venice. Cheers," they all said in unison as they lifted their beers and took a much needed swig.

"Now isn't this just Utopia?" Crum said as he threw his left leg over his right.

"It is for us. We live in the great country of Australia boo, while these Americans are left to suffer in the wake of the election," John said with an ounce of snobbishness.

The upcoming election had been all anyone ever wanted to talk about with Luke and Chris—the close race between Senators John McCain and Barrack Obama was under a global microscope.

"They'll sure be in hell if McCain wins," Crum said. Molly nodded her head in agreement.

"Why do you say that?" Luke asked.

"Because, Lucas, if he wins, the heart of Alaska becomes your "Vicey"." Crum answered.

"And considering McCain's, what, eighty?" Molly interjected.

"Seventy-two or seventy-three I think," John tried to recall.

"Well, whatever the number, he's old. If that ticker gives out while he's in office, Miss Sarah Palin becomes the President of the United States, or Hell, as Crum pointed out."

"Well, that's a bit exaggerated, isn't it?" Chris said with a roll of his eyes. Luke smiled. "And McCain's not going to win."

"Oh please, share your political strategy with us," Molly conceded.

"I mean, I hope he doesn't. It's the lesser of the two evils. I think we are screwed from either side," Chris began as Luke listened heavily—Chris never entertained his political thoughts in recent conversations with fellow travelers. "On one hand you have the aging Republican from Arizona who can't even count how many homes he owns, and on the other hand you have the new, fresh African-American Obama who has spent the entire election playing off of McCain's mistakes, rather than offering any solutions to the issues at hand."

"Which are?" Crum asked.

"Take Iraq for one. During the primaries, McCain shot his own foot by saying he could see American troops in Iraq for the next fifty to one hundred years. Yeah, that strikes a chord with most American mothers. Americans wanted the war when they were pissed— when they were angry that blood was shed on American soil. It's been seven years. It's time to move on." The group nodded heads while constructing their own rebuttals or side comments. John was going to interject but Chris continued. "And Obama, his campaign is geared towards having the troops out of Iraq within a calendar year of him taking office. Now how the fuck is he going to do that?"

"True, true." Molly said. "You can't really pull the troops out can you? Not with all of that oil to lose."

"Well, most of the oil is in Saudi Arabia," Crum corrected her.

"I know that, you twit. The war in "Iraq" is just symbolic. It's not just in Iraq now is it? It's really war on the Middle East."

"It shouldn't be about oil anyway," John interjected. "Those wells are running dry. All the new oil is in Siberia. Tons of it. Russia is coming back, just watch."

"I don't think it matters. We're going to have troops over there for a long time—it just comes down to a game of liars poker, and who's the better player between Obama and McCain." Chris said as he finished his beer and reached in one of the plastic bags for another one.

"It must be costing you guys a fortune. Waging this war and all—I'm glad to you see you guys still having a little left over for a bout in Europe." Crum said lifting his beer.

"The economy is turning to shit," Chris started again as he popped the top of his second beer. "Do you guys know what our unemployment rate is?"

"Around 9%," John answered.

"That's right. When Clinton was in office, we were hovering around 3%," Chris said. "Bush really bent us all over."

"That's funny, mate, I always thought Clinton was the one who did all the bending over," Crum joked. The whole group had a laugh.

"Well, at least you guys passed your bailout bill—something around $700 million." Molly commented.

"But what's that going to do?" Chris asked. "If we bail out the major banks, we just solve the problem for now. The banks may get back to even, but it's not a long-term solution. If things don't get better, a couple years down the road, every person and their uncle will be looking to refinance their cars, homes, and loans. The banks will have to say "no" eventually—then a ripple affect will occur that hits the middle class with an unnerving blow."

"You mean the housing market?" Molly asked curiously.

"That, small to medium businesses, the construction industry—anything that is considered a secondary luxury will be affected."

"Secondary luxury?" Crum asked.

"Fitness centers, automobiles, new construction, vacations—all those industries will get hit really hard."

"You can always move to Australia. People without jobs still manage to buy a pint." Joked John as the others laughed.

"We might have to."

"It's funny you brought up Clinton," Molly started to say as John and Crum reached for new beers. "People were so quick to impeach him after his fiasco—but certainly they wouldn't now."

"Explain," Chris said.

"Well you say the unemployment rate was at an all time low, and for a lot of major American cities, the late nineties, and early two thousands was the time of major growth. Capitalism at its finest."

"Agreed. What's your point?" Chris asked.

"Well people are fickle then aren't they? I'm sure if you put out a poll to ask registered voters, 'would you forgive Clinton's "brownie poke" fiasco if you could have him back in the White House?' they would all certainly say 'yes.' There's something very sad about that, isn't there?"

"It's because, at the time, everyone was doing

just fine," stated Chris. "And holding onto their convictions seemed to be the right thing to do."

"He was hardly impeached anyway," Crum said. "It was a technicality for the archives—he still stayed in office for all of his eighth year."

"John, can you grab me another beer?" Luke asked as he held out his empty can, which John exchanged for a full one.

"I almost forgot you're here," Molly joked. "Do you have anything to say on the subject, oh Prince of Wisdom?" Luke grinned at her sourness.

"What's to say that hasn't been said already?"

"A lot of things. With all the beer you brought up here, we're going to be out here till Chris falls down into the canal anyway, so you might as well spit it up," Crum blurted out.

"I'm not falling into the canal," Chris quickly corrected him. Luke took a moment to think about what he would say—he had a revised indignation for people who spoke without thinking.

"Well, I think it all comes down to knowledge of purpose," he started.

"There we go. Go on," John said egging him on as he repositioned himself as if to watch an ensuing show of some sort.

"I think this is an incredibly righteous thing we're doing here, don't you?"

"What? Drinking beer and smoking 'fags' on the patio of a sanctuary?" Joked Molly. A few chuckles and wide smiles spread throughout the group.

"No." Luke said as he paused for a beat. "This. This conversation. This journey we're all on. How many people who know what they're talking about are sitting around having these conversations?"

"Well, I'm not exactly sure we know what we're talking about," Crum said smiling.

"But even if we don't, we've giving into the power of discussion. All too often people confuse the difference between a good discussion and a declaration. A good discussion has give and take; it has two or more parties that listen to all the ideas; but most of all, it doesn't pressure, but rather offers something. All people would rather be offered something compared to being forced to take something, or worse, getting something taken from them. A declaration does just that. They are told a perspective, told a belief—it is not offered to them. Some people declare things with such a nastiness, that it belittles their opposition, thus taking away their voice." Luke could see he had the groups' attention as they slowly nodded their head's in agreement.

"I think more people during these election times need to look at purpose above all things. To me, the most important purpose is our individual purpose. Each person must take care of himself or herself in a way that will ensure the highest quality of life. You hear a lot of complaining about political issues during a campaign, but how many people write letters or emails to their state senators or governor voicing those complaints? How many people attend rallies, and volunteer time at informative booths to support their chosen candidate? The answer is a staggeringly small percentage of people. I would venture the greater number of American citizens have no idea who they are voting for and why they are voting for them in the first place."

"True story," Chris said in support of his claim.

"People also need to look at the purpose of who they are supporting. I love watching the debates— because I can't wait to see who shows the most character at the stand. Too much of the debate is spent ragging on the ideals of the opposition rather than offering solutions to dictated problems. I look for the person showing the most passion or charisma—rather than the speaker who shows little or no excitement at all. A presidential candidate is not applying for a management position at a Smoothie King—they are fighting for the chance to be the leader of the free world—a position that should not be won over meaningless debates of 'he said, she said'."

"As a country the first thing we need to be fighting for is to stop the bar from getting any lower then it already is. Education is suffering because of this. Our students are hurt by poor education. Illiteracy is at an all-time high—we're toppling after being the innovator of progress. Our health care system is becoming a Tower of Babel—no one can understand it, and no one can afford it. We live in a day and age that sees the rich getting richer, the poor getting poorer, but the ones suffering most are the middle class. An honest laborer has nothing to show for his efforts these days, and that is monumentally depressing."

"I hate to say it, but Chris is right. It's the lesser of two evils." Chris held up his beer as if to indicate a small bow. "Neither one of these candidates inspire me—they don't make me dare to dream big dreams. "Change" is a big part of Obama's campaign—but to quote a famous reverend he 'leans on the color of his own skin rather then the content of his own character'. And McCain, he seems like just another tailored Political-Machine puppet—ready to appease the party, rather than uphold the highest of ethical standards. It's a wash. Either way, the U.S. is in a great deal of trouble for at least the next four years."

Luke could feel a vibration in his pocket. Pulling out his Blackberry, Luke opened up his email account. Seeing that he had one new message in his inbox, he smiled knowing exactly who sent it.

"So, your absentee ballot then." John said in the direction of Luke. Luke looked up and noticed he still held the group's attention.

"My what?" he asked.

"Your absentee ballot. Who'd you vote for then?"

"I wrote in Jed Bartlet."

"Who?"

"Jed Bartlet, from "The West Wing"—his speeches always gave me the chills."

40.

22/10/08 08:40
Hotel Di Armi

In a rare moment Peter chuckled to himself as he shook his head. He knew all too well about Jed Bartlet and Luke's reference to "The West Wing." It had been their favorite show to watch when Luke was in high school. In fact, it was one of the few traditions they kept in their bachelor home.

Peter always thought Aaron Sorkin, the creator of "West Wing", should have run for president. He thought only a man of the highest caliber could create a character as rich and prophetic as Jed Bartlet. In fairness, Aaron Sorkin had Martin Sheen to thank for bringing his words to life; but still, his words were scripted in a way that a wondering soul with only the ability to read could most likely bring an audience to their knees—Jed Bartlet was absolutely captivating. He

270

was a dynamic president with unparalleled knowledge and wisdom. But only in a sad world do real people wish they were led by fictitious T.V. show characters.

Politics.

Peter scoffed. He didn't care for politicians, and evidenced by Luke's absentee ballot, neither did he.

Yet again, Peter thought about Luke's style in the previous entry—his writing was evolving, but not in a good way—it was actually getting worse. The way in which he wrote with exact detail was beginning to lessen—the whole picture was breaking into fractions, to what extent Peter couldn't tell. He didn't know if Luke had suddenly awakened one morning and decided to write less or if it was simply a time issue—either way, Peter really wished he had Luke's Blackberry.

When a shadow cast over the journal, Peter looked up to see a smiling Chris heading in his direction. He was dressed in jeans, his worn Nike cross trainers he'd been wearing across Europe, a long sleeved white t-shirt, and his patented backwards Oregon Ducks baseball cap.

Peter suddenly felt emotional for the young man—his heart bled for him. Chris had always been on the bad side of a bad break: his father, his mother riddled with old pain and sharp regret, and his sisters were probably as "at risk" as he was. And here he was, smiling, probably at the site of the beautiful morning. Peter wondered if Luke had anything to do with that—he wondered if his son had managed to reach this hard-boiled boy. Whatever the case, Peter had a fondness for Chris he hoped could cultivate into a lasting friendship.

"Good morning," Peter said.

"Hey, how are you holding up?" Chris asked as he grabbed a plate and put a croissant on it.

"I'm doing well. Better." Chris grabbed a bran muffin and moved to sit next to Peter.

"Yeah?" Chris asked as he sat down in an armchair to Peter's left.

"Yeah. I also want to thank you for last night. It was a long day, and you helped me find a small amount of peace at the end of it."

"Oh. Don't thank me. I meant every word of it."

"And I have to say that I'm sorry."

"For what?"

"Well," Peter began slowly, "In all this commotion nobody's really stopped to ask you about how you're holding up. You were Luke's friend—in all of his entries I can see how much you grew together over the last three weeks."

"It was kind of forced. Anytime you travel with someone over a long period of time like that it creates a bond—especially with how little alone time we had. I can't remember very many times we were separated, and when we were, it wasn't for very long; except that one day in Rome." Peter furrowed his brow.

"What happened in Rome?" He asked inquisitively.

"You haven't read that far? Or did Luke not write about it?" Chris asked as he pointed to the journal.

Peter opened the journal and turned to the next page. The entry dated *"10/8"*—the title read:

"Rome and Nikki"

Peter looked at Chris who was now devouring his breakfast riddled with unnecessary carbohydrates.

"Who's Nikki?" Peter asked.

"No, you'll have to read to find out. I know who Nikki was to me, but I have no idea who Nikki was to Luke. That one day I spoke about—she and Luke spent it together while I hung out with her friend Olivia."

"You don't think..." Peter trailed off as he insinuated the obvious.

"Just read," Chris responded with a smile. "We'll talk about it after." Peter slowly lowered his gaze to the journal as Chris stood up and walked over to replenish his plate. Peter felt something in his stomach—a feeling that was preventing him from diving into Luke's diary without a second thought—Peter was actually nervous.

41.

08/10/08 14:22
Rome, Italy

Luke had recently learned the word that helped define love all too well. It was a code of conduct; it was a form of training for the mind to resist all temptations. Without it, love may never endure. Love is entirely too fragile—the word itself is overused in the English language. People love ice cream. People love their pets. People love to go fishing. But without this one word, people can almost instantaneously change their mind about what they love. Like a person who loves ice cream, if they were to try tiramisu gelato in Venice there's a great possibility their loyalty may shift.

Luke knew love needed devotion.

He knew he couldn't just love Saskia, but he needed to be devoted to her as well. To do this he would insistently look at the smallest details of his life to display the grand gesture of devotion Saskia most inherently deserved. The half-heart shaped necklace never left his neck the second after he put it on. During their summer of separation, Saskia sent Luke a postcard from Munich; the same postcard he used as bookmark in every book he read. He felt the postcard had a shared energy—he imagined when Saskia picked it out she was thinking of him. He imagined when she wrote on it and put it in a drop box, the thought of him filled her mind with happiness. So Luke looked at it daily—the energy and love she used while picking it out and sending it to him was the same energy he felt when he held it in his fingers while examining it. It would have been easy for him when he received the postcard to read its contents, smile, and systematically shove it in some junk drawer, never to be seen again. But that is the problem with most people, isn't it? A gesture out of love and devotion is almost always taken for granted and overlooked. The postcard needed to become symbolic of their love for each other—nothing would be too small or too insignificant to be viewed in a greater way.

Rome had proven to be a formidable foe in testing Luke's devotion for Saskia. Daily emails kept them engaged, communicating, and excited for their planned reunion in Cinque Terre. But in the current moment, Luke had to cling to his convictions, as his devotion for the woman he wanted to spend the rest of his life with would be tested in a soul-inspiring way.

After a few great days in Venice with the circus Australians, Chris and Luke headed south to Bari. Luke had always wanted to go to Sicily, but Bari was as far south as their Eurorail passes could take them. It was decided after Venice, that Chris and Luke would use their few days in Bari for strict rest and relaxation. They spent two days and three nights in the basement lounge of a regional YMCA watching subtitled movies and drinking sparkling water. After viewing "Dazed and Confused" and a few Jimmy Stewart films, the two made their way to Rome.

On the train ride, Chris finally spoke up about his growing concern for Luke's health. Luke hadn't been sleeping more then two or three hours a night, and it was beginning to weaken his entire body—some mornings he barely felt strong enough to get out of bed. It was decided upon arriving in Rome they would seek a physician who could prescribe some sleeping pills so Luke could get some rest.

Luke didn't want to be hassled with miles of paperwork filled with international regulations about prescription drugs, but seeing Chris's concern for his well-being, he quickly relented. After checking into *La Torre*, the six-story hotel of their choosing, the two set off to find a pharmacy. When they located a pharmacy on the corner of *Via dei Cestari* and *Via Minerva*, next to the Pantheon, Luke and Chris walked in and asked for a list of nearby physicians. The pharmacist, who spoke relatively good English, asked them what they needed. Luke told him he had not been sleeping well, and he was in need of a doctor's prescription for sleeping medication. The pharmacist said it wouldn't be necessary and handed him a full bottle of Temazepam and charged Luke fifty euros.

Chris thought the whole ordeal was fantastic, but Luke was weary of it all—a hypnotic like Temazepam had been strictly outlawed in the States for over-the-counter use. Chris casually reminded him that he was "no longer in the states" and the two left it at that. For the next two nights, Luke slept like a tranquilized animal.

After three days of exploring the Vatican City, the Coliseum, and the Pantheon, Luke and Chris got ready to go on a pub crawl they found advertised in a flier on the hotel's bulletin board. Since the two were no strangers to loud social experiences, they thought it would be a great way to meet a few travelers like themselves while exploring the city's nightlife. So Luke and Chris zigzagged their way through the western district of ancient Rome to the *Hotel Rinasciment*, the meeting place for all those interested in becoming obliterated by the seven ensuing stops—they don't call it a pub crawl for nothing. At 19:00, exactly, the group started walking down the *Via Del Pellegrino*. The first stop was *Cesar Sri*—an ideal starting point for it's namesake and mixed euro shots. Over the course of the next three hours the group jumped around between *Cesar Sri*, *Ktesios*, *Le Grenier Sri*, *Al Bric Sri*, and *Nuyorica Sri*. By the time Luke and Chris got to *Nuyorica Sri*, the fellow number of crawlers had reduced considerably. Chris made the comment of his uncertainty of whether or not the fact he and Luke were still standing and fairly sober was a good thing—it seemed their drinking practice had put them in good form.

The *Nuyorica Sri* was more of a wine bar than a pub. The prices were fairly inexpensive, but the atmosphere required a certain restraint. Luke didn't mind, in fact, he welcomed it—for almost three hours he'd been in a position of yelling just to be heard in conversation—he hated that. Nevertheless, he and Chris sat with a couple from Sweden, drinking tall Peroni's in a mug. The Swedes, Johan and Sarah, were in Rome for a few days before returning to their home in Halmstad. Sarah was a touch heavyset, but still beautiful with her dark eyes and mysterious confidence. Johan was a pleasant fellow—he actually let Sarah do most of the talking, but at key times inserted his own questions and comments to show his awareness. The four of them were currently talking about the Coliseum.

"I had to nearly drag Luke out of bed yesterday to make it to the Coliseum at a decent hour," Chris shot out.

"Hey, they call it beauty sleep for a reason," Luke joked.

"Was there a long line when you got there?" Sarah asked.

"No. We got there by ten and it took fifteen minutes at the most to get in." Chris replied.

"It was also drizzling a bit, so some people were probably turned off by the weather."

"It's gorgeous isn't it?" Sarah asked, more rhetorically then anything.

"I always thought it would be bigger," Chris commented.

"It was big at the time. I'm sure if one of those ancient Romans were to see one of our *futbol* arenas their eyes would pop out of their heads."

"Probably," Luke said as he noticed Johan yawning. "Johan, you alright?"

"Yes, of course. This place is just a little bit lighter then the others isn't it?" Chris looked around at the casual conversations happening around them. Luke figured the crawl would probably end there as a result of expired endurance. Luke looked at Chris who had his eyes fixed on something.

"Luke," Chris started. "What's really lacking in this place?"

"Napa Valley wine." He joked.

"No." Chris shot back before realizing he missed something. "What?"

"Nothing. What's this place lacking my friend?"

"Music," he said informatively.

Luke, surprisingly, hadn't noticed. But when he focused his attention beyond the chaotic chorus of voices, Chris was certainly right. There wasn't any music—not even the courtesy elevator music you find in mundane book shops.

"You're right. There's not even a terrible flute playing anywhere," Luke said looking around. Then his eyes caught what Chris had been staring at. Behind Luke sitting flush against a wall was a piano. The piano had a vertical microphone angled down over the seat as if they had missed an earlier performance before they got there. Luke looked at Chris with a slight roll of his eyes.

"Come on," Chris instantly begged.

"No," Luke shot back.

"What?" Sarah asked.

"Nothing," Luke said.

"Luke, which I can't say for sure since I have never gotten to witness it, is a very talented musician." Chris announced.

"Oh, really?" Johan said with a smile.

"Oh, come on Luke," Sarah beckoned him. "This place could use a little livening up. Give us our second wind."

"Come on Luke," Chris begged like a four year old. "I'll sleep in the lobby tonight. You'll get the room all to yourself. Promise."

"The room all to myself if I play a song?"

"Absolutely. Scout's honor." He said holding up two fingers to his forehead before adding weakly, "I was never a scout though."

Luke was not a shy entertainer by any stretch of the imagination—his old Bruin nights testified to that. He was making a show of pretentiousness for Chris, Sarah, and Johan for no reason at all, really. The truth was, as soon as his eyes saw the piano, he couldn't wait to start playing. Seeing a piano sitting untouched with the cover board over the keys was like watching junior varsity girls' basketball—he simply couldn't stand the sight of it.

"Alright," Luke conceded standing up out of his seat and stretching his back out. "What shall it be then? Should I rock this joint or what?"

"I don't know what you should play, or what you can play, but remember that you're in Italy. Not everyone knows every American band. You have to play something that is pretty damn popular if people are going to have fun with it."

"Got it," Luke said after he thought for a moment. He picked up his beer and headed for the piano as he heard Chris say to Johan and Sarah, "this ought to be good." After he maneuvered his way through the crowd of young drunk bystanders, he uncovered the keys and turned on the sound system. He noticed a bartender looking at him with a bit of suspicion, but Luke waved him off, as if to say everything was fine.

After tapping the microphone and hearing the taps over the speakers above, Luke spoke to the crowd who had begun noticing the upcoming entertainment.

"Good evening to all you pub crawlers," Luke started as he began softly stroking the keys in background music. He could see Chris smiling at the table. "My name is Luke Sebastian and I have a song to share with you. It's a song about friendship; it's a song about getting the chance to get away. I don't know how many of you even understand me," Luke paused and laughed as he heard a bunch of "hoot's" to acknowledge they did. "And I don't know where you come from, but let it all go tonight, for one reason, and one reason only, because..." Luke started pounding on the keys as a few cheers went into the air as he started singing.

Making your way in the world today
takes everything you've got.
Taking a break from all your worries sure would help
a lot. Wouldn't you like to get away?

Luke could hear the wild cheers while his voice rang throughout the bar. Luke had a beautiful singing voice, and this song, he knew extremely well since the day he sang it in his sixth grade talent show. Gary Portnoy had been one of his mother's favorite singers, and the theme song for "Cheers" had been a longtime favorite of Luke's as well. Glancing over at his table, Luke could see Chris, Johan, and Sarah on their feet, along with everyone else in the bar.

All those nights when you've got no lights,
the check is in the mail;
and your little angel Hung the cat up by its tail;
and your third fiance didn't show.

Luke then shouted to the rousing audience who joined in, "Everyone!" Everyone pounded their hands down on the bar twice to go along with the beat for the popular chorus.

Sometimes you want to go,
where everybody knows your name,
and they're always glad you came; you want to be
where you can see, Our troubles are all the same;
You want to be where everybody knows your name.

After the chorus, there was a thunderous burst of laughter and whistles. The once stagnant crowd was standing together, some people putting their arms around each other. Luke played a quick bridge before singing the second verse—the crowd at this point knew their part as the chorus, so they quieted down to hear Luke sing.

Roll out of bed, Mr. Coffee's dead; The morning's

looking bright;
And your shrink ran off to Europe,
And didn't even write;
And your husband wants to be a girl;

Everyone joined in at their part, as Luke again pounded down on the keys for bravado.

Be glad there's one place in the world Where
everybody knows your name,
and they're always glad you came;
You want to go where people know,
people are all the same;
You want to go where everybody knows your name.

Luke played the bridge with energy and excitement. When the time for the ever-important trumpet came up, Luke pushed his lips together and created the trumpet sound on his own into the microphone. Sounding pretty good, the crowd erupted in surprise cheers and laughter. Luke could see Chris jumping up and down in excitement—it seemed everyone in the room was having an absolute blast, and Luke was happy to be helping in the process. When Luke wanted the crowd of people to sing the chorus while he impersonated the trumpet, he pointed at them, and they finished the song.

Where everybody knows your name,
And they're always glad you came;
Where everybody knows your name,
And they're always glad you came..

Luke then slowed his fingers down, softly the notes through the melody until he sang *a capella* :

You want to go where people know,
people are all the same;
You want to go where everybody knows your name.

As Luke hit the final few chords, the crowd burst into applause, some people even chanting his name. Luke wheeled around on the bench and bowed his head a couple of times. It was then he noticed the two girls standing next to Chris—one engaged in a conversation with him, while the other stole glances at Luke. Luke kept smiling as the crowd's applause wore down, and the bartender, on cue, turned on some music to fill the void of energy in the air.

As Luke picked up his beer and strode back to his seat, a few fans slapped him on the shoulder and shook his hand. Once he reached the table, Sarah gave him a big hug and Johan shook his hand.

"Well done!" Sarah exclaimed. "That was great."

"Did you hear everyone?" Johan asked. "I'm sure they could hear the singing at the coliseum."

"Maybe," Luke said with a smile. "I'm just glad everyone joined in to drown out my terrible voice." Sarah rolled her eyes.

"Oh, come off it. You're a regular Luciano Pavarotti, aren't you?"

"Not quite," Luke said as he felt a hand grab his shoulder. Turning around he faced Chris and the two young women he was speaking to.

"Yeah," Luke said.

"Bro, that was amazing."

"Yeah, really good," the young woman on the left said. They were American.

"Yeah, Luke, this is Olivia," Chris said as Olivia stuck out her hand. She was a pretty red-haired girl, probably in her mid twenties. Luke shook her hand and smiled. "And this is her friend, Nikki."

"Nice to meet you," Luke said as he held out his hand. Nikki did the same and smiled. Luke took a deep breath. Nikki was, and to all men is, the mistress extraordinaire—a title reserved for the one woman you don't want to meet when you are devoted and in love with someone else. To paint a clearer picture, she was flawless. Her beautiful straight blonde hair gently swept her shoulders while her soft hazel eyes dared any man not to stare at them. Her face showed promise that her mother still looked twenty-five as it held not a single blemish, not a single scratch in the whole of its statuesque beauty. Nikki's body stood toe to toe with Saskia's—both women shared an edge over all the other women in the world—they were God's top two creations. Now in what order, heaven help any man to decide. But Luke didn't gawk—he shook her hand and took his seat across from Sarah and Johan. The next twenty minutes he sat conversing with his new Swedish friends, he could feel two eyes burning a hole into his back, hazel eyes that now screamed at him to notice.

"Are you always going to walk two feet ahead of me?" Nikki asked as Luke kept his distance. He and Nikki had just reached the main entrance of the Roman Forum on *V. dei Fori Imperiali*, at *Largo Corrado Ricci*, halfway between *P. Venezia* and the Coliseum. Luke didn't quite know how he got into the situation of being alone with her, but it happened.

The night before, after his performance at the *Nuyorica Sri*, Chris convinced Olivia and Nikki to join the rest of the crawl, which lasted well into the night. Chris ended up staying in Olivia's hotel room, serving both his scout's honor promise to Luke if he played and his need to be a chauvinist male that can't just look without touching.

Before Luke parted with Nikki, Chris, and Olivia at

the end of the night, he agreed to walk the Roman Forum with her, allowing Chris and Olivia the chance to spend the day together, doing, whatever the imagination can bare to conjure.

"I'm sorry. I'm just a bit of speed walker," he replied without letting her close the gap between them.

"Then slow down," she begged as she grabbed his arm. "The Roman Empire was built over centuries—we can at least take a day to observe its beauty."

Super, Luke thought to himself. Not only did this girl stop traffic with her attractiveness, but she was intelligent as well. Luke consciously kept his eyes at the level of her face to keep from staring at, well, all the other parts of her. On that particular walk through the forum, the slight northeastern wind had brought a small chill over Rome—Nikki combated it by wearing black stretch spandex that dove into her black knee high boots. Seeing as it wasn't necessary for a trench coat, her grey long-sleeved hooded shirt didn't cover her more than perfect Brazilian style ass—the main reason Luke walked ahead of her rather then behind.

"You're right," Luke said summoning some courage that was supposed to get him through the day unscathed. "I just wanted to get the blood flowing, you know?" She smiled. He looked around for the stoppage of cars.

"What do you do, Luke?"

"Nothing, at the moment," he replied as they continued down the path towards the historic ruins. "I graduated business from UCLA, with a music minor. I've always wanted to find a way to stay in the music industry somehow."

"Well, play. Sing. You were fantastic last night."

"Thank you."

"I mean it, you were really good. I don't think there was a person in the whole club with the ability to shut you out."

"Well—" he started to say bashfully.

"I mean, it was only one song, but it turned a boring time into a beehive of activity. I thought you were brilliant." Luke could feel her eyes swarming all over him. His conscience told him to sprint away, but he didn't want to be rude, and furthermore, he didn't want to feel like he couldn't trust himself when he wasn't with Saskia.

"What about you? What's your story?" Luke asked.

"Well, I just got done with graduate school. I got my PhD in biomedicine from the University of Pennsylvania. I just accepted a job in the research department at Johns Hopkins in their Autoimmune Disease Research Center starting next month. I figured in between school and the rest of my life, there's no better idea than to travel around Italy."

"Very impressive, Dr. Nikki," Luke said as he actually thought, *Oh God, Oh God, get me out of here.*

"Oh please. Don't call me that. I don't know if I'll ever want anyone calling me Dr. Stanton."

"Nikki Stanton? Luke Sebastian. Pleased to meet you."

"I know. You told all of Italy your full name last night. I love your name. It's very cute."

"How can a name be cute?"

"It can," she said with a flare. "When a name just roles off your tongue like yours does, Luke Sebastian; it's cute." Luke smiled at her excitement.

"I don't buy it," he said in rebuttal. "A name is just a name."

"No. Come on, Luke."

"What?"

"A name is not just a name. Did you ever see "The Crucible", with Daniel Day-Lewis playing John

Proctor?" Luke shook his head no. "Oh my God you have to see it. Do you know the story of the "The Crucible"?"

"I'm sorry, I don't."

"It's one of Arthur Miller's best plays. Too many people think it's dry, but it takes a true actor to deliver Miller's message."

"Which is?" Luke asked as he put his hands in his jean pockets.

"Oh, sorry—the story is about the Salem Witchcraft trials—Miller wrote it as an allegory for McCarthyism. Do you know what I'm referring to?"

"Yeah," Luke lied. She was on a different level than him at the moment.

"The part I'm referring to is when John Proctor must sign a statement confessing his witness to witchcraft thus saving himself from being hanged. But he can't do it—because the judge needs a written confession for his records, and Proctor can't part with a false confession signed with his name. When they demand his written confession, on paper, he says he would rather perish at the stake, because he can't have his name in connection with the conspiracy to hang innocent people for a crime they didn't commit. He screams to the judge who wants to know why he won't part with the written confession, "Because it is my name! Because I can't have another one!"

Luke smiled. He certainly loved listening to her passion as she spoke. She was clearly more than what met the eye—her beauty magnified by her articulate nature filled with knowledge and originality.

"And what is your purpose for telling me this?" Luke prodded for more.

"You said there is nothing special about a name. You're wrong. Your name is everything—it is your brand, your stamp, your proclamation of identity."

"Okay..." he trailed off to prompt for even more.

"Okay? Don't play dumb," she said with a little annoyance in her voice.

"I say "okay" because I want you to keep going."

"Okay," she said with a chuckle as she leaned in. "What do you want me to keep going with?"

"How does a man with the name," Luke paused for a second, "say, Claude Butler—how does he make his name more beautiful?"

"With grace, knowledge, or tyranny. Think of all the famous names throughout history. "Alexander The Great" is what his followers shouted in his wake. "Benjamin Franklin" is always pronounced in its entirety out of respect for his innovations, and Genghis Khan and Adolf Hitler are known for their created empires. Of course a name can have a negative connotation, but it is within the individual's grasp to create such a distinction."

"You should go on Jeopardy," Luke joked prompting Nikki to roll her eyes.

"Thanks," she said sarcastically.

"I'm just messing with you," Luke tried to backtrack, and then added after a pause. "I agree."

The two walked in silent observance of the ancient ruins around them as they approached the *Basilica Aemilia*. The large columns stood out against the cloudy sky. Luke hoped for an intrusion in the form of a vibration in his pocket, but Nikki dashed his hopes as she broke the silence.

"Luke," she began, her voice softer now. "Why don't you ever want to look at me?"

Luke stopped his forward progress as Nikki moved a few more steps before turning and facing him—his avoidance was apparently grossly obvious.

"Nikki—"he started to explain before she interrupted him.

"I mean, you stare off in the distance like you're

afraid of something. What is it about me you find so repul—"

"I'm engaged," he interrupted her. He didn't want to be coy with her—it was time to stop all of the misdirection.

"Oh," she said as her eyes widened with understanding before she regained her composure. "So you can't even look at me?"

"Nikki, come on," Luke protested. "Look at you. You're the example of beautiful. Every guy in Rome would gouge his eye out to stand next to you."

"Every guy but you, that is?"

"Maybe you didn't hear me, I'm engaged," Luke said coolly, hoping the label would turn his appearance as to that of a leper.

"So. Is she here, hiding behind a column, watching your every move?"

"No," he said with a fake smile.

"Then what is it about you? I don't get it—did you decide to hop around Europe clinging to your necklace aiming to bypass the power of spontaneity?"

Luke stood in idle shock—he hadn't noticed his necklace was even visible tucked into his black colored dress shirt. He didn't try to hide it, but her awareness of it, combined with her forward form of questioning startled him.

"What do you want from me?"

"By the power of Athena, nothing that you don't want yourself." she replied as she stretched her fingers down to her thighs.

"I think you have the wrong impression of me."

"Really? So you have a fiancée that you're undeniably devoted to that you just up and left alone so you could parade around Europe with Chris?"

"It's not like that. Saskia—" he started to say when she cut him off again.

"Saskia? So that's her name. Pretty name. And what do you think Saskia is doing right now?"

Luke was almost repulsed by her change in attitude. He couldn't understand what was going on. *What is with this girl?* He thought to himself.

"Hold on," Luke said as he calculated his position.

"Luke, I want you. Bad. When I saw you playing the piano last night, I couldn't help myself. Every inch of me wanted you—you have no idea."

Luke started to feel mildly uncomfortable.

"If I told you that you had the chance to take me back to your room, and have me, and I mean all of me— what would you say?"

"No," Luke said without a moment's hesitation. Nikki just stared at him. Their eyes were locked together for what seemed like an eternity before a small smirk spread across her face.

"He told me you'd say that."

Luke's mouth opened to show his befuddled state.

"Who told you I'd say that?" He asked almost pervasively.

"Chris."

All at once, Luke understood. *That son of a bitch*, he thought. *He set me up.*

"Chris," he repeated. She nodded her head with a smile. Luke laughed out loud as he turned away from her to rub his eyes back to reality.

"Not that I wouldn't entertain the idea myself," she started to say. "I mean, you're something else, but I'm a lady Luke. And I respect another lady's prize."

"So this whole thing..." Luke said more as a question.

"Was to test your loyalty."

He couldn't believe it. Devotion. She had said the word, not him. In that moment he thought about Saskia's smile—how when her frozen visage stole his heart the world was a complete place. *No, Nikki may be one of God's elite, but she would have to wait in the wings of Saskia.*

"You're evil," Luke threw at her.

"I know." She smiled. He smiled. For the first time that day the shared a mutual respect, grounded in the information she had learned about the previous evening—Luke was a one woman man. "I do have to confess this. I don't know Saskia, and I barely know you, but I can tell you, she is an incredibly lucky girl. I mean that."

"Thank you," Luke said, grinning ear to ear. "But really, I'm the lucky one, trust me." Luke then motioned with his head as if to say the two should keep walking. Complying, she began walking with him, keeping in mind the respected bubble of Saskia's personal property.

"Are you even a doctor?" Luke asked as the sun broke through the clouds.

"Oh yeah, all that was true." She responded.

"You should've been an actress."

42.

22/10/08 09:27
Hotel di Armi

The end—"Rome" was the last entry in Luke's

journal. Peter thumbed through the rest of the remaining pages only to find every single one of them blank. Chris was sitting in the chair next to him, waiting.

"So that's it?" Peter asks as he turned his attention to the young man.

"Where did it end?" Chris asked as he spoke through his hands.

"His day with Nikki at the forum—the stunt you pulled."

"It wasn't a stunt—it was a test." Chris replied.

"What are you, an elementary school teacher?" Peter said as he rolled his eyes and sat back in the couch. Chris smirked.

"No," he started to say, choosing his words a little more carefully. "When Olivia, Nikki, and I got to their hotel, Nikki started asking all these questions about Luke—she was very interested in him. Every girl was interested in him, but in every city we went to, every time we would be around beautiful girls, Luke would disappear. I didn't know if it was one of two things—that he didn't want to be put in a position to cheat, or if he didn't trust himself not to cheat."

"Luke would never have cheated on Saskia," Peter said with a wave of his hand.

"And you know this, how?" Chris pressed as he sat back into his armchair. Peter knew he had a point—he didn't know much about his son at all before he read the two journals.

"I don't know," he said sheepishly.

"Everything you read in those journals was the real Luke—I don't doubt that. But I was with him. I couldn't tell if he trusted himself. And believe me when I say, I told Nikki about everything that night; I told her all about Luke and his relationship with Saskia. I mean, his story made Olivia like me more, I think. They fell in love with him through my version of his story—just like I fell in love with Saskia through his."

Peter just stared off into the distance while he listened to Chris. He knew he was right—he didn't exactly approve of Chris's decision to test Luke with Nikki, but Chris and Peter both shared the same thought about Luke and Saskia—they had something special.

"It was actually more Nikki's idea," Chris continued. "She said she would see for herself how deep his devotion went. And Peter, you should have seen this girl." Peter looked up and raised his brow.

"A ten?" He asked.

"More like a twenty. She was the girl I was staring at when they walked into the bar, but she had her eyes on Luke, and I had gotten used to that. And when they met up with us later that night for dinner, and I saw what she was wearing, I told myself, 'okay, if Luke cheated on Saskia, nobody would blame him'."

"You're an idiot," Peter said in his slumped position.

"I know," Chris said as he paused. "But you will never know the impact it had on me to find out he didn't. I felt proud. I think I felt the way a younger brother feels when he really looks up to an older brother." Chris's words began to lose their air as he choked up. "I will never forget Luke for that. He was the teacher, not me."

Peter shook his head, as Chris exhaled his emotions away.

"It seemed too easy for him, didn't it?"

"Yeah," Chris replied.

"And after Rome?"

"We came straight here. I know why now, with Saskia meeting him and all, but at the time it was strange. Luke was so adamant about getting here. But I will tell you this, on that train ride; I don't think I ever looked over at Luke when he wasn't smiling from ear to

292

ear. I can only wish we all get to see what he saw." This time it was Peter who took the deep exhale when Chris asked him the hardest question he ever had to answer. "Was it like that for you and Luke's mom?"

Peter thought about it for a few moments before looking at Chris. "No. I doubt it was close at all."

Shortly after Peter's conversation with Chris, Roberto showed up and told them it was time to go. Peter asked him about the report from Munich concerning Saskia, and Roberto told him it should be arriving later in the afternoon. He asked Peter if he wanted to wait for it, but Peter decided they could view it when they returned, if indeed, it had already arrived.

The trail from Monterosso Al Mare to the neighboring city of Vernazza is a treacherous hike for a sixty year-old man who was more prone to sitting in his recliner than working out. Peter turned to his motivations for energy, and let the adrenaline guide him even though he knew he would suffer the consequences later. With Roberto in the lead, Peter followed, while Chris headed up the rear. Before they set off, Peter asked about James Russo, and Roberto told him he'd seen him back to his truck and bid him farewell. Peter recalled James offering to help them the next day but knew he had done all he could, and silently whispered his thanks to him as they set off down the trail.

The cliff-side trail hugging the Mediterranean Sea was a vertical juggernaut—in some places the trail was only wide enough for a single body to pass through. The winding and twisting stone pathways were difficult on Peter's feet as he trudged along with the ocean to his right at all times. At the most vertical ascents, large stone slabs were spaced to create stairs that at some points only tread a mere four to five inches in depth.

Peter thought about the incredible effort it must have taken for path developers over the centuries to create all the natural stone retaining walls, vertical steps, and matted pathways twisting and turning around the cliff. Cinque Terre was famous for it's inability to be reached by car, which made the feat even more incredible for their lack of modern equipment. Thousands of hands, combined with ache and sweat, created the trails so many enjoyed as it provided one of the most serene and breathtaking views of the Italian coastline.

Along the way, Peter was able to keep his mind off the treacherous path by explaining to Roberto his findings in the entries he read. Chris offered insight to the gaps of time between the entries, but listened carefully to Peter's synopsis as many of the entries included details from outside of his view.

After an hour of hiking, the three men reached a summit of sorts. Roberto stopped them to take a break.

"How are you doing Peter?" he asked with a touch of fatigue.

"I'm fine," Peter replied. He pulled out bottled water from the side pocket of his black pack on his shoulders. "How much further?"

"Twenty minutes at most. Around this bend the path goes to Vernazza, but we are going up there," Roberto noted as he pointed up a side staircase leading around group of olive trees. "The last twenty minutes are the most hard. It is a steep incline to the top of the hill. The Spaniard's home is at the top, above his olive tree terrace."

"Jesus," Peter began. "How does he get his olives down to the towns?"

"He brings them down in potato sacks."

"Shit, no?" Chris said in exasperation at the thought of it.

"Oh yes," Roberto replied. "These olive harvesters

are incredible people, and they have been doing it for a very long time."

"And he has a bar up there?" Peter asked.

"Yes. Just like potato sacks, only one box of supplies goes up at a time. He might have a thirty year old bottle of *Ramazzotti*."

"What's that?" Chris asked interested.

"Italian liquor." Roberto smiled.

Peter looked up at the cliff. His journey up to that point had led him to believe they would find the answers they were looking for once they reached the top—but he couldn't shake a feeling that pitted in the heart of his stomach—a feeling of darkness that he had never seen before. He recalled the day before when Roberto told him not to get his hopes up, reminding him not to chase a phantom killer. He couldn't be chasing a phantom killer though, because Luke was dead; something had killed him, Peter just didn't know what yet.

"Let's go," Peter said putting the bottle of water away without realizing he hadn't taken a drink.

43.

22/10/08 11:23
Ristorante Sulla Scogliera

"Papa," a young voice yelled from behind the kneeling Alonso Eloy.

"Did you find it?" Alonso asked in his native tongue to his son from the house. Alonso was stretching a damaged net sliced by a tree limb from the previous night's storm. Alonso considered himself blessed—only three nets had been damaged, and considering the fury of the storm, that was a good sign. The nets were important on the terraced slope to catch the maturing olives, and prevent them from tumbling down the rocky terrain.

"Yes, Papa," Jacobo announced as he reached him. "Here is the extra thread."

"Good job, and thank you Jacobo," Alonso said as he patted his young son on the shoulder.

"Will you let me do it?" Jacobo asked. "I know how." Alonso stood up and straightened his very strong back.

"You do, do you?" He asked as a small smile crept over his face.

"Yes. I have watched you do it many times." Jacobo said confidently.

"Did you finish your schooling?" Alonso asked sternly.

"Yes. I did all my arithmetic, and wrote a summary of the first chapters of *Don Quixote de la Manche.*"

"You did? Maybe I should go read it before I let

you help me with the nets," Alonso said taking a step up the slope before Jacobo grabbed his hand.

"Alonso Quixano turns himself into a knight and calls himself, "Don Quixote de la Manche." Jacobo began to recite. "He also names his little horse "Rocinante." One morning at an inn nearby, which he thinks is a castle, he asks the innkeeper to dub him a knight, and—
"

"Jacobo, I believe you." Alonso said laughing. "I will let you help me if you promise me we'll work on your Italian after supper. Deal?"

"Deal, Papa." Jacobo said heavy with excitement as his father handed him the thread which he began to unravel.

"And don't forget to keep the knots very tight," he reminded him.

"I won't Papa," Jacobo replied.

Through a small clearing to the right of an olive tree Alonso could see three men ascending the slope— one of the men he noticed to be Captain Caligno, the head of Cinque Terre police. Alonso's memory was sharp, and he remembered meeting him a few times before.

"Jacobo, go to the house and pull down the chairs. We have guests," he said as Jacobo looked up and saw the three men.

"Yes, Papa," Jacobo said as he turned to run up the slope towards the house.

"*Bueno sera, Captain.*" Alonso said as the three men drew near.

"*Bueno sera,*" the Captain said in response as the two continued their conversation in Italian.

"What brings you up the cliff?" Alonso asked curiously.

"We don't mean to intrude during the heart of harvest," Roberto said politely. "I have reason to believe you held a meeting with a young American a few days ago—his name was Luke Sebastian."

"Was?" Alonso asked as he shifted his stance a little.

"He was found dead on the path below four days ago. The man behind me is Peter Sebastain, his father."

Alonso instantly felt his heart sink when he heard the Captian's words. Only days before the young American stood where his father stood, alive and well.

"Yes, I met with him. I considered him a friend," Alonso replied, grief spreading across his face.

"May we come inside and ask you a few questions?" The Captain asked.

"Yes, of course," Alonso replied as he held out his hand in the direction of his home. The Captain nodded his thanks. As the men stepped forward, Alonso locked eyes with the older man standing behind the Captain— his eyes were the saddest he had ever seen on a man, and Alonso instantly felt his pain.

Peter didn't know exactly what Roberto was saying to the Spaniard, but he could guess. Although Roberto vouched for the man, Peter still wondered if the Spaniard was responsible for Luke's death—he had, after all, been one of the few people to come in contact with Luke shortly before his body had been found on the trail. But when Roberto started moving towards the house, Peter and the Spaniard locked eyes for a moment, and in his eyes Peter could see a great deal of pain.

Peter had seen the young boy run ahead to the house as they drew closer, and maybe it was the internal communication between two fathers, but Peter somehow knew the Spaniard felt heavily for him when he found out about Luke's death.

Was there even one person Luke didn't touch in

some way? Peter asked himself.

As they reached the house, Peter noticed the very modest living conditions of the Spaniards. The wooden porch wrapping around the front door was made of old, rotting wood that would soon need to be replacing. The front door led to an open room that housed a small bar with two shelves behind it stocked with beer, sparkling water, juice, and Italian liquors. A lone window was on the opposite wall with a neon "Pilsner" sign hung in the center to serve as a beacon for hikers who no doubt camped on the cliff summit. The Spaniard quickly went behind the bar to grab three sparkling waters for the exhausted men. When he set the bottles down on the table, Roberto made the introductions.

"Peter, this is Alonso Eloy, and the boy is his son, Jacobo." Peter held out his hand as he shook Alonso's hand.

"It's nice to meet you," Peter said as Roberto translated his greeting. Alonso said something in response, and Peter waited for the translation.

"He says it's a pleasure to meet you and he is very sorry for your loss. He considers your son a friend."

"Thank you," Peter said as the four men sat down. Alonso turned to Jacobo, said something, and the boy ran down the hall to a room and shut the door.

"How did you know my son?" Peter asked as Roberto translated. Peter knew he would need to be patient to allow Roberto to translate what Alonso was saying.

"He says he met Luke on the night of the thirteenth." Peter said as Chris stole a glance at Peter. "Luke had been hiking alone and he ran into Jacobo down on the trail. Jacobo said he could get some water at their house, and Luke obliged."

"The thirteenth," Chris spoke up. "We had only been here a day. In fact, we hiked all four trails earlier that day."

"Did you and Luke separate?" Peter asked.

"No. We hiked all four trails together," Chris started to say before stopping as a realization struck him. "I took a nap. I took a nap after we got back to the hotel. Ask him what time Luke was here."

Roberto turned to Alonso and asked him the question. Alonso responded.

"Around 17:00."

"He came back," Chris said as his mouth hung open. "He came back up the trail. Why would he do that?"

A quick moment of silence was disrupted by a high *ping*. Everyone stole glances at each other before they heard it again. And again. Chris suddenly looked down—the sound was coming from his pocket. Pulling out his cell phone he looked up at Peter.

"My phone. There's reception up here," Chris said as he examined the front screen of his phone. "It's not very good service, it looks like it goes in and out; but you can definitely send a message up here."

Peter exhaled. It was all coming together. Luke hiked up the cliff to send messages to Saskia on his Blackberry.

"How many times did Luke come up here?" Peter asked. When Roberto heard Alonso's response, he turned to Peter.

"Every night for five nights." Peter's eyes went wide.

"The seventeenth—you're saying Luke was here the night of the seventeenth?" Peter shot across the table. Alonso didn't need a translation—he just nodded, yes.

"Tell me about it. Tell me everything about Luke's visits." Peter said. "What did you and my son talk about?"

300

44.

16/10/08 18:20
Ristorante Sulla Scogliera

Luke sat across the table from Alonso and Jacobo. Over the last four days he had come to look forward to the time he spent with them. The father and son intrigued Luke with such affection for one another. When Luke and Alonso spoke in private, Alonso bragged about how proud he was of his son. Since he was home-schooled, Alonso kept a very watchful eye on his son's progress, and to say he was smart would be a drastic understatement. Jacobo was also a very strong boy—he never seemed to fear anything. When Alonso asked him to do something, he took the request head on as his new challenge. Even now, as they sat at the table, Alonso was quizzing him on his day's lessons, and Jacobo was smiling wide as he knew the answers because his father told him he needed to know them.

Luke thought about his father back home. He knew he would need to return home at some point so they could sit down and talk, not as men, but as father and son. Over his short travels, Luke had quickly come to realize that life was too short to hate his one and only father—Chris had taught him that lesson.

As Alonso kept quizzing Jacobo on his schoolwork Luke returned his attention to his Blackberry sitting on the table. He had already read the email once, but he wanted to read it again:

My Luke,

Why does my bed have to be the loneliest place I have ever been? Why does the pillow next to me cease to have your dent? Why do I fear for you ever second you are not with me? Luke, what have you done to me?

You should answer these questions for I have many times. From the moment I saw you, I knew I wanted you to be the company of my life; from the first time I heard your voice, I knew I wanted your head next to mine, your blue eyes burning a hole into my heart. We spent our entire lives apart, but in a few moments together, I have been the held in the gaze of a love that would drive a mad person sane.

What is out there, Luke? Everything? Nothing? You once told me about a song you had written about a man who gained everything—who was the same man who had nothing at all. Did he have our love Luke? Because to me, that is everything. And if you were to tell me that now that I know what this feels like that I have nothing at all I would call you mad. But don't worry, like I said, I would only have to kiss you to turn you sane again. We are on top of the world, and it is the best place I have ever been.

I cannot wait to see you the morning after next. My train leaves Munich at 19:00. It goes through Trento, Verona, before stopping at Genoa. From there I will switch trains to Monterosso Al Mare, and into your arms. And believe me, I cannot wait for your arms to hold me safe once again. 6:10 Luke—that's when I get in. Don't be late. My prayers are with you.

A Kiss Lasting Forever,

Your Saskia

A kiss lasting forever—a farewell Luke read that weakened his knees and sent shivers down his spine.

Saskia was beyond her youth and more. She had a lustrous way of publishing her thoughts that promised the second coming of the romantic age. Luke dreamed of the days he would sit down as an old man telling the youth of tomorrow of a better time, when a man and a woman sat beyond the realm of possibility scribbling their thoughts that expressed the feelings of giants. He dreamed of a time that God would show Himself in a ray of light for all to see, so they may bask in His glory. And then, only then, could any common man whisper those two names that found that light in each other—the light of eternal love. Damn the day that light is extinguished, for so is the hope for all mankind. For only in love did Luke feel all creations truly served a purpose.

And so on the morning of the eighteenth, Saskia would arrive to fall into Luke's arms, and sitting in Alonso's home he could barely stand the wait.

Having replied to Saskia's message, Luke powered down his phone and sat observing the father and son.

"It is time for you to go to bed," Alonso said to Jacobo in their native tongue of Spain. Luke had loved his ability to speak Spanish with Alonso and Jacobo—having studied it for six years; he found their conversations a great tool for strengthening his second language.

"Can Luke tuck me in?" Jacobo asked his father as he closed his books and stood up from the table.

"Ask him yourself." Alonso replied.

"Will you tuck me into bed?" Jacobo asked politely. Luke smiled at the boy. He never had a little brother, but if he did, he would want him to be just like Jacobo.

"Absolutely."

"Hurry and get changed, Jacobo. Go. Make sure you clean your teeth," Alonso said as the smiling Jacobo ran down the hall to his room. Luke laughed at his excitement.

"You have a great son," Luke said to Alonso.

"Yes, he's a good boy. He takes after his mother."

"Alonso, I don't want to be rude, but can I ask what happened to his mother?" Luke asked leaning forward at the table.

"She died giving birth to him." Alonso replied.

"I am so sorry."

"My Teresa was a great woman—she knew how to make me happy. She had a beautiful smile—always laughing and telling jokes. She would always say, 'Alonso, if you do not see me smiling at night, you will not find me alive in the morning.' It takes a strong woman to understand what that means."

"She sounds great." Luke said with a smile.

"And poor Jacobo—his only knowledge of her is through an old man's stories—but my best memory of her is in his beautiful face." Alonso paused for a moment. "The doctor gave her a choice—it was either her or him, and she chose him. And although she was only a mother for a moment, she was the very best mother there could be." Luke sat in silence. Matthew the English professor's first rule: a tragedy through death.

"And over the years I have been haunted by a question—would I change the decision, if it were mine? What man can answer this question? If it were a choice between good and evil, that is easy and fair—but a choice between a wife and a son, the only choice, I'm afraid, is to choose my own life."

Luke shook his head—he acknowledged Alonso's pain, and in doing so, acknowledged his father's pain. As a fourteen-year-old boy, Luke still remembered the exact feeling he had when he watched his mother die right in front of his eyes. He knew of one greater pain than witnessing his mother's death, and that was the pain he caused his father by never telling him the truth.

"Only in the world of mice and men are cowards shown and feelings sent."

"But what about your Saskia?" Alonso asked. "She is almost here, yes?"

"In two days. She'll be here the morning after next." Luke answered with a smile. "I was going to bring her to meet you and Jacobo."

"No, you mustn't. The hike is too difficult."

"No, I know she wants to meet you. I've written about you in emails."

"You two will already have too much to do. And Jacobo and I have a lot of work with the new harvest."

"Alonso, no—" Luke started to insist before Alonso cut him off.

"When she arrives, do not bring her here. We look forward to your visits, but you must do me a favor." A small smile swept across Alonso's face, replacing the pain from the memory of his late wife. "You must take her on the ferry to Manarola. When you get off, climb the steps to the main street and head east towards the end of the city. Just before you reach the tunnel, there will be a staircase on the left that takes you high up into the hills. About ten minutes up the stairs, there will be an old gate that looks like it belongs near a cemetery. Go through it and walk down the grassy slope till you get to a huge rock embedded in the hillside. Stay there and watch the sun go down over the horizon."

"Why?" Luke asked Alonso.

"Because that is where I asked Teresa to marry me." Alonso said with a grin. "Do you promise?"

"I promise," Luke replied.

"Now go tuck my Jacobo in bed, he needs to sleep." Alonso said as he pulled a book closer to him.

Luke got up from the table and patted Alonso on the shoulder as he passed him by. Luke opened the door to Jacobo's room to find Jacobo laying in bed with the light on.

"Hey, my brother. Are you ready for bed?"

"Can I sleep with the light on?" Jacobo asked.

"Do you usually sleep with the light on?" Luke asked.

"No, Papa doesn't let me." Jacobo responded. Luke felt used—Jacobo had only asked him to tuck him in to get what he wanted.

"Then you can't tonight."

"Okay," Jacobo said dejectedly as he rolled over away from Luke. Luke smiled and exhaled heavily as he pulled his wallet out of his rear pocket. Opening it he took out a small photo from the hidden slot behind his driver's license.

"But I think I have something that will help you," Luke said to Jacobo. Jacobo slowly rolled over to face Luke.

"You do?" He asked.

"Yeah. But you have to promise me that you'll take really good care of it."

"I promise," Jacobo said sitting up. His eyes were wide with wonder.

"Okay," Luke said as he handed Jacobo the photo. Jacobo studied the photo for a minute. It was the photo of a woman with long curly brown hair and beautiful blue eyes.

"Who is it?" Jacobo asked.

"It's an angel," Luke responded, "An angel that will watch over you like she has watched over me."

"Really? A real angel?" Jacobo asked.

"Yeah. A real angel," Luke whispered.

45.

Ristorante Sulla Scogliera

An angel? Peter thought to himself. *What is he talking about?*

"Can you get Jacobo to bring that photo to me?" Peter asked politely. Roberto translated, and Alonso nodded as he stood up from the table and headed down the corridor. As he did that Peter reflected on Luke's timeline. "He still didn't say anything about the seventeenth, but Saskia was due to get in at 6:10 on the eighteenth."

"Yes, and if he was here the night of the seventeenth," Roberto added. "Then he was here very late—around midnight."

"Maybe longer; we need to ask Alonso." Then Peter turned his attention to Chris. "And how did you not notice him slipping off for hours at a time to hike a damn trail?"

"I don't know," Chris said dejectedly as he bowed his head. Peter didn't mean to lash out at him, so he patted Chris's leg.

"I'm sorry. Don't worry about it. It's not your fault." Peter said convincingly. He turned to see Alonso walking back into the open room holding a small square photo in his hand. Handing it to Peter, Alonso took his seat.

Peter examined the photo he had seen more than a thousand times before. The picture of Mary had been taken when Jake and Luke were kids. Peter never knew Luke kept a copy of it in his wallet.

Luke and I share the same angel. Peter thought to himself. He didn't want to explain to everyone the picture was of his late wife, because then Alonso would surely make Jacobo give it to Peter. This was not Peter's angel to give—in his opinion Luke had offered a great gift to the small boy, and it was not Peter's gift to retract. Clearing his throat, Peter poised himself.

"Thank you," Peter said to Alonso as he handed the photo back. "You may give this back to Jacobo."

"Are you sure?" Roberto asked.

"Yes. It is irrelevant to the case," Peter tried to sound judicial.

Roberto spoke as Alonso shook his head and smiled, leaving the photo face down on the table for the moment.

"Ask him if there was anything else from that night," Peter said to Roberto. Alonso listened and then added a short response.

"He says Luke came out and asked for a piece of paper and pen," Roberto said, wondering if it held any relevance.

"Why?" Peter asked.

"Luke wanted to write something down. Alonso says it looked like he wrote a letter to someone."

Peter thought that was odd. Luke had his journal, why would he write someone a letter? Especially when he had his Blackberry to write emails to anyone he wanted.

"So he wrote a letter; and then what?" Peter asked. Alonso spoke without prompting from Roberto. Peter gathered Alonso understood more of their conversation then he thought.

"He says that was it. Luke wrote the letter, and wished him a good evening." Roberto replied.

"And he's sure?" Peter asked for certainty. Alonso thought for a moment and then spoke briefly.

308

"Luke also asked if he could come the next night, but much later, and probably stay until the early morning." Roberto repeated.

"So what happened the next night? The night of the seventeenth?" Peter asked as he leaned forward in his chair.

46.

17/10/08 23:41
Ristorante Sulla Scogliera

Luke knocked on the front door to Alonso's home. Alonso had told him to do so quietly so he didn't wake up Jacobo as it was so late into the evening. Alonso would normally be in a deep sleep at that time of night, but Luke had asked him permission if he could come late, and Alonso had complied.

Luke could hear footsteps creak over the old floorboards of the wood home as Alonso opened the door.

"*Hola mi buen amigo,*" Luke said as he and Alonso shook hands. Alonso, dressed in his sleepwear, smiled.

"*Venga en y salgo del frio,*" Alonso said quickly as Luke stepped inside.

"Thank you," Luke continued. "And again, I'm sorry to come calling so late."

"You're fine. Anything I can do to help. Please, sit." Alonso said as he shut the door and pulled down two chairs sitting atop the tables. "Can I get you anything? Water?"

"Water would be great, and I will pay you of course," Luke said as he sat down in one of the chairs.

"Of course you won't. You are my friend, and my guest, not my customer." Alonso said with a smile.

"Did you have any customers tonight?" Luke asked.

"I did. I had a small group come around noon. They almost drank the last bit of *Ramazzotti* I had. I wouldn't be surprised to find them at the bottom of the ocean by now."

Luke smiled weakly. He placed his head in his hands and rubbed his temples. He had been getting short migraines recently—small spurts of sharp pain would make his head throb.

"What is wrong with your head?" Alonso asked, noticing Luke's grimace.

"Nothing. I have been getting some headaches recently—probably from all the elevation changes over the last few days," he joked. Alonso set bottled water in front Luke and sat down across from him.

"Would you like a shot of liquor to aid the pain?" Alonso asked. On the cliffs of Cinque Terre, a shot of liquor was a bit of a "cure-all".

"No," Luke said as he opened the bottled water. "I'll be fine. Thank you for offering Alonso."

"So, what brings you here tonight?" Alonso asked.

"I hate to say it, but I'm waiting for a message from Saskia. She said she would message me when she got to Verona." Alonso looked at him with a look of questioning pity.

"I hate to ask, but what purpose does this serve?"

"What?" Luke asked.

"Sitting here waiting for a message from Saskia when she gets to Verona. Verona is only a couple hours away—you will get the email, head down the cliff, and she will almost be there."

"Yeah..." Luke replied wondering what the question is.

"Why don't you go to sleep, Luke?" Alonso asked.

"I can't sleep," Luke started to say. "I know she's coming here, right now, and everything is going to be great—but,"

"But what?" Alonso asked.

"I have this feeling...I don't know, I've been feeling it all day. This terrible feeling inside that has caused me to worry...I don't know—I just need to stay here and wait for the message. Just to know she's okay. In Verona."

"Okay," Alonso said as he patted Luke's leg. "You sit here and wait for your message then. Don't worry, she will be fine. The trains are very safe—you know this." Luke shook his head.

"I know."

"You sit here and wait for your Saskia's message, and I will go dream about owning an Olive terrace that is right next to town." Alonso spoke as he stood up and stretched his back. Luke laughed at his comment.

"Thank you."

"Goodnight, Luke." Alonso said as he moved towards the hallway.

"Goodnight, Alonso."

47.

22/10/08 12:27
Ristorante Sulla Scogliera

"And that's it?" Peter asked after Roberto finished. "You went to bed, and that was the last time you saw Luke?"

Alonso nodded his head, and then stood up out of his chair. Walking behind the bar, he opened a small drawer that had a box inside it. Alonso carried the box over to the table and opened it as he spoke.

"He says, when he woke up, he found this on the floor." Roberto repeated. Alonso pulled out a rectangular phone.

Luke's Blackberry.

Alonso handed the Blackberry to Peter as he frowned—they were living in a world that only half-existed—because all their stories about Luke contained a main character no longer was alive. Even now, as Peter was being handed Luke's phone, he felt a connection breaking somehow. Luke's Blackberry had been his connection to Saskia.

"Why did he leave this here?" Peter asked out loud to no one directly as his eyes stared at the screen.

"He wouldn't have left it somewhere for no reason," Chris shot back. "He wouldn't even let me use it on the trip. That thing was sacred to him."

"Yes, but maybe in his haste to get to Saskia's train, he left it here by mistake." Roberto added as he turned and said something to Alonso. Alonso then stood up and pointed to the floor in a certain spot—and then

312

pointed to the chair Chris was seated in.

"Why would that make a difference?" Chris asked.

Peter could hear them talking, but he couldn't make out what any of them were saying. His eyes and thoughts remained glued to the Blackberry as he held the power button. A red light flashed in the top right corner as the screen illuminated, "AT&T". After a few seconds, the home screen appeared—a beautiful young woman in the background. Peter smiled—it had been the picture Luke described in his journal. Saskia was standing next to the Bayern Lion in Munich.

Peter scrolled the roller ball to the "Messages" folder. Clicking on it, he saw a long list of dated entries, all by the same email address:

saskia.e.1990@yahoo.com.

Peter was only concerned about the last entry—dated, "_16/10/08_". Clicking on it, it began.

My Luke, Why does my bed have to be...

Peter read the entry in its entirety. He thought it was beautiful and romantic, but at the moment, fairly useless. Peter wondered why it was the last email Luke had received—surely Saskia would've wanted to write him the day of her trip, right?

Come on Peter, think. He thought to himself. _Why wouldn't she write him an email the day of? Let's take Saskia. She was coming on her fall break—no doubt right after school. That's why she took the night train. So she goes to school, goes home and packs, maybe she was already packed. She goes to the train station...she was early. Saskia would have gone early. Maybe, she didn't have email on her phone._

Working the problem out in his head, Peter

pressed the "back" button on Luke's Blackberry. Going back to the home screen, he clicked on the file that said "SMS and MMS"—the file that stores all text messages. Luke wouldn't have wanted he and Saskia sending text messages during his trip because it was more expensive. But, Peter knew from one of his employees who took a trip to Greece, that AT&T offers a fairly inexpensive International package that offers free Internet use, and a small number of complimentary text messages. Peter concluded Luke switched his package before flying out to Munich.

When he clicked on the text message icon, a new list of messages displayed on the screen; again, all from the same sender, "Saskia Einreiner". Peter focused his eyes on the last received message reading, "7:03 Saskia Einr... I'm on the..." Peter clicked on the message to read the contents in its entirety.

Oct 17, 2008 7:03:22 PM
I'm on the train. I'm so excited!!! ☺ I can't wait to see you. I'll text you when I get to Verona. Ich Liebe Dich! MUAH

As Peter read he got the message, but the time-line was all he cared about. None of it was adding up. Luke never received a message in his waiting time at Alonso's home. There was the possibility of a message being erased, but it seemed unlikely with the events thus far.

Peter hardly noticed when Roberto's cell phone rang.

"E non avete sentito niente durante la notte? Non lo avete sentito mai alzarti persino per andare alla stanza da bagno?" Roberto asked Alonzo.

314

Roberto hadn't really noticed Peter sitting with his head down at the end of the table—he and Chris had been asking Alonso specific questions about the night of the seventeenth. He figured any details could prompt new ideas, and new ideas could lead to answers.

All of the sudden, Roberto felt his phone vibrate on his hip, followed by a loud *ring, ring, ring*. Knowing by the tone it was an incoming call, Roberto picked it up.

"*Caligno,*" he said to the caller. Unable to clearly hear his lieutenant's voice through the static caused by the low reception, Roberto stood up and began walking towards the door. "Hold on, I'm moving to a place with better reception," he said in Italian.

Roberto walked down the wooden deck steps, and out into the open area before the steep descent down the slope.

"Hello. Hello. Can you hear me. Yes, I can hear you. Yes. Go ahead," Roberto said as he listened. After a few seconds he exclaimed, "What? When!?"

Peter continued staring at the home screen of the Blackberry. He looked at each icon again: "Messages, SMS and MMS, Media, Contacts, and Calender." He looked at each file; the media held a few pictures and one ringtone; the contacts held every phone number Luke saved in his phone, but nothing looked unusual; and the calendar didn't have a single entry in—Luke, apparently, didn't keep a calendar.

Think Peter, he yelled at himself as he rubbed the back of his head. *What else is there? Who else would he have talked....*

The thought hit him with a flash—Peter then pushed the green phone button. The home screen shifted to a call log list—the last being to Luke's voicemail, dated "10/18 4:11 am".

Peter didn't waste any time as he scrolled down through the options and selected, "Call Voicemail." Putting the phone to his ear, he listened to the voice of an Operator.

"Main Menu, to listen to your messages press one. To—"

Peter pressed one, and again held the phone up to his ear.

"First skipped message. From, an outside caller. October eighteenth, four, eleven. AM."

Peter could barely hear Roberto shouting his name from outside the house—he didn't care. He concentrated his hearing to the voice that followed the operator. It was a man's voice—he had an accent that Peter couldn't geographically place. There was a deep sadness in his voice—a deep, dark, sadness. A sadness in a voice Peter hadn't heard for almost ten years.

"Luke. It's Otto. I don't know how to say this to you...Luke, it's about Saskia...She's..."

48.

17/10/08 20:10
Train 0187
Trento, Italy

Glancing down at her hands, Saskia noticed the

moisture in her palms. She was hours away from seeing Luke but she couldn't stop feeling nervous. Luke had this hold on her that kept her from feeling how she used to feel. She no longer wanted the independence desired by most eighteen year old young men and women—she didn't need to be free to roam about the new adult world with a rebellious nature. She felt like her year spent in America served that purpose up until she saw this young musician playing the guitar at a college concert.

Saskia knew her age. She knew it was abnormal for a girl of her youth to be so deep into her affections— to feel so much happiness when she heard a single name. Most girls her age claim they know love and happiness—they talk about it day and night like a telethon, almost as if the goal is to convince you to believe what they're saying so you can buy into the purpose. Saskia didn't want to be like any other girl, because she knew she was different. She knew she had the real, honest-to-God love that poets would spend a lifetime trying to depict. So when it came down to convincing others that her heart was, indeed, someone else's, she showed everyone instead of telling them. When her mother, Tuvia, asked about Luke, she answered no more than what the question required, but remained honest to the end. When she would see a picture of Luke, she wouldn't brag about his handsomeness, but she wouldn't stop her face from beaming like the reflection of the sun on the damp horizon.

Saskia believed in the Bible. She believed firmly in The First Epistle of Paul the Apostle to the Corinthians. She read daily chapter seven—the principals of a good marriage in preparation of a lifetime of happiness with her Luke. Soon, very soon, her body would not be hers as she would freely give it up to her lover, and he would freely give up his to her. For many reasons Saskia thanked God for Luke's divinity—she felt that although Luke was still finding his way to an exact point, he was still on the path of righteousness. She believed his soul was good—she believed his intentions were that of a man who would turn the other cheek, and love his neighbor as himself—not because he was a coward, but because he dared not strike a coward back, throwing himself into the same lot.

Saskia believed the world was a changing place—it evolved for the better and it evolved for the worse. The worse being the lowering bar of ethical standards; she always thought a person back then would be abhorred by contemporary youths, but the person right now could overly inspire the person back then. The right being the outbreak of emotional acceptance; a person can love whomever they want, whenever they want, for as long as they want, until the end of their natural days.

And even now as Saskia sat on the train, she listened to her daily devotion on her iPod—a playlist Luke had sent her over their summer of separation. A smile stretched across her face, as she awaited the passage of time. Saskia had worn Luke's favorite outfit, and done her hair in his favorite way. She carefully put on her make-up to ensure its perfection—her spying sisters witness to her efforts. Her family that accompanied her to the train station had called her *Prinzessin von Luke*. She hugged each of them before waving her goodbye as her train pulled slowly away from the station.

"Only in the world of Mice and Men are cowards shown and feelings sent," Saskia said to herself. She loved Luke's quote. The world of mice as cowards, and the world of men as true lovers.

Saskia had been on the train for four hours when the voice over the intercom prompted her to remove her headphones.

"Excusez-moi des dames et le monsieur, peut j'avoir votre attention svp. Le chemin de fer sert d'équipier éprouvent des difficultés avec les voies, nous forçant à nous arrêter dans Trento. Un système d'autobus a été mis en place pour vous éviter autour des dommages, et sur votre chemin à Vernona. Merci et nous sommes désolés pour ce dérangement." The voice said overhead.

Saskia wasn't trying to hide her confusion. The voice had been in French—a language she was very distant from. She listened carefully and could make out bits and pieces about a "bus", "Trento", and "Verona" , but that was it.

A man sitting a few rows away from her could see her confusion. He was a middle aged man, slightly overweight. He had a slight scruffiness to him. The whole train ride he had spent the time reading a newspaper, occasionally sharing glances with Saskia. He stood up as Saskia could feel the de-acceleration from the train.

"Excusez-moi," he said. *"Parlez-vous français? Anglais?"*

"English?" Saskia asked to the possible cognate.

"Yes, English. I speak good English," the man said.

"Saskia," she said to the man holding out her balmy hands.

"Viggo," the man said as he held out his. When Saskia shook his hand, she noticed he had the coldest hands she'd ever felt.

"What did they say about the train? Why are we slowing down?" Saskia asked curiously.

"There is a problem on one of the tracks. They are fixing it. Where are you heading?" The man asked.

"Verona, then on to Cinque Terre." Saskia replied.

"Verona, me too," the man said with a smile. "The

announcement said that all those going to Milano are to get on a bus outside of Trento, which is where we are heading now."

Saskia hadn't recalled hearing "Milano" during the announcement but she thought she could be mistaken.

"And for those going to Verona?"

"We are to wait for a second train that will take us straight to Verona from Trento. It will be a faster train, so we will actually get to Verona faster then scheduled." This made Saskia smile—if she got to Verona ahead of schedule, she knew she could catch a quicker train to Cinque Terre and surprise Luke with her early arrival.

The train slowed down to a small "passenger" station with a loan sign at the head of two poles fixed in the cement. The sign read "*Trento*". When the train came to a complete stop, Saskia saw the slew of passengers exit their cars and head for the exit sign. Being a late train, there were not more then fifty of them. But as more and more passengers headed for the exit, Saskia found she and Viggo were the only one's staying on the platform.

"There are a lot of people going to Milano," Saskia commented. Viggo was a few meters away, lighting a cigarette.

"Yes. I can see that."

After the all the passengers had gotten off the train, three train marshals stepped out and began trolling the empty cars for sleeping passengers, and left-behinds. When one of the marshals saw Viggo and Saskia standing there, she called out to them.

Viggo stepped up, and spoke for the both of them, quickly walking towards the marshal, rather than let her get close to them. After the two spoke for a brief while, Viggo turned and started walking back towards Saskia as the marshal boarded the last cart as the train slowly crept out of the station in the direction they had come.

"What did she say?" Saskia asked.

"She said the next train will be here shortly. She was also surprised that we were the only ones continuing on to Verona." Viggo said.

"No kidding," Saskia said as she surveyed her surroundings. The track they had come down was labeled "1". There was also a track "2", and track "3". It made sense to Saskia—they were working on a mechanical problem on track "1" and they would catch a train heading down track "2" or "3". To get to tracks "2" and "3", there was a flight of stairs that led down into a tunnel underneith the tracks—being a very common thing in Europe, Saskia was actually glad to have Viggo there. If she were alone, she would've probably been terrified.

"Did she say which track the train would be coming down?"

Viggo looked up at her from his staring contest at his cigarette and exhaled a plume of smoke. His jaw clenched as he licked the corner of his mouth and bit down on his lower lip.

"Yeah. She did," he said with a heavy breath. "Track 3."

"Okay," Saskia said as she re-adjusted her purse, and pulled up the handle to her suitcase on wheels. "Then let's go over there."

"Yeah," Viggo said as he put his cigarette out. She watched him scratch the stubble on his neck before taking a step forward. "And did you say where you're from?"

"No. I'm from *Munchen*. You?" Saskia asked as they headed for the stairs.

"*Lyon*, in the western district of France," Viggo said as he casually put his hands in his pocket. "And you are heading to Cinque Terre?"

"I am." Saskia replied as they descended the stairs into the tunnel. The tunnel had three overhead lights complimented by the wash of moonlight creeping down the two stairwells leading to the other tracks.

"And why are you traveling alone?" Viggo asked curiously, his frozen gaze staring straight ahead.

"I am meeting my fiancé there," Saskia revealed, although she didn't want to. She continued to speak despite getting this very strange feeling at the heart of her stomach. Saskia looked at her watch. It said: 23:52. "He is waiting for me..." she trailed off as she noticed Viggo not walking beside her anymore. She stopped when she heard the *click*. She didn't know what it was when she heard it, but she instantly recognized it when she felt it.

Viggo's heavy, hard hand reach around her body and grabbed her left arm—a thick covered forearm powered her body against his broad chest. The stubble on his face dug into the side of her head, as she gasped at how fast it all happened. And despite the lighting-like surprise of the assault, she felt one thing at a time; the hand, the forearm, the chest, the stubble, and then the sharp tip touching her abdomen, followed by the searing edge of the four-inch switchblade.

The pain didn't instantly come, but when it did, Saskia let out a wail that God himself couldn't ignore.

And I can't, tell you, enough,

Saskia screamed from the top of her lungs as she tried to pull away from Viggo's grasp. "PLEASE! STOP!" They wrestled as she started sobbing uncontrollably.

How much I feel in love,

Saskia managed to break her right arm free as

322

she planted her elbow as hard as she could into Viggo's face—causing two things; he momentarily lost his grip on her, and she fractured her right elbow.

And what we are, it feels, so right,

Saskia kept screaming, "HELP! SOMEONE HELP! PLEASE!" She sprinted ahead a few steps before Viggo grabbed the back of her shirt and ripped it down, tearing it from the top right shoulder to her punctured abdomen that was now beginning to bleed out. When he grabbed and ripped Luke's favorite shirt, Saskia was sent tumbling to the ground as she scrapped her knees against the cold pavement.

Take me, and be, my goodnight.

Racing to her feet, Saskia thought she could make a sprint for the track "2" staircase. "SOMEONE PLEASE! HELP ME!" Her cries echoed in the underground chamber. "HELP ME!"

After taking one hard step, she thought she could make it, so she powered all of her energy into the next step—but when she did so, the coldest hand she had ever felt reached around her neck, and flung her body against the wall. With her body pinned by his left arm, Saskia could feel the stabbing sensation again, this time into her left rib cage, just below her exposed black bra Luke told her to wear because it was his favorite.

Be my light, be my bride.

The second stab punctured Saskia's left lung causing her to panic with every breath as it began to fill with blood. She continued to push against Viggo's impossible hold with her left arm and fractured right elbow with all of her might. She gasped for air, but continued to fight his strength with all the energy she could summon. Lifting her eyes, she stared into her assaulters cold, dark visage. In his eyes, she begged for a reason to why he was doing this to her. "Please," she barely was able to whimper. "Don't do this, I beg you."

Time froze as they just stared into each other's eyes—Saskia's fighting to stay open. Then Viggo whispered, "I'm sorry," as he removed his blade from her left side, and let her fading body drop to the ground. Saskia fell on her right elbow which sent a fury of pain to combine with the two puncture wounds now bubbling red water features on her torso. She could see Viggo grab her purse and suitcase which had been thrown around in a frenzy in midst of the assault.

All he wanted was her *things*.

Saskia tried to pull herself up to her knees, but every movement sent a thousand sharp pains coursing through her body. Her breathing was becoming more and more irregular—her quickened heart pumping the ill advised blood out of her body as well as into her lungs.

And when her head was down for just a second, she felt the cold hand reach to her neck and grab hold of her silver necklace. She reacted quickly and wrapped her bloodied hand around the front of the chain holding the sacred half-heart pendant. They reached a standstill of force, as she wouldn't let go of the necklace he wanted to claim. She was willing to let the sterling silver slice through her hands and bones before she would let go. "Not this!" She seethed. And then again in a scream."NOT THIS!"

Please, be my wife.

And then she was alone. Her eyes, blurry with tears, avoided the site of her staining blood spreading across her torn short. She fought her own body for air—the oxygen all around her but her lungs incapable of capturing it.

She tried for a last time to stand—but in her weakened state, all she could do was lean against the wall. She wanted to vomit. She needed to urinate. Clouds began forming in her mind—her thoughts becoming more and more unclear. She thought about the blood in her hair—she had tried so hard to make it look perfect for Luke, and on top of it all his favorite outfit was now ripped, torn, and stained with blood.

Saskia curled over on her right shoulder, as she tucked her arm into her stomach, hoping to stop the pain that was now fading away with her consciousness. She reached up with her left hand and pulled the half-heart shaped pendent into view. She stared at it. She thought about Luke, his hair that waved over his face, and his blue eyes that matched the sky. She thought about their time together—how happy he made her feel.

And then she couldn't breath anymore. She knew it was the end. She looked up as her tears ceased—their salty taste lingering on her lips. Saskia didn't waste her last moments. She knew she had to think fast, so she shared a thought for everyone in her life that she loved. Mental images of her father, her mother, her brothers, and her sisters filled her mind. One by one she prayed for their safety, and for their future happiness and salvation. She then asked for God to stay with her until the end, and then gently carry her home if it was His will to do so. And then she asked for His forgiveness for not letting Him be her last thought. She knew He'd understand.

Her last thought she saved for Luke. Luke Sebastian. The man of her dreams. She had planned to spend the rest of her life in his arms, and thought it was eternally sad it had to be cut short by the selfishness of one man. She never thought it wasn't fair though—she would never think it wasn't fair. Because she knew that in knowing Luke for a short time, that she lived for a lifetime.

Panic started to creep in as her body was in desperate need of oxygen. And then her song crept into her head. His beautiful hands plucking the beautiful strings—his eyes closed as he sang to the angels. His question embedded in the most beautiful melody she had ever heard.

Please, be my wife.

Yes, she thought. *Yes. I'll love you forever.*

And then she was gone. Her lifeless body lay in the tomb of some discreet tunnel—her hand clenching to the silver chain around her neck—her blood spreading across the cold earth shared by mice and men.

49.

22/10/08 13:01
Ristorante Sulla Scogliera

The world moved in slow motion as Peter felt the phone slipping from his fingers after he heard the message of Saskia's death. He could see Roberto rushing to the door; a scared Chris seated next to him;

a disheartened Alonso still dealing with the new grief of Luke's death. Four men from opposite parts of the world stood together in a room watching time stand still.

When the phone finally hit the table, Peter clenched his grief stricken heart until his hand formed a fist—he couldn't help it. The thought of Luke standing in that room, receiving the news of Saskia's deadly assault made Peter feel as distraught as the day he got the call that Mary died. Peter's hardened heart had been broken again after learning about Luke's death, but now he wept uncontrollably for the tragic and brutal loss of Luke's dear Saskia. He wept until his voice cracked, and his eyes dried as his tears dripped from his quivering chin.

"Peter," Roberto whispered as he drew closer. Peter brought himself to look into Roberto's eyes, which were damp with tears of his own.

"Do you...?" Peter trailed off as Roberto nodded his head to answer the difficult question. Chris sat quietly in confusion.

"What's going on? Peter, what did you hear?"

Peter turned to Chris, but couldn't bring himself to tell him. Roberto knelt beside him.

"Saskia," he began slowly in almost a whisper. "Was found stabbed to death in Trento, Italy four days ago."

Chris's mouth hung open in total shock. He started shaking his head as if to shake the truth away.

Peter took a deep breath.

"Luke received a message from Saskia's father early that morning he was found on the trail." Peter tried to hold his composure together. "The last message he got, was to find out that Saskia had been murdered."

"*Dio maschile*," Roberto said softly.

Peter could start to see the final piece of the puzzle. As each second passed, he almost saw himself as a rare art connoisseur finally stepping away from a masterpiece depicting tragedy. Perspective became very important, as Luke had no one witness his final moments. The only way Peter thought he could grasp what happened to his son was to think like his son.

Luke had left behind two volumes of his most intricate thoughts on the treasures of the world. Peter not only read them, he believed in them. He believed, from reading about the last six months of his son's life, that in his death, Luke taught him more about life than he could possibly have ever learned on his own.

Peter hadn't noticed that Chris had taken a small, orange pill container out of Alonso's box. Peter also hadn't noticed Chris telling Roberto they were Luke's. He just stood up out of his chair and faced the door.

Alright Luke, Peter said to himself. *How did it happen?*

Luke had taken a couple of sleeping pills to ease the headache he was having—the tension building between his temples had become more then he could bare. When the message finally came through he was sleeping in his chair, the bottle of pills on the table. The time was 04:11.

"Okay, he was right here," Peter said. "It was 4:11 in the morning."

Chris, Roberto, and Alonso sat in quiet compliance to whatever was going to happen next.

"Is the moon really bright at night?" Peter asked, not even turning away from the door.

"Peter—" Roberto started to say.

"Is the moon really bright at night!" Peter shouted at him.

"Yes, yes it is." Roberto answered immediately.

"Let's go," Peter said as he grabbed his black pack

and hurried out the front door.

Luke's eyes welled with tears as he ran from Alonso's home. The narrow path was slightly illuminated in the heart of the night. When Luke reached a small, level pad on the descent, he leaned against a long retaining wall that separated Alonso's land from the public national park of Cinque Terre.

Luke's heart raced as he sobbed in chaotic increments. His onslaught of depression weakened his muscles—his hands shook uncontrollably. He didn't know where he was going. He didn't know what to do. But he kept running down the rapidly descending slope.

Peter heard Roberto and Chris screaming after him as he continued to move swiftly down the trail. He maneuvered his feet as he kept a watchful eye of each step as he concentrated all of his energy to moving quickly, and safely down the determined path.

When he reached a small level pad that sat next to a long natural stone retaining wall that served as Alonso's property line, he paused to catch his breath. He looked around, but saw nothing, so he continued.

Luke reached the base of Alonso's path and spilled onto the open, common path that everyday hikers used to travel between Monterosso Al Mare and Vernazza. To his right was a trail he knew; to his right was Chris and Hotel di Armi; to his right was the passenger unloading platform he was supposed to meet Saskia at in two hours; to his right was his life that was supposed to be the greatest thing anyone had ever known; to his right…was all lost.

Luke continued to sob in bursts as his emotions grew more and more unstable. His mind raced. The overwhelming feeling was driving him insane. His

329

migraine continued to throb. In between sobs he reached for his Temazepam, but quickly realized in his haste to get away from the house, he'd left them behind.

Instead of going right. Luke turned left.

Peter broke onto the main trail almost wheezing from a lack of oxygen. He bent over in frustration, before straightening his body to allow his lungs to take complete, full breaths. He could hear Roberto and Chris as they approached—he figured they would easily catch up to his aging pace. When they broke through to the path, Peter was relentless.

"Where? Where!" Peter screamed. Roberto took a second to catch his breath.

"To the left. Around the bend. You will see the cross."

Peter looked at him as the sweat rolled down his face. "Cross? What cross?" Peter asked furiously. "Someone put it there for Luke?"

"No," Roberto said calmly. "It has been there for over a hundred years."

Peter glared at both men. They knew not to follow.

Luke had been planning to take Saskia to the cross—he knew she would love it.

When he rounded the corner, he slowed down to a walk. His jaw wouldn't stop clenching in his continuing agony. Images of Saskia kept flashing in his mind. He couldn't imagine how lonely she must have felt the moments before her death. His face kept cringing as his hands turned into fists.

Slowly, ever so slowly, he approached the cross. When he got close, he knelt in front of it—his outward breaths screeching as he continued to die inside.

330

Peter didn't know what to expect when he turned the corner. Roberto had said there was a cross, but when Peter finally saw it, he didn't think it would be what it was.

The "cross" was a tree.

It wasn't just a tall trunk with only two branches stemming from it—it was a trunk that had perfect symmetry with two perfectly even branches protruding from its sides. The most miraculous part was the bulk in the middle. Peter could see what looked like arms, legs, hands, feet, and the head of Jesus Christ. The natural aesthetic of the tree looked like the biblical depictions of Jesus Christ being crucified on the cross.

Peter walk slowly towards it. He then noticed a great deal of other things—things he had seen before.

The pictures, he thought.

Peter recalled the pictures Roberto showed him at the Pizzeria in Genoa. He remembered the picture taken about ten feet away, three feet off the ground. When he got to the right distance, he knelt to his knees. His eyes sat at the same level the picture had been taken from. He could understand why he didn't see the cross—in the photo, all he could see was the base stump.

Peter continued to wrestle with his thoughts. *Luke came to the cross. He and Chris had already seen it. They hiked all four trails when they got here.*

Peter crawled on all fours to the exact spot Luke's body was found. Putting his hand on the earth where Luke's head was, Peter closed his eyes. He then lay on his back—his head side by side with Luke's ghost. Peter wanted to lie next to his son's spirit.

After a few minutes of silence, Peter opened his eyes.

Standing up, Peter took off down the path towards the bend. When he got to Roberto and Chris, they were leaning patiently along the wall. Peter looked at both of them confidently, and gave a slight nod of his head.

"Let's go see the autopsy report. I need to know what happened."

50.

22/10/08 14:52
Hotel di Armi

"Give it to me," Peter said when Roberto came into the lobby with the report in his hand.

Having descended the trail as fast as they could, Roberto told Chris and Peter to go straight to the hotel and rest for a few minutes while he got the report from the small police office on the south side of the city.

"I haven't read it," Roberto said, "But remember—
"

Roberto stopped as Peter held up his hand. Peter didn't want to hear another word until he looked at the report. He wanted to make sense of the very last part—the last ten minutes of Luke's life.

As Roberto handed him the brown folder, Peter saw Chris enter the lobby. Roberto took a seat on one of the armchairs, and Chris did the same—together they sat in silence as Peter pulled out the report. He almost smiled to himself when he read the cause of death.

Luke stared at the cross from his knees as the full moon cast shadows from the limbs across his face. His blue eyes were crusted as his sobs subsided to heavy wheezing.

Unable and unwilling to move, Luke could feel the shift within him. He didn't know exactly what was going on, but every man can tell when they are minutes away from the end of their life.

"I'll just read it to you," Peter said to Chris and Roberto after he finished reading. "Lucas Joseph Sebastian died at a presumed time of death of 04:38, the 18th day of October, in the year, 2008."

"An increasing amount of *carbon monoxide* build up in Luke's *alveoli* from excessive amounts of unprecedented smoking caused inflammation in his lungs. After, what appears to be a mild hemorrhage of the *hypothalamus*, a mild stroke caused a periodic brain malfunction that induced *alveolar hypoventilation*, also known as Acute Respiratory Distress Syndrome (ARDS)..."

Luke's head continued to throb as his lockjaw continued to get worse. The overwhelming pain pushed him forward onto his forearms. Every breath he took got harder and harder while his right arm started to shake uncontrollably.

Luke didn't cry for help. He didn't get up to run— he had nowhere to run. Luke didn't have a fight in him. His thoughts remained on Saskia which eased his pain— the medication the same as the poison. He thought about every minute he got to spend with her; the day he first met her; the walk through the park; the first time he took her to his flat; the night he proposed at the consulate; the way she looked at him when they first locked eyes at the airport; and their last kiss standing at her door.

"Due to the combination of the *carbon monoxide* and the foreign Hypnotic, Temazapam, Luke developed slight case of Heart Arrythmia—this slowed his heart rate well below 40 beats per minute (bpm)."

Luke felt a stabbing pain in his chest as he keeled over. In what felt like a complete deconstruction of his inner body, Luke calmly lay on his back to open his wind tunnel as wide as it could stretch—this allowed him to capture a few last breaths on his way to the other side of things.

Luke could see the stars through treetops that gently swayed with the rhythmic gusts that blew throughout the hillside. Luke thought about her hair; he thought about her eyes; he thought about her smooth skin that formed against his the times they lay naked in bed together; he thought about her soft lips; he thought about her laughter; and he thought about her gentle fingers flowing through his hair.

"With the precise timing of the Acute Respiratory Distress, the Heart Arrhythmia, and the Hypothalamus Hemorrhage, Luke developed a rare case of Stress Induced Cardiomyopathy (SIC), which is the sudden weakening of the *myocardium*—the major muscle of the heart—this caused the *myocardium* to bulge out of ventricular domain, the equivalent to a massive heart attack."

Luke knew this was it. He could start to feel himself pulling away. He never wondered how he got to this point—he just assumed that only a just God would take him away as soon as he took his Saskia.

334

Luke wasn't scared. He knew he would be home soon.

Luke took his final breath. He concentrated his mind. He wanted to save a thought for him, his father, because he never really told him how much he loved him. So much wasted time.

Luke scanned the treetops one more time before using the last ounce of energy he had to pull his left hand up to his chest to reach for the half-heart shaped pendant protruding through his shirt. With his other hand, he pointed to the shining star through the opening in the tree.

Saskia, he thought for the last time. I'll love you forever.

Peter sat down on the couch as Roberto and Chris kept their eyes on his every move. Peter ran his fingers through his fading hair, as he set the report on the table in front of him.

"The other name for Stress Induced Cardiomyopathy," Peter said slowly, "is dying from a Broken Heart."

Peter let his words sink in as he heard the other two collectively exhale their emotions. Each grown man had tears welling in their eyes, but couldn't bring themselves to shed them. Peter was the first one to outwardly smile, as Roberto nodded his head in approval. It was up to each individual to determine whether or not this explanation would suffice.

To Peter, there could be no better way.

Peter got up from the couch and headed to the lobby window. Outside, the warm sun cast down on the beach, the waves gently pouring into the shore. Peter watched as the townspeople went about their everyday lives—moving in a controlled chaos from one spot to another, completely oblivious to what was going on.

"Peter," Chris beckoned. "Are you okay?"

Peter heard the question but he didn't have a response. Was he okay? He supposed he was by comparison to others. He was doing better than Luke. Luke, his tragic son, whose heart couldn't bear to live without Saskia.

"Peter," Chris said again.

"Yeah," Peter finally acknowledged him.

"What do you want to do now?"

"What do I want to do now?" Peter snuffed the question. "I want to...I want to...die myself." Peter's cynicism didn't draw a response as he continued. "I want to turn the clock back and start last week over again. What I want is my son back. I want fair. It eludes me in the present moment." Peter turned to his audience and leaned back against the windowsill as he folded his arms across his chest. "I want to kick a chair and let it make me feel better, but it wont. I want to punch a hole in the wall, but the penetration would be in the wrong place. It's my mind...my thoughts. My son is dead. I know this. I've already cried about that. The initial shock was near enough to kill me; that pain, I wish upon no one. But the enduring pain...now that is something else all together. Reading his journals while the ink is still drying...it fools me. It makes me think, I was "this" close. We were just around the bend from him when he died, and minutes, no seconds, was the difference. But that's so far from the actual truth. The truth is I was the distance from here to my home, and the time was years. Years. I was years away from Luke. And this was my own fault."

Peter paused, as the other two remained silent.

"I've spent the last few days reading his journals, researching my own son like he was some topic in a damn book report. When all I had to do was be a better father, which I had the chance to do for twenty-three years...so I hate to repeat myself but I was years away from saving my son...what am I... The," Peter stammered. "The thought I keep having is this glaring image that I can't see Luke at Christmas. I can't call him on his birthday, or call him to tell him that I'm sending some more of his mail home, because his former high school music teacher doesn't have his new address. I'm not going to be able to have him drive home for two hours of nonsense talk and cold pizza with his miserable old man...All the, or I should say, the very few things I did for my son which made me the father I am; I can't even look forward to those things. I lost him...I lost him. It's completely this time. I don't have the opportunity to call him. And that my friends, that fact is haunting. It is haunting for a father. It is haunting for me. And I know that I am just filling your ears with my regurgitated thoughts, but I need you to realize something. In Luke's death, we have all glorified his thoughts, his character, and his morals. We have made him out to be this professor of love and life, but he actually was very ordinary. He," Peter continued with a more panicked voice then before. "He chewed his food with his mouth wide open, and I could never get him to do his laundry or clean his bathroom, and Luke always felt he knew the answer to everything. He was the king of talking back, and the Lord knows he punished me with his words...he has to be described as ordinary. He has to take some fault in his death; the drinking, smoking, the sleeping pills, and his obsession with Saskia...that has to bring him down doesn't it? His story is so sad...that has to bring him down to earth, doesn't it?"

"No. No it doesn't. Because he was my son. He was my boy. He chewed with his mouth open, but his smile could change the mood of a room. He hated cleaning, but his advice could send a young man home to his family to change the future for the better," Peter said gesturing to Chris. "And he may have spoken back to me time and time again, but at least he had a voice. No, he wasn't ordinary to me. And if you two haven't heard me yet, hear me now, your boys, Roberto, and your family, Chris, they aren't ordinary to you. They deserve a special place."

Peter then slowly shook his head to agree with his own sentiment. "Yes, they deserve a special place. I lost Luke because I forgot that. I did. And now, I have to live with that grief. I do."

51.

22/10/08 20:10
Riomaggiore, Italy

Roberto slipped quietly through his front door into the tidy kitchen he knew his son Petri had cleaned while his mother was out of town.

Placing his bag on the counter he noticed a new decoration on his refrigerator. On a blank white canvas, four figures stood on a hill facing the setting sun. The figures were labeled, "*Papa, Mama, Petri, Elmo*." All four figures were holding hands.

Roberto swallowed hard the emotions he found difficult to contain. Only hours earlier he had said goodbye to his new American friend.

"You can always stay here," Roberto said to Peter as they stood at the Riomaggiore Central Station depot.

"No," Peter said with a small, forced smile. "I can't stay here. But I'll come visit."

"I want to say again, I am very sorry for your loss."

Roberto let his apology sink in as Peter looked around for a moment before he answered with a question.

"Do you know what you can do for me?"

"What is that?" Roberto asked as he took off his Aviator sunglasses to look Peter in the eyes.

"You can go home and spend time your two little boys. Make sure you tell them you love them. That's what you can do for me. Be better than me. Do better then I did."

Peter then smiled. A real smile.

"You got it," Roberto replied as the two men hugged.

Roberto then watched Peter get on the train with Chris to head to the airport. He knew there would be another body to examine, and another family to console; but he didn't think there would be another case like Luke's.

It was special. It was tragic.

As Roberto walked down a small hallway, he stopped in front of the first door on the right and peered into the room. In their beds, Petri and Elmo were fast asleep.

Not forgetting his promise to Peter, Roberto crawled into bed with his little Elmo—the hard cast on his elbow sitting on top of the covers. Elmo shifted a little bit before opening his eyes. He looked at his father and smiled.

"*Ti amo Papa*," Elmo said quietly as he closed his

eyes again. Roberto let his emotion go, crying into the warm blanket resting on Elmo's back.

"*Ti amo, Elmo.*"

52.

10/23/08 3:07 A.M.
Sacramento, California

Peter yawned as the cab driver drove Peter home through the streets of Sacramento. The surrounding neighborhood was quiet as the brisk morning air held morning dew visibly moving past the street lamps.

Peter was exhausted. His flight from Fiumicino International had been like a twelve hour bus ride in which he stared out the window alone in his own thoughts. Peter could feel the ache in every joint and muscle in his body—the gash on his arm began to close nicely, but the tenderness had yet to fade. Peter figured a warm bath and a few aspirin would help immensely, but he hardly looked forward to them. He had a hard time looking forward to anything—but yet he knew he couldn't give up. Chris had said something to him just before they separated to their respective gates.

"Well, I guess this is it," Chris said as he pulled his arms through the straps, hoisting the large pack on his back.

"You have my number," Peter said with a smile. "Don't be afraid to check in from time to time."

"I will," Chris responded. And then he added after a pause, "It shouldn't be like this, you know. You and I should've met at their wedding, or something."

Peter nodded his head and then shook it immediately after. "Yeah," was all he mustered out.

"You know, I wish my father was like you. I mean that."

"Thank you. You're a good kid. Take care of your family."

"I will."

The two hugged, and then they walked in opposite directions.

I wish my father were more like you, Peter replayed in his head. He didn't know what he'd done, if anything, in the last forty-eight hours. And if he had done something, did it even matter?

"It's up here on the right," Peter told the cabdriver who pulled the cab to the side of the curb.

Peter paid his fare and tipped a little extra, thanking the driver as he pulled away from the house. Peter had to use the hidden key tucked safely under a loose red brick on the far right side of his walkway, because his keys were in the suitcase at the bottom of the Mediterranean Sea.

Roberto had told Peter before he flew out that all of his things would be sent to his home in a couple of weeks; all of Luke's belongings, copies of the reports, and Peter's suitcase once it was fished out with Roberto's car.

Peter opened his front door as he entered the usual silence of lifeless objects awaiting their owner. His home, which at one point was full of voices and the laughter of two young boys, was now cold, quiet, and empty.

Peter picked up his small pile of accumulating mail and turned on the lights leading to the kitchen. Setting the mail on the table Peter walked over to the thermostat and turned on the heat. Crossing over to a drawer organized with miscellaneous things, Peter pulled out his extra pair of reading glasses. Setting them on the table, he walked over to the refrigerator and pulled out a jug of orange juice.

Unable to stand the silence, Peter picked up his mail, his glasses, and his freshly poured glass of juice and moved into the living room. Setting his contents on the table next to his molded armchair, Peter shuffled over to the sound system and turned on his favorite mix of classical music, letting the sound of organs, violins, harps, and flutes fill the air.

Walking back to his armchair, Peter began sorting through the mail. One by one he looked at each envelope as he sorted them into piles.

Bill. Bill. Trash. Trash. Bill. Trash. Trash...

Peter froze when he came across a letter.

The postage was from Italy. The handwriting he knew all too well. In the top left corner, the sender's name was perfectly scrawled in legible handwriting with high arching "A's". Peter almost began crying again when he noticed name in the center followed by *Dad* in parenthesis.

The letter, written by Luke, must have just crossed paths with Peter as he flew to Italy. Peter recalled Alonso saying Luke had asked him for paper, and written a letter the night of the sixteenth. He never suspected that letter could be for him.

Carefully sliding his index finger through the back crease of the envelope, Peter began to slowly and carefully tear the top fold. Reaching into the envelope, Peter pulled out the letter and unfolded the page.

Before he began reading, Peter reached over and turned on the side lamp—he wanted the room to be as illuminated as possible. Examining the letter, he could see the single sheet of paper filled with text, both front and back. Peter's heart began to speed up as he felt nervous once again. This was not one of Luke's journal entries—it was a direct message to Peter, a last letter from a son to his father. Peter began to read each word carefully, making sure he didn't skip a single speck of specifically placed ink.

10/16

Dad,

I want to start out by saying I am safe, and I am in relatively good health. I am currently in a small Italian city called Monterosso Al Mare—one of the five small Cliffside cities that make of the Cinque Terre Providence. Each morning I wake up facing the Mediterranean Sea as it glistens and beckons my attention—calling me to notice the wonder of Mother Nature far greater then myself.

I am sorry for writing you a letter. I actually don't know your email address, and if you could send me an email to lsebastian18@gmail.com, I could store it, and we could stay in communication while I'm over here.

I'm stalling, Dad. I have two main reasons why I'm writing you this letter today. The first I will merely skim, for it is a conversation I've wanted to (and tried) to have with you for almost four months now. I don't know if you remember our last conversation, but I must apologize for my outburst—for my vague lecture of pointed assumptions of your personal happiness. Dad, I

343

am sorry for the way I spoke to you. I actually didn't come to you that day to talk about losing Rochelle—I actually came to tell you about my gaining of Saskia. You do not know the name or the face that fits the name, but I swear, over time, you will grow to love her as much as I do. Saskia is my fiancée...she is my everything in this world. She is my teacher, she is my soul, she is my reason...and I can't wait for you to meet her.

In these last four months I have come to learn I will never meet or come to love anyone like Saskia ever again. She is my one and only—just like you are my one and only father. I only get one father, and you are not a disappointment at all. You are a great father—you have always been one, and will always be one. I am just sorry you had to have two terrible sons like Jake and me.

Peter looked up from the letter as tears began to crawl down his face. As he read, he wondered if the misery would ever end—if his tears would one day cease to exist. Reading Luke's letter, his heart began to break.

Dad, I must now tell you something I should have told you years ago. I need to tell you about the truth of how mom died—what happened that day has more to it than you have ever known. And I feel, before I can start being the son I've always wanted to be, that I need to be honest with you for the first time in almost ten years.

Where to begin? Do you remember the morning of the accident? Jake was sick, and that's why mom was driving me to school. That morning at breakfast, I don't know if you remember how tired mom was. You asked her how the late PTA meeting went, and she started telling you all the details, and reasons why it took her so long to get home. I just sat and listened. I watched you two; a married couple of twenty years, methodically

344

going about your morning. Before you left for work, I noticed how you and mom kissed each other. The kiss was meaningless...like it was an obligation, especially from mom.

Well mom took me to school that morning. And I finally caved. I had been helping her keep her secret without her knowing for entirely too long. And so as we pulled out of the driveway in the Land rover, I was the one who started the last conversation anyone would have with my mother...

53.

03/23/99 7:21 AM
Sacramento, California

Luke put on his seatbelt as his mom backed the blue Landrover out of the driveway. His silence around her had begun to build of late—a silence caused by the secret he knew, but dared not to bring up till that morning. He didn't know how to ask her, or to tell her, so he decided to be cautious.

"Mom," his young voice cracked as it continued to

make its way through puberty.

"Yes," Mary responded sweetly as she kept her hands at ten and two.

"How was the meeting the last night? The PTA meeting."

"Good, honey. We got a lot done. I think some of the parents are really digging into improving your standardized testing. The pencil and paper tests have to go."

"Did Mike's mom go?" Luke asked, beginning to position his rooks around the queen.

"No, actually. Gloria didn't make it." She responded coolly.

"What about Reed's parents? The Smiths; they are really into PTA I hear."

"Yeah," Mary said with a slightly weakened tone. "They were there."

"Yeah? Because Reed sits next to me in Biology."

"Oh," Mary responded. Luke let their comments sit in the air for a second.

"I'm sure we'll have a lot to talk about, like what he did while his parent's were gone till midnight."

Mary straightened her back—Luke could tell she was instantly uncomfortable.

"Well, Luke—"She began to say before he interrupted her.

"Where were you last night, mom?" Luke asked, as his voice grew sturdier.

"I told you sweetheart, I was at a PTA meeting."

"Mom, where were you last night?"

Mary couldn't bring herself to look at her son as she continued to drive.

"Luke—"

"Were you with Mr. Hadley again?" Mary's eyes went wide with shock.

"How do you..." Mary trailed off as her voice was

near a whisper.

"I've known for about a month."

"How?" Mary asked.

"Elizabeth Keeling saw you at Harper's out in Folsom the night you went on your Women's Retreat. She was out there with her family on the way back from a soccer game in Colfax. She saw you two kiss."

Luke could tell his mother was in shock. She had no idea anyone ever knew about her affair with Scott Hadley, Luke's freshman English teacher.

"Have you..." Mary began as she bit her upper lip. "Have you said anything to Jake, or your father?"

Luke shook his head. "No. But you need to. You need to tell Dad, Mom. You need to tell him."

Luke could feel his anger building. For too long he sat on the secret of his mom's affair, hoping she would get over it quickly, and they could all stay together as a happy family.

"Luke, I can't."

"Yes, you can. And you will. You have to tell Dad!"

"Luke, it's not that simple."

"Why? Why is not that simple? This is what happens, right? You cheat on dad, and then you leave him! Jake's graduating, but you explain to me that I need to make a decision on who I want to live with!"

Mary began to cry as she listened to her youngest son's rant.

"No, no that's not it."

"Then what! Then what, Mom?"

"I can't tell your father!"

Luke screamed "Why?" as he heard the beginning of his favorite classical song.

Mary screamed back that it was because she loved his father as she hit the steering wheel with her hand.

"Because you love him?" Luke exclaimed. "You

love my Dad and so you cheat on him?"

Mary slowed the Land rover to the stop sign, and seeing no one behind her, shifted into park.

"I love your father," she started to say as she cried. "I don't love Scott Hadley. I just...Things are so tough with your Dad right now at work. He's always gone..." Mary turned to Luke as the mascara ran down her face. "He's never home. I get so lonely, sometimes Luke. I can't tell your father. He's my husband. He's the only one I want."

Luke could feel his own tears running down his cheeks. His mother was breaking his heart. He thought about his father, his hard working father who at that moment was stacking shelves so Luke and his mother had a roof over their heads.

Luke couldn't betray the one honest man left in the world.

"Mom, I love you. But you have tell Dad..." Luke trailed off as he sniffed his tears away. "You have to tell Dad, or I will."

After he gave his mom the ultimatum of a lifetime, Luke pushed open the passenger car door, and got out of the car. He could hear his mother screaming in unison with Andrea Bocelli's operatic intervals.

Luke ran across the crosswalk ahead of the parked Land rover containing his screaming mother. He turned when he heard the honking as the tires squealed to catch up with him.

And that's when it happened. Mary's split second decision to put her car in drive and speed up to catch her angry son had killed her. Luke watched his mother as the three-ton garbage truck smashed into her like a wrecking ball into a phone booth.

Mary was killed instantly—the secret affair along with her.

54.

10/23/08 4:17 AM
Sacramento, California

Peter was in shock.

He didn't know how to handle what Luke was telling him. For so many years he wondered what happened that day. He never suspected the truth. Mary had been engaged in an affair. And Luke, Luke had been the one who tried to put an end to it.

Peter suddenly remembered his last conversation with Luke before he left. He remembered screaming at him, blaming him for Mary's death. How foolish could an old man be?

Peter returned his attention to the letter—a few more paragraphs remained.

I'm sorry to have to tell you this way. I kept this from you because I thought it was the right thing to do. I saw how much you loved Mom. And telling you would only bring you unnecessary pain. But you've held on too long, Dad. There is so much out here for you to see, for you to love, and for you to live for.

As hard as the truth may be—Mom sped up to me because she couldn't bare the thought of me telling you the truth. She loved you with all her heart, Dad. She just got lost somewhere along the way, that's all. And looking back now, we all made mistakes; you spent more time at work than with your family; mom made poor decisions; and I turned myself off to you after her death, which you resented me for.

But it's all going to change, dad. We're going to

change. I'm writing this to you because I think it's the only way I can truly get you to hear my words, to see my heart. I want you to be a big part of my life—my life with Saskia. I want you to be the best grandfather, the best father in-law, and best father from here on out and into the future.

I love you, Dad, I can't wait to sit down with you and tell you all of the extraordinary things that have happened in my life. And I can't wait for you to meet Saskia.

I love you,
Luke

Peter pressed the letter to his chest as his faced folded together in pain. Luke had wanted everything Peter now wanted—a loving relationship between father and son.

Peter sat in complete silence for what seemed like an eternity. The music in the background gently moved in and out of his conscience. A soft piano could be heard, as it harmonized with a string of violins to create a feeling of warmth. Peter's drying eyes closed as he let his thoughts go with the music. The violins faded to the punctuated rhythm of the piano, as the beautiful melody could be heard alone and separate, almost exact—like a lone burning candle in a room without light.

Peter kept his eyes closed as he thought about his son. Luke was that candle, a bright spot amongst the darkening times.

As Peter listened to the music, he could feel his son's spirit all around him. Luke was in every note—his warmth was in every count of one, two, three, and four—as Peter gently swayed his composure-like hands in the air.

He smiled.

In that one moment, there absolutely nothing

wrong with the world.

Peter got up from his chair and walked into the kitchen, grabbing the cordless phone off the hook as he passed it by. Walking over to the far end of the counter, he scrolled through his address book until he found the number he was looking for.

After dialing the number, the phone rang four times before he heard the tired voice he was expecting.

"Hello?" the voice said.

"Jake..." Peter's voice trailed off as he took a deep breath.

"Dad?"

"Jake, I love you."

Epilogue

18/10/09 14:12
Monterosso Al Mare

Peter looked out into the many faces. It had taken him a long time to assemble and prepare the event that was currently taking place.

After his return home from Italy, Peter sold his hardware store and moved to New Hampshire. Peter decided he wanted to be a part of Jake and his family's life. He had no reason to stay in Sacramento, so he quietly packed up his belongings, sold his business and home, and moved into a small one-bedroom cottage thirty minutes outside of Concord. Peter visited Jake and his expecting wife Emily twice a week. They would have family dinners on Tuesday nights, and would attend church together on Sundays.

Peter found going to church a very powerful tool in helping him rebuild his fractured spirit. The devastating losses of Luke and Mary had been more crippling to his soul than he could have every expected. But the relationships he built with his church community slowly lifted him off the ground and onto his own two feet. As each day passed, his whole world expanded— the sun was brighter, the sky was bluer, and his once broken heart began to fill with a deep love and purpose. It had been Luke that first showed him the light, but after a while, he couldn't credit only Luke for his revamped spirit. Jake, Emily, God, the church, and his continued relationships with Roberto and Chris showed Peter how to truly and deeply love.

One day, at Jake's home in Concord, Peter

informed Jake and Emily of his intentions for Luke's one-year anniversary of his death. Jake instantly agreed to help him, both in preparations and with finances.

So here Peter stood, looking out into the many faces, some he knew well, some he didn't. Standing with him at the cross between Monterosso Al Mare and Vernazza was Roberto, his wife Ella, Petri, Elmo; Chris and his mother, Peggy with his two sisters, Jane and Lisa; Otto and his wife Tuvia, and their children Jonus, Timo, Hanna, and Mia; Paul from Wales, and his new girlfriend Jasmine; Dr. Matthew Gerhard and his wife Alexis; John and Molly, alongside Crum; Rochelle Dobbs and her new fiancé Chris, with her parents Rick and Paula; the Swedes Johan and Sarah standing next to Olivia and Nikki; Alonso and Jacobo Eloy: and Jake and Emily with their new two-month old son, Luke.

Each person held a lit candle. They had placed two small memorial crosses at the base of the tree, one cross with a picture of Saskia and the other a picture of Luke. Surrounding the two cross memorials were bouquets of flowers and handwritten letters placed in envelops, never to be read.

Peter stood between the two memorials, and faced the crowd.

"I'd like to thank you all for coming," he began. "I would also like to thank Roberto for getting permission for us to be up here. I must especially thank Jake for spending an un-godly sum to get you all out here."

Peter paused as he smiled at Jake, who just nodded his head.

"A year ago today, was a tragic day that none of us could have predicted. The deaths of both Luke and Saskia were a call to all of us—it weakened our hearts, our minds, and our souls. For me, personally, it was the day that changed my life. Because of what they stood for, together. I know, in their own special way, Luke and

Saskia influenced each and every one of you here today. They touched your hearts with their loving words, kindness, and spirituality."

Peter handed his candle to Jake in exchange for a brown leather journal he held in his hand. Peter put on his reading glasses that hung around his neck.

"I want to read for you all an insert from Luke's journal, dated on the eighth of October, last year—right around the time Nikki tried to seduce Luke."

The crowd let out a gentle laughter as Nikki smiled and nodded her head at Peter. Word of Luke and Saskia's story had spread throughout the group and into the world like a wildfire after their deaths.

Peter cleared his throat as he began to read.

"Luke writes, 'She gives me light, she gives me strength. I would move a mountain if she asked it of me. In all the world I hope for one thing, one unifying thing, and my hope is this; that each man finds his own Saskia, and each woman to find their own Luke; for together, we bring out the best versions of ourselves. Without her, I am incomplete. Without me, she feels an empty void that is far too great to fill. But together, with help from a higher power I strive to understand, we are two clouds joined as one, floating above the earth. We love greatly, and therefore hold the key to everything, and beyond.'"

Peter took off his glasses, and looked up at the smiling crowd.

"Did you hear his message? Did you feel it? Those two knew something that a lot of people miss. The greatest thing you'll ever know and understand is rooted in love. There will never be a greater story than Luke's, and there will never be a better example of the power of love than the love shared between he and Saskia."

Peter then handed the journal back to Jake. Standing in front of the silent audience, Peter pulled out two sterling silver necklaces from his pocket. The two necklaces shared a pendent, that when put together revealed a whole heart with an engraved "S" in the center.

Peter walked over to the cross tree, and hung the two necklaces together on a loan nail safely secured in the crevasse at Jesus' feet. When he did so, he retreated back and stood next to Jake, taking his candle in his hands once again.

Peter then heard Chris count out loud on cue. "One, two, three," he said as the voices started singing as one, some reading from a small sheet they'd received earlier, others singing from memory.

Making your way in the world today
takes everything you've got.
Taking a break from all your worries sure would help
a lot. Wouldn't you like to get away?

Peter looked around him as people sang the fun song Luke sang to amuse a crowd in Rome. There was a legend of a song that Luke wrote for Saskia—Peter would have loved to tribute it at their memorial service, but no one knew the words. He thought it was probably for the best—Luke's romantic legacy may have been published and left behind, but his one song for Saskia would die with him.

Knowing the song would dull, Peter told everyone to sing the first verse and a lone chorus—he thought it was tasteful, and knew it would give enough time for everyone to properly think about and pray for Luke and Saskia.

Sometimes you want to go where
everybody knows your name,
and they're always glad you came; you want to be

355

where you can see, our troubles are all the same;
you want to be where everybody knows your name.

And then once more, for good measure.

You want to be where you can see,
our troubles are all the same;
you want to be where everybody knows your name.

And then Peter led the group to blowing out their candles—the extinguished fumes moving in the wind—the silent exhale of momentary sadness erupted into a chorus of stories shared between family and friends. The spoken words about the two distant lovers and how they found each other in a day, but loved each other for an eternity.

THE AUTHOR

Caleb Kearns graduated from Linfield College with Dual B.A.'s in Creative Writing and Theatre Arts. *A Journal Away From Life* is his first full-length fiction novel.

Kearns currently lives in Charlotte, North Carolina where he works as a stonemason.

Printed in Great Britain
by Amazon.co.uk, Ltd.,
Marston Gate.